PRA   OF

When We Met

D0726055

A. L. Jac

"Exquisite, beautiful, poignant—A. L. Jackson is in a league of her own!"
—#1 *New York Times* bestselling author S. C. Stephens

Molly McAdams

"Kicks off with a bang and holds nothing back. You'll be enthralled, romanced by the wonderfully spun tale of love and acceptance."
—#1 *New York Times* bestselling author Jennifer L. Armentrout

Tiffany King

"Funny, real, moving, and passionate . . . a MUST READ for New Adult contemporary romance fans."
—*New York Times* bestselling author Samantha Young

Christina Lee

"Pure NA goodness . . . turns the classic model on its head, making it new and oh so compelling."
—*New York Times* bestselling author Jasinda Wilder

ALSO BY A. L. JACKSON
Come to Me Quietly
Come to Me Softly

ALSO BY MOLLY MCADAMS
Sharing You
Letting Go

ALSO BY TIFFANY KING
No Attachments
Misunderstandings

ALSO BY CHRISTINA LEE
All of You
Before You Break
Whisper to Me
Promise Me This

when we met

A. L. Jackson

Molly McAdams

Tiffany King

Christina Lee

 New American Library

New American Library
Published by the Penguin Group
Penguin Group (USA) LLC, 375 Hudson Street,
New York, New York 10014

USA | Canada | UK | Ireland | Australia | New Zealand | India | South Africa | China
penguin.com
A Penguin Random House Company

First published by New American Library,
a division of Penguin Group (USA) LLC

First Printing, November 2014

LIBRARY OF CONGRESS CATALOGING-IN-PUBLICATION DATA:
When we met/A. L. Jackson, Molly McAdams, Tiffany King, Christina Lee.
    p. cm.
ISBN 978-0-451-47192-5 (softcover)
1. College students—Fiction. 2. Young women—Fiction. 3. College stories. I. Jackson, A. L.
II. McAdams, Molly. III. King, Tiffany. IV. Lee, Christina
PS648.C64W47   2014
813'.0108352375—dc23   2014020210

Printed in the United States of America
10 9 8 7 6 5 4 3 2 1

Set in Bell MT
Designed by Spring Hoteling

contents

behind her eyes

A. L. Jackson

prologue

isha hugged herself around her middle. Chills raced down her spine and crystallized the blood in her veins. She felt sick. So sick. Tears streamed from her eyes fast and hard, dripping from her chin as she bent at the waist and cried toward the ground. As she stood in the front yard of his house, confronting him with the video she'd found, her body trembled with a shock of grief. "How could you do this to me?"

Hunter laughed, a sound of insult as it rumbled up his throat and passed through the smug smile curling his lips. He inclined his head to capture her attention up from her own feet. Like a deer blinded by the light, she froze, locked in the clutches of the blue gaze she'd once thought so tender and kind. Now those eyes simmered with derision.

"Knew you had it in you, Misha." His voice raked the taunt, cutting her deeper with each biting word. "The good girl act . . . I saw right through it. You're just as easy as the rest of the sluts around here, aren't you?" His face twisted with morbid satisfaction. "Of course that amazing fuck was worth the hundred dollars I had on the line."

"A h-h-h-hundred dollars?" She stuttered over the question, her tongue thick as she tried to force the words around the shame clogging her throat. Confusion and disbelief spun with the heartbreak. Her knees went weak.

Hunter moved closer, his nose an inch from hers. "A h-h-h-hundred dollars?" he mocked, pouring salt into her oldest wounds.

Misha sucked in a pained breath and squeezed her eyes shut.

"What? Do you think you're worth more than that?"

Misha recoiled from the insult.

He might as well have slapped her.

He'd already ruined her life.

Abruptly he straightened and took two steps back. "Because you're not." He released a lazy chuckle, casually running a hand through his blond hair like she meant nothing at all. Then he turned and left her there.

The sob she struggled to hold in broke free, and Misha stumbled over the patchy lawn as heartbreak tore through her.

Betrayal and humiliation penetrated all the way to her bones. Horror flamed her heated cheeks, streams of tears flowing like a river of fire scalding her flaming flesh. But this heat was nothing like the blush that kissed her skin with shyness, the way the crimson colored her face when the slightest bit of attention was cast on her.

No.

Because this? This was anguish.

Misha couldn't fathom the viciousness, couldn't comprehend that one person could be so cruel. She'd believed he'd cared about her. Loved her. He'd promised her she was everything.

Turned out she was just a pawn in some sick, twisted game.

chapter one

Misha

Three months later

What am I doing here?

I looked up at the dusty blue two-story house—the house I'd shared with three other girls, Indy, Courtney, and Chloe, during my sophomore year. Nostalgia billowed through me on a soft wave. I'd loved so much of my time here, learning how to spread my wings, to fly on my own without the shelter of my parents, who'd made it their lifelong duty to protect me from the vile dangers of this world.

My head shook with remorse. It hadn't taken me long to be ensnared in its traps, had it?

After Hunter's betrayal, I'd run straight home to Wisconsin and right into my mother's waiting arms. Completely crushed. I'd sworn to never return here, too ashamed to be seen walking the halls of the university I'd attended in Ann Arbor, Michigan, since my freshman year of college.

Summer had passed in some kind of blur, my heart searching for a way to mend after it had been shattered beyond recognition. No longer did I fully recognize myself. The endless smile was wiped from my mouth and the naive trust I'd held in this world disintegrated into nothing.

But here I was, back in Michigan, standing in the driveway of the house I shared with my roommates. As much as I didn't want to look, I couldn't stop my gaze from wandering, latching warily on to the dingy white house next door.

Nausea pooled in my stomach as my eyes were drawn up the side of the house to the last window on the second floor. Behind that window was the room where I'd given Hunter my innocence. My hand fisted at my side, all of me protesting that thought. No. Where Hunter had *stolen* my innocence. Behind that window was where he'd hurt me, humiliated and shamed me.

For all my life I'd seen the best in people. My mother had always told me it was what made me who I was, why I glowed and smiled and shed a radiant light on the rest of the world. She said it was what made me good and begged me to never let it go.

Hunter taught me it just made me a fool.

"There you are."

Tearing my eyes away, I turned to Indy as she stepped out onto the front porch of the house. Red hair whipped around her face, green eyes watching me where I stood at the end of the walkway.

"It's about time you got here. It's Happy Hour and we're making drinks. Get your ass inside."

I felt the heat rush to my face, and I chewed at my bottom lip, grabbed the two suitcases I'd taken from my car, and began to haul them behind me.

Happy Hour.

Ha.

I hadn't truly been happy since I left this place three months ago.

Junior year started in just three days. I didn't think I'd be a part of it, resigning myself to giving up my dreams and transferring to a small school in Wisconsin, never turning back. Indy had convinced me I was wrong. She'd been betrayed, too, her jerk of a boyfriend hurting her, and she needed me back in the house. Just as much as I needed to be here.

I'd missed it. Now that I was here, I could admit that I knew I didn't want to run away. By my doing so, all I had accomplished was allowing Hunter to win his nasty game.

He'd stolen something precious from me. I wouldn't let him steal the internship I'd worked so hard for, too. Helping the kids there was the most important thing in my life, the one true thing that had called me back to Michigan. I couldn't rid those innocent little faces from swirling through my mind, those little kids being the ones I planned on dedicating my life to.

No, I wouldn't allow him to steal them, too.

The final key had been Indy telling me Hunter had been booted from the house next door, voted out when his three roommates found out he was the one who'd been responsible.

My heart warmed in a way I thought was no longer possible. I still couldn't believe they'd taken up my side, supported me after I'd been so gullible.

It didn't mean I loved the idea of someone else there, living in that room where I had been played like a cheap, worn-out piano.

Condemned.

That was what I wanted it to be. The room should be taped off and boarded up so no one could enter its repulsive walls. Even better, pummeled into a million tiny pieces by a wrecking ball. Maybe then the memory of what had happened there would be pulverized along with it.

I knew he would still roam the campus, that some people would think me someone I was not, that there would be times when I'd bear the brunt of the curse he'd cast on me. But I took comfort in knowing I wouldn't have to witness that same smug, self-satisfied expression he'd looked at me with when I confronted him, when he laughed and mocked me, tossing me aside like a piece of trash.

Never again would I allow myself to fall prey to a guy like that. Lesson learned—the hard way.

I ascended the five wooden steps to the covered porch, my suitcases bouncing as I dragged them up behind me. I let them go and
hugged Indy.

"I'm so glad you're here," she whispered near my ear.

I squeezed her tighter, sad the two of us were sharing in some kind
of brokenhearted kinship.

"I'm so sorry to hear about Dean," I mumbled into her shoulder.

"Me, too." She pulled away, swiping away a tear. She gestured toward the door. "Come on, let's get your stuff inside and then we need
to catch up."

I followed her through the front door. Inside, the main room was
cramped with three couches. We spent a lot of time here, watching TV,
lounging, and talking, sometimes studying, and this was where our
friends hung out when they came over.

One of our other roommates, Chloe, sat on one of the couches,
typing furiously on her laptop. She glanced up, squealed when she saw
me in the doorway. "You're back!"

She set her laptop aside and hopped up to welcome me.

I hugged her. "Thanks for letting me come back."

"Pshh . . ." She smiled a playful smile, waves of her short blond hair
swishing around her face. "Like we wanted to go through the trouble
of looking for a new roommate."

Courtney, the last of my roommates, ducked her head through the
opening to the kitchen. "Misha's back!" Her statement was no question,
but tossed out in a loud greeting. "You don't know how glad I am that
Indy was able to drag you back here where you belong."

There was no question they were working to play it light, to pretend like this heaviness didn't surround me, like tears wouldn't fall at
the drop of a dime or at the mention of his name.

"I'm glad to be back," I forced myself to say, doing my best to make
it the truth. I smiled softly at them all. "I'm going to go upstairs and
get settled."

Courtney nodded. "Just let us know if you need anything. Indy and

I are making drinks. We require your presence in . . ." She studied her watchless wrist. "Oh . . . two point five minutes."

I giggled, feeling another flare of redness seep to my cheeks, and I self-consciously blew back a thick black curl that had fallen in my face. "How about five?"

"Deal."

I headed upstairs. On each side of the hall were two doors, four bedrooms taking up the second floor. Straight back at the end of the hall was a bathroom and a door to the side that led up to the open attic. We'd stuffed it full of pillows of every size, the floor just one huge, soft, squishy mess. I loved to escape to its quiet sanctuary, to maybe get lost in a book, to set myself free in my imagination.

After Hunter, I was sure I'd be hiding out up there a lot, stowed and locked away from all the things I didn't want to face.

Sadness swallowed me when I opened the second door on the right and let myself into my small room. Everything was how I'd left it, minus the pictures I'd torn from the walls and the belongings I'd shoved into plastic bags that night three months ago when I left as quickly as I could, completely broken and having no clue how I'd go on, sure I would never come back to this place I loved.

Standing in the silence of my room, I made a resolution that I now would go on.

And I'd never allow myself to be so vulnerable again.

chapter two

Misha

Sucking in a steadying breath, I hiked my backpack higher up on my shoulders. My hand fluttered on the front doorknob. The cool metal beneath my palm passed through me like some kind of warning I couldn't shake.

My first class of the semester started in an hour. I knew I had to make it out this door, hold my chin up, and face the world that I . . . well . . . the world I really didn't want to face.

But I hadn't come back here to be a coward, to become some kind of pathetic, reclusive girl who holed herself up in her room like I'd been doing since I came back to this house three days ago. I hated feeling like this, my heart all twisted up in my ribs, pounding so hard I was pretty sure I could see it beating under my shirt. Nerves wobbled my legs, my breaths heaving as they panted in and out of my parted lips.

I can do this.

I forced myself to turn the knob and stepped out onto the covered porch. The soles of my shoes thudded on the wooden floor, echoing as I propelled myself across the deck.

I can do this, I chanted over and over, my lips moving without sound as I studied my feet.

At the edge of the porch, I stepped down onto the top step and into the light. The light I hadn't seen in days, my blinds drawn and my room cloaked in shadows for too long, the overbearing darkness filling me with melancholy and fear and questions of whether I really should have returned.

Now rays of shimmering sunlight beat down, wrapping me up in a soft hug of warmth, embracing my pale skin. Goose bumps lifted on my arms as the days I'd spent in dread seemed to clash with the greeting of the sun.

I lifted my face to the sky, my eyes dropping closed as I relished the sweet feel of the cool breeze and warm sun that tickled gentle fingers of comfort across my face.

And I stood in awed welcome of the day.

Winter would be here soon enough, ushering in the cold. This beautiful day was a stark reminder that I couldn't allow Hunter to steal the best of life from me. Hiding in my room just meant I was again allowing him to take another piece of myself by giving in to the worry and questions.

I pulled the deepest breath into the well of my lungs. Clean, crisp air filled me up like a soothing balm that could be inhaled, a tangible solace that could be tucked somewhere deep inside myself, becoming a vital piece of who I was.

Something I hadn't felt in so long stirred in my heart. A swirl of joy blossomed in my belly, sending a swell of appreciation right along with it. A feeling that everything might just be okay quietly slipped through my body on a hushed wave.

"I can do this," I whispered again, only this time I uttered it aloud, the encouragement ringing through my ears to give a boost of confidence to my downtrodden spirit.

This time I believed it.

Slowly my eyes blinked open to the bright blue canopy above, and I shook myself off, skipped down the steps. I headed down the walkway leading away from the house, my face downturned and focused on my white canvas shoes.

Awareness prickled along my spine, lifting the hairs at the nape of my neck. On its own accord, my head drifted to the side where the upheaval of energy radiated, barreling into every last one of my senses.

I slowed to a stop.

It was doubtful anything in this world could have forced me to keep walking.

My lips parted in surprise, and a little "Oh" dropped from my mouth. My heart stuttered and all the heat of the sun landed square on my face, my cheeks flaming so hot I felt it burn somewhere in my stomach.

In the driveway next door sat a car I'd never seen before, one I didn't recognize, one there was no question I would have remembered had it ever appeared in my sight. It was completely blacked out . . . all of it . . . the windows and the wheels and the body. It looked fast and dangerous and set off all kinds of bells in my head, every last one of them screaming a blaring warning.

Trouble.

But the car wasn't what had me trapped. It was the guy tucked under the hood, hovering over the powerful engine, who had frozen me to the spot. The guy braced the wide span of his arms over the entirety of it, holding himself up and craning his head to the side as he stared across the short distance at me. The shaggy thatch of dark brown hair that flopped over his forehead did nothing to obstruct the unsettling intensity of his hazel eyes. Even in the space between us, I knew they were mostly green, but the sun caught flecks of gold that made them seem to glimmer with mischief.

He was wearing nothing but a pair of snug-fitting jeans, his strong chest and arms bare, the sheen of sweat covering it glistening in the sun, just enough to accentuate every ripple of muscle he had exposed.

Oh. My. God.

I chewed at my lip and attempted to look away, but my gaze was all tangled with his, locked up and wrenched tight with the eyes that seemed to be holding all of my functions hostage—eyes that were narrowed and burning with curiosity.

A lump grew in my throat.

Did he recognize me?

Shame scorched me all the way to my core.

Still I couldn't look away.

Without taking his gaze from me, he pulled himself from under the hood. He grabbed a rag as he propped his hip up on the edge of his car, meticulous as he began to wipe the grease from his hands.

Seconds passed, or maybe hours, I wasn't sure, everything a blur as my body waged a war with my mind, every rational thought I had sent to slay the fearful fascination this stranger sent speeding through my veins. Just looking at him had set the million butterflies that had lain dormant in my stomach scattering. They fluttered fast, teasing me with the unwanted attraction my traitor body was giving in to with just a glimpse of a cute boy.

Cute boy.

Ha.

This guy . . . man . . . whatever you wanted to call him . . . wasn't cute.

He looked like some sort of avenging angel. Too beautiful to be real. Maybe he was here to collect my soul, to make me pay for the sins Hunter had led me into.

Those butterflies dipped and dove when he spoke, his voice deep and rough, no doubt created for the sole purpose of enticing guileless girls into temptation. "So, are you just going to stand there and stare at me all day, or are you going to introduce yourself?"

Flustered, I shook my head, blinking as I took a stumbling step away from him, my mouth dropping open just a little more.

I spent a dumbfounded moment trying to process his words.

Did he really just say what I think he did?

What an arrogant jerk.

"I think you have a little something . . . right here," he continued. With his index finger, he tapped at the cocky, curled-up edge of his lips, teasing me as he wiped the imaginary drool from the corner of his mouth. His taunting touch left behind a smudge of grease on his gorgeous face.

Dirty.

That thought ratcheted up my confusion a thousandfold, just like that wrench he'd been wielding against the bolt in the engine of his car. I was pretty sure this guy could twist me so tight he'd strip me bare.

I'd been screwed enough. Not again.

"Y-y-you were looking first," I stammered over the lame defense, my voice strained and sounding a little too much like a petulant child's.

Damn it! He had me hot and bothered in places I didn't even know existed.

His head tipped to the side, tossing locks of his dark brown hair around his face. Then he shrugged. There was nothing I could do to stop my eyes from traveling to the defined planes of his chest.

I swallowed hard and tried to get my bearings.

Oh man, oh man, oh man. Not good.

It was like the bait that lured prey to the sharp teeth of a trap, too tempting to resist. Everything about the movement was predatory.

I could almost smell him, all man and grease and sex.

"So what if I was?" he asked, nonchalant, that rough voice tossing the contention out without the slightest hint of shame. He cocked an eyebrow as his eyes made a slow pass down my body.

I almost gasped in relief when he released me from the chains of his stare. Of course, he just dragged his attention right back up, and those searing eyes made me their prisoner again.

"You did look at yourself in the mirror this morning, didn't you? You can hardly blame me."

Redness bloomed hot and fast, and I let my hair fall in my face, obstructing the reaction I had to this boy.

Er . . . man or god or whatever he was.

Stupid. Stupid. Stupid.

I refused to take his grimy come-on as a compliment.

I wanted to stomp my foot and tell him so. Instead I just stood there with my mouth still hanging open like some kind of blubbering fool.

He pushed himself from his car.

Panic thudded my pulse.

I wasn't sure I could handle this guy getting any closer than he already was.

His expression shifted again, his head steadily drifting to the side as he approached, like he was doing his best to dig around in my thoughts.

I wasn't letting him go there. Instead I dug around in myself for courage, lifting my trembling chin as if I were brave instead of the shivering coward I felt like.

"Do you really need an introduction?" I asked with almost a sneer. "Figured you'd already know who I am." Spitting out those words took up the last of my pride, and I was suddenly feeling like a fraud, saying things like someone I was not. My eyes flew to the ground, and I studied a weed growing up through a crack in the pathway as I said a silent prayer that he didn't *know*. Obviously I didn't want anyone to know, this blight something I wished I could obliterate from history.

But him?

Something inside me twisted. I would do anything to be spared that humiliation.

I peeked up through the veil of my hair when I noticed him gesture behind me. That mischief was back in his eyes, only this time it was lighter, like their potency was no longer a threat. He grinned. "I'm no genius, but based on the fact that you just came out of that house wearing a backpack on the first day of classes, I'm going to go out on a limb and say you're one of my new neighbors."

He'd turned casual, which was about the last thing I was feeling.

"But do you know my name?" I demanded, my hand curling into a fist at my side.

Do you know my face? was what I was really asking, almost begging him to relieve me of the burden.

"Well, let's see . . . Kier filled me in on all the neighbors." He lifted his gaze to the sky, as if he were thinking back to their conversation.

Kier was one of the guys who lived next door, quiet, nice. I'd always liked him. I was close to feeling relieved, because I felt almost positive he wouldn't divulge my secret.

New guy raised his hand and lifted his index finger. "Chloe." He held up a second. "Indy." He continued on, checking off all of us girls. "Misha and Courtney." A smirk twisted up one side of his mouth. "Guess I'd feel pretty confident betting on the fact that you belong to one of those names."

Discomfort shifted my feet, and I finally forced my name around the lump this guy had seemed to permanently wedge at the base of my throat. "M-M-Misha." I tucked an errant curl blowing around in my face behind my ear, my nod shy and unsure. "I'm M-M-Misha. Misha Crosse."

His eyes narrowed again, studying. Then he shook his head, raking his plump bottom lip between his teeth. He freed it with an easy smile.

Dear Lord.

"Darryn. Darryn Wild." He stuck his hand out between us. I eyed it warily. Those bells were ringing. *Don't touch. Off-limits. Danger.*

But he was smiling this cute smile, and my hand tingled, twitching toward his. What could a handshake hurt?

"Oh, come on, Misha, I know you want to touch me." This time, he didn't touch the corner of his mouth but reached out to touch mine.

Shivers raced down my spine and sent something tumbling around in my stomach that I didn't want to recognize, and I prayed another prayer that the drool he lifted from my face was imaginary, too.

At this point, I wasn't so sure.

Fantastic. The guys next door had just traded one asshole for another. And to think for a second I'd almost been duped into thinking he was nice.

I didn't like it, didn't like thinking this jerk was sleeping in Hunter's room, didn't like his things there or his thoughts there or his ripped, muscled body stretched out like Satan's seduction across that bed.

And I really couldn't stand the cocky grin that was playing all over one side of his perfect mouth.

But mostly I just hated that he managed to make me feel this way.

One of these days I was going to learn to trust my instincts. I'd had them that night with Hunter, this feeling sparking inside me, alerting me that something was off.

No day like the present.

"You wish," I spat at him, doing my best to sound intimidating and not like some scared little creature who wanted to find a rock to hide behind.

My eyes made a pass over the yard, wishing that overnight a huge boulder had miraculously been dropped into our yard.

Nope.

No such luck.

He laughed, the sound thick and throaty and arrogant. Part of me wanted to smack him, while the other part wanted to beg him to do it again.

Damn it!

Damn him.

"I wish, huh?" He eyed me up and down. "Yeah, I guess I do."

I huffed, and he chuckled again.

Refusing to submit myself to his torture any longer, I turned and stomped away, scolding myself under my breath. "Stupid, stupid, stupid," I ranted, my lips moving silently as I pounded down the sidewalk toward campus. Mounds of curls bounced angrily around my face as I left Darryn Wild staring behind me. "I hate boys," I muttered hard. "Jerks. Every last one of them."

I was so angry he'd managed to make me stutter and stumble all over myself.

It didn't matter if he was the prettiest thing I'd ever seen.

No way, not a chance.

I'd been there before.

And I wasn't about to go there again.

chapter three

Darryn

couldn't wipe the smile from my face as I watched her storm away. Thick, heavy black curls bounced all around her shoulders and down her back, her little hands twisted up in the tightest fists at her sides.

Like a feisty little kitten with a cute button nose and wide curious eyes, skittish and scared and completely naive.

Pretty sure I could have said *boo* and she would have run.

I chewed at my lip, fighting the grin.

Yeah, I knew her.

Knew her face and her name and that fucking incredible body, all curvy and full and just about the most damned perfect thing I'd ever seen.

Why I lied when she'd asked me such a pointed question, I didn't know. I knew exactly what she'd been referring to, that video I'd been trying to get off my mind for the last month. But it was like she'd been pleading with those huge, hopeful eyes—brown eyes so dark they were nearly as black as her hair—to spare her, like a lie would be so much easier than the truth.

Or maybe it was because she was nothing like I expected. I expected some raving hot bitch, all sass and sex and mile-long legs, with pouty full lips and vacant black eyes.

What I wasn't expecting was a girl who blushed so red I was pretty sure she was going to incinerate with just the slightest hint of attention. Didn't expect a girl who stuttered over her own damned name.

God, I'd just spent the last five minutes being a total ass to her, egging her on, but I couldn't help it. Every time she blushed, my dick stirred to life and my heart pounded a little too hard, this girl some kind of sweet contradiction, all sexy and shy and so damned adorable I wanted to wrap her up in my arms and never let her go. Couldn't tell if I wanted to haul her off to snuggle up on the couch or tear all her clothes from her and teach her every dirty trick I knew.

But it became clear really fast.

This girl didn't do dirty.

For a fleeting second, my eyes shot up to the room I'd rented out when Hunter was canned. Yeah. I knew him, too.

Anger spiked deep in my gut, and I sucked in a breath as I turned back to the curly mane of black stalking away from me, no doubt still cursing my name.

Hunter.

I was hit with the intense need to take the asshole out.

He needed to pay for treating a girl as sweet as Misha the way he had.

Guilt reared its ugly head, sneering at me, reminding me I was just as bad as the rest of them.

How many times had I fantasized about kissing the hell out of that pouty mouth? About my hands palming her hips while she rode me, her hair falling over her shoulders, just brushing over her full tits as I looked up at her while she drove me right out of my mind with pleasure?

Misha peeked back at me, her eyes going wide when she caught me still standing there ogling her as she walked away. For a second I saw her little kitty claws come out, like she was about to make a valiant attempt to protect her sweet little self, before she gave herself over to all the insecurities swimming so visibly in her eyes. But then she just ducked her head and rushed to turn the corner.

I shook my head, tossed my rag back to the engine of my car, and chuckled aloud. Thought I'd had a finger on her. Wasn't even close.

But one thing hadn't changed.

I still wanted to kiss the hell out of that pouty mouth.

chapter four

Misha

My phone vibrated in my back pocket. I pulled it out and squinted at the screen as I navigated through the drove of students who were spilling out of the lecture hall.

A small smile pulled at my mouth when I read the needy message from Indy.

COFFEE?!?!

I tapped out a quick reply.

`Be there in two :)`

Changing course, I pushed through the throbbing herd of bodies, heading for Common Grounds, the little coffee shop Indy and I had made a habit of frequenting between classes last year. School had started last week. Indy was still having a really rough time after her breakup with Dean, and I was doing my best to spend as much time with my friend as I could, hoping my presence would ease her mind in some way. She'd worried me this last weekend, coming home so blitzed out I didn't think she even knew her own name.

My days?

I risked peeking up at the faces that blazed by me without a care. There was no hint of recognition, not a soul who paid me any mind. Relief slipped through me, just under the surface of my skin, a buzzing gratitude flooding me as I gave thanks for the mercy I'd somehow been granted. I'd settled into some kind of routine, keeping my head down and my focus entirely on school and my internship. Each day that passed with no one saying anything to me just gave me another boost of confidence, an affirmation that I really belonged here.

Seeing my kids yesterday was confirmation.

I'd walked into that building and all of them had run up to me, calling my name as they laughed and smiled and hugged my legs.

Being with them was worth any amount of discomfort I might suffer here. Those kids . . . they were where I belonged.

I swung open the glass door and stepped into the bustling coffee shop. I inhaled deeply, hit with the overwhelming scent of coffee, warmth infiltrating my chest.

Yum.

The small space overflowed with people. Students clamored to get their caffeine fix as they rushed to get to the next place they needed to be. I popped up on my toes, craning my neck as I looked for the shock of red hair that could only belong to my friend.

"Hi." It was uttered right next to my ear.

"Ah!" I jumped and spun around, finding Indy standing there grinning at me.

"Oh." I flattened my hand on my chest. "You scared me."

She rolled her green eyes. "How you can be startled in the middle of a busy store in broad daylight is beyond me."

"Don't judge me . . . I have keen senses." I smiled up at her, tucking a thick lock of hair behind my ear as I looked back down.

She laughed lightly. "Whatever you want to call it." She knocked into my side. "Come on, let's get some coffee. I thought I'd pass out or possibly die of boredom in my economics class. I need caffeine, and now."

We headed to the counter, Indy in front of me. She ordered her usual, and I stepped up after her and did the same.

Waiting for our drinks, we spent a couple of minutes chatting about nothing, the two of us almost feeling normal as we caught up on things that really didn't matter. For a moment it felt like things were back to the way they had been before our lives were upended by two guys who hadn't deserved either of us, two people who didn't think twice about breaking a heart or fracturing someone's spirit.

"Indy," the barista called, pushing the paper cup in her direction.

"Oh yes . . . gimme, gimme, gimme." Indy grabbed her coffee and winked at me as she backed away. "I'll find us a place to sit."

"I'll find you," I called as she disappeared into the fray.

I stayed in the mass of people milling around waiting for their drinks, turned to study my shifting feet while I listened for my name.

"Misha."

I stepped up and stretched my hand out for my cup when another darted over my shoulder. A big hand wrapped around my cup and snagged it from the counter.

What in the . . . ?

"H-h-hey, that's mi—" I started to say as I whirled around. I stopped short when I met with the hazel eyes smirking back at me.

Redness rushed to my face.

Oh, who was I kidding? Every inch of my skin lit up like a chili pepper, flaming and burning and shouting out all my insecurities.

Damn him.

I'd managed to dodge him for the last week, peeking out the window to make sure the coast was clear before I rushed out the door and down the sidewalk. The last thing I needed was another awkward exchange like he'd somehow dragged me into last week. I didn't need to be scrutinized and teased, and I sure didn't need to find out just how far this guy's jerk-off ways went.

Of course my belly had a whole different idea about the situation, all those butterflies doing a little choreographed happy dance when my eyes fell on the glorious display standing just inches away from me.

Glorious?

Ugh.

Stupid. Stupid. Stupid.

I couldn't stand this guy, couldn't stand the way he tugged and twisted at me like he had some magnetic pull, spinning me up, no doubt with the intention of spitting me out.

"Hey yourself," he said, holding on to my cup like he had an inherent right to it.

This time I couldn't help stamping my foot, indignant. What a jerk. "That's mine," I said, hating that it came out sounding all petulant again. "It says so right there." I pointed to the *Misha* scrawled messily along the side of the cup, rocking back on my heels as I crossed my arms over my chest.

"Obviously." His brow shot up with the sarcasm, before he lifted my cup to his nose and sniffed. "God . . . what are you drinking? A gallon of sugar? This isn't coffee. This is a liquid candy bar."

"It's none of your business what I'm drinking." *So there*, I added in my head, fighting the urge to stick my tongue out at him.

He drove me crazy, made me feel like a little girl fighting with a bully who'd stolen my favorite toy.

I'd dealt with enough bullies in my life.

He chuckled and rubbed his chin. I got locked on the movement of his fingers, my mouth falling slightly agape as he tugged and scratched at the stubble on his jaw. He was so close, and I could feel myself getting sucked in his direction, that aroma that had assaulted me the other day stronger, but this time it was all man and soap and sex—all Darryn Wild. I trembled. Oh God.

Catching me, he smirked.

Damn him.

Why did he have to be so beautiful?

"Give it," I demanded, just wanting to get my coffee so I could get the heck away from him.

"Darryn," the girl behind the counter called. He turned away from me. Seeing his face caught her off guard, and her eyes widened with appreciation as she stood there and blatantly devoured him with her gaze. Apparently no one was immune to him. He didn't even spare her a second's glance. He snatched up his coffee, holding both cups tucked up close to the strength of his chest.

"Are you going to give me my coffee or do I have to buy another one?" I said in surrender, giving up his game because I didn't have the will to play it.

He blinked back at me like I was crazy. "Of course I'm going to give you back your coffee. I was just being the gentleman like I am and was going to carry it to our table for you."

I felt the disbelief take over my expression. A gentleman? Yeah, right. Then the rest of what he'd said sank in. "Our table?" I asked, a challenge bleeding into the words.

"Our table," he deadpanned. Those hazel eyes did that shimmer thing again, where they danced and sang with mischief, all jubilant mayhem on my erratic heart.

"You wouldn't even shake my hand last week. Now you owe me."

My chin lifted in defiance. "You're insane," I said.

"And you"—he handed me my coffee, before he reached up and plucked at my bottom lip with the pad of his index finger—"hurt my feelings."

And I knew it was all just a ploy, this boy-man-god or whatever he was manipulating me, my flesh so easily turned to putty, aching for him to take those big hands and mold me into whatever he wanted me to be.

Those alarms started ringing like loud, clashing cymbals struck right near my ears, the off-key chorus hosted by the betrayal that had changed something intrinsic inside me.

Part of me wanted to give in to what it was Darryn was making me feel. But that was the problem. Because if I was honest with myself, what he made me feel most was scared. The feelings of desire he awoke in me just reminded me of how vulnerable and foolish I'd been in Hunter's deceptive hands. I didn't want to be that girl anymore. I wanted to be stronger and smarter and wiser.

"I seriously doubt that, Darryn Wild, because guys like you don't have feelings."

But as soon as the words were out, I realized one thing I hated more than sounding naive was sounding like a bitch.

Anger scored me deep. Hunter. I hated him most of all. He'd done this to me and made me this way.

For a split second Darryn's face transformed, flashing with something that looked like pain, shutters dimming the mischief in his eyes. Then he slowly nodded through a forced smirk. Again, he tapped the side of my mouth, a reminder of the effect he knew he had on me. "I guess we don't, do we?"

He backed away, left me watching him as he spun around and pushed his way through the coffee shop toward the exit.

On a heavy sigh, I turned and plodded to where Indy waited for me. I slumped down in the plush chair next to her.

"Oh. My. God. Was that our new neighbor you were talking to?"

I scrunched up my nose, shifted to tuck my leg under me, and let my hair fall down the side of my face to block Darryn's view.

"Yes." My whisper was all scratchy and self-conscious.

"Holy hell. I only saw him from a distance when he was moving in. I thought he was pretty then. . . ." She trailed off suggestively. Her eyebrows disappeared under her bangs. "Looks like he's into you."

I huffed. "All I need is another beautiful jerk to take advantage of me. No, thank you."

Of course I was the one feeling like a jerk after what I said to him.

But judging by the effect Darryn had on me, I was pretty sure he was much more dangerous than Hunter ever was.

Hazardous to my health.

Awareness tugged at me, that same feeling from last week, the weight of his presence strong and unyielding. Helpless, I let my attention travel where it was led—where he stood facing me with his back leaned up against the door. A small smile curved his lips, something that almost appeared regretful, something true and soft, and for the first time I thought I saw something real in Darryn Wild. Then he flipped that asshole switch, and a wide, cocky grin blotted out all traces of anything sweet. He shot me this wicked, unruly wink before he backed out of the shop, dipping his head as he hit the sidewalk. I just stared as the door fell closed behind him.

My heart all of a sudden decided to agree with my stomach and indulged in a little flip-flop in rhythm with the patter of quick, uneven beats in my chest. That presence that felt too overbearing, too over-whelming and heavy and intense, was suddenly gone, leaving a void in its place.

Scratch that. The guy was lethal.

Deadly.

I planted my face into my palms, frantic as I shook my head in them. *Stupid. Stupid. Stupid.*

"Oh, Misha, don't fool yourself. Hunter has nothing on Darryn Wild." *Hunter* dropped from Indy's mouth like a vulgar word.

I agreed on all accounts.

She giggled, sipped at her coffee, her voice all a tease as she sang, "Someone is crushing hard on the boy next door."

My chest heated above my heart, splashing crimson all over my skin.

I wasn't, was I? Not after everything I'd been through. Boys were trouble and I didn't need any more of that.

I sucked my bottom lip between my teeth, worried it as my eyes slanted to the huge plate-glass windows that looked out toward the campus, unable to stop myself from wondering where he'd gone and what would have happened had I taken him up on his offer to hang out with him. I still had no idea how to make sense of him, or what part of him was genuine, if any was at all.

Indy snorted, cutting into my thoughts. "You should see your face right now. Whatever questions are running through that pretty little head of yours"—she leaned over the small, round table, lifted her fin-ger, and circled it around my face—"you've got your answer right here, and I'm pretty sure it's a resounding yes."

chapter five

Misha

yanked at the pull-cord of the lawn mower. It sputtered but didn't turn over. I dug my foot into the ground for leverage, giving it a good pull, a little grunt included. Another sputter.

Grrr . . .

I looked up to the blue sky, praying for some miracle that would bring this piece of junk to life. I sucked in a breath, gripped the handle in my hand, and gave it my all.

Nope.

Nothing.

I kicked the mower with the side of my sneaker. "You dumb piece of junk . . . would you give me a break and work? Come on, please." My voice lowered to a whispered plea on the last, like I could cajole something inanimate into cooperating. I jerked it, the engine spinning, then chugging as it ran out of steam.

"Damn it," I cursed under my breath, throwing my hands in the air as I stalked around the overgrown lawn, wondering how in the heck I'd manage to get this impossible chore done using a thirty-year-old machine. I'd take scrubbing toilets over this any day, because me and motors just didn't seem to mix.

Behind me, the wooden fence that rose around our tiny backyard rattled. Startled, I froze as I felt more than saw the shadow of movement pass behind me.

I tore myself from the shock and twisted to look over my shoulder, gasping when I saw Darryn drop into our yard, landing on his feet, crouched down, one hand propping himself on the ground for balance, like he was humbled in the deepest bow. Slowly he lifted his head as he straightened, looked up at me with those hazel eyes, hard and intense and brimming with concern.

A rush of dizziness swirled through my overheated head, and I figured I was seconds from fainting.

Yep.

Just like I'd thought.

Avenging angel.

I gaped at his glory. Again, the boy-man-god lacked a shirt, his golden chest much too proud to be inhibited by something so ignoble as fabric. His jeans rode low, the cut of his abs so delicious I had the overwhelming urge to taste them. My mouth watered, and I was imagining tracing my tongue over the rock-hard grooves and planes.

"What are you doing?" His voice cut into my daydream, the throaty question filled with disbelief.

My head snapped up. Mortification climbed to my face when I realized I'd been staring. I blinked away the stupor, having no clue what he was talking about until I followed the trail of his attention to the beaten-down pile of junk sitting in the middle of the lawn.

Slowly I untwisted myself from the pretzel I was in, turning to face him, shifting on my feet as I watched him approach the lawn mower as if it were an injured animal.

"Um . . . trying to mow?" I said, the words almost a question as they flowed out with a tilt of my head. I squinted, trying to understand where the overt distress he was wearing like a cloak was coming from.

He settled his long body down to kneel on a single knee next to the mower, studying the motor as if it were alive, and his mouth moved as if he were having some kind of secret conversation with the hunk of metal.

He looked over his shoulder at me, sparkling hazel eyes narrowing in skepticism. "And kicking the crap out of the poor thing is going to help how?"

"Um . . . ," I stammered again, frowning at how Darryn seemed to be bleeding sympathy for the old equipment that had become the bane of our house. Each of the four of us roommates would gladly pay good money to get out of the weekly mowing job we rotated around on the cleaning schedule, but the problem was that none of us was willing to take money to do it an extra time. "This isn't my favorite job."

The sight of the old mower sitting slumped in the middle of the lawn, buried in the too-long blades of grass, seemed proof enough.

He turned back to the mower. Craning his head, he poked around, muttering under his breath, "And what in God's name are you doing out here trying to mow?" He unscrewed the gas cap, shook it around, looking for the source.

I wrung my hands together. "It's my chore this week," I explained, feeling the little flush of a grin come to my mouth with the idea of Darryn in my backyard, all that confusion from last week when I'd seen him in the coffee shop barely registering with the relief at him flying in unannounced and without summons to my rescue. I chewed at my lip, and for a second I decided to give up the war I seemed to fight every time Darryn came into my view, and mumbled quietly, "Thank you for coming to help me."

"Ha, I'm not here to save you." He flashed me this brilliant, teasing smile, the one that twisted me all up in knots and tossed me right into an endless, spiraling swoon.

Oh God.

He inclined his head, still grinning. "I'm here to save this poor machine that you're trying to kill."

I frowned as my gaze landed on the rusted metal. There was no stopping my light-headed giggle. "I think you're too late. It's already dead," I whispered in feigned mourning, slowly shaking my head with remorse.

Darryn stared up at me, those mischievous eyes glinting as they stepped up to play partner to that delirium-inducing grin.

And I swear to God, I saw them, these little sparks shooting through the air, like darts of energy impaling me all over my sun-drenched skin.

Oh. I kind of jumped. *That felt good.*

Damn him.

Because there was no denying it. Being around Darryn Wild *felt* good.

He pulled a wrench from his back pocket, as if this boy-man-god was magic, superpowered with an enchanted bag of tricks always at hand. He held it up, wielding it in my direction. "Oh, I think there's hope yet."

He turned away from me and went to work, and I edged in, prompted by the demands of the butterflies in my stomach. I stood over him, probably driving him out of his mind with annoyance as I leaned over his shoulder, watching him. His strong hands were adept and his mind obviously knowledgeable as he tinkered with bolts and wires and little parts that I wouldn't begin to recognize.

"All this thing needs is a little TLC." He eyed me seriously. "You can't just leave stuff like this out to rot. It needs to be maintained. *Taken care of.*" Then he winked. "The way every girl deserves to be."

I reddened at his blatant innuendo, chewing a hole in my lip as I turned back to watch him work.

"Ah, there we go," he mumbled to himself as he seemed to find whatever the problem was. He twisted a couple of wires.

I took a stumbling step back when he suddenly stood, his towering presence too much for me to handle up close like he was. Delight danced all over his face as he wrapped his hand around the handle, his lithe body rippling as he leaned down and cranked it to life. The engine roared.

And we just stood there staring at each other, both of us grinning, me feeling all self-conscious and shy while Darryn was so obviously proud, the air filled with the deafening rumble of the mower and the buildup of the energy sizzling between us.

"Thank you," I said, the sincere words swallowed up by the loud churn of the mower, though I knew Darryn understood what I'd said.

Slowly he nodded as he seemed to get twisted up in the same tension pounding through my system.

A breeze blew in, stirring through my hair, whipping the thick locks around my face. Tentatively Darryn reached out. His hand hovered in indecision, before he gave in and gathered a thick curl to rub between the pads of his fingers, like he needed to feel the texture and weight of it. All the while, he never looked away from me. And this time . . . this time the softness in his expression, the same look I'd witnessed at the coffee shop, didn't evaporate in a flash. It wasn't just a flicker of good that scattered fast to reveal a boy who was so obviously bad.

He shook his head as if he were trying to make sense of something, before he averted his eyes from mine to watch himself tuck the loose strand behind my ear. I shivered when he let his fingertips flutter down the side of my neck, just barely brushing my sensitive skin. He released a ragged exhale when he trailed them lower, across my collarbone to the center of my hammering chest. Fire singed me through with the vibration of his gentle touch.

And was he? Obviously bad? For a second I wanted to suspend it, to disbelieve it, to reject the idea because something about him made me want and ache, made me want what I'd sworn to avoid.

Indy was right.

I was crushing hard on the boy next door.

He stilled with his fingers just grazing my exposed skin, and those hazel eyes latched on to mine. Endless moments passed in a blur as my gaze got all tangled with his.

Something wistful played around his mouth, something like regret and longing that melded with the gentle curve of lips. "Beautiful," he whispered, the sound swallowed by the ceaseless drone of the mower, but so overtly clear as I swallowed the word down. My wounded heart wanted to believe that someone would truly see me that way, and not like the sick joke I saw when I looked in the mirror in the morning.

Creases wrinkled at the sides of his eyes, making him appear both younger and older, different. Making *me* feel different, still scared and unsure—but there was no mistaking the flicker of hope that lit somewhere inside me.

Again he reached up to touch the trembling edge of my mouth. Though this time it wasn't a taunt, not a tease, not something meant to twist me up with confusion and fear.

It was just sweet.

Simple as that.

He dropped his hand and took a step back, seeming almost as confused and flustered as I was, before he turned and jogged across the yard. He scaled the fence in one stride, his feet landing on the top of the wooden planks, sending him sailing over to the other side.

chapter six

Darryn

A stream of sun bled through the slit running down the middle of my bedroom curtains, a slash of bright light blaring directly into my face. I squeezed my eyes tight against it. Flopping to my stomach, I yanked a pillow over my head, making a valiant attempt at shutting it out, begging for more sleep. Just one more minute, and I'd be fine.

But it was no use.

The light had already roused me from sleep.

All right, so the problem was clear. I was *aroused*.

Big difference. Bigger problem.

Groaning, I threw the pillow to the floor and flopped over onto my back, taking up a staring contest with the pitted ceiling above.

My dick was throbbing, standing at full attention, all too interested in the lingering images that I couldn't shake from my mind.

I flung my arm over my eyes. As if that would help.

Maybe the problem was the fact that I'd been dreaming about porcelain skin and inky hair, about the feel of her touch and the light in her smile.

Maybe the problem was the girl next door.

Maybe the problem was Misha.

Goddamn, this girl had done me in, burrowed herself like a tiny, nagging burr that had gotten just under the surface of my skin until she'd flamed into an all-out itch. Gotten to me. I couldn't get that beautiful face out of my mind and there was nothing in hell I could do to purge the sweet sound of her voice from my ears. It flooded through me like warmth, all this lust and need mixed up with some kind of twisted infatuation.

But that wasn't just it.

Yeah, I wanted to get lost in that body, make her scream and moan my name. My chest tightened. Shit, I couldn't wait to hear the way it'd sound slipping from her lips.

But none of that was really a problem.

The problem was I'd be content just to take up a little bit of her space.

I'd started to make excuses to be out front when I knew she'd be leaving or coming home, excuses to talk to her and make her blush and cause her to fumble all over herself the way she always did.

It was the fucking cutest thing I'd ever seen, the way she got all nervous and stuttered, how the red would come stampeding in the second she did.

I crammed the heel of my hand in my eye. *Shit. Shit. Shit.*

Realization slowly took hold.

I liked her.

Pressure throbbed at my ribs.

Fuck me, I liked her.

It was killing me to know where she wandered off to in the afternoon, heading in the opposite direction from campus, when she'd come home nearly giddy, smiling this unending smile that I'd come to crave. Hounding her didn't work, and neither did flattering her with all these little compliments that made her squirm. She remained tight-lipped, which only made me want to know more.

God, but more than all of that? I wanted to erase the pain I'd catch lingering in her eyes. I knew it now, what it was, what flared in those searing pools of the deepest black when she was speared with an errant thought like an arrow, like I could somehow feel it when it pierced her, too.

Shame.

It killed me that she felt that way, and I was dying to wipe away that look of distrust with my touch. Show her there was nothing for her to be ashamed of. I wanted her to know she was beautiful and good and anyone who made her feel anything less than that was nothing but a fool.

Images flashed, and I grunted as I was slammed with a vision of Misha straddling me on this bed. The soft slope of her neck was all exposed as she threw her head back, thick curls cascading down in waves that brushed along my thighs, her body all stretched out as she drove me right to the edge. Pleasure rocked through every hardened inch of my body, ecstasy hitting me somewhere deep.

But then she looked down at me. And those eyes were no longer hollow, they weren't edged with sadness or creased in confusion, and not for a second did they flash with fear. They glowed with affection as she stared down at me.

Guilt gripped me by the throat, and I squeezed my eyes shut, choking on it, trying to purge the fantasy from my mind. It made me feel like an asshole, like some kind of perverted voyeur, picturing her this way.

But I didn't know how to stop.

I raked a hand over my face. Fuck. I just wanted her to trust me.

How the hell did this timid girl next door manage to make my body beg? She didn't have a single clue how badly I wanted her or how deep my thoughts went. Guess there'd always been something about her, something that had struck me before she lifted her face to the sky that first morning of classes, soaking the sun in as if it was somehow feeding her soul. Something that drew me to her.

I recognized it now.

Misha didn't even know and she didn't need to. I'd protect her. Collect everything due to her. Lay it at her feet.

At least I owed her that.

chapter seven

Misha

"Misha, if you don't hurry up I'm going to come up there and drag you down here." Laughter and loud voices and impatient calls rose from the first floor, Indy's voice lifting above them all as she shouted at me for what had to be the hundredth time.

"I'm coming," I hollered in the direction of my bedroom door that stood wide-open behind me. "Sheesh," I added under my breath.

"I heard that!"

With a soft giggle, I turned, letting my gaze wander over myself in the full-length mirror set up in the corner of my room. Uncertainty tickled my nerves, and there was no mistaking the self-conscious flush that bloomed hot on the exposed skin on my chest, before it blazed a path up my neck to settle where it always landed—right on the apples of my cheeks.

I was wearing skinny jeans and heels with a shimmery silver and black shirt that fell off one shoulder, my long hair sprayed into shiny ringlets that spilled over my shoulders and down my back. Months ago, I'd bought this outfit to wear out with Hunter, thinking it was sexy and cute, and I'd hoped it would make me feel confident and pretty. It was something so out of character for me and I'd wanted to do something special for him, to make him proud to have me on his arm when we went out with his friends.

Too bad I didn't get a chance to wear it before he drove that treacherous knife right into the center of my back.

I'd had the intense urge to set fire to these clothes. To watch them burn up so I'd have no reminders left of who I'd tried to make myself be for him.

I wouldn't change for anyone.

Never again.

But I realized wearing something that made me feel pretty didn't change me. Pride had hit me hard when I slipped into these clothes. Not because of the way they made me look, even though I felt *good* in them, but because they were no longer for him.

I chewed my lip, shifted to look at myself in the mirror.

"Forget him," I whispered to myself.

Tonight I was finally letting Hunter go. It wasn't because I missed him and loved him and was letting my broken heart heal. I didn't feel any of those things. I knew it now, knew picking a guy like him was just me trying to fit in, to be more like the girls I thought I was supposed to fit in with.

But what he'd done had hurt me.

And today I would finally let go of all that pain.

"Misha!" Indy shouted again.

Grinning, I grabbed my little purse from my bed. "All right . . . all right! I'm coming! Don't get your panties all in a bind."

I headed out my door, doing my best not to wobble on my four-inch heels.

"Who said I was wearing any?" she shot back as I carefully maneuvered down the stairs. So maybe the shoes weren't exactly me, and I was much more comfortable in my sneakers, but I liked them, so I was wearing them, and I didn't care what anyone else had to say.

Chuckling at her, I clung to the railing as I made my way to the bottom floor. When I got downstairs, I found all three of my room-mates in the kitchen. Courtney was pouring amber liquid into tiny shot glasses, one round ready to get the night started.

Indy grinned in my direction. "Cheers!" she said as she handed a shot glass to me.

"Cheers!" The three of us lifted our glasses and tossed them back, Chloe sitting out the drinking like she always did. I was actually sur-prised she'd agreed to come out with us at all tonight.

Liquid burned a fiery path down my throat, and I forced myself to swallow, doing my best not to choke on it and spew it right back out. My face screwed up with the awful taste when it settled in my stomach. "Ugh . . . that is terrible. Why are we doing this again?"

"Just a little preamble. Tonight we're letting go."

"To tonight." Courtney poured us one more round. We clinked glasses, toasting us. In unison, we slammed them down on the counter, grinning like fools as we swiped the backs of our hands over our mouths.

Was I tipsy off two shots? I wobbled on my heels, giggled more.

Oh yeah. I wasn't exactly what you'd call a *drinker.* But I loved the fuzzy feeling that swept through my body, the way my nerves became subdued and thoughts of Hunter became nothing but a distant memory.

The four of us filed out into the night. A dark canopy kissed with twinkling stars covered us like an embrace from high above. We laughed and talked the entire ten-minute walk to the club. It'd been a very long time since I felt so good.

We were ushered in, and I felt like I stepped into a whole new world when I entered through the wide double doors. Music pulsed, heavy and loud, colorful lights throbbing with the beat. Bright strobes flashed over the crush of bodies on the dance floor, people moving against each other, completely free.

As free as I felt.

Indy tugged at my hand. "Let's hit the bar. I need another drink before I go anywhere near that mess of people."

Funny, because I felt drawn to it, like the only thing I wanted to do was get mixed up in it. Just for tonight, I wanted to get lost.

I let her lead me through the throng, Courtney and Chloe just ahead. The three of us partook of another shot.

I slammed my glass down as I forced my drink to stay in my stomach. "Gah! That's the last one for me." I furiously shook my head. "Whew."

Indy smirked at me. "Lightweight."

And that I was.

My head spun, and the music blared, calling me into it. I began to shake my hips right at the bar. "Come dance with me!" I prodded, yanking at my friends' arms.

"I'm in." Courtney linked her elbow with mine. The two of us were giggling as we pushed through the groups huddled up close to the bar and wound our way into the middle of dance floor, where we completely cut loose.

Sweaty bodies beat around us, but I couldn't even begin to mind. We danced for minutes, or hours, I didn't know. All I knew was I was having the best time I'd had in so long, and I no longer felt like the pariah, like someone people would whisper about.

Because no one here knew.

A month had passed since I returned to campus, and not one person had uttered a word to me about what had happened.

Courtney started dancing with some random guy, and she cast me a telling smile as she turned away. I returned an accepting grin, giving her the go-ahead before I lifted my face toward the high ceiling that strummed with lights. Colors flashed across my face and lit up behind my closed eyes, and I completely gave myself over to my newfound freedom.

I was lost in the crowd, but still I felt it strike me. Tension infiltrated the already heavy air, thickening it more, making it difficult to breathe. I felt them, eyes watching me dance, traveling my curves as I moved.

A burst of modesty tried to crack the surface of the buzz that sedated my mind.

But tonight, it couldn't touch me.

Because I welcomed it. I wanted him to see me.

God, how much time had I spent dreaming of him? Darryn Wild, that boy-man-god who'd stolen so many of my thoughts, that teasing smile that did something to me I'd never felt before, made me shy in a way I liked, like he saw beneath all the red to the girl below.

Now I could feel him, his eyes all over me, caressing me slowly, up and down.

I let all my insecurities drift away as I swayed in time to the music, in sync with the throb of the crowd and the intermittent lights that glowed against my lids.

A charged moment passed, before strong hands found my hips and gripped them from behind. For a beat, I stiffened, before I again gave in to this sublime release. And again, *he* felt good. Right. All this intense energy that ricocheted between us wrapped me up in a frenzy of nerves, alight and alive. The smell of him took me whole, all soap and man and sex.

Oh God.

My heart beat frantically, racing to keep up with my thoughts that were spiraling out of control.

A shimmer of fear slithered through me, before he pulled my back into the safety of his firm chest.

And that was what I felt.

Safe.

With him, and I didn't know why, and I was searching inside myself for resolve, for the commitment I'd made to never allow myself to be so easily played again.

But it was just out of my reach.

Darryn held me close, our bodies moving in time, like we shared the same breath, the same space. I leaned back, my head on his shoulder as his face found the curve of my neck. Chills sped, spinning my body into a violent cataclysm of need. He let his hands roam, palms pressing hard as he ran them down the front of my legs, spanning them wide as he trailed them back up to my hips and over my stomach.

Fingertips dipped into my ribs as he slid them up the curve of my sides, and he lifted my arms as he went, in the same fluid motion fastening my hands around the back of his neck.

All those butterflies scattered, a clash of discordant wings that fluttered haphazardly through my insides, leaving my stomach in a coiled mess of confusion and need.

Why him? Why now?

Holding me close, he brushed his mouth over the shell of my ear, his whispered words injected directly to my manic heart. "Goddamn, Misha. What are you trying to do to me?"

I suddenly found it impossible to breathe, because it was him who was slowly undoing all the fibers of reservation woven through my weakened spirit.

"Can't get you off my mind." He leaned in closer, his hand sweeping up my stomach. Fingers brushed between my breasts, and I released a sharp gasp.

"Been dying to touch you," he murmured low. He began to prod me back, slowly leading me away from the heaving bodies on the dance floor. The riot of the crowd bled into black as he edged us through the club, his roaming hands leaving me completely stripped of any defenses. Walls rose on each side of us as he drew me backward into the darkened hallway. Darryn pulled me into its depths, before he suddenly spun me in his hold and pinned my back up against the wall.

And it wasn't fear I felt when I looked at up at him, captured by those hazel eyes that were more intense than anything I'd ever seen as they searched me frantically, his hands just as frantic when he twisted his fingers through the locks of my hair on both sides of my head.

It was desire.

He yanked me against him, tilting my chin up by the force of his hold in my hair.

I grunted.

"Tell me you want me, too," he demanded in a pained whisper, his eyes flying across my face. "Tell me you lie in bed at night and when you close your eyes, you see me. Because all I can see is you."

Shock punched all the air from my lungs, and my mouth dropped open—I was stunned by his blatant admission.

That gaze darted to my parted lips and back to my eyes, our bodies heaving with the tension that continued to wind us higher and higher.

Shivers lifted on a swollen wave and broke over my skin with a heated rush of desire.

And I wanted to laugh through the haze of alcohol. Because none of this made a lick of sense, how this boy-man-god could say things like he could see right inside my mind, like he'd just mimicked my most secret thoughts, ones of him that I couldn't escape every single time I closed my eyes, how he could make me feel like nothing else in this world mattered except for his hands on me—right here, right now.

Just for tonight, he made me want to be brave.

Even in my heels, I had to push to my toes to reach his mouth, but it was me who closed the distance, me who seemed desperate to feel.

His reaction was immediate, and his breath rushed across my face as his body crushed mine to the wall. His mouth overtook mine, unyielding, his tongue demanding as he swiped it across my teeth, then dove in to tangle with mine, assaulting me with long, hard strokes.

Trembles rolled through me, and my knees went weak, because whatever desperation I'd had to feel his mouth against mine paled in comparison to the recklessness he devoured me with now. His hands and mouth and the racing beat of his heart consumed all my senses.

Shaking, I kissed him with all abandon, like this was the one chance I had, like it was the one moment I'd been granted to feel like this—like I was important and beautiful and somehow this gorgeous man could want me for who I was and it didn't stem from the infamy Hunter had cast like a bounty on my head.

Hunter.

The errant thought of him caused a resurrection of my insecurities, the memories blossoming full as I thought back to the way Hunter had initially made me feel. When Hunter first asked me out, I'd been so shy and scared, sure no one would pay any interest to the small-town girl who'd been sheltered all her life. Hunter had showered attention on me, and I'd clung to the way it made me feel.

Special.

Sickness coiled in my stomach.

Because again, I was feeling it, although Hunter hadn't come close to skimming the magnitude of what Darryn had bounding through my veins.

Fear took hold.

God, what was I doing? Rushing into the same thing as I'd done with Hunter? Desperate to feel? Desperate to please?

I couldn't do this again.

I managed to wriggle my hands between our bodies that were plastered together, and there was nothing I could do to stop the whimper that escaped my throat at the feel of his chest under my hands. Darryn did something to me, touched me somewhere deep inside that I didn't even recognize, drew me in, tempted me.

Stupid. Stupid. Stupid.

Hadn't I been humiliated enough?

With trembling hands, I nudged him back. He only kissed me harder, like he again could read my thoughts and that tongue was at work to convince me to trust him.

Moisture gathered in my eyes, this time my hands firm as I pushed him. "P-p-please, stop."

I could feel him submitting as he stumbled back, not by my force, but by a force of his own as he tore himself away. His entire body vibrated with what roared through mine, this desire that pooled so heavily in my core.

I pressed my hand to my mouth, as if I could contain it all, as if there were a chance I could stop the outpouring of emotion Darryn had brought on me. He filled my thoughts with need and want. Made me feel beautiful and good and not like a stupid little girl. But the fear was so much greater than all of that, molding the idea of Darryn Wild into nothing but a threat. All the warnings about boys like Hunter my mother had ever hammered into my head were ringing out.

Danger. Bad. Hurt.

I couldn't go through that again.

Even if walking away from Darryn now felt like I was ripping away something essential to my soul.

"Misha," he started to say in a grating voice, taking a pleading step forward.

I stuck my hand out to stop him. "Don't. Please. I can't do this."

"You can't or you don't want to?" he challenged, fisting his hands at his sides, like he didn't know what to do with the energy barreling through him any more than I did.

Mine manifested as tears streaming hot and fast down my face.

Oh God, did I want to.

"Can't," I whispered, shaking my head.

Couldn't go through this again.

Regret flashed in his eyes, like he could see straight through me, like he knew exactly what I was thinking and why I was pushing him away.

If only he really knew.

He wouldn't want me then.

"I have to go." I turned to flee. He grabbed me around my wrist and spun me around. His hands found my face. For a flash, agony took over his expression as he hesitantly pulled me closer. This time his kiss was slow, fueled by passion. It cut me so much deeper than the frenzied kiss we'd given ourselves over to minutes before, because this one spoke of what could be, of what I'd always dreamed of as a little girl before Hunter showed me just how cruel this world could be.

I surrendered to it and kissed him with everything I wished I could be, before I ripped myself away. Standing there panting, I stared at him and said, "I'm so sorry."

Swallowing hard, I took two steps back, watching something that looked like anger flare in the depths of Darryn's eyes. Harshly, he blinked. "Yeah, so am I."

chapter eight

Darryn

Fuck.

It was official.

I was a creeper.

Not the *I'm going to drag you into an alley and slit your throat* kind of creeper.

More like the *I'm going to drag you into an alley and kiss you senseless and leave you begging my name* kind of creeper.

Different, right?

I sure as hell hoped so.

Because this was the low I'd stooped to.

Trailing her from a distance, I kept my eye on the mass of black curls that bobbed through the surging crowd on the sidewalk while doing my best to remain hidden.

Misha Crosse had done this to me. Made me a little bit crazy and left me partaking in tactics I'd never consider for another girl. Clearly she knew I was pursuing her, the way she kept peering over her shoulder, keen eyes searching through the horde of people as she sought out my presence.

Like she could feel me.

That same insane way I could feel her.

She didn't appear so much scared as she did wary. The thought of her being afraid of me made me sick, although I knew she was fearful in an entirely different way. I'd never damage a hair on her head. I think she knew that. But it was that weakened heart the girl was protecting.

But that *kiss*. That searing, shattering kiss? I thought I couldn't get her out of my mind before. After that kiss this weekend, she was all I could think about. The way she felt. The way she tasted. She'd singed through all those exterior layers of indifference that covered me up in callousness, straight down to splay open wide the deepest part of me.

God, I wanted her. Wanted to fix her and hold her and promise her I'd never let anyone hurt her.

But she wouldn't give me the chance.

Misha had been avoiding me at all costs. Sneaking from her house when she thought I wouldn't see her, leaving me standing outside their front door like a lovesick fool when I knocked, had me pacing when she didn't return the text messages I'd sent after I begged her number off one of her roommates.

That girl was pretending she wasn't affected.

But I knew better.

I'd felt everything when she kissed me, when she kissed me like she could taste freedom, like she'd finally found what she'd been searching for.

I had, that was for damned sure.

I could kiss a thousand girls and not one of them could stir up a modicum of the feeling Misha had brought to a full boil in me in one singular touch.

To be honest, it scared me a little, just how intense it was.

I mean, shit, here I was, basically stalking this girl, looking for a moment to talk to her. Chasing her. And I would have let it go . . . let her go . . . if I hadn't witnessed what I'd seen so clearly on her face last weekend at the club, like she was begging me to somehow make it better and she was just too scared to ask, too many doubts holding her back.

There was no place inside me that could ignore that silent plea.

I'd gotten lucky and seen her slipping out the door this evening. She'd walked in the opposite direction of campus, heading to whatever secret place she stole to those evenings when she came back with a smile flooding her precious face.

Maybe I'd get to see it now, where she went, and from afar I could experience what brought her joy.

Every part of me screamed that I wanted to bring it to her, too.

Joy.

My heart squeezed.

How had this girl gotten so far under my skin? Like she'd come out of nowhere, a rogue wave that had barreled over me unseen, dragging me under. And there was no coming back up.

Misha suddenly cut through the crowd. On the left, she swung open a large plate-glass door nestled along the row of businesses lining the bustling walkway. She disappeared inside. Swallowing, I wove a little faster through the crush of people on the sidewalk, anxious not to lose her, more anxious to make out the sign hanging over the door.

I squinted.

CHILDREN'S LANGUAGE AND SPEECH PATHOLOGY.

Frowning, I cupped my hands around my eyes and pressed them to the hazy glass, peering inside to the large, open space.

So it wasn't the most inconspicuous move. But what the hell? It wasn't like she hadn't already known I was there.

Chairs lined the walls of the front room, and a reception area sat to the far back in the center. White double doors rested on each side of it, passageways to what I could only assume would be some sort of clinic-style rooms behind them.

But none of those things were what interested me.

It was Misha.

She stood facing away, lost in an army of all these little kids that were probably four or five years old circling her legs, their faces all lit up with excitement as they smiled up at her.

Like she was their light.

Guess she had that way about her.

People who I could only assume were their parents sat in chairs that were placed along the walls, watching with soft smiles on their faces while Misha and another girl I'd never seen before, although she had to be close to Misha's age, gathered all the kids and started playing these games with them. Enraptured, the kids all went along with the instructions, grinning through their small faces, tossing their heads back as they roared with laughter, Misha tickling and loving and smiling so wide it twisted me up tight and my breath got caught right in the center of my throat.

She was always stunning. Beautiful. But seeing her there, so happy amid all those kids?

I rubbed at my chest.

I didn't know what to make of her or what I felt. Why I was so intrigued.

Why I was *hooked.*

Images made an unwelcome pass through my mind. Every fantasy I'd ever had of her slammed me with guilt. Because I never should have witnessed her that way. Not like that. Not with *him.*

Anger built inside me, interlocking with that shame Misha wore like a broken crown on her head.

My fists clenched.

All of it just pissed me off.

This girl was innocent. I could feel it radiating from her, saturating her being.

Thoughts of the interactions Misha and I had shared eddied through my vision, this flustered girl who stumbled all over herself, *stuttered* over her own damned name.

I looked back to the glass. With pure affection, Misha dragged her fingers through the red curls of a little boy who had some sort of device stuck to his head with wires coming from it that ran to his ear. Giggling, he grinned up at her.

She spoke and laughed, leading them through a bunch of different activities.

Working with them, but not like it was *work*, but because it was her passion.

All of this? It meant something to her.

And I had the desperate need to mean something to her, too.

chapter nine

Misha

I read below the dim bulb attached to the generic floor lamp that was set up next to my bed. Sighing, I shifted, tucking my bent legs up closer to my chest while I adjusted the huge textbook on my lap. I rested back on the wooden headboard, going through the last two chapters in my psychology textbook, reviewing yet again all the material that would be covered on our test tomorrow.

Tonight had been good.

I'd been with my kids. Seeing their smiling faces always reminded me why I was here, giving me that encouragement to continue on.

Things had been difficult lately.

Well, lately meant since the moment Darryn Wild had come like a battering ram into my life, battering his way right into my heart.

Said muscle skipped and pattered, just a knee-jerk reaction that came with every thought of him, like a little thundered affirmation of my stupidity.

I liked being around him.

Way too much.

I liked the way he made me feel, liked the way he looked at me. God, I barely knew him, and still I liked everything about him.

But kissing him this last weekend? It'd shaken something loose in me that I was doing everything in my power to ignore.

It didn't matter if I wanted to ignore it or not. It was there.

What I wouldn't do to be normal. Maybe then I could embrace it. *Normal.*

I scoffed, shifting my book as I struggled to focus on the words bleeding across the page.

What did that even mean?

But whatever it was, it wasn't me. I never had felt that way, at least. My parents had worked so hard to ensure that I grew up living a *normal* life, but all their efforts had only made me feel the opposite. They didn't mean to hinder me, to stunt my emotional growth, to narrow my developing mind.

But they'd done it nonetheless.

Still I wished I wasn't this awkward little girl who didn't have the first clue how to traverse the normal path of a college student.

Here I had made that one bold attempt with Hunter. And what did I do? Failed miserably. I'd been foolish enough to think I could just shuck it from my consciousness like a pair of dirty socks, leave it behind. One touch from Darryn had proven that theory wrong, and all those doubts came flooding back.

What if he was the same kind of guy as Hunter?

Every time Darryn came close, all those danger bells started ringing.

So I pretended I didn't feel the pulsating ache in my chest when I thought of him. I wanted him. So much. And that scared me.

Bitterness shook my head. I was so tired of being scared, of being fearful people were watching me, worrying they were judging me. When would it ever stop?

Two soft knocks at my door stalled my reading, not that I was doing much of it.

I barely glanced up when I called, "Come in," figuring it was one of my roommates.

The door cracked open. I gasped when all those darts of energy pinged against the boxed-in barriers of my walls, that tangible tension that seemed to follow him like a broiling summer storm spreading out to saturate every inch of my room. Only now they were amplified, driven by the frustration of what I had cut too short.

My legs flew from my chest and flat onto the mattress, and I splayed my book across my lap as if it would afford me some sort of cover. All I was wearing was a pair of black boy-short panties and a tank top, no bra, my hair loose.

Exposed and vulnerable.

And he was there, that boy-man-god standing in my open doorway.

Beautiful. Commanding. Potent.

Heat rushed and sped, covering every inch of my skin, smoldering on my neck and face. I felt myself glow like an ember under his gaze as he devoured me with his eyes, the same way he'd done with his mouth and hands and tongue this last weekend.

Oh. God.

A tremor traveled my body, dripping like melting ice as it slipped down my spine.

Hesitation held him back, like he was coming to some sort of decision, his steely gaze so intense I found myself at a loss for words. I had no power to make them form on my lips. Even if I could, I didn't know what to say, because part of me was screaming at him to leave, to demand to know how he made it this far, invading my private space where I hid away.

The other part was just begging him to come near.

Apparently that was the part he heard.

Without a sound he stepped inside. He didn't look away from me as he blindly snapped the door shut behind him and twisted the lock.

I gulped for the nonexistent air.

It was almost too much, being with him this way, drowning in the intensity of his presence.

He said nothing as he crossed the room.

Desire throbbed between my legs, a sensation that was a little bit foreign and a whole lot terrifying. I swallowed down the knot that formed in my throat. Finally I managed to force the words from the dried-out cavern of my mouth. "Wh-wh-what are you doing in here?" I sat forward, blinking through the stupor. "Y-you shouldn't be here."

The smallest of smirks lifted one side of his mouth as he tilted his head, not so cocky as self-assured. He dropped to his knees at the side of my bed. Without warning, he grabbed me by the outside of my legs, dragging me to the edge of the mattress, and he nestled between my bare thighs as his stomach pressed to the burning heat of my center.

I yelped, this tiny sound of resistance that was really an utterance of surrender.

"Yes, I should," he murmured as he looked at me, his warm hand cupping my face, his thumb stroking my cheek.

Oh. Lord.

Defenseless.

That was the way he left me, a shivering mess of nerves in his arms as he stared up at me.

He leaned forward and pressed his mouth to mine. Softly. I whimpered but gave in, succumbed as he tugged at my bottom lip with his mouth before his tongue made a slow pass against mine.

Fire.

I let my hands wander over the planes of his chest and shoulders, my body jerking with pleasure as I felt his quiver beneath my touch.

"God, Misha," rumbled up his throat as he rose onto his knees and deepened the kiss, pulling back before he dove in again, teasing us both with the idea of what we could be together. He gripped my face and whispered at my mouth, "I can't stay away from you anymore. Can't go one more night without knowing you're mine."

Inside, that timid girl shrank, but still I kissed him in between all her words that I couldn't keep from tumbling out. "I c-c-can't, Darryn . . . can't do this . . . can't be what you want me to be. . . . I'm not ready for this."

He pulled away a fraction. Both of his hands tangled in my hair, not letting me go. "Then tell me what you're ready for . . . anything. I just want to mean something to you."

His words nearly tore me apart.

I wanted that so badly, to *really* mean something to someone.

He'd just reflected it back.

And the truth was, I wanted to mean something to him.

"I'm scared," I admitted, stretching out a shaky hand and tracing the lines of his face. I trembled doing it, disbelief radiating to my bones that I was touching him. That he was here. And he wanted me.

"I can't just jump into something with you, Darryn. I don't even know you . . . a-a-and . . . and . . . I've been . . ." I paused, looked to the wall as I chewed at my lip and the red flushed hot. Maybe one day, as my trust grew, as he showed me what was happening between us was real, I'd tell him. Tell him everything. He needed to know. But for now, I settled on what I could bear. "I've been *hurt*." I cast it from my mouth like a dirty confession.

A soft sigh filtered from his mouth, and he lifted himself up higher on his knees, bringing us level, nose-to-nose and face-to-face. He smiled slow. "We don't have to rush, Misha, but we can't ignore this, either. Just tell me . . . tell me you're mine. That you want to be. Be my girl . . . and I'll be satisfied to take whatever comes along with that."

I didn't mean to cry, but I couldn't stop the wetness that gathered in my eyes and streaked like a deluge of relief down my face. I'd cried so much these last months, but this was just a rush of emotion, all this sweet joy that was mixed up with all my fear.

I nodded through a soggy smile. "I want to be," I whispered breathlessly.

God, I wanted to be.

His.

Satisfaction danced all over his beautiful face, before Darryn branded me with a searing, close-mouthed kiss.

It stole my breath.

He chuckled a little, pecked my lips again and ran his fingers through my hair. "You are perfect."

"Hardly." But I couldn't help but smile, and that smile only grew as he slowly rose, crawling over me and onto my bed, taking me with him.

Laying us down, he tucked me into his side. The warm breath from his mouth seeped out at my temple when he exhaled and splayed his big hand wide across my belly.

Those butterflies swayed in a lazy dance.

Never in my life had I felt so secure.

"Tell me about where you went tonight," he said, nudging the side of my face with his nose.

I frowned, but really, I already knew. He'd been there. I'd thought I felt him following me, but I could never catch a glimpse of him among the roiling throng of bodies that had flocked along the busy sidewalk during rush hour.

I should have been angry. Offended that he would be so bold as to follow me.

But again, it made me feel special. Like I meant something to him, the way he wanted to mean something to me. And he did. God, he did. That scared me, too.

"I—I—I . . ."

He gave me a squeeze of reassurance. "Hey, it's okay. You can trust me."

I swallowed and found my voice, but I had to press my face into his chest to make the words form, and even when they did, they were barely more than a breath. "Have you . . . did you notice I sometimes stutter?"

He hooked his finger under my chin and pulled my face up, forcing me to look at him. A quirk of his brow told me he had indeed. "Yeah, and it's really fucking cute."

Sadness shook my head, because I knew he really didn't understand. "It's not cute, Darryn." I licked my lips. "For years my parents tried to have a baby. They'd given up, and then there was me. They were older when they finally had me, and of course they became super protective. When I was four, my mom had to go back to work, but they didn't want to put me in day care. They thought the best solution would be for me to stay with our neighbor next door, a woman they'd known for several years."

When my voice got choppy, Darryn pulled me closer, like he knew I was having a difficult time getting this out.

"They wanted me close to home, where my mom knew I was safe. But I wasn't safe," I whispered, the words sounding like my darkest secret.

Gentle fingers brushed up and down my arms, silently encouraging me to go on.

"I really don't remember everything that happened. . . . I just see these little blips . . . pictures that flash through my mind that are hazy and unclear. The woman . . . sh-sh-she was just . . . cruel-hearted. She liked it when I was scared and when I'd cry. She'd make me sit in the dark closet all day and when I'd cry she'd smack me around. What I remember best is the anxiety I felt every time my mom dropped me off at her house. And how she threatened me not to tell my mom and dad."

Darryn pulled back, leaving a fraction of space between us as we lay on our sides. He just stared across at me, everything in his gaze protective. "I'm not sure I want to hear this story," he admitted, sadness coloring his tone, though he smiled a sympathetic smile. He brushed his thumb along my jaw. "But I need to . . . just don't blame me if I run out your door and have to kick someone's ass."

I laughed quietly, a sound that I hoped somehow told him that I was okay, that this woman hadn't scarred my heart even if she had scarred something in the deepest recesses of my mind. "N-n-no . . . my parents already took care of that. It didn't take long for them to realize what was going on in that woman's house because I started acting so differently. But that was the problem . . . I just . . . stopped talking."

Lines creased Darryn's brow as his eyes narrowed, like he was slowly catching on.

"The therapist said it was because of the trauma and s-s-something was triggered in my brain that wouldn't allow me t-t-to talk." Attempting a joke, I lightened my voice, hating that my tongue was so tied. "Guess her threats to hurt me if I told worked just fine. Apparently if you get annoyed with my voice, you can smack me around a little bit and I'll shut right up."

Darryn just frowned. "Not funny," he scolded.

Okay, so maybe not, but I hated the thought of this boy who'd chased me down as if I was something special, something he couldn't be without, instead looking at me with pity.

"M-my parents . . . they got me into therapy, both to help with my emotional trauma and to help me to begin to talk. But once I started talking again, I stuttered. Badly." I shrugged, embarrassed but somehow still at ease with baring myself to him. "In some ways, the worst part was watching my parents worry about me. They loved me so much."

Softness pulled at his lips. "How could they not?"

Palpitations rocked my heart. This boy-man-god and his glorious body had even sweeter words, words that teased me with what sounded like a promise. I was done for.

I pressed my hand flat to his chest, just because I wanted to feel him, to connect, because I was intent on finishing my story. At least the part I could tell him. "I . . . I think they felt so guilty over what happened to me, they overreacted. They pulled me out of public school and my mom homeschooled me. I grew so comfortable in the shelter of my parents' house with no other kids around, I got to the point where I was afraid to leave it. The truth is, I never really learned how to function comfortably in public situations. I learned to control my stuttering for the most part, unless I'm excited or nervous. But still, I stayed under my parents' protective wings, until I came here for college."

He kissed my forehead, and I snuggled farther into him, resting my head in the crook of his arm. "It was a big deal for me to come to Michigan. My parents were terrified they wouldn't be close to keep an eye on me. But I knew I had to make a change or I'd always be dependent on them. The first year here, I barely spoke to anyone, just watched and observed and went to my classes, but my confidence slowly grew. Then when I moved in here, Indy became my first real friend. It's been so good for me."

Remorse left me with a heavy sigh. "But that doesn't mean I haven't let people take advantage of me. I always see the best in people. T-trust them when they don't deserve it. *That's* why I'm scared," I emphasized, twining our fingers together with our free hands, praying he could understand where all my reservations stemmed from.

Because I hadn't had a bad life. I'd just had circumstances that made me different.

"And the center today?" he asked, lifting our hands up between us, studying the contrast of our skin in the dim light of my room, mine almost white against his golden tan.

A wide smile took over my face. "Those are my kids . . . they all have hearing or speech disorders of one kind or another. It's a support group I run . . . more fun for them than anything, a safe place where they all feel they belong. But it's my internship, too, part of my school-work for my degree."

"Your degree?"

"Speech pathologist," I said, almost shy. "For children. I just want to help them. . . . I overcame so much when I was little, and some really wonderful people helped me. Now I want to help other kids the same way." I drew my shoulder up to my ear in a self-conscious shrug. "It fits, don't you think?"

A low chuckle rumbled up his chest, and he kissed the back of my hand, our fingers still twisted together. "Yeah, it definitely fits." The intense emotion in his hazel eyes deepened, flashed with something I didn't quite recognize, almost a blend of anger and devotion. "It all makes sense now."

Darryn pushed his weight to one of his hands, moving over me. Slowly I rolled onto my back, led by his motion, that strong chest hovering over me with his body still off to my side. My nerve endings ratcheted up, all those darts of energy rapid-firing across my skin as his eyes changed and everything between us became charged, heightened to a level I'd never experienced. One that had me trembling below him.

He touched my face. "You're amazing, Misha."

Heat blazed up my throat, and Darryn dipped down, pressing his mouth to the oversensitive skin. He trailed kisses up and down along the hollow of my neck, up to beneath my ear.

I whimpered, and he brought his mouth to mine, shifting his weight over me, his knee wedged between my thighs. "Is this okay?" he asked, leaning back to run his hands down my sides.

"Yes."

He continued his assault, kissing every exposed inch of skin on my chest and shoulders, moving to my face, trailing sweet kisses over my closed lids. He ran his nose down between the swell of my breasts exposed over the top of my tank.

"And this?" he whispered, almost urgently—almost as urgently as the need stampeding through my veins. "Tell me when to stop, because I don't know if I can trust myself not to push you too far. You have no idea how badly I want you."

And the crazy thing was I didn't want him to stop, but I needed him to. I pulled back, tipping my head to force him to look at me. All that shyness came rushing to my face, flaming with the fire he'd set inside me. I blinked, murmuring my plea. "Just . . . respect me . . . Be patient with me." My tongue darted out to my lips. "Above all, be honest with me."

He hefted the air from his lungs, and again I was slammed with all that was Darryn—all soap and sex and man.

He pulled back and settled down at my side. And right there, in that one action, he earned a huge piece of my trust. Because he did know when to stop. He could have continued, and I would have let him. But he didn't.

He pulled me into the sanctuary of his arms, right up against his beating heart. "I'll take care of you, Misha," he said. The words sounded like the most solemn of promises.

Maybe my boy-man-god really was my avenging angel. Darryn the Destroyer. Sent to rescue me. To slay all the beasts that had held me captive.

I guess I really wanted a fairy tale, after all.

chapter ten

Misha

"Oh my gosh . . . stop!" I pled. Breathless giggles built up in my belly and rolled through my entire body before they spilled from my mouth.

My cries only encouraged Darryn. Hazel eyes gleamed with all that mischief, and his deft fingers made another assault on my sides, tickling my ribs. It might have hurt if being near him didn't feel so good.

I flailed and kicked my legs, howling with laughter as I twisted and turned and tried to pull myself out of his reach.

Darryn only leaned in farther, pinning my back to the small table in the nook of his kitchen. "You asked for it."

"You're going to make me pee my pants," I yelped, thinking that just might do the trick considering that our bodies were in a very compromised position, his overpowering mine as I struggled under him.

No such luck.

"Really?" he dared, leaning in a little farther, digging in a little deeper. "Come on, let's see it, Misha." His smell enveloped me like a big, huge hug. A hug that came with an overwhelming surge of desire. Because who could blame me?

This boy-man-god was mine.

He'd been mine for more than a month.

Was it wrong it'd been the single best month of my life?

Darryn pulled back a fraction, just enough to allow me to drag a gulping breath into my lungs. Even though he had me at his mercy, there was so much softness in his eyes, so much restraint in his hands, so much goodness in his heart, I knew he'd never hurt me. There was no mistaking it.

He pushed back and dragged the hem of my shirt up, exposing my stomach. His mouth went for my side, tickling me in a whole new way as he suckled at my skin.

I squealed, my hips doing their best to buck Darryn from me, but there was nothing I could do to stop him from leaving his mark.

He pulled back and glanced up at me with a smirk before he turned back to his handiwork. "Perfect," he said, rubbing his thumb over the flaming skin that he'd exposed just above my hip.

I wondered if it could possibly be as red as my face.

So yeah, he was still a total punk. Arrogant and sly. But God help me if I didn't like that about him, too.

He'd told me a month ago he just wanted to mean something to me.

Little did he know he was slowly becoming everything.

I sobered a little, reaching out to brush my fingers through the flop of hair that had fallen on his forehead. Slowly he helped me up to sitting, and he plopped down on a chair in front of where my legs dangled off the side of the table, wedging himself between my knees. He looked up at me, his expression so sweet it twisted something loose inside my heart. A smile pulled at his mouth, and he touched my chin, tilting it, quietly inspecting my face. "I love that blush," he whispered, fluttering his fingers over it like he wished it were palpable, something tangible he could ball up in his hand and hide away.

I felt so exposed, yet so adored. "Do you know what I love?"

His eyes glimmered. "What?"

I ran my thumb across his bottom lip. "This mouth." I leaned in and placed a kiss on it, so soft I hoped it spoke a thousand words that I wasn't ready to say. Or maybe it was just three.

I love you.

It was there, screaming out from my heart. But even as I thought them, all those feelings of vulnerability came barreling in, warning me against feeling something so strong for someone I'd only been dating for a month. But I couldn't stop my feelings or change them. I couldn't help the way he made me feel. Couldn't help that his arms were my favorite place. Couldn't help that his mouth was my favorite flavor and his voice was my favorite song.

His tongue was all warm when he swept it against my mouth, and tingles spread through me like a wildfire. "Mm," he moaned, "not as much as I love yours."

I tilted my head and parted my lips, welcoming the rush of his heat as he took over my mouth, the way his tongue danced and played before he closed his mouth over my lips, before they opened again and the kiss only deepened.

With both hands, he palmed my breasts over my T-shirt, urging a moan from somewhere in the deepest part of my spirit, before his fingers hooked in my collar and pulled my shirt down to expose me.

I gasped.

Sure, I was wearing a bra. But that didn't mean I didn't feel laid bare.

I could feel the heat emanating from my chest, the burning red I knew was flaming on all that skin Darryn had just brought out into the light.

Darryn looked up at me, wetting his swollen lips with his tongue, hunger and hard-won restraint so vivid in his eyes. "Too much?" he asked as the worry floated into his strained voice, his question guarded as he let his hands wander over the lacy cups of my bra, so slowly, giving me time to react. Time to clamp my hands over his to stop him the way I usually did, when I'd beg him to be patient even though he'd never given me any reason to feel I needed to plea.

He always understood and never pushed me any further than where I wanted to go.

And I knew he probably thought me a blushing virgin, the reason for all these pesky layers of clothing we had to maintain.

Which really wasn't all that far from the truth. Except for that one monstrous mistake I'd made. As much as I wanted it all swept up and tossed away like forgotten litter from my past, I knew he needed to know, and things couldn't go much further between us before he did. How deceitful would that be? Me leading this man into thinking I was some kind of unsullied damsel. Pure and clean. What a joke.

Darryn ran his hands up my sides, all those little darts of energy injected directly into my skin.

Oh God.

Did I ever want him to touch me.

Every day Darryn made me trust him more. Showed me why it was okay to give in.

Today, for the first time, I didn't stop his exploration. I welcomed his hands that touched and caressed. Hands that I thought maybe even loved. Even if it were over the constraints of a flimsy piece of fabric.

But just then, I heard the sound of the front door banging open, and I stiffened. My hands clapped over my chest to cover myself up as one of Darryn's roommates walked into their house. He was still in the front room, but he was close enough to burst the bubble Darryn and I had been floating in.

Darryn groaned and dropped his head to my chest, the chest that he'd discreetly covered back up. "Maybe we should take this up to my room," he mumbled.

"I . . . I—I'm s-s-sorry. I can't go up there." I fumbled over words I couldn't seem to form, searching for an explanation for why I was such a freak. "I—I . . ."

It wasn't like we hadn't been alone in my room a hundred times.

But when Darryn pulled away, it was like he already understood what was holding me back from making my way up those steps. Anger darkened his eyes, just for a flash, before he raked a hand through his hair and sighed a heavy sound of surrender. "It's fine, baby. You don't have to explain anything to me. I get it."

It left me unsettled, because I knew he really didn't *get* it. He had no clue.

I shifted on the hard surface of the table, wanting to be brave and just tell him. Hating myself for being a coward and not saying anything.

But the truth was, I didn't want to lose him.

Just the thought squeezed my heart.

I reached out and cupped his cheek, my voice soft. "Please be patient with me."

He took my hand from his face and pressed it to his mouth. "I already told you I'd take whatever came with you being my girl. The only thing I hate is you being afraid of me. Because I promise, I'll never hurt you."

But it wasn't Darryn I was afraid of facing.

I was afraid of facing the humiliation that had been born in that room. Hated that any moment I spent there with Darryn would be tainted by memories of Hunter.

Darryn pulled me to the edge of the table and wrapped his arms around my waist, his head resting just below my breasts. He looked up at me, the gold of his eyes prominent in the rays of sunlight slanting in through the window. "I just want you to trust me."

I tickled my fingers down the back of his neck, and he released a raspy breath. And I did trust him.

I knew it now. Knew he was different from Hunter. Knew Darryn cared about me, maybe the way I cared about him.

I could feel him slipping deeper into me the way I felt myself falling further into him.

I wanted to show him how much he meant to me.

Tell him.

But would he feel the same about me when he knew?

I let him pull me ever closer, his hot body all pressed up to mine. Flames licked up the walls of my stomach, sending needy waves of heat through my body, a feeling I'd only ever experienced with Darryn.

Indy had definitely been right. Hunter didn't have anything on Darryn.

Every part of me was begging for more of him.

His hand clutched my side like he couldn't bear the thought of letting go. "Can't get enough of you, Misha," he whispered, his nose making a pass along the underside of my breast. Shock waves jolted through my system.

Soon I would give him all of me.

The truth. My heart. My body.

Because I knew Darryn would never make me a fool.

chapter eleven

Misha

The doorbell rang and I skipped to the door. I swung it open to Darryn. He rested his shoulder up on the doorjamb, this boy-man-god larger than life, the sun swallowing him up from behind in a halo of blazing light as he stood as a silhouette in my doorway.

My pulse stuttered.

Oh God.

So pretty.

Darryn stepped forward, bringing his face into focus. He was biting at his bottom lip with all that mischief playing in his eyes. Damn him. He knew exactly the effect he had on me.

Then everything about him softened, and he wound his fingers through my hair and brought his hand to the back of my neck. He tugged me forward to place a sweet kiss at the corner of my mouth. I shook a little as his nose slipped along the angle of my jaw. He breathed me in, and there was no mistaking the shudder that rolled down his spine.

I felt a little giddy, struck light-headed by this joy. Guess I liked that I had the same kind of effect on him, too.

"You ready to go, baby?" The words came out all low and rough.

Uh, yeah. I'd go anywhere with him.

I beamed up at him, picked my backpack up off the floor, and hoisted it farther on my shoulders. "Yep. All set. Let's get this day over with. I have two exams and a presentation. I was ready for today to be over before it even started."

Darryn chuckled as he tossed his arm over my shoulders, guiding me out of the house and closing the door behind us, leading us in the direction of campus. "You're going to do great." He glanced down at me. "Don't think I've seen anyone study the way you do. You make all the rest of us look bad."

"Pshh." I waved him off, swaying a little into his side as we walked wound up in each other. "My classes are just rough. If I didn't study this much, I'd for sure fail, and the last thing I want is to have to take any of these classes over again. No, thank you."

He kissed my temple. "Smart girl."

I grinned up at him. "I like to think so." I attempted a wink, but I was pretty sure it was one long blink.

Darryn howled, his laughter so thick I felt it seeping into my chest. "You are too much, Misha Crosse. You know that?"

We walked like this most days, stealing a few moments close together before we both had to go our separate ways to our different classes. We grabbed just a few minutes together, laughing and goofing around. It was the perfect way to start the day, with his face one of the first things I saw every morning, before he tucked me to his side and walked us toward campus, like I was a piece of him and he was a part of me.

I exhaled in contentment, and Darryn pulled me closer. I felt no hesitation snuggling farther into him. It was beginning to get colder, the fall air turning crisp, the leaves beginning to change. I lifted my face to the cool breeze and just relished the turn of the season, and this turn in my life.

I'd been so fearful about coming back to school. And look at the way things had turned out. What if I'd refused Indy's invitation and instead stayed in the suffocating safety of my parents' house, attending a community college, giving up my kids, my goals for the future?

Losing all that would be awful. But the most horrifying part of it all would be the fact that I would never have met this man had I not stepped out and been brave.

I made the decision right then and there, that was what I finally needed to be.

Brave.

Darryn seemed to sense my inner turmoil, and he somehow managed to pull me even tighter to his body. "What are you thinking about?"

I chanced peeking up at him. Nerves tumbled through my stomach, a chaotic scramble of fear and insecurities and hope. I smiled, and it felt almost forced. "Just thinking about you," I said.

He chuckled, and he buried his face in my neck, leaving a little trail of fire where he nibbled his lips along my skin. "You better be thinking of me, since I can't think of anything else but you." He squeezed my side. "What do you say we make it a date night? Go grab a bite to eat and maybe catch a movie or something?"

"Yeah, that would be great." I chewed at my lip, and the rush of redness I felt blossom on my face had nothing to do with the shyness that had plagued me my whole life, but instead was the stark evidence of the true worry I felt at finally telling Darryn. "I actually have been needing to talk to you about something," I confessed quietly.

He frowned and slowed, stopping fully to turn and face me. His head canted to the side as he studied my expression. "I don't think I like the sound of that, Misha. You aren't letting me take you to dinner with the intention of breaking my heart, are you?" He said it causally, playfully, but I didn't miss the undertone of fear that laced his words. His own insecurities were evident in the unease that sparked in his eyes.

I loved all of Darryn's confidence, craved it almost, after all the years I'd lacked it myself. But the truth was, I liked the vulnerability he was now wearing, too. It made him seem real. Genuine. This boy-man-god, in all his glory, the one who stole my breath just as easily as he'd stolen my heart, was not just a figment of my overactive imagination.

"I couldn't possibly break your heart," I whispered, averting my gaze to pluck a piece of fuzz from his shirt.

It was my heart on the line.

With caution, I peered up at him, feeling so shy and exposed. But I had to finally lay it all out. Trust him so he could trust me.

Was I really ready for this? To lay myself bare? At his feet?

Would he trample all over my heart when he knew?

Was it worth the chance?

"You just need to know something about me before we go any further."

His expression turned unreadable, but I felt every single one of the muscles in his body fire, rigid as they flexed, tension winding him tight.

For a moment, I thought he was . . . angry?

Darryn softened, and he lifted his hands, touched my face so softly. Still it scorched me through. "Nothing you can tell me will change the way I feel about you," he promised, locking our gazes. My breaths turned ragged as he backed me up against the wall of the lecture hall building.

His promise infiltrated my spirit, and I swallowed hard, nodding before I lifted myself to my toes and pressed my mouth to his. It was meant to be innocent, sweet, but Darryn deepened it, swiping his tongue across the seam of my mouth. On a gasp, I opened, then melted as he pinned me to the wall with that glorious body. His tongue skimmed and danced and played against mine with an intensity that I wasn't close to expecting.

Darryn, the one who'd saved something inside me.

And I felt it pumping, full of life, full of hope, my heart so full I thought it would burst right in my chest.

He pulled back, fisted his hands in my jacket collar, and jerked me toward him. His voice was fierce at my face. "Nothing," he promised again.

Then he turned and left me standing there, panting, as I watched him disappear in the hustle of students emerging from another class.

Thankfully I had the support of the wall to keep me from dropping to my knees.

Dear. Lord.

I bit at my lip, fighting against the satisfied smile.

"You got some of that for me?"

The voice barely cut into my senses, and I blinked, wondering if it had really been intended for me, but something inside me was sure it had. I turned my head toward the sound of it, and a guy I'd never seen before stood ten feet away, looking directly at me.

"Should have known better than to have bet against Hunter, but something about you looking all innocent in the picture he had of you had me laying down my money in your favor."

Hunter.

The mention of his name punched me in the gut. I clutched my stomach, bent at the middle. My heart careened to a stop, tightening in my chest in a ball and making it impossible to breathe. I tried to, but I couldn't get anything down as the air got locked in my throat. I felt light-headed. Sick.

So long. It'd been so long and no one had said a word. I guess I had started to believe no one ever would.

I struggled to draw a breath into my lungs. But the air was gone as the realization of what this stranger was implying seeped into my consciousness.

"You owe me," he said, like he had the right to even speak to me, and he took a step forward. Confidence dripped from him, that sickening kind that made people choke on it, it was so overbearing and wrong. "Why don't you come back to my place and I can show you exactly how you can make it up to me?"

Horrified, I felt my mouth drop open in the same second that tears sprang to my eyes, so heavy they blurred my vision of the guy leering at me like I was a nothing, just a plaything to be used up and tossed aside.

Just like Hunter had made me out to be.

Finally something broke, and air raked into my lungs, and I struggled to speak. "D-d-don't t-t-talk t-t-t-o me. . . ."

He laughed at my expense. "Don't worry, baby, talking is definitely not what I have in mind."

I had to get out of here. Escape.

I squeezed my eyes closed, wishing I could disappear, and instead forced my feet to work. I stumbled as I pushed from the wall, an overbearing weight crushing my shoulders.

It hurt. Oh my God, it hurt.

Frantic, I tore through a group of people standing in my way, desperate to keep myself together until I made it home.

"Hey, watch it."

I didn't even respond, just propelled myself forward, through the outer campus halls and out onto the street. I ran as fast as my feet could take me, my eyes blinded by tears and my heart broken by shame.

I flew into the house and upstairs. Slamming my door shut behind me, I threw myself on the bed. I buried my face in my pillow.

And I completely fell apart.

chapter twelve

Misha

"Baby, what's wrong?"

Darryn rushed to my bed when I lifted my face. I'd been crying for so long my eyes hurt, my entire face puffy and sore and burning.

I didn't want him to see me like this. "Just go," I mumbled into my pillow as I turned in the other direction.

This afternoon, he'd texted me what seemed a hundred times, first to solidify our date plans, then with progressive worry when I didn't return any of his messages.

But how could I face him? Tell him?

All that confidence I'd felt this morning was long forgotten. It had only been a fantasy. Because I'd seen the results of what Hunter had done, had seen it in the way that guy had looked at me back in the hall, as if I meant nothing and I could be used up any way he deemed fit.

How could Darryn see me any differently?

Darryn's footsteps treaded tentatively across the room, and I could almost feel the force of his breaths as he heaved them from his lungs and out into the darkness of my room. I pressed my face deeper into my pillow, silently begging it to swallow me up.

I couldn't do this.

The bed dipped with Darryn's weight, and he placed a soothing hand on my back.

I shivered, wishing I had the strength to push him away. But all the comfort of his touch slipped along my skin, penetrating deep. I squeezed my eyes shut and choked over a sob brought on by the kindness in Darryn's gesture.

He rubbed me up and down, all these soft little sounds tumbling from his lips. "Shh . . . baby . . . shh . . . it's okay. You're going to be okay."

I thought I'd cried enough today that I'd used up all my tears. But no. Darryn showing up here only brought a new onslaught of them, these hot, fat tears that poured from my aching eyes, because God, this hurt so bad, Darryn here, making all these promises that seemed so impossible.

Not after today.

"Tell me what happened," he murmured in encouragement near my ear. His breath felt cold against my skin where it met with the endless streams of fiery tears flooding down my face. He leaned in closer, sweeping his mouth across the wetness, gathering my tears up with his lips.

I shuddered.

Oh God.

I couldn't handle this, but I wanted it all the same. Wanted him to take care of me. To make it better.

My avenging angel.

Sent to rescue me from all the wrongs of this world.

He kissed me on my neck, his voice so sure as he released it against the shell of my ear. "I'm here now, baby. Nothing can hurt you. I've got you."

Grief shook my chest.

Darryn slowly rolled me onto my back, and I stared up at him staring down at me. He watched me with all his compassion.

My voice was hoarse. "It h-h-hurts," I tried to get out, my mouth so dry as I forced the admission from my tongue.

It hurts.

For a flash, the hazel of his eyes pulsed with aggression, an imprisoned rage. But his expression was contrary to what flamed in his eyes. The lines edging the set of his grim mouth promised me it didn't matter. That like he'd promised me earlier, no matter what I had to say to him, it wouldn't change the way he felt.

But I no longer felt like telling him.

I couldn't. Not now.

I just needed him to make me feel better, to cover up all the ache.

I gripped him by the back of the neck and pulled him down to me, desperation behind the ferocity of my kiss.

Darryn froze, then made a veiled attempt to push away, but I just pulled him closer. "Please. Make me feel better. Take this away from me. Just for tonight."

His nose was an inch from mine, his eyes frantic as they roved all over my face, everywhere and nowhere at once. Confusion and fear lined his, like maybe he felt compelled to save me from myself.

From this decision.

But this decision had already been made.

I wanted him to have me. No words could assuage the hurt and humiliation, the shame Hunter had brought on my name.

No one else but Darryn—his touch, his mouth, his body.

I needed it.

"Please," I whimpered, arching up. My hips met his like a plea. *Please.*

Agony twisted up his face for the briefest moment, before he succumbed and dropped to his elbows, caging me.

And I knew . . . knew I'd never be free of him.

And I didn't want to be.

A frenzy lit in him as soon as our bodies aligned, and he rocked against my core. Need spiraled through my stomach, dropping low, throbbing a discordant beat between my thighs. I felt myself grow aroused. Wet. And I wanted to be embarrassed because I thought maybe he could feel it. But with him? I couldn't. With him I didn't feel ashamed.

"Oh God," I moaned, my hips lifting from the bed to meet him, the roughness of the seam of his jeans rubbing against me. "Please."

Darryn ran his hands down my sides and slipped them under my shirt. His palms were hot and desperate, and I didn't stop him when he lifted it and slowly pulled it over my head, for the first time allowing him to peel a piece of clothing from my body.

Darryn shifted his weight to his knees, hovering over me, taking all of me in. His eyes dropped from my eyes, to my mouth, before they roamed over the redness that burned my skin.

My fingers were shaking as I dragged them down his back and to the hem of his shirt. I pulled it over his head. Darryn dropped back down, bringing his skin flush against mine. He felt both soft and hard, rippled muscle and strength that eased over me like a downy blanket, sent to comfort and protect.

My whole body sang, the horrors of this afternoon clashing with how safe Darryn made me feel. Trust flowed from my body in waves, as it arched and begged and bucked into his.

"I need to feel you . . . need to feel you everywhere," I pled, raking my greedy nails down Darryn's back.

He groaned, his hoarse voice vibrating against my neck. "Fuck, Misha . . . baby . . . God, I need you, too. You don't know how much."

His thick erection strained through his jeans, and I rubbed against it, letting him know that I understood, promising my intentions were the same.

I needed him.

All of him.

He rolled onto his back and pulled me on top of him. He pushed me back so I was straddling his waist. Darryn stared up at me, keeping almost all of his attention on my face, but he kept stealing these glances down my body, at the bra that was still covering up my breasts, at my chest that heaved and my stomach that clenched.

I reached back and flicked open the clasp on my bra, and my head tipped back as I let the straps slide down my arms.

Because I wanted him to see me. All of me. To understand that he was the only one I ever wanted to see me this way. That all of this should have belonged to him and I never should have given it away.

Regret filled up every crevice of my heart, and I wished . . . wished it'd been him, that the first time I'd had sex it hadn't been all a ploy to bring me to my knees, just a wicked game played by wicked boys.

I wished I'd been cherished.

Loved.

Like I was sure Darryn was loving me now.

Darryn moaned as he grabbed me by the hips, pressing me firmly against him. "Can't wait to be inside you."

All that energy fired, pinged across the confines of my room, and clashed in an all-out war with the hurt of this afternoon. Everything felt so heavy and light. Blinding.

I wanted Darryn to take it all away.

I rocked over him, and on a ragged hiss, he gripped me tighter. Darryn pinched his eyes closed as if he'd been tripped, caught somewhere in his own painful thoughts.

"Wanna kill him, Misha . . . wanna hurt him for making you feel this way. For making you think you need to be ashamed."

His words slammed into my consciousness. Images flashed. Me in a position so much like this, my breasts bared and my head thrown back.

I knew what it looked like in the video. Like I was lost in passion, like I'd wanted to be exposed, set on display. Like I was desperate for attention.

But I'd been in pain, both physically and emotionally. It had been my first time and Hunter had just rammed inside me before I was ready, after he'd persuaded me to ride him because he said that was the only way he liked it.

All of those warning bells had been going off, and I knew something was so off, because I didn't feel loved or safe.

The worst part of it all was that he'd convinced me to let him take a picture. At least that was what I thought it was, because he'd actually been recording me.

A bet that he could get a virgin on top and a picture to prove it.

That's all it'd been. A joke.

Horrified, I felt like every cell in my body froze, before it began to shake uncontrollably. I fell forward, keeping myself braced on the strength of Darryn's chest before I crumbled.

I wanted to blink away the image, to assign it to coincidence.

But there was no mistaking Darryn's words. He said he wanted to kill Hunter . . . for making me ashamed.

Darryn knew. He'd lied to me.

His eyes flew open as if he'd just realized the slip he made. He looked up at me with panic strewn all over his face.

"What did you just say?" I demanded, dread whipping through my entire being, a cold chill biting my skin.

I shivered and did my best to swallow down the nausea that rushed up my throat.

Rapidly, Darryn blinked and shook his head, as if he were searching for something to say.

For an excuse.

Oh my God.

No.

I scrambled in an effort to get away. Darryn grabbed my wrist, trying to yank me back onto the bed, but I jerked it away and fell to my knees on the floor. "Don't touch me. Don't you dare touch me."

I fisted the edge of the sheet and ripped it from the bed, clutched it to my front as if it could shield me from all the pain that tore me in two. Violently.

If I thought I hurt this afternoon? Or that night months ago when Hunter had stood there, laughing at me, taunting me, telling me I was nothing but a fool?

It didn't come close to touching this.

I forced myself to climb to my unsteady feet, backing into the wall with the thin sheet crumpled in front of me.

Darryn slowly stood from the bed but stayed there at the edge, his shoulders dropped low as if it would give him some sort of edge, fool me into thinking he wasn't just as vicious as the rest of them.

"You knew?" I begged through a whisper, praying he'd deny it, all the while knowing if he did, it would be another lie.

His throat bobbed heavily as he swallowed, and he nodded. "Yes." The word was rough and ripped through my soul.

A cry shot from my throat before I could stop it, and I slammed my hand over my mouth, trying to keep it in.

But there was no keeping this heartbreak from pouring free.

"Misha . . ." He took a step forward. "Listen to me. I knew, yes, but—"

"Just sh-sh-shut up. Shut up!" My voice cracked. "I c-c-can't believe you'd do this to me. C-c-can't believe you'd stoop so low."

"Misha," he pled, taking another step forward. "It's not what you think."

"Did you bet?" My chin quivered with the question.

Remorse made a slow pass through his body, and he shook his head. "No . . . of course not. But I need to be honest with you . . . I was there the first night he made the bet with all the guys." He swallowed again. "And I was there two days later when he brought the video over. I watched it with them."

Agony twisted up my face, and I attempted to take a step back, but only backed into the wall. "Y-y-you . . . you were there? You laughed with them? While they made me a joke?"

Was that the kind of guy he was? Just as cruel, just as mean as the others?

"No" flew from his mouth. "Never. The night the bets were made . . . Hunter was drunk, spouting off his mouth like he always does. He started talking shit about how easily he could have this new girl he started dating, claiming you were a virgin. Then he showed us a picture of you and you were so sexy. Beautiful. And I thought there wasn't a chance that you hadn't been with someone before. I didn't believe him. I just thought it was more of his stupid games, so I didn't give it a second thought. All the rest of the assholes at the party tossed in money, saying he didn't have a chance with you. It got out of hand . . . all of them started throwing out different things he had to make you do."

And I could feel my heart crumbling. Splintering into a thousand pieces.

"Two days later, he brought over his *proof.* I tried to talk him out of it when he loaded the video to that site." He squeezed his eyes closed. "But once it was there, I couldn't stop watching it because there was something about you that drew me to you. Then when I saw you out front that day, I knew you were nothing like any of those guys played you out to be."

I felt so dirty. Filthy. Like I could feel it crawling all over the surface of my skin. I wanted to scrape it away. "Get out," I said as firmly as I could, feeling my heart cracking a little more. Because I had thought he was different. I had wanted him to be different.

"Misha . . . please. I'm so sorry."

"Get out!" I repeated. *"Get out!"* I screamed.

Darryn winced, then backed away. He started for the door, paused to look back at me. "I fell in love with you, Misha. I'm sorry it all started at the hands of an asshole. But I'm not him. And you are definitely not that girl."

He just stood there. So beautiful.

I wanted to believe him.

But he was dishonest. A liar. And he had made me out to be a fool. Again.

"Go," I whispered quietly, but there was no question he heard.

He nodded, then stepped out my door.

chapter thirteen

Misha

ndy jerked the covers down. Bright light burned my eyes, and I grappled for the end of my comforter and dragged it back over my head.

"Come on, get out of bed, you have got to stop moping around," she said.

I groaned a little more, securing the blanket tight around my body. "No. And I'm not moping."

I was pretty sure the act of "moping" required walking, and since I'd basically been confined to my bed for the last seven days, I could swear none of that had been going on.

Indy yanked the comforter back just as hard. "Yes, you *are* moping, and yes, you *are* getting out of this bed. It's been seven days. Enough already."

So maybe Indy and I dealt with our pain differently. She went out, partied it out of her system.

I wallowed in it.

"It's not enough when it still hurts."

Sympathy softened her face when I reluctantly peeked up at her.

She ran her fingers through my tangled hair. I hadn't washed it in days. "I know, sweetie. But I can't let you stay in here any longer. It's unhealthy. Besides, the big game is tonight and Courtney wants all of us to come into Gruby's. Her friend Amber has a table reserved for us and everything. It'll be fun . . . take your mind off him for a while."

I was certain it would most definitely *not* be fun, and even more assuredly it would do nothing to rid my mind of what plagued it.

Darryn.

I loved him and hated him, those two emotions all balled up into a big old mess of emotion that sat like a gloomy lump right smack in the center of my chest.

I still couldn't make sense of it, why he would lie, other than the truth that he was playing the exact same game Hunter had been. I couldn't believe he even knew him. Associated with him. They'd been *friends.* That in itself felt like the worst kind of betrayal. That every time he'd held me . . . kissed me . . . just months before he'd been sitting around a table with Hunter while he plotted the demise of my innocence.

"Come on, babe. Get up. Take a shower. You'll feel so much better after you do. I promise we won't stay long, but I can't let you lie around like this any longer. You wouldn't let me do it, so unless you want me to drag your ass out of that bed by force, you need to get up."

I tossed the covers aside. "Fine."

Indy grinned. "See, that wasn't so hard."

Uh, yes, it was. She had no clue.

My entire body ached when I rolled over to the edge of my bed and placed my feet on the floor. I gathered a change of clothes and headed to the bathroom. I turned the faucet as hot as it would go and let the tiny room fill up with steam that I breathed in, hoping the warmth could chase the cold from my soul.

I stayed in the shower for too long, until my skin was red and shriveled and I had a very irate roommate pounding on the other side of the door.

"I didn't pull you from one hiding spot to let you sneak off to another. Get out of the shower. We're leaving in five minutes."

Shaking my head, I turned off the faucet and climbed from the shower, toweled off, and halfheartedly dressed.

Ha.

Halfheartedly.

Not even close.

None of my heart was in this.

But I guessed I had little choice in the matter.

Indy banged at the door again.

I went back into my room and shoved my feet in a pair of boots, glancing out at the waning day through the slats in my window. The sky was filled with winter clouds that had taken over Michigan the last two days, the approaching twilight just as dreary as I felt.

I hauled myself out of my room and downstairs. "Fine, I'm ready."

Chloe, Indy, and I pulled on jackets and filed out the door onto the sidewalk. I struggled to keep up with them as they chatted and laughed, feeling none of the excitement that poured from them as they talked about the game going on tonight and how cool it was our football team was so close to winning the championships. Tonight's away game would be broadcast live on cable, which of course Gruby's would be playing proudly tonight.

Rain threatened and teased, spitting little droplets of water that chilled me all the way to my bones. Warily, I peeked up at the sky, my face immediately pelted with stinging dots of frigid water.

Great.

It had just started to really rain by the time we made it to the sports bar. We rushed inside with our heads ducked, pulled our wet jackets off, and shook them out as we stepped up to the hostess station.

Amber, Courtney's friend, saw us from across the room, and she wove through the overflowing crowd, the dim-lit room so thick with bodies that people stood along the walls and gathered in groups around tables.

"There you guys are! Courtney has been waiting for you." She grinned and grabbed some menus. "Come on, I have you in my section."

We followed her, and I kept my head down, no longer feeling that ease that I'd so foolishly given myself over to in the last two months, thinking that no one here knew my face. It'd only been proven last week by the jerk who'd accosted me outside my building. All week I hadn't made it to class, unable to face what was waiting for me outside the doors. If someone confronted me about it again? I wouldn't know how to survive it.

But Indy was right. I couldn't just keep hiding. That was the girl I'd been my entire life. Always seeking out the places where I felt most comfortable. Taking paths with the least risk. Doing everything in my power to shy away from anything that would make me nervous or apprehensive.

No doubt what I was feeling now was much more than just unease.

This was physical pain, pain that had been inflicted cruelly, everything about it unfair.

But what could I do short of running back to my parents?

That was no longer an option.

I settled into one of the barstools at the high round table, and accepted the menu from Amber. "Thank you."

"No problem," she said, "just let me know what you guys want. The kitchen is pretty backed up since it's so busy, but I'll try to get a rush on it."

Mumbling another quiet thank-you, I turned to study the menu. I hadn't eaten in days, and my body felt weak. Tired. I knew it was about time I started to pick up the pieces and took care of myself.

Darryn had destroyed something deep inside and I needed to figure out how to begin fixing it.

I suppressed my mocking laughter, all of it aimed at myself.

Darryn the Destroyer.

Some fairy tale he'd turned out to be.

Turned out he'd been sent to ruin another piece of me.

My chest tightened as sadness pooled in my belly. And that was the truth of it. It made me sad, because I missed him. Missed his face, missed all that arrogance that endeared him to me, the way he joked and laughed. Most of all, I missed the way he'd made me feel.

Sighing, I shoved it off and forced myself to try and enjoy the time with my friends. We ordered, and Amber brought me a beer that I had no stomach for. Still I sipped at it and tried to relax in the boisterous mood of the bar, the lights dimmed and the huge television screens streaming the game. Cheers rang out, everyone there to support our team. People would jump to their feet and grip their heads on the tricky plays and boo when our team fumbled or the vying team gained on them.

No one even seemed to know I was there. I'd disappeared. Become invisible. Just like I wanted to be. I let my mind wander with the noise, and I sank into the first calm I'd felt in days.

"Well, look who's here." The voice came from behind, just at my shoulder. It sent fear slicking icy tendrils down my spine, leaving a frozen path in its wake.

I shook and a knot formed in my throat. I hadn't seen him since that night when I found out what he'd done, when I'd confronted him, trying to be brave when all I'd felt like was a stupid little girl.

All I wanted was to curl into a ball under the table.

Instead I sat stock-still, all except for the rush of goose bumps that lifted in warning on my neck when his vile presence encroached on me from behind. Something triggered my senses, and I was assaulted by memories of the smell in his room, ones I could only attribute to Hunter. Something threatening—vulgar and depraved. It flooded my nostrils and manifested as nausea in my stomach.

"Been too long, Misha." Hunter laughed, a taunting sound that took me back to that night and how deeply he had hurt me.

Anger and shame billowed through me, but I kept myself still and gave him no response. Maybe if I ignored him long enough he would leave me alone.

I should have known a jerk like Hunter would not give up.

He ran his hand along my shoulder and gripped me by the back of the neck, as if he had some sort of God-given right to touch me.

I cringed and tried to fling off the perversity of his touch.

I choked as he gripped me tighter.

And the tears came.

God, I didn't want to cry, I didn't want to be that naive little girl that cowered in front of him.

But I couldn't stop the tears from breaking free. Heated, they raced down my face and dripped from my chin. I didn't wipe them away, praying he couldn't see them in the dark.

"Aw . . . are you crying?" he said as if it were sympathy, but he said it loud, so the people around him would hear. He was begging for an audience, the way he always did.

My hands fisted.

Maybe it was Hunter who was the coward, so insecure he needed to steal the attention of others around him to make him feel good.

Not at my expense. Not ever again.

"L-l-leave me a-a-alone," I tried to get out of my shaking throat, my tongue all twisted and thick.

The motion seemed to jar Indy from the game, and her eyes narrowed when she turned and found Hunter looming over my shoulder. He paid her no mind, just continued to degrade me.

"Oh . . . come on, M-M-M-M-Misha," Hunter drew out, digging the knife a little deeper. I could almost feel myself bleeding out. "Know how much you like me. Let's say you and me go for another round. Maybe this time you won't be so shy."

Vomit lifted in my throat, and I swallowed it down.

By now, Hunter had garnered that attention he was always hungry for, and all the tables surrounding us had tuned in on us, curious eyes peering our way. I could feel them, watching.

"I wouldn't mind a little retake," he almost shouted, his obnoxious laughter ringing through the room.

"L-l-leave me alone."

Indy leaned toward him, her brow all pinched up in a scowl. "Take a hint, Hunter. She doesn't want anything to do with you, so why don't you get your sorry ass away from her? Like she'd ever let a pathetic asshole loser like you touch her again."

"Fuck you," he hissed in her direction, and he twisted his hand in my hair, tight enough that it made me yelp. "The only two people this concerns are me and Misha."

And I hated . . . hated him that he thought he had even an ounce of control over me, hated that he made my heart pound in fear and my stomach turn with sickness. I refused to allow him this.

"L-l-let me g-g-go."

"I'll let you go when I'm ready to."

My heart hammered with a flutter of energy that suddenly swirled around me, movement at my side that I couldn't process, but I saw Hunter's eyes widen with something like shock. A fist rammed into the side of his face. I screamed in both relief and confusion, my eyes going wide as Hunter's head violently rocked to the side, his hand releasing its hold in my hair as he stumbled back.

"Wrong." Darryn stood just off to my side, seething, flexing his fists while Hunter rubbed at his jaw. "You let go of her when she tells you to."

Darryn glanced over at me as if he were in pain, as if seeing me here hurt him just as badly as Hunter had been hurting me.

Completely caught off guard and confused by the rage boiling in Darryn's body, Hunter seemed flustered. He rubbed at his jaw. "What the fuck, dude? You just fucking punched me."

Darryn sneered at him. "And I'll gladly do it again if I ever find you anywhere near her," Darryn growled. He took a menacing step forward, his jaw clenched tight in warning. "You got me?"

Hunter chuckled when his eyes darted between the two of us, like he was slowly catching on. "Oh, I got it. Your turn to take her for a ride."

Rage filled Darryn's eyes, and he rushed forward, gaining speed as he rammed into Hunter. Hunter flew back into the table. The table toppled over, wood crashed on the hard floor, and mugs flew to the ground, shattering when they hit. Hunter landed on top of it all. Everyone scattered, a rush of voices and screams and people jumping out of the way.

Darren dove for Hunter, straddling him as he landed blow after blow. "Stay the fuck away from her, you got me? Stay. Away." He fisted his hands in Hunter's shirt, lifted him from the floor, and then slammed him back down. "If anyone *ever* says one word to her about that video . . . if anyone even thinks about it . . . I'm going to hold you personally responsible. You understand what I'm telling you?"

Hunter groaned, nodding weakly.

I backed away, shaking, trying to catch my breath and make sense of what Darryn had done.

Indy came over and reached to wrap me in her arms.

I shook her off. "I need some air . . . just . . . I'm fine."

Reluctantly she nodded, then released me. "I'll be right here if you need me."

I ran outside. Rain poured from above. Freezing cold water drenched my hair and face, soaked through my T-shirt. Overcome, I dropped to my knees, weeping as I bent toward the loose-pebbled ground of the parking lot. Chills rolled through my body, and my teeth chattered.

The door flew open, and Darryn came running out. He skidded to a stop when he saw me on the ground, the anger on his face transforming with remorse and sorrow.

The rain continued to spill from the sky, dousing his hair and soaking into his clothes. Long chunks of his light bangs clung to his forehead, all of his questions sweeping across his face as he watched me with caution.

My boy-man-god. My avenging angel. All that skin wet and glistening under the streetlamps that glinted in the driving rain.

I gasped when he seemed to win whatever war was raging inside him, and he jogged to me and scooped me into his arms. He hoisted me high up and hugged me to his chest. "I've got you."

He began to walk away from the bar, his feet urgent as he carried me without looking back. Behind us, every sound bled away into nothing until all I could hear was the erratic beat of Darryn's heart where my ear rested against his chest.

He leaned down and tenderly brushed his lips across my forehead. "I love you," he murmured, never stopping his stride. "Not gonna let him hurt you. Not ever again, Misha. Not ever again."

His steps never faltered as he carried me toward our neighborhood. He started to turn up the walkway to my house, and I clutched his shirt. "Take me to your house . . . to your room."

He hesitated, looking between me and the window on the second floor of his house, weighing what was right, maybe weighing if I was thinking clearly or not.

"Please . . . just . . . I need to go there. To face what Hunter did to me there."

Slowly he nodded in understanding. "Okay."

He hefted me a little more securely into his arms and quickly made his way into his house. Inside, everything was quiet and dark. He carried me up the stairs, cautious as he twisted his bedroom doorknob without ever letting me go. The door slowly swung open to the room where I'd allowed Hunter to take advantage of me.

But had it ever really been my fault? Was trust such a bad thing?

My pulse was all thready and harsh, clattering around in my rib cage as my spirit came to the realization.

Because I wanted to be that girl, the one who trusted with everything she had and loved with every piece of her spirit.

I didn't want to be scared or hard or filled with hatred. I didn't want to miss out on what this world had to offer because there were some in it who would rather hurt than cling to the good.

And as Darryn stood there with me in his arms in his doorway, I knew that was exactly what I was doing, my hands in fists in his shirt and my face buried in the perfect warmth of his chest.

I was clinging to the good.

"Are you okay?" he asked.

"Yes."

Darryn carried me in and set me on his bed. He climbed down to his knees, all of his movements watchful and slow, assuring me I didn't have to be afraid.

No longer would I allow myself to be.

"Let's get you out of these wet clothes."

I nodded but made no move to help him as he took charge, unlaced my soaked boots, and pulled them from my feet. He dropped them to the floor, turned to peel off my socks and my jeans. His smile was both timid and reassuring when he glanced up at me. Gently he gathered the hem of my shirt, his eyes filled with devotion as he slowly removed it. Leaving me in my panties and bra, he pulled a fresh T-shirt from his drawer. He said nothing as he settled it over my body.

It swallowed me, it was so big, but I knew it fit perfectly. The way Darryn perfectly fit me.

He shed his own clothes, down to his underwear, then lifted the blankets. "Climb under," he whispered.

I slipped in, and I felt my entire body sigh in relief when he got in beside me and pulled me into his arms.

He brushed his fingers through my hair, his mouth pressed to the top of my head as he murmured quietly, "Please forgive me, Misha . . . for lying to you the first day I met you. I didn't mean to hurt you." His lips moved slowly as he brought them to my ear. "I love you . . . I meant it when I told you the other day. I fell in love with this sweet, shy, beautiful girl . . . She's the same one who was in that video . . . one who trusts and loves and sees the world unlike anyone I've ever met. Don't ever be ashamed of who you are."

And I let go, sobbing in his arms, let it all out, because he *knew*— and he still loved me. I cried because I'd spent so much time hating the girl I was instead of embracing her. Instead of finding someone who accepted her.

I guess I needed to accept myself first.

He leaned forward, his touch tender as he wiped all my tears away.

Pulling back, I stared up at him. "I love you, Darryn. So much. I should have told you, too, but I was so scared you wouldn't want me anymore once you found out."

"Not possible," he said, kissing me tenderly. "Not for a second. Not for a day."

He pulled me impossibly closer, my entire body tucked against the warmth of his and my head pressed to the strong, even beat of his heart. "Sleep, sweet girl. I'm here. And I'm never going to let you go."

chapter fourteen

Misha

I tied a towel under my arms and studied myself in the foggy mirror as I pulled a brush through my thick, curly hair. It was so strange looking at myself so differently, finally seeing myself for who I was rather than the person I thought I'd wanted to be.

Naive.

Maybe I was. Maybe I would always be.

But through my experiences I knew I could no longer count myself a fool. Now I knew it was okay to be looking at things through trusting eyes, although I'd just be looking a little closer. Examining intentions without losing the heart of who I was.

Who I knew I really wanted to be.

I cast myself a soft smile, before I unlocked the bathroom door and padded out to Darryn's closed one. I'd spent the last two days here, pretty much in his bed with his arms around me. All day yesterday we'd just talked and watched movies, a strong sense of calm and belonging filling me up with every second I spent with him.

Oh yeah.

And kissing.

A whole lot of it, too. We'd given ourselves over to relearning each other with the walls we'd put up to protect our secrets crumbled to the ground. No longer were there barriers between us, and it just felt good to bask in the entirety of his presence, complete and without pretenses or truths concealed. I'd just relished all that golden light that reflected something both dangerous and perfect in Darryn. My protector. My gorgeous avenging angel.

My boy-man-god who stole my breath.

My heart.

I twisted the knob and his door swung open. Darryn sat on the edge of his bed, wearing only his underwear, his hair still damp from his own shower. His chest flexed with strength, and his lips turned up at the edges, the softest of smiles taking him over as he caught me standing in his doorway taking him in.

Who could blame me?

Darryn chased a wave of redness from where his perusal began, at my bare legs, as his eyes caressed every inch of my skin. My thighs shook when he stared at them a beat longer than the rest. I could feel the heat of my blush, heading north just ahead of his stare, as if my body were preparing itself for the desperate need that would grow in me as Darryn's gaze caressed up my skin. Finally he brought those hazel eyes all the way to my face.

"Can't believe my fantasy is standing right there at my door."

I shook with his honesty, with his blatant desire as he greedily looked at me.

I edged forward, and with each step I took, Darryn lifted his face a little more, tilting his head back as I came to stand between his legs. All those little darts of energy flew, fired, and fed the frenzy that was steadily building between us.

For two nights I'd slept in his bed with all those pesky layers of clothing still firmly set in place.

Darryn reached up and cupped my face. "My fantasy because I never thought I'd get the chance to love someone like you . . . my heart because I'd never thought I'd find someone I was ready to love." A soft smile pulled at one side of his mouth, and his tongue darted out to wet his lips. "But you . . . you've become everything."

He brushed his thumb across my bottom lip, and my tongue flitted out, just teasing his fingertip as it made a gentle pass. "Misha," he whispered hoarsely.

I opened my mouth and sucked his thumb into my mouth.

"Shit," he hissed, his jaw clenching as I pulled his thumb deeper inside my mouth, as I sucked and kissed. "What are you doing?" He choked over the question.

I couldn't stop my gaze from slipping down over his wide shoulders to his taut stomach, finally drawn to find his erection that was straining at the thin material of his underwear.

My stomach tightened, and all those butterflies flapped and flew. A tumble of nerves tripped through every inch of my body as all of this pent-up desire broke free and beat frantically through my veins.

Darryn's expression darkened with lust, and his hazel eyes flamed the most intense green.

As hard as I listened, no bells were going off in my head, no warning to get away and get away fast. All I could hear was the rapid beat of my heart that escalated with each breath I took, all of the affection I felt for this man bursting free.

I released Darryn's thumb, and he stared up at me, panting as I undid the knot that held the towel under my arms. It dropped to the floor at my feet.

Darryn exhaled, heavy and hard, and though it seemed impossible, his eyes darkened more, desire evident in every cell of his body as he let his gaze drop and wander.

And I didn't feel self-conscious or shy.

I felt beautiful.

Like this was right.

I braced myself on Darryn's shoulders and leaned in close enough to brush my lips across his. For a second it was just soft brushes and lingering caresses, before we completely caught fire.

Darryn wound his arms around my waist, and in one movement, he lifted me from my feet and had my back pinned to his bed. And that glorious body was hovering over mine, caging me in and still making me feel the safest that I'd ever been.

"Are you sure you want this, Misha? I told you I'd wait as long as you needed me to, so you need to let me know what you're thinking right now because I'm not sure my body is thinking the same thing you are."

I wet my lips, searching his eyes and finding all the love I wanted to see staring back at me. "I asked you to be patient with me . . . respect me . . . to be honest with me." I fluttered my fingertips down his face and across his mouth, and Darryn gently kissed each of them as they passed. "You've been all those things. Even in your lie there was honesty, and I know you'll never take advantage of me. I trust you."

"You don't know how badly I wanted to hear those words."

Darryn descended on me, his kiss everywhere, on my mouth and my jaw and my neck. I gasped when he went for my breast, drawing my nipple into the well of his wet mouth.

Flames tore through my insides. "Oh my God," I whimpered, burying my hands in his hair, gripping and clutching while Darryn ignited something inside me I'd never felt before. It was all-around consuming, this untamed feeling that built and spread in the pit of my stomach, growing, begging for more.

I rocked against him, asking for it.

"I know, baby, I've got you."

I whimpered when he pushed his weight back to his knees, and his head dropped below his shoulders as he slowly worked down my abdomen, kissing under my belly button, raking his lips over to my hip and down the outside of my leg.

My head spun when I realized Darryn was suddenly fully kneeling between my legs, heat searing me from the inside out. Without a doubt, my milky skin was glowing red, a flush of desire and a surge of warmth.

He looked up at me, his expression fueled by lust, but a lust that went so much deeper than just the physical. Like he wanted to consume me, heart and body and soul.

"P-p-please." The word scraped up my throat and left my mouth on a barely constrained plea.

Because Darryn owned every single one of those parts of me.

He dove in, his tongue making a deep pass through my folds.

"Darryn," I cried out, his name sung like praise.

I had no idea anything could feel so good.

Until he turned all his attentions to that little spot that throbbed and begged, just as needy as the incoherent words that were tumbling from my mouth. "Darryn," I whimpered. "I don't . . . I—I—I—"

"Shh." His voice vibrated against my slick flesh, and that was it.

I came undone. And I thought I understood the meaning of an orgasm, what all the hype was about, but I had no clue. Pleasure tore through me at the surety of Darryn's touch. Wave after wave, I was rocked in a jumbled state of pure bliss.

Before I could catch my breath, Darryn was on his knees, pushing his underwear down his thighs and kicking them aside.

What little air I could find was knocked free. Gaping, I couldn't look away. I was struck dumb . . . silenced when all that was Darryn was revealed to me.

This boy-man-god was so beautiful that he left me in an almost terrified state of awe, because every part of Darryn had been master-fully created. My mouth ran dry as I tentatively reached out, my fingers trembling along the underside of his massive erection.

I watched in fascination as Darryn jerked, and his face twisted up in an almost tortured pleasure-pain.

"Careful," he warned.

Redness lit on my face, and I bit at my lip, maybe feeling a little too proud that I caused this kind of reaction in him.

Darryn leaned over and dug through the little drawer beside his bed. His expression was all earnest and fierce. He kept his eyes trained on mine as he rolled on a condom. I shook as he settled his perfect body over mine.

I was pinned beneath him, though much of his weight rested on his elbows, our chests touching as the beat of our hearts worked to catch up with one another, each pulse racing faster than the last.

Darryn ran his fingers through my hair. He smiled the softest smile. "You're shaking," he murmured in quiet understanding, a question almost hitched at the end.

Are you okay?

I shifted so our bodies were aligned.

"I'm nervous," I admitted quietly, licking my lips to rid myself of some of the nerves that were stampeding out of control. "My first time wasn't exactly the best experience of my life . . . and I want . . . I—I—I want this to be different."

Darryn shifted to take my hand, threading his fingers through my mine and tucking our hands up between us. He kissed across my knuckles, his breath like a soft breeze of reassurance that was pumped directly into my spirit.

"This *is* different." He kissed my wrist, running his nose along the underside as if to draw me in, to bring me closer than we already were. "It's different because when I look at you, I don't see some girl who is a weak victim. What I see is a girl who is so strong that she overcomes every cruel and unfair obstacle placed in her way. It's different because I see someone to be cherished rather than someone to be used."

Affection played through his eyes. "It's different because I'm in love with you . . . desperately." He trailed his fingers down my face, and hooked his finger under my chin, tilting my mouth up to his. "And I see it when you look at me, that you feel the same. That you're loving me as much as I'm loving you. That means everything is different."

Slowly he pressed himself into me. All the air left me in one sharp gasp as my body accepted all of him, stretching me, filling me so full it would almost have hurt if it didn't feel so unbelievably good.

"This is me giving you all of me. Forever." He pulled away, before he rocked back into me with one firm thrust.

This time when Darryn pulled back, I lifted my hips to meet the force of his as he drove himself deep into me.

"I want to mean everything," he said.

I wrapped my legs around his hips and gave him my all, whimpered and moaned as he wound that feeling back into the deepest, most secret place inside me.

"Everything," I promised through my ragged pants as Darryn worked his body over mine. All those darts of energy sparked, a live charge shot straight into my heart. It spiraled down to my core, and I felt it building with every surge of his body.

"I love you," I whispered just before he tilted his hips and took me hard. Another wave of ecstasy swallowed me whole, stealing my breath and mind.

Darryn pushed and strained, groaning loud as his body tensed, his own pleasure rolling in tremors through all his brimming strength, his muscles bunched and coiled in his release.

For a few moments, Darryn remained still, gathering his breath, before he pushed up with his hands on either side of my head, his nose an inch from mine. His eyes were almost wild as he stared down at me with a look of pure possession.

I'd become his.

My avenging angel.

The one who'd been sent not to destroy but to expose something vital that had been so difficult for me to see.

To show me it was okay to be me.

saving me

Molly McAdams

prologue

Indy

Swiping at my wet cheeks, I drove past the house I shared with three girls not far from campus during the school year, and kept going until I pulled up outside Dean's frat house. I wasn't supposed to be coming back to Ann Arbor for a couple more days. But Dean was already here, and, well, there was apparently nothing left for me in Chicago anymore.

My parents had made that all too clear when I'd come home from the gym this morning to find my suitcases on the driveway. A note pinned to one of them had said *We can't keep pretending everything's okay*, and the locks on the door had been changed.

Gone for an hour at the gym—and they changed the locks and packed all my stuff. They'd obviously been busy carrying out plans they'd had for who knew how long.

Through my tears and depressed-to-angry mood swings, I'd made the drive to Ann Arbor, Michigan, in only three hours, and remembered maybe five minutes of that. But none of that mattered now. As I let myself in the stale, funky-smelling frat house, I was already breathing easier knowing I was seconds away from being in Dean's arms. He would make everything better—he always had over the last two years.

Jogging up the stairs, I worried for a second about looking like a disaster when I was about to see Dean for the first time in months, but I knew he'd already seen me at my lowest. A red, blotchy face and workout clothes weren't going to faze him right now.

As I opened the door to his room at the end of the hall, my already shaky smile immediately fell, and I froze with one foot inside his bedroom. After the day I'd had, I wasn't comprehending what I was seeing. I wasn't getting the memo that I needed to do something. Like leave. Or scream. Or cry some more. Something. Anything. I just stood there staring—Dean not even noticing me through the music blasting in his room as he repeatedly drove into some girl I'd never seen before.

When everything seemed to snap back into reality, I grabbed at the docking station on the dresser near the door and launched it across the room—the music immediately stopped and was replaced by my voice.

"What the fuck are you doing?" I screamed.

The girl shrieked and shoved Dean back before trying to cover herself. "Get out of here!"

"Indy!" Dean yelled, and looked around wildly for a few seconds before coming toward me. "Indy, oh my God!"

"Don't touch me! Don't you dare fucking touch— You're not even wearing a condom!" I didn't know why that was the important issue right then, and I didn't know why my gaze had flashed down. But that stupid, simple fact was what had the tears falling. He always wore a condom; he was obsessive about being safe.

"Get her out of here!" the girl demanded.

Dean stopped his advance for a second to snap, "Babe, shut up!"

"Babe?" I choked out, and looked away, holding my hands out in front of me to block my view of his junk just in case I turned around again. I'd seen him naked too many times to count. I knew that area of him intimately. But right now it was like a stranger was standing in front of me.

"Indy," he crooned, his voice much closer.

"Tell me this isn't happening. Tell me this isn't fucking happening, Dean!"

"Just listen—"

"We were going to get married one day. You're supposed to love me. You just told me last night that you love me. What—I don't—what the hell happened?"

He sighed heavily. "I just . . . Why are you even here? I thought you weren't coming back until Saturday."

I dropped my hands and looked at him, a look of disbelief covering my face. "Obviously I'm back early! Don't put this on me! It doesn't matter if I'm here now, or if I'd waited until Saturday. You were just screwing someone else! How long has this been going on? And for the love of God, will you two please put some damn clothes on?"

"You need to leave," the girl said, sneering.

"I'm his girlfriend!" I screeched, my voice echoing off the walls as I shot a glare at her that I wished could kill.

"Look," Dean said softly, and moved forward to grip my arms. "I was going to wait until you got back to talk to you, I just couldn't upset you while you were having to deal with your parents. It's just—"

"No," I pled. "No, don't do this."

"It's just not working out, Indy. I love you, but I'm not *in* love with you anymore."

My sobs finally broke free from my chest, and when Dean tried to pull me into his arms, I pushed away from him. "Why would you say the things you've said to me? Just a few nights ago you brought up getting engaged. Why? You can't—you can't tell me you're not in love with me anymore!"

"Jesus Christ," the girl complained. "He was trying to make things easy on you then, and he's trying to let you down easy now. Dean was feeding you that bullshit while his cock was in my mouth. The talk about getting engaged? Sweetheart, it's already happened, just not to you." She held up her left hand, and my head jerked back.

"What?" I couldn't breathe. All the air had been sucked from the room. This wasn't happening. This whole day was a prank, or a nightmare. Something. I looked at Dean, but he was staring past me with a blank expression.

"Do you think this was just something over the summer?" she continued. "This has been going on almost as long as the two of you have. I didn't mind letting you think you had him, because I knew he'd be mine in the end."

"You're lying," I breathed. "Dean." His name fell like a plea from my lips. I needed him to tell me this was all a lie. But he still wouldn't look at me.

"Why wouldn't I be sure of us? After all, you already confirmed something else. He's never worn a condom with me. Doesn't sound like it was the same with you. And seeing as you didn't seem to have a clue about me, but I knew all about you . . . it wasn't hard to figure."

She wrapped the sheet around her body as she stood from the bed and pointed toward the door. "Now you need to go. It's finally our time. The days of having to listen to Dean bitch about how useless, needy, and frustrating you are are behind us."

I bent forward, grabbing at my stomach when it felt like the air had been knocked from me. I looked up to Dean, once again hoping he would deny what was happening—what she was saying. But there was nothing on his face that hinted otherwise.

"All he's been doing for the last two years is putting up with the mess that is your life. He's done, and I'm done letting you pretend you have him. His ring is on my finger, and his last name will be mine. His baby is in my body. And you have no more claim on him, or right to be here. Leave."

My head snapped to the left to look at her, and my eyes dropped to her hidden torso. There was no indication that she was pregnant—but after everything else, I had no reason not to believe her. My life *was* a mess. I was always wondering why a guy like Dean would stay with me after everything I'd been through. I had considered myself lucky.

I'd been wrong.

He'd just been biding his time.

chapter one

Indy

Two and a half months later

I was frozen somewhere between getting out of the chair and standing—my empty cup of coffee in one hand, my purse hanging uselessly in the other. My mouth and eyes were wide with horror as I stared at them from across the warm coffee shop. They hadn't seen me yet, and I hoped like hell they wouldn't. But I couldn't seem to stop staring, just like every time I saw them together. Only this time she had a very obvious baby belly. It had jutted out considerably in the couple of weeks since I'd last seen her. *Vanessa*, as I'd come to learn—and loathe. Dean had his hands on her belly, his lips pressed to her neck; her diamond was shining subtly in the dim lighting of the shop like it was mocking me or something.

They looked ridiculously happy. And that probably killed me as much as it did to see him caressing her stomach. I glanced up at his handsome, smiling face and once again wished I'd actually broken his nose when I punched him that day in his room. Given him a reminder of what he'd done to me every time he looked in the mirror. But no broken nose. No *nothing* on that stupid, perfect face.

I sat roughly back in my chair and quickly put on my large sunglasses. Like that would help. Like they wouldn't see my hair and know it was me. Who else had hair as naturally red as mine?

"Indy." Misha, one of my housemates, wiggled her fingers in front of my face before her body blocked my view of them. "What are you doing? Do you feel okay?"

"No," I panted. "I need to get out of here."

"What's wrong?" she asked a little louder, concern lacing her words. "What can I do?"

"Just shh! Don't draw attention to us," I whispered, and her dark eyes widened.

She barely glanced over her shoulder before her entire body went rigid. "Oh."

"Yeah, 'oh.' Let's go. We need to go. Like right now."

"Back door." She nodded in the direction behind me, and I stood and turned at the same time, keeping my head down as I did.

"Indy!"

"Balls," I whispered harshly, and turned back around to see a guy approaching me—and just past him Vanessa and Dean were staring at me with wide eyes.

"Hey," the guy said. "I didn't even see you in here until you stood up. Are you going to the party?"

Do I know this guy? "Uh, what party?"

He gave me a look, amusement dancing in his eyes. "At your neighbors' house."

Apparently I do. Unfortunately this wasn't uncommon lately. After running out of Dean's frat house at the end of August, I'd called Misha to see if she was on her way back to Ann Arbor, only to find she hadn't planned on coming back after what had happened between her and Hunter last year. But I hadn't been about to let her hide away, and I'd needed my friend to cry to, and stand tall with me this year. She'd stood tall, and I was so proud of her . . . Me, not so much. Misha ended up meeting Darryn, a new guy next door, and I'd just tried to lose myself during every party.

Everyone thought I was showing my wild side and finally letting loose since I wasn't with Dean anymore, but they couldn't have been more wrong. I wanted to forget Dean, I wanted to forget everything about him and our time together—so I drank until I did just that. The downside of that was times like this. I didn't remember those nights, which meant I sure as hell didn't remember the people I'd met or interacted with.

"Most likely . . . ?" I responded awkwardly. "Are you going to stalk me if I do?"

A grin tugged at his lips as he stepped closer. "Don't you want me to?" he asked huskily, and his arm wrapped around my waist just before his lips fell on mine.

My eyebrows rose, and my eyes widened. Before I could gather myself enough to push him away, he was stepping back. "Wha—"

"I'll see you tonight," he said confidently. Turning, he walked back a few tables and sat down where there were a couple of people studying.

I gaped after him for long seconds before turning to leave with Misha, only to find Dean and Vanessa still staring at me. Vanessa with a satisfied smirk, Dean with a raised eyebrow and an annoyed look on his face.

I needed to get out of there before I did something stupid like cry. I needed to get to that party so I could try to have fun as I drank away memories of Dean as I had done every weekend since I'd walked in on him and Vanessa.

"I don't know what the hell just happened," I hissed as Misha and I walked out the back door of the coffee shop.

"What do you mean?" She looked over at me with her dark eyes, her expression telling me she really had no clue what I meant.

"That"—I pointed behind us—"in there, that guy. I don't know him, and I don't know why he ki—"

She laughed in that soft, quiet way of hers and shook her head—her dark curls bouncing around her face. "Oh, I'm pretty sure you know him, Indy. Quite well, in fact."

My face fell as we got in her car. "Oh no, no."

"Oh yes, yes."

"I've slept with him?"

"Uh-huh."

"I just saw Dean and Vanessa and her stupid, pregnant stomach. And a guy I don't know—or remember—kissed me. And Dean was there. And—I need a drink. Or five," I groaned, and slumped down in the passenger seat.

Misha sighed. "That's usually how the night starts out when you end up sleeping with him or someone else—and then you never seem to remember it."

I sat back up quickly. "Someone else?" I nearly shouted. "Where are you and Darryn when this is happening? Why don't you stop me from sleeping with guys I won't remember the next morning? And why are you just telling me all this *now*?"

"It's not like we don't try, and based on how drunk you get and the things you say, you don't want anyone telling you about what you do when you're drunk," she whispered, her tone indicating she was done with this conversation, and judging from it, I wondered just how many times they'd tried to stop me from myself when I drank.

Six hours later I'd successfully put Dean and Vanessa out of my mind, had lost twice and won once at beer pong, had beat three frat guys at downing six shots the fastest, and had eaten half a loaf of warm, fresh garlic bread.

Wait. What the hell?

"Who gave me bread?" I yelled, and looked around at everyone before tearing off another piece of the soft disgustingness and shoving it in my mouth.

Despite not knowing where it came from, I kept the foil-covered loaf firmly in my grip. I was going to gain five pounds off this alone, and I didn't care at all right now. Someone started moving against me, and I automatically began moving to the music—half loaf and beer still in hand.

A deep chuckle vibrated against my neck. "What's that you got there, Indy?"

My eyebrows rose, and my eyes opened sluggishly. "Hmm?"

The person behind me tapped my bread, and I snatched it away from him, holding it close to my chest. "It's my present. It's delicious and soft and melts in my mouth, and you can't have any."

He pressed his body closer to mine, his hands gripping my hips. "You know what else melts in your mouth," he said suggestively.

"M&M's?" I asked with false naivety before laughing loudly and turning to look at him. "I don't know you, either," I mused, a smile on my face. "But I do know you, don't I?"

The handsome guy nodded. "We definitely know each other, Indy." His body was still moving to the music—as was mine—and his head dipped to kiss behind my ear.

I pushed at his chest, and giggled. *Why am I giggling? I'm not a giggler. Am I? Garlic bread plus hot guy plus drinking equals the giggles. Oh God, drinking makes me do math problems.* "No." I drew out the word. "I promised Misha I'd be a good girl."

A grin tugged at his lips. "You weren't last week."

"Last week, huh?" I tilted forward as I studied his eyes, and clapped my bread and cup together. "You're really hot. Go, me."

He huffed out a laugh, his expression morphing into something other than the heated look he'd been giving me. He looked confused and kind of shocked. I didn't blame him—I'd already been mauled by the guy from the coffee shop about an hour ago, and now there was this guy in front of me. I was beginning to wonder how many more guys I'd run into tonight who I'd been hooking up with over the past couple of months. Even through the haze of my drunken mind, I was disgusted with myself.

I wasn't this girl, never had been. I'd lost my virginity to Dean and had planned on being with him forever. Multiple partners weren't my thing. Drunken hookups weren't my thing. Actually . . . getting drunk at all wasn't my thing.

And now I was frowning.

"Uh, am I missing something?" he asked, and I frowned harder as I wished I remembered him. He really was cute.

I could have gotten his name, I could have walked with him back to my room next door . . . but I didn't want to fuel this side of me he thought he knew.

I held up my beer and half loaf and smiled. "Cheers." Turning, I walked away from unknown guy number two and stumbled my way to the hall on the first floor to find the bathroom.

It shouldn't be that hard. This house was built exactly like ours, and I'd spent enough time in this house that I knew it as well as I knew my own. But the walls were spinning sideways and tilting forward, and my bread was starting to smell like bananas, so . . . yeah, difficulty level in finding the bathroom was at an all-time high.

After one miss, I hit a door that was locked and smacked the hand holding the loaf against the door. "Hurry," I whined, as I kept smacking my hand against the door.

It was official. I turned into a three-year-old when I was drunk. Note to self before I drank again: I'm an annoying drunk.

"Bathroom!" I whined again, and went to take a sip of my beer, but my cup was suddenly empty. "Lame. So much lame in that cup."

The door swung open, revealing a flushed couple, and I grinned widely at them. "Hope you used protection," I sang as I stepped into the bathroom and they hurried out. I'm sure tomorrow I would be grossed out that I used a restroom after people just got done doing unmentionables in it.

After leaving the bathroom with more bread in my mouth, I looked to the left and my eyes narrowed on a closed door. On my right, the music was loud, and the people at the party were even louder. But something about that door called to me.

Rolling up the top of the foil again, I went to the door, twisted the handle, and put all my weight into it, expecting it to be locked.

It wasn't.

I stumbled in, a giggle bubbling up from my chest as I gripped the doorknob and my bread like a lifeline, trying to keep myself vertical.

"Whoa—shit," I laughed, and straightened.

There was a sigh behind me. "Guess it's time to go home?"

I whirled around and fell back into the wall from my too-fast movement, the familiar guy lying on the bed darted up like he could save me from over there.

"Definitely time to go home."

"You scared the shit out of me!" I hissed.

"Really, Indy?" he said on a soft laugh, his hand rubbing the back of his neck as he stood up.

My frown was back. "You know me, too?"

He sent me a patient smile. "Not really."

"But you know my name," I prompted.

"Yeah, well—yeah. Come on, let's get you home."

I pointed at him and gasped. "Casey!"

His face fell. "No."

"Cain?"

"No." He reached me then and put one arm behind my back. "Hold on to your bread, Indy." And that was the only warning I had before I was in his arms and he was walking me out of the room and down the hall.

"But that was your room. You live here, right?"

"Yep."

"Keith?"

His lips twitched as he stepped out of the house. "No."

"You're the quiet one. I don't ever see you because . . . because I don't see you. You're never at the parties, and you don't talk to anyone."

"I'm talking to you now."

I tore some bread off and used it to point at him before shoving it in my mouth. "That you are," I said around the bread. "Chris?" I guessed when we were in my house.

"No."

"I'm on the second floor."

"I know."

My brow furrowed as I studied him. He wasn't looking at me, just looking straight ahead. His black hair looked like it had been styled by running his hand through it, and his eyes looked dark from the lack of light in the house—but somehow, I don't know how, I knew they would look like honey in the light.

By the time we got to my room, I was chewing on more bread, still studying him, and he was trying to keep his breathing steady even though his arms were shaking from having carried me so far.

"Here we are."

"Hello, room, I've missed you!" I called out, and he actually laughed. My head whipped back around to look at him, my voice filled with awe. "I've never heard you laugh."

"There's a first for everything, isn't there?"

"I guess. Can you tell me your name?"

His face fell into a serious mask as he laid me down on my bed, kneeling at the side of it. "You know my name. You just don't want to remember it right now."

"That's ridiculous. Why wouldn't I remember it if I knew it?"

"Great question, isn't it?"

I grabbed for more bread, and he took it out of my hands. I pouted but didn't comment on that. "You're confusing."

"I know," he said on a sigh. "Get changed. I'll go—"

Oh no. Guy number three. "Apparently drinking brings out my inner slut, and I'm sorry if we've had sex before, but I don't want to and I promised Misha I wouldn't."

"We haven't, and I'm not trying to have sex with you, Indy," he whispered, his eyes burning into mine.

Then why was he here? Why did he know where my room was? He wasn't shy like Misha. He was just quiet . . . like he'd rather not be a part of whatever everyone else was doing, and our conversations never interested him. I couldn't remember ever speaking to him before tonight.

I inhaled a soft gasp. "You gave me the bread." It hadn't been a question, and I didn't know how I knew. I didn't even remember receiving the bread. I just remembered having it all of a sudden. But even without his confirmation, I knew without a doubt that this guy gave me the bread.

He looked away for a few seconds before sending me a brief, strained smile. "Yeah, I did."

"Why?"

"That's not important right now. Just get changed and get some sleep. I'll leave water and aspirin on your nightstand, okay?"

Before I could respond, he straightened and quickly walked out of my bedroom. I heard his footsteps on the hardwood floor before the sound descended the stairs.

After kicking off my shoes, I tugged off my jeans and threw them over the side of the bed before tearing off my long-sleeved shirt and bra—leaving me in only a camisole and a pair of lacy underwear. I had my makeup on and I felt grimy and gross, but now that I was in bed I couldn't even think of getting up to turn my light off, let alone to take a shower. I jerked at my comforter until it was covering me, and rolled over on my stomach, wrapping my arms around the pillow I rested my head on.

A minute later I heard footsteps on the stairs again. Before I knew it, the handsome boy from next door was walking into my room. He didn't say anything as he set down a glass of water and bottle of aspirin, and it was when he straightened and turned to leave that I just knew.

"Kier?" I called before he could switch off my bedroom light.

His body stilled, and he looked over his shoulder at me, a soft smile tugging at the corners of his mouth. "Yeah, Indy?"

"Thank you."

"Anytime."

"I swear I'll remember you tomorrow."

The smile fell, and a sad look touched his face. "Good night."

"Night," I whispered when he shut off the light and walked quietly out of my room and away from me.

I fell asleep trying to commit everything about Kier to memory, and chanting over and over again that in the morning I would go to him and prove I remembered him.

Kier

"Hey, excuse me?"

I paused midstep and shut my eyes. That voice. That fucking voice that belonged to a girl who refused to remember me, refused to remember parts of her life for reasons I'd probably never understand. The girl who refused to leave my damn mind.

I ground my jaw and turned, already knowing I'd find her looking apologetic for stopping me—and there she was. Hands covering her mouth, eyebrows drawn together as she bounced on the balls of her feet once.

"I'm so sorry. I'm sure you're busy, and I don't really know you—I mean, we're neighbors, but we don't talk. And anyway, I need your help, or someone's help," she rambled. "I shouldn't have bothered you." Her cheeks filled with heat, and my lips twitched up.

"You're not bothering me."

"Are you sure?"

"Positive, what do you need?"

"Um, my car"—she hooked her thumb over her shoulder, and then turned to look at it—"is dead. I need someone to jump it so I can get to class. I only have one today, but I have an exam that I can't afford to miss."

I grimaced. "I don't have cables." *Lie.* "But I'll give you a ride. I'm heading to campus and will only be there for an hour or so. I'll drive you back."

She chewed on her bottom lip for a second. "I don't want to inconvenience you."

"You're not, come on." Not waiting for her, I turned and walked over to my SUV, and was actually surprised when I'd started it and she was sliding into the passenger seat. I hadn't expected her to come that easily.

"Kyle, right?" she asked, her face excited as she waited for my answer.

My lips tilted up again. "No."

"Oh God. I'm sorry."

My eyes bounced over her face for a few seconds, taking in the redness there from the cold air outside, and her embarrassment. It was adorable on her. She ran a hand through her waist-length red hair, and her green eyes darted back to mine as she pulled the sleeves of her sweatshirt over her fingers.

"Kier," I offered.

Recognition flashed in her bright eyes. "Right! I know I've heard that. You'd think I'd remember an awesome name like that."

You'd think you'd remember a lot, I thought. I wanted to tell her she'd promised me four days ago that she would remember me, but there was no point. She promised me that almost every Saturday night. So I didn't respond, just pulled out onto the street and concentrated on driving.

"Um, my name's Indy," she said when I was looking for a parking spot. Her voice was so unsure, and I knew she thought she was bothering me again. One glance at her red cheeks confirmed it.

For a redhead, she didn't have a lot of what you'd expect to find. She had tan skin and no freckles. But goddamn, could this girl blush when she wasn't drinking.

"I know."

"You do?" Her eyebrows drew together.

After I pulled into a space, I turned to look at her and winked. "It's hard to forget an awesome name like that."

She blushed harder, and I couldn't help it. I laughed.

Her green eyes went wide. "Oh my God. I don't think I've ever heard you laugh."

Of course you haven't, I thought sarcastically. Taking my keys out of the ignition, I raised an eyebrow at her. "Well, there's a first for everything, isn't there?"

"Yeah, I guess there is." She gave me a strange look and huffed a soft laugh. "I just had the weirdest sense of déjà vu. Have you ever had that?"

"Every week," I muttered. "What do you say we go get this bullshit test out of the way?"

"Tell me about—wait. We?"

"Yeah. We. We have the same class, Indy."

Her face fell. "Where have I been?"

I got out of the SUV and shook my head. "I ask myself that all the time."

She rushed around the back to join me, her face pinched together in confusion. "Wait, how did I not know this?"

I shrugged and started walking with her at my side. It felt weird. Instinctively I wanted to pull her up into my arms and carry her, but this was different. She wasn't wasted, she wasn't about to forget this conversation, and she wasn't trying to feed me bread. This was normal—just her. For the first time in the year since the girls moved into the house next to us, she was trying to have a conversation with me—sober.

"It's a big class. It's not hard to miss someone."

"But we're neighbors," she argued, and then muttered to herself, "Well, I guess this goes back to the whole us-never-talking thing."

"I'm talking to you now."

She looked up at me with a smile on her face, her green eyes narrowed like she was trying to figure me out. "That you are."

We walked in silence the rest of the way to the lecture hall, but every minute or so I'd catch her looking at me out of the corner of my eye—that same curious expression on her beautiful face.

Grabbing the door, I opened it and held it for her as she walked in, but she paused in the doorway. She stared straight ahead for a few seconds before turning to look at me, her mouth open like she was going to say something. But instead she closed her mouth without speaking and her eyebrows bunched together again.

With a slight shake of her head, she exhaled audibly and shrugged. "Good luck, Kier."

"You, too."

I watched her turn and walk into the room, walking toward the middle where she usually sat with a group of girls. I went to my normal spot in the back left corner and sank into my seat as I pulled out my phone, waiting for when the professor would come in.

My thumb paused on the screen of my phone when a bag was dropped a couple of chairs down, followed by a long leg stretching over the back of the row of chairs. Long red hair shielded her face as she hopped over and plopped down into the seat next to mine. Brushing her hair away from her face, she glanced at me, a small smile playing at her lips before she stared straight ahead.

She didn't say anything, and neither did I. Because not only had the professor just walked in and already begun passing out Scantrons, but there was nothing to say in that moment. I fought back my own smile.

Indy was coming to me sober.

chapter two

Indy

stepped back as one of my housemates, Chloe, ran through the house to leave for work, and called out a good-bye before I heard the door shut. Walking through the kitchen, I pulled my thick hair up into a messy bun on top of my head and grabbed a soda before joining Misha and my third housemate, Courtney, in the living room.

Neither was talking. The TV was on a music channel, but it was turned down low as they both did homework. I knew I needed to finish this paper, but I couldn't concentrate on it . . . All I could think about was Kier and how weird it had been to talk to him today. How I'd felt like I'd known him—how every time he spoke, I had the craziest sense of déjà vu . . . like we'd already had that same conversation before. But that was ridiculous; he never talked to anyone, including me. He was absurdly quiet. Not just in comparison to the other guys next door, but compared to anyone.

With a huff, I tried to push thoughts of him out of my mind and pulled my laptop onto my crossed legs, determined to finish this stupid paper. Twenty minutes later, I had written the word *the* and was staring blankly at the screen . . . only seeing a pair of honey-gold eyes, a too-perfect smile, and black, messy hair.

"Misha," I whispered. Why I was whispering, I had no clue.

"Hmm?" She raised an eyebrow and tilted her head in my direction but didn't look up from her laptop.

"Misha," I repeated, this time harder.

She looked up at me this time. "Yeah?"

"What do you know about Kier?"

Both eyebrows shot up, but she didn't say anything.

"Kier—neighbor, Kier—lives with Darryn. Really quiet, doesn't ever talk."

"I know who he is. He's actually really nice. I'm just surprised you know him."

I sat back against the couch and made a face. "Why?"

"Because—well, because like you said. He doesn't talk."

"But you just said he's really nice. Which means you've talked to him."

She shrugged and looked back at her laptop. "Only a couple times, and it was just a few words. I think I only heard him talk because I was sitting there with Darryn." Her dark eyes flickered over to me. "Why are you asking about him?"

"He drove me to class today. Apparently we have a class together and I had no idea. And he didn't talk a lot, but he talked. It was weird. Nice, but weird." When I looked up, Misha was just staring at me. "What?"

"Nothing."

"You're looking at me weird. It's not nothing. Is there something about him I should know? Is he a creeper or something?"

Misha laughed softly. "I doubt he would be living with the guys if he were. From what Darryn says, he just doesn't talk a lot."

"Do you know why? Because he doesn't seem shy." And why was I so interested in knowing about Kier all of a sudden?

She shook her head and looked back down at her laptop. "Not shy. Just isn't one for talking, that's what I know." Her fingers began moving over the keys again, and my shoulders sagged in defeat.

I wanted to know why he was so cryptic, and why I felt like I knew him and could trust him when I hadn't said more than five words to him before this afternoon. I wanted to know why he gave me little, knowing smiles like I was missing some private joke that I was supposed to be in on.

None of it made sense. He didn't make sense. But for the life of me I wanted to make sense out of what was pulling me to him.

My feet pounded rhythmically against the concrete, and my breath came out in puffs of little clouds in front of me as I pushed to finish the last bit of my run the next morning. I'd barely slept last night as I went over every detail of every word that had passed Kier's lips, and I was paying for it this morning. Even cutting half a mile off my normal distance, I felt like I had tried to run double what I normally did.

Three more blocks . . . three more blocks, I chanted to myself. *Two more.* Even the music blaring through my earbuds couldn't pump me up enough to finish hard. I didn't even know what song was playing as I tried not to collapse. Just then, my eyes caught the paper tucked under my windshield wipers, and I stopped running.

Looking around the empty street as I walked over to my car, I had one of those flashes. Like I was about to be in a bad horror movie, and people were screaming, "Don't go over there! Run away!"

I rolled my eyes and ripped the paper away from the windshield. Unfolding it, I read the words twice, my heart pounding harder than it had been during my run.

We tried jumping it, still wouldn't start. Went and got you a new battery, she's running great now.

My lower legs had been a weird, stinging mix of cool and hot as the freezing air blew around me, and I knew my ears, nose, and cheeks had been bright red from the cold and my run—but now I didn't feel the cold. I didn't feel the shakiness from pushing myself even though I'd been too exhausted for my run this morning. My cheeks were now filled with heat as I just stood there staring at the paper, my breathing too fast as I thought about what he'd done for me.

Embarrassment and wonder coursed through my body and I slowly turned my head to look up at the house next to ours. People didn't take care of me. Not anymore. Dean had been there for me when I broke and fell too far when it felt like my entire world was crashing down on me—but it'd been a lie. And this? This was different. This was . . . too much.

I walked up to their house on shaky legs, the note clenched tightly in my fist as I stood at the front door for a few seconds before knocking. When there was no answer, I knocked again, harder this time. Less than a minute later, Kier answered the door.

"You . . . ," I whispered, and pointed behind me in the direction of my car.

"Indy?"

I ground my jaw when my eyes began to sting, and when no words could make it past the tightness in my throat, I launched myself at him—throwing my arms around his waist and burying my head in his chest. "Thank you," I choked out.

He laughed awkwardly, and hesitantly wrapped one of his arms around my back. Pressing his closed fist under my chin, he leaned away from me and tilted my head back so he could look at me. "For what?"

Unwrapping the arm holding the note, I held my hand up between us. "My car. You fixed it. Thank you. You didn't have to do that. Please tell me how much it cost. I'll pay you back."

Kier released me, and his lips tilted up in the corners. "As much as I love having a beautiful girl throw herself at me . . . I didn't fix your car."

I blinked quickly. "What?"

"I didn't fix your car, Indy." He shrugged. "That was Darryn and Misha. I saw them working on it when I came back from an early class this morning."

My face fell, and I took a step back. Oh. My. God. I'd been so wrapped up in the enigma standing in front of me that I'd started making *everything* about him. "Oh my God," I breathed. "I'm so sorry, I just—oh God." I dropped my head to stare at the porch, my eyes wide with mortification.

"Indy, it's fine. I'm glad your car's running now."

I nodded, not looking back up at him. "Uh, I'll, uh . . . see you later." Never. I never wanted him to see me again. The girl who didn't even know he was in her class. The girl who launched herself at him for *apparently* no reason. The girl who couldn't remember his name.

Turning, I jogged down the few steps and took off for our house. I slammed the door behind me, still running until I found Misha and her boyfriend at the table in the kitchen.

"Are you okay?" she asked, and stood, her expression worried.

"No—yes—I just, oh my God." I pointed in the direction of the house next to ours and looked at Darryn. "I thought . . . I'm such an idiot," I groaned, and sagged against the counter.

"Because none of that made sense," Darryn said.

I laughed lamely and covered my face with my hands. "I know. I'm full of win this morning." Looking back at them, I took a deep breath and hoped I could make them understand how grateful I was for what they had done. "Thank you both so much for fixing my car. Please tell me how much the battery cost and I'll pay you back."

They gave each other a look, and Darryn glanced at me before his eyes darted to the floor. "Uh, we—"

"Just think of it as a late birthday present," Misha said, cutting him off before shooting Darryn a look.

"I can't, that's too much."

"Well, you're going to have to. Because I won't be telling you how much it cost."

"Misha," I complained, but knew she wasn't going to give on this. "If I wasn't covered in sweat right now, I'd hug you both." It hit me then that I'd just hugged Kier. *Oh God, kill me now.*

A small smile crossed her face. "No need, really."

"Thank you guys, again." Pushing away from the counter, I went upstairs to shower and try to forget how badly I'd just humiliated my-self. I'd gotten halfway through my junior year without talking to Kier. It wouldn't be that hard to go back to how it had been before yesterday.

• • •

A nd it hadn't been hard. Well, it had, and it hadn't. It'd been nine days since I thanked him for the battery he hadn't even bought for me, but it'd been impossible to forget about the quiet guy next door. I looked for him during the party at their house a couple of days later, but before long I'd gotten lost in drinking games—not that I would have said anything if I had seen him. And even though I knew he was in the back left corner of the lecture hall in our class on Monday and Wednesday, I refused to look back there, even though everything in me was screaming to do so. I didn't remember anything from those classes other than once they were over, I'd let out a relieved breath.

After looking for him for a few minutes at the neighbors' party tonight, I'd given up. It was stupid to look for him. I'd never seen him at one of these parties anyway. For all I knew, he wasn't even here to-night. He could be at work if he had a job; he could be out with his girlfriend—oh my God. He could have a girlfriend.

"He could have a girlfriend!" I said out loud, and the guy I was curled up against on the couch gave me a funny look.

"What?"

I threw my hands up in the air. "This whole time I've been— Where the fuck did this bread come from?"

The guy laughed loudly, and curled his arm around my waist. "Baby, you are wasted. You keep forgetting about it, but you've been holding it for an hour at least."

I stared at the gold foil as I leaned away from his body. I didn't like the way he called me "baby." "Did you give this bread to me?"

"No, and you won't let anyone touch it." He pulled me back toward him, his mouth going to my ear. "Let's get out of here."

"Mm. No, no." I made a sound of disapproval as I scrambled away from him and off the couch, taking a few seconds to get myself steady when I was standing.

Holding the bread close to my chest, I moved through the tightly packed bodies, needing air. I don't know why I didn't go toward the front door. It would have made more sense to leave and go to my house, but before I knew what I was doing, I was standing in front of a door in the hall on the first floor.

"Safe room," I mumbled to myself, and tapped my finger against the wood.

Unrolling the top of the foil, I tore off a piece of the warm bread and put it in my mouth as I continued to stare at the door, like if I stood there long enough, it would do something for me.

It didn't.

I let my forehead fall roughly against the door and whined, "Stupid safe room. You didn't go all wardrobe on me and lead me to Narnia."

The door swung open and I stumbled forward.

"Shit—I got you," a deep voice grunted as a pair of arms caught me and helped get me standing again. "Guess it's time to go home?"

I looked up and gasped. "You. You have a girlfriend!"

Golden eyes widened with shock. "What?"

"You have a girlfriend, don't you?"

"No, I don't have a girlfriend."

"You don't?" I breathed, and staggered closer to his body. His hands tightened on my upper arms to keep me where I was. My lips fell into a pout. "And you didn't fix my car."

He laughed softly and moved to wrap one arm around my back. "Hold on to your bread, Indy."

I held up the bag and shrugged. "I don't know where it came from," I murmured. "But it's delicious."

"I bet it is. Up you go." He lifted me into his arms, and I squealed.

"No, no! No!" I said sternly, my eyebrows slamming down.

"If you're in my room, then it's time to get you back to yours."

My face fell, and I kept my eyes trained on the bread in my hands as he walked us down the hall, through the people at the party, and out the door. "I bothered you. In your room. That was your room, not Narnia."

He missed a step and tightened his grip on me as loud laughs burst from his chest. "Narnia? What the hell did you drink tonight, Indy?"

I tried to glare at him, but I probably just looked like a three-year-old not getting her way. "It was the safe door. It was supposed to be magic," I whispered. "No magic."

He did stop walking then. "What did you just say?"

"No magic," I repeated.

"Before that."

I stared at his face for a few seconds before popping a piece of bread in my mouth. "I don't remember," I said honestly. "Why are you carrying me?"

"Because you would fall otherwise."

"Nu-uh."

"You did the first night," he grumbled, and looked away.

I stopped chewing. "What first night?"

"It doesn't matter." He began walking again, his hardened eyes straight ahead.

"Cookie?" I asked when we walked into my house.

He snorted as he kicked the front door to my house shut. "You've called me a lot of names, but that's definitely a new one. No."

"I know your name," I said, and held up my hand. "Do you *want* a cookie?"

His dark eyebrows pinched together. "That's bread, Indy, not a cookie."

I looked at the bread and frowned before offering it back up to him. "It'll be our secret," I whispered. "We can pretend it's a cookie."

He smiled wryly at me before dipping his head and biting the food out of my hand. "Amazing cookie."

I watched his mouth as he chewed, and didn't know if I should be embarrassed by the fact that my breathing was heavy now. "My room is—"

"On the second floor," he finished for me. "I know."

"How'd you know that?"

"Why'd you call my door the safe door?" he countered, his eyes flicking to my face for a second before he began climbing the stairs with me still in his arms.

This felt familiar . . . and right. But that couldn't be right, because I'd only talked to Kier twice, a week and a half ago.

"Indy?"

"Hmm?"

"Why did you call my door the safe door?"

"When did I call it that?"

He exhaled heavily but didn't say anything else as he finished walking up the stairs and straight into my room. My eyebrows pinched together, and I wondered again how he knew where my room was, but before I could ask, he was lowering me onto the bed and pulling the bread from my hands.

"This is mine," I complained, and tried to pull it back toward me.

"I know it is, but I'm betting you have about five minutes before you're asleep. And you don't want to fall asleep with garlic bread in your hands, do you?"

"Yes! Yes, I do!"

A bright smile crossed his face as he uncurled my fingers, one by one. "No, you don't." Once it was in his hand, he straightened and looked down at me, his gaze lingering on my face for a few seconds. "I'll be back in a couple minutes. Get changed."

"For what?"

He stopped midturn and looked back at me. "To go to sleep."

"But I'm not tired," I insisted when he walked away. He didn't respond. "I'm not."

I wanted to talk to him. I wanted to know why he never talked to anyone, and why he didn't have a girlfriend. I wanted to know why he sat in the back of the class, how he knew where my room was, and why he wasn't the one to fix my car. I wanted to know if he'd been as consumed in thoughts of me the last week and a half as I'd been in thoughts of him.

Unzipping my hoodie, I yanked at the sleeves and fought with the material until it was off my arms and on the floor. Then I grabbed my long-sleeved shirt. But that proved to be much more difficult to deal with. I ended up on my side with one arm hanging out of the hole where my head was supposed to go, and the other caught up in the material along with my head before giving up.

I didn't need to get undressed anyway, and it was oddly comfortable. Or that could've been because I was drunk and any position would be comfortable, but my eyes were already shutting, even though I knew I wanted to stay awake to talk to Kier.

My eyes were shut and my breathing was deep when I heard a low laugh followed by the sound of glass being set down on wood. "Kier?"

"Yeah, Indy?"

"My shirt attacked me," I mumbled before letting myself go back to the place where sleep was calling me.

"I can see that."

His hands were touching my arms, maneuvering them through the correct holes of the shirt as he tried to pull it off my body. When he was done, he moved me back so I was lying on the pillows, and I heard his footsteps cross my room before the light behind my eyelids disappeared.

My eyes cracked open, then shut again as he lifted one of my legs to tug my boot off. "Are you staying?"

"No," he said as the other boot slid off, a dull thud sounding in the otherwise quiet room when it hit the floor. I was so close to sleep that the sound seemed miles away.

I felt a pull on the button of my jeans, and groggily slapped at his hands. "No," I protested, and tried to open my eyes.

"Don't kick me, Indy. You're safe with me. Safe door, remember?" Kier's voice filled my head seconds before his hands touched my ankles, grabbing the bottoms of my jeans and pulling them down.

"No, no," I said louder, panic filling my voice as my eyes finally snapped open.

Kier let my pants fall to the floor as he pushed my legs onto the bed and pulled the comforter over my body, his eyes never once on any part of me as he did so. When I was covered, he glanced at me and cupped my cheek. "Get some sleep, sweetheart."

He turned and walked from my room, shutting the door behind him as he did. But before he left, his fingers twisted the lock on the doorknob, and I knew he'd made it a safe door. He hadn't been about to take advantage of me. He was taking care of me, and he was making sure no one was getting in my room tonight.

chapter three

Kier

I jogged down the steps of the house and hurried over to my SUV. As I neared the end of the walkway, movement to my right captured my eye, and I paused when I saw Indy slowing from her run. Her eyes widened before she glanced away, and she looked like she was trying to figure out a way to avoid seeing me.

Two weekends of her remembering my name, but nothing had changed during those weeks. It was painfully awkward to see her now, especially after the morning I'd had Darryn and Misha make Indy believe they'd been the ones to fix her car instead of me. But I hadn't wanted her to know, just like I didn't need her to know about how I took care of her every Saturday night. Until she figured it out, there was no point in talking to her about it.

I glanced at my SUV before looking at her again, a grimace tugging at my lips as I decided against what I knew was the right thing to do. "I thought you'd be gone for Thanksgiving break," I said when she got a little closer.

"We still have classes for a couple days."

"And? Most people skip them so they can actually have a full week off."

Her green eyes fell to the straps of my backpack before she looked to the ground. "You're not."

"My parents aren't big on celebrating Thanksgiving." Or any holiday for that matter, including birthdays. "They take a trip every year instead, so there isn't much of a point in going home."

"Without you?" she asked, her eyebrows pinching together when she looked back up at me.

"Most years."

"That's sad."

I laughed. It might have been sad when I was ten, but now it was normal. "Not really. Have your parents ever taken a trip without you?" She didn't respond for a few seconds, but finally nodded. "That's all it is. We just don't do the whole traditional holiday thing, never have. When are you gonna head home?"

"I'm not."

She looked uncomfortable, so I didn't press for anything else. When she looked at the ground again, I took that as a cue to leave and turned to walk back to my car.

"What is it about you?"

I paused but didn't turn around for a few moments, and then it was only to look over my shoulder.

"I don't know you. Other than right now we've only talked to each other twice and it was for a handful of minutes, but I feel like I know you. I feel—I don't know how to explain it," she huffed, and a frustrated smile crossed her face. "I'm about to embarrass the hell out of myself, but I don't care anymore. I feel like when I'm near you, I'm safe, and it makes *no* sense to me. It is the weirdest feeling to have with someone I only know three things about."

My eyebrows rose at that and I turned to fully face her. "Three?"

"Yes. *Three* things. Your name is Kier, you're extremely quiet, and you are the biggest puzzle I've ever tried to figure out."

"*I'm* the puzzle?"

"Yes!" she said in exasperation.

That had to have been the most backward statement I'd ever heard. "And why am I a puzzle?"

"Because of what I just told you. I don't know you, you don't even talk to anyone, and I feel safe when you're near me! Why is that? I feel like I'm going crazy because all I've been able to think about for these past two weeks is you, and how every time you open your mouth it's like déjà vu, and I just—I don't know what's happening." Her green eyes were massive and she looked like she was on the edge of losing her shit.

I took a few steps toward her and lowered my voice. "Calm down, Indy. You're fine."

"I just don't understand," she said loudly, the pitch of her voice rising. "Do you believe in past lives?" she asked suddenly.

I paused, a laugh slipping past my lips. "I'm sorry, what?"

"Past lives? Like that whole stupid YOLO saying is really just bullshit, because we're about to get another shot down the road?"

I tried to contain my smile, but she was really fucking adorable when she was like this. "What does that have to do with what you're freaking out over?"

"In stories with soul mates they find each other no matter what in every life. And it's like they have a weird connection they can't explain."

I closed the distance between us and dropped my head so I was looking directly into her eyes. "Are you saying we're soul mates?"

"No!" she said, horror lacing her voice, her cheeks filling with heat.

"I think you were," I teased.

"I wasn't, I was just saying that in stories . . . I don't know what I'm saying, okay? But I don't get what's going on with us!"

"So now there's an us?"

"Oh my God," she whispered. "I need to stop talking."

I laughed and took a step back. "I'm teasing you, Indy. And no, I don't believe in past lives. I think we have this one, and that's it."

She sighed, and her body visibly relaxed. When she spoke again, she sounded exhausted—and in a way, defeated. "I don't, either, but I can't figure out how to explain this feeling like I know you."

I ground my jaw for a few seconds as her green eyes held mine. "Because maybe you do know me. You're just not ready to remember why."

Her mouth popped open and an audible huff blew past her lips. "What does that even mean?"

"You'll understand when *you* think you're ready, Indy. That's all you need to know for now."

Before I could say anything else, and before she could ask more questions, I got into my SUV and drove away.

Indy

I climbed the stairs up to the attic the next afternoon, enjoying and hating this time alone. I wasn't leaving for break, but I'd been skipping my classes anyway. I wanted to be alone, *needed* to be alone. But being alone was also a dangerous thing for me—especially when Thanksgiving was two days away.

It didn't matter that it was the wrong day. It didn't matter that I'd already broken down on Saturday—the actual two-year anniversary—and that for the first time in the last two years I'd chosen to forget him rather than grieve for him. It was just that it was *that damn day*.

It just had to be on a holiday. One that was widely celebrated and changed dates every year—almost as if to torture us that much more. Like, *hey—you have* two *anniversaries for this fucked-up day. Not just one. Congratulations, you.* But, at the same time, I feared the year that Thanksgiving fell on the twenty-second again. I would view that day like a bad omen. Only bad would come on that day; I was sure of it.

As I climbed onto the dozens of multisized and colored pillows and blankets that covered the entire floor of our attic, I fought with the knowledge that I needed to be around people. That I should go to a Starbucks at the very least.

Both Chloe and Courtney worked so much that they weren't going home this break—and I doubted they would go home over winter break. But even though they were still at the house, they weren't ever here. And with Misha gone, the last couple of days had been practically impossible to get through.

Urges that felt more like repulsive cravings coursed through my body, and my hands impulsively curled into fists as the muscles in my thighs tightened in anticipation for something that wouldn't come. A soul-deep ache and longing filled my chest, echoed by a much smaller ache to have Dean here, helping me through this. This was the first time I was facing the anniversary alone, and a part of me was terrified I didn't know *how* to get through it by myself.

No wonder Dean had cheated and left me. *Mess* was a nice way of describing my life and me.

I rolled onto my side and curled my knees up to my chest as I tried to hold myself together. I fought with myself to stay here—to not run to someone to make them fix everything. To fix me. Chanting to myself over and over that I just needed to keep breathing through the pain, through the urges, through the grief.

I loved this attic. I loved how quiet and comfortable it was. And now, when all I wanted to do was panic over being alone, I told myself this was what I needed. Quiet. Alone. Peace. No one could fix what had happened. No one could fix me. I needed to do this by myself.

I'd finally been able to stop my damaging form of grief, and hadn't realized that I'd just replaced it with Dean until we were over. The pride of stopping hadn't lasted long when I'd started drowning out memories of Dean with drinking.

One form of fucked-up coping to another.

One helping me feel like I could take some of *his* pain away.

The other making me forget that everyone had given up on me.

But not once in the last two years had I tried to forget *him*. Not once until this past Saturday . . . and I hated that I'd spit on his memory that way. Two years without him—and instead of drinking to forget about Dean and my parents like I had been doing, I drank to forget my own twin brother.

I was a mess. I was drowning. I felt so fucking lost and was tired of pretending that everything was okay. And for the first time in two years, I was trying to pull myself up without using someone else, and I knew I was failing.

But I wouldn't go back to where I'd been. I couldn't. No matter the amount of pain and craving to make it go away, Ian would hate me if he knew what I'd done after his death.

So until I was sure I was okay, I wasn't leaving this attic. I couldn't put myself near any temptation. No one was home; no one would hear my anguished cries. The pillows, blankets, and memories of Ian were all I needed right now.

My eyes cracked open sometime later. The room around me was dark except for the glow of the streetlights filtering in through the attic's window. My bladder was full, my eyes hurt from crying for hours, and my body was sore from the tension of restraining myself from giving in to my cravings. I licked at my dry lips and reached around me for another blanket before pulling it on top of the other two already surrounding me. It was freezing up here.

Just as my eyes started shutting again, I heard a deep voice call my name. I held my breath and didn't move as I heard muted voices talking back and forth, and then the sound of quick feet climbing. Before I knew what was happening, the door to the attic opened.

"Where's the li—"

"Don't turn it on," I pled.

"Oh!" Courtney gasped. "God, you scared me! I was coming up to see if you were in here, but still."

"I'm here." *Obviously. That was stupid, Indy.*

"I have to go back to work, but that quiet guy from next door is here looking for you," she said in a singsong voice.

My heart pounded as I thought about my embarrassing conversation with Kier yesterday. "Did he say why?"

"No," she said, drawing out the word.

"Uh, can you tell him I'm not here?"

"I guess. If you really want me to."

"I really want you to."

She sighed and didn't say anything for a few seconds. "Okay. Well, I'll be back late. Text me if you need anything."

"Bye," I mumbled into the pillow.

I tried going back to sleep after she left and I heard the front door shut, but I couldn't. I had to pee, and now that I'd been awake for more than a few minutes, my stomach was letting me know how neglected it felt. With a groan, I pushed myself awkwardly off the pillows, letting the blankets fall off me, and stumbled my way over to the door and down the stairs. After using the bathroom, I had begun walking toward the main stairs leading to the first floor when something caught my eye, and I paused.

Turning to look on my left, I noticed a light coming through my cracked-open door and raised an eyebrow. I had a bad habit of leaving my door wide-open, and I hated having lights on.

Trying to remain as quiet as possible in the old house, I tiptoed toward my room and held my breath as I reached my door, trying to listen for signs of anyone in there. When I didn't hear any, I pushed the door open, ready to scream, or run, or turn full-on ninja.

My shoulders sagged and all the air left my chest in a depressed huff when I found nothing in my room out of place. It was super anticlimactic.

I walked out of my room and turned toward the stairs, and a scream tore through my chest as I stumbled back before tripping over myself and falling hard on my butt.

"Are you okay?"

"Why are you here?" I yelled, my breathing ragged as I stared at Kier's worried face, his arm outstretched like he'd been about to catch me.

"I was waiting for you." He leaned closer to help me up.

"So you wait for people by popping up out of nowhere and scaring the shit out of them?"

"Didn't mean to scare you. I was just coming back upstairs."

I sighed heavily and pressed a hand to my chest. "Christ, you about gave me a heart attack. Have you been in my bedroom?"

He glanced at my door and shrugged. "Yeah."

"Do you have a habit of inviting yourself to wait for people in their rooms?"

His lips tilted up on one side in a charming, lopsided smirk. "Uh, not exactly. Your housemate told me she didn't think you'd be upstairs much longer and to wait in your room. I'd been in there, but I realized I left my phone in my car, so I went to get it and was coming back."

"Traitor," I hissed.

"Excuse me?"

"She was supposed to tell you I wasn't here."

Kier didn't look hurt or shocked by this. His smirk just turned into a full-on grin. *Ass.* "She told me that, too."

I crossed my arms under my chest and glared at him. "What all did she tell you?"

"First, are you okay? That looked like it hurt."

"I'm fine," I said through gritted teeth.

His golden eyes danced. "All right. She came downstairs, said you'd told her to tell me you were gone even though you were hiding out upstairs in the pillow room—whatever the fuck a pillow room is—and she thought you'd been up there for a while and probably wouldn't last in there much longer, so to wait for you in your room."

"Lovely," I groaned.

"What's a pillow room?"

"It's a room full of pillows."

His expression went deadpan for a few seconds before he rolled his eyes and sighed. "Anyway. I wanted to check on you."

I'd started turning away from him, but at his admission, my head snapped back to look at him. "Why?"

"Because of yesterday."

My cheeks burned and I took a self-conscious step back. "What about it?"

"You were obviously freaking out, and I don't think I made it easier for you. So I wanted to see how you were doing."

"I'm fine."

He studied my face for a few seconds. "Are you sure about that?"

I broke down most of yesterday and today. No, I'm not fine. "Positive."

"Indy . . . ," he mumbled, his tone conveying his disbelief.

I had humiliated myself in front of this guy yesterday, and after the days I'd been having, I didn't need him bringing that humiliation back up. "Did you need something else? As much as I appreciate you checking up on me, I'm fine, and I'm kind of busy."

Kier's head jerked back and his eyebrows rose. "Look, I'm sorry if I embarrassed you yest—"

"For a guy who doesn't talk a lot, you've sure seemed to do nothing but talk the last couple days. I'm sorry, but I need you to leave."

Even as I said the words, I wanted to take them back. I didn't want Kier to leave. I wanted him to keep talking to me. I wanted to know everything about him. I wanted this safe feeling to never go away, but I hated knowing he could see how close I was to breaking for the second time today. I hated knowing he probably thought I was some ridiculous girl. And right now . . . right now—no matter how much I wanted him here—I needed to be alone.

With a small nod, he took two steps backward before turning and walking down the stairs.

I didn't even wait until I heard the front door shut. Ignoring the hunger pains in my stomach, I turned and bolted up the stairs and into the attic as the sadistic cravings got to be too much and a tortured sob burst from my chest.

I tripped over pillows and blankets, falling onto a mass of more of the same as hard sobs racked my body and tears streamed down my cheeks. My hands fisted, and I pressed them against the tops of my thighs as I chanted the words over and over again until sleep finally claimed me.

I won't do it. I can't. For Ian. For me. I won't do it. I can't. For Ian. For me.

chapter four

Kier

I spent the entire next day doing nothing but thinking about Indy and the way she'd looked when I saw her the day before. It wasn't hard to miss the bloodshot eyes and blotchy cheeks, but she hadn't even wanted to talk about our conversation from the morning before—and I know that had been my fault. But if she wouldn't talk to me about that, I knew bringing up the fact that she looked like she'd been crying would only make everything worse.

But I couldn't stop thinking about her. I couldn't stop wondering what had been wrong. I couldn't stop the need I felt to go take care of her. Just like I'd always felt with her. From the beginning there'd been something about her, something calling me to her—to protect her. Only now I was having more and more trouble staying away from her. Like today. It'd been storming all day, the temperatures borderline freezing, and the lightning and thunder constant. Obviously she wasn't alone in her house like I was, but her housemate had mentioned something about two of them being at work all day, and I figured today would be the same. So she was alone again and I'd been thinking of a hundred different excuses to show up like I had done yesterday. Keep her safe from the storm—douche line. Bring her food—which I didn't have any of. Take her out—which I doubted she would agree to. Ask her if she was ready to actually *remember* me—but I knew I couldn't.

I was reaching, and I knew it. I needed to stop. I just didn't know if I could.

I sat up quickly on my bed when the power went out in the house. After waiting a few seconds without it flickering back on, I fell back and raked my hands down my face.

"Fucking perfect."

Slapping my hand around on my bed until I found my phone, I slid my thumb across the screen to light my way so I could go check the breaker in this old house. I stopped when I realized there was no light coming in my window from outside, either.

Walking over to it, I looked out the blinds to find a dark street that only lit up from the random lightning. Glancing to the left, I saw Indy's car parked in front of their house, and fought with myself for only a minute before I was pulling on a hoodie and jacket. With a douche line or not, I was going over there and keeping her safe from the motherfucking storm.

I ran through the rain and up the stairs to the girls' porch just as the front door opened, revealing Indy with wide eyes, like she'd just been caught.

"Kier," she breathed.

This was such a bad idea. "Uh . . ." *I'm checking on you again. I'm protecting you like the badass I'm not.* "I wanted to see you."

Her lips curved up. "You wanted to see me?"

"Yeah," I said on a defeated sigh.

"Even after the way I treated you yesterday, and embarrassed myself the day before, and I could go on to the other times we've spoken . . ." She started to laugh, but jolted when a bolt of lightning flashed, almost immediately followed by a deafening clap of thunder.

"Yeah, still wanted to see you. But if you're going some—"

She stepped back, holding the door wider. "I was coming to you. You just beat me to it."

I kept my eyes trained on her as I walked into the house, not missing the way she was looking everywhere but at me as I did. I was used to the drunken Indy forgetting me, and the sober and adorable-as-sin Indy—but I wasn't used to what I'd encountered yesterday, and I wanted to know what had made her act that way. I wanted to fix it. I wanted to make sure it never happened again.

"So you—" I started at the same time she blurted, "I'm so sorry, Kier. I—wait, what were you about to say?"

I smiled even though I doubted she could see me clearly. "I was just trying to figure out why you were coming to see me."

There was a long pause. The only sound was our breathing, the rain against the house, and the occasional thunder. When she spoke again, her words were soft and slow. "I needed to apologize for yesterday, and . . ."

"And?" I prompted.

"And I didn't want to be alone tonight," she breathed.

My heart beat harder in my chest and heat flooded my veins, but I tried to stop my initial reaction. Telling myself that if her housemates had been here, she wouldn't have come looking for me, and that it was possible she would have gone to any of the guys in my house. But it was damn hard to keep telling myself that when she'd been coming to me sober for the second time.

When I didn't respond, she huffed. "I can't see you very well, so I can't try to figure out what you're thinking and it's bothering me."

I bit back a smile and reached out until the tips of my fingers brushed her stomach. Her muscles contracted at the contact, but she didn't pull away. I let my fingers trail across her stomach until I found one of her arms, and then I slid my hand down her soft skin and intertwined my fingers with hers.

"Well, then, you won't be alone."

Her breathing deepened and she curled her fingers around mine, and my body relaxed at the simple movement. "What *is it* about you?" she asked.

Even though she'd asked me before, I knew this question wasn't meant for me. Just her tone told me she'd asked herself that question at least a hundred times, and I wondered what answer she'd started coming up with.

"I told you—"

"When I'm ready."

I swallowed roughly and nodded in the dark room. "Yeah."

"And you're not going to tell me when exactly it is that I *will* be ready?"

"No."

"But I still feel safe with you."

God, I hope so.

Indy cleared her throat and took a step back, her grip on my hand tightening as she did. "The pillow room has a lot of blankets. I, uh, don't really feel comfortable having you in my room yet—even though you were already in there yesterday. But it's comfortable up there, and even though it's probably colder up there than the rest of the house, we'll be able to stay warm."

If only she had any clue how many times I'd been in her room. My lips twitched into a smile. "Lead the way."

After stumbling our way up one flight of stairs, down the hall, and then up more stairs, she suddenly paused in front of me.

"I wasn't joking when I said it's full of pillows. We didn't turn this room into a bedroom. The carpet is covered with dozens of pillows, and there are probably another dozen blankets at least in here. You have to walk very carefully or you'll trip and go down."

"Okay . . ." I could see enough so I could make out the silhouette of her body, and the lumpiness of the floor, but that was about it.

She started walking painfully slowly, and after she took a few calculated steps, I took two—and immediately fell, taking her down with me.

"What the hell kind of death trap is this room?" I grunted into the mass I'd fallen into, half of which felt like a pillow, and half of which seemed to be a blanket. At least the landing was soft.

Indy was laughing so hard she didn't respond for a few seconds. "I told you to be careful where you walked!"

"I was!"

"Obviously not." There was a rustling noise before the blanket was yanked out from underneath me. "If you find blankets, grab them."

"You just took mine."

She huffed. "You'll find more. Come on, it's freezing up here, and it's only going to get worse the longer the power stays out."

Not wanting to risk standing, I crawled around on the pillows, grabbing anything that felt like a blanket as I moved toward where Indy was already waiting by the window. I could see her silhouette and breaths coming out in little white puffs.

"I think I got five?"

"I got six," she said as she began wrapping blankets around herself.

Dropping mine, I wrapped the ones she'd collected around her until she was completely covered. "You look like a burrito."

Her soft laugh filled the space between us. "I can't move my arms."

"Doesn't matter, you don't need to. At least you'll be warm."

"Oh, there's no doubt of that." She smiled at me in the dark room before frowning. "But now I can't make you look like a burrito."

"I don't want to be a burrito. I wouldn't be able to move my arms."

"What the hell, Kier?"

I laughed and grabbed the blankets I'd dropped. "You'll get over it."

After I covered myself, we huddled closer together and talked for an hour about classes, housemates, and why she had always been afraid to say anything to me since she never saw me talking to anyone. Like I'd known it would, that topic led to her asking again why she felt safe with me, and when I couldn't give her an answer, she stayed quiet for a few minutes.

"I haven't felt safe in a long time," she finally admitted softly, and then shook her head. "I don't mean I've felt like I was in danger or any-thing. I just—I've felt—it's hard to explain. . . ."

I just waited.

"I've felt like I was on the verge of destroying myself for so long, and I just couldn't stop. It made me feel like I was drowning, and even when I thought I had people helping me keep it together, they weren't. And they never made me feel as at peace as you do just by being near me. This feeling is so different—such a nice change. Like I've said, I don't know how to begin to explain it, but it's just this feeling I have around you."

And this was it. That tone. It was the same one she'd had yesterday when I tried to talk to her and she asked me to leave. And I knew at that moment that she was ready to know about all those Saturday nights I'd been taking care of her. I didn't know how I knew; I just knew wherever this conversation was leading this time, it would lead there. She'd told me she'd felt safe before, but never like that. Every-thing was different this time.

She laughed awkwardly. "I don't even know why I'm bringing this up. I know you won't tell me why."

"It's because all I want to do is take care of you," I said before I could stop myself, and risked a glance at her wide eyes.

"Wh-what? Take care of me?" She laughed. "Kier. You don't even know me. I'm—I'm a mess. I'm apparently a slut—"

"Don't. Don't say that about yourself."

"You don't know—"

"Yeah, Indy, I do." I held her gaze for a minute and watched as she bit down on her bottom lip, like she was trying to stop herself from saying something. "Destroying yourself . . . ," I mumbled, echoing her words, and let that hang in the air for a few seconds. Taking a deep breath, I looked away as I said, "Indy, you always seem so surprised that you're hearing me talk—or you say something about how I'm quiet. And yeah, I'll admit I don't talk to a lot of people—and last year, we didn't talk at all. But we've talked a lot over the last three months, more than you realize. That's not the only difference in this year, though. I saw you at the parties at our house last year, and you were never like how you are now. You're wild; you're out of control. You're with multiple guys, and you never remember a thing."

"How do you know that?" she asked, her voice shocked, but just barely above a whisper. "You're never there."

I kept speaking like she hadn't said anything. "You say you feel like you're on the verge of destroying yourself, and Saturday nights are the first thing that come to mind, Indy. Because, although no one can stop you from drinking, or doing whatever you want to do . . . I know you don't like who you are when you drink."

"How could you possibly know that?"

"Same reason I know which room is yours. Same reason you stumble into my room at some point during every party. It never fails, you end up in there, and we go through the whole thing all over. You trying to remember my name, me carrying you over here to your room, you figuring out I gave you the bread and wondering why."

"Safe room," she mumbled to herself, her mouth forming a perfect *O* when it hit her. "You leave the water and pills, too, don't you?"

It hadn't been a question, so I didn't answer. I just sat there as her mind worked around the information she'd just been given, and everything she was trying to piece together.

"Are you the one who locks my bedroom door?" she asked after a couple of minutes.

I nodded. "People know you live next door. They see me carrying you out of my house and returning not even ten minutes later alone. I don't trust someone not to take advantage of that."

"But why—why would you do that for me? I don't remember any of—" She cut off suddenly, her face blank for a split second. "And why don't I ever remember it? I don't get that drunk, Kier!"

"You're right, you don't get that drunk. You're definitely drunk, but not to the point where you wouldn't remember *anything* from the night before. The first couple times I thought you were doing it just to be . . . I don't know, I thought you just wanted someone to take care of you. So I did. But then I realized you really had no clue. After the last three months of it, all I've been able to come up with is I think you block out these nights in your mind. Like there's already something bad about them, so the rest of it you just decide to forget as well."

Her face went blank, and she didn't respond for a long time, but I knew I was right. "Dean . . . I drink to forget Dean." She sighed raggedly. "He was—"

"I know who he was to you," I said, clenching my jaw and cutting her off.

"You do?" she asked, shock coating her words.

Of course I did. Every time I saw him on campus, I wanted to punch the bastard. "There was a party a few weeks into the school year, and it was the second night you stumbled into my room. After I got you in bed, you started sobbing, saying you were disgusted with yourself. You'd slept with some guy and said, 'It didn't work—my heart still hurts,' and told me all about Dean. When the next two weeks went by with similar results, I started buying you the bread. Partly because it would absorb some of the alcohol you were drinking, and also because the first three weeks before you fell asleep you kept complaining because you didn't understand why the world was suddenly banning garlic bread, and all you wanted was to find some. Some weeks you eat it and stay away from guys. Some weeks you stumble into my room without it, and those are the nights you cry again."

"That's really . . . embarrassing. Oh my God," she groaned. "And after all that, how could you sit there and tell me I'm not acting like a slut?"

I glared at her and resisted the urge to shake her. "Did you not hear me? I know you don't like who you are when you're like that. You *tell* me you disgust yourself. I see you when you're sober, Indy, and I know you're not that girl. You're trying to forget someone, and you're wasted whenever you do something."

"Like that makes it okay?"

"No," I answered honestly. "But you—the way you are, the way you honestly block all of this from your mind, I think that proves you're not a slut. You said you feel like you're drowning, and to be honest, that's kind of a perfect word."

"Did you fix my car, yes or no?"

"Yes," I said hesitantly, and she laughed without humor.

"Then why did you tell me it wasn't you? Why did Misha say it was her?"

I looked away for a second before saying, "Misha and Darryn are the only ones who have figured out what I've been doing every week. I don't talk to them about it, but they've figured it out. And I needed help getting into your car to fix it the other morning. Misha knows you weren't ready to know I was helping you. She was just protecting you."

Even in the dark room I could see when her jaw started trembling and tears filled her eyes. "So all of this, this whole feeling safe with you, has just been an illusion? A product of not remembering certain nights, but for some reason, remembering to come to your room?"

"If that's how you want to see it."

"How else would I see it?" she nearly yelled.

"Sober, you feel safe near me, drawn to me. Drunk, you feel the same way. You came to me the first time, second time, third, and so on. Nights you don't remember at all. But you still came to me. You knew I was safe, and that's all I needed to know to keep taking care of you."

"God!" she cried. "Why would you keep doing that week after week?"

"Because someone had to let you know."

Her eyebrows pinched together in confusion as a line of tears fell down one of her cheeks. "Know what?"

"That you mean a lot more than you think you do. You don't seem to think very highly of yourself—and I don't know why—but you're wrong. Whatever it is, you're wrong . . . and Dean was an idiot to let you go."

A soft cry burst from her chest, and when I started moving toward her, her voice stopped me. "Don't! Please don't."

I sat back and watched helplessly as she tried to pull herself together underneath all those blankets.

"I want that to be true . . . but it's just not," she whispered. She didn't say it like she was searching for more compliments. Every word had so much truth and pain behind it, the admission had me rubbing at my chest as I shook my head in confusion.

"Indy . . ."

"Thank you for taking care of me, and trying to protect me from myself, but I told you, I'm a mess. My life? It's . . . God, Kier, it's beyond complicated, and so many people have already given up on me—it's not long before you will, too."

"And what makes you think that?"

"Because there's no reason for you not to. The people who were supposed to be there for me through anything gave up on me. Why *wouldn't* you?"

My breathing deepened as frustration pumped through me, and I had to wait until I had it under control before I responded to her. "Well, you're not giving me much of a chance to prove myself, are you? You've already determined that *you'll* disappoint *me*. That's a new one." My lips quirked up on one side in a sarcastic smirk. "So this time it really is 'it's not you, it's me'? And we're not even dating."

"Kier . . . ," she protested. "You don't understand."

"You're right, Indy. I don't." I began shrugging off all the blankets, and her eyes widened. "No matter what you think about yourself, I see differently. See, I don't talk to people unless I want to give them my time. And, God, Indy, I want to give you my time. But I *see* people, and I sure as hell see you. I may not know what's hurting you, I may not know why you're destroying yourself, but I still fucking see you. I see that you need someone to save you from yourself." When I had all the blankets off me, I carefully stood, never taking my eyes off her pained expression. "And I'll still be that guy. I'm *still* that safe place, and I'll still be there ready to take care of you if you find you can't handle whatever's going on and you start trying to destroy yourself again. But I won't listen to you basically tell me you're not worth being saved. Because that? I don't believe that for a goddamn second."

"You don't understand what you're saying," she said as I turned to leave, and I looked back at her.

"No, I do. If I'm capable, I will save you every time, Indy. Believe that, if nothing else. I don't need or expect anything in return. I'm doing this because it's what you deserve and what I want to do for you."

"I want you! You consume me in a way I've never experienced even though up until ten minutes ago it didn't make sense! I want the feeling you give me to never end, but there's no way—"

I dropped to my knees in front of her and cupped her cheeks in my hands and brought my mouth down onto hers. "Don't finish that," I growled against her lips before kissing her again.

Her mouth moved easily against mine, and when I traced my tongue against her lips, they parted on a soft inhale, allowing me access to tease her tongue with my own.

"I need to be able to touch you," she pled before deepening the kiss, and I released her cheeks to begin quickly, and awkwardly, pulling down the blankets I'd wrapped around her.

Once her arms were free, I laid her back on the pillows and hovered over her body for a few seconds before relaxing on top of her. An annoyed groan sounded in the back of her throat when she tried to move her legs, but the six blankets wrapped—and now tangled— around her lower body prevented the movement.

Moving back enough so I could look down into her eyes, I shook my head and whispered, "Nothing is ever guaranteed, but you can't write us off before you even give me a chance to prove that I can be good for you."

That pained look was back in her eyes. "I have a feeling that you would be. I've *had* that feeling. But that doesn't mean that I'll be good for you."

I brushed my lips against hers, everything in my body yelling to taste her again. "Let me be the judge of that."

Fresh tears welled up in her eyes, and my body tightened as I prepared to make my case again. Instead of the resistance I was coming to expect, she choked out, "My brother died. Two years ago last Saturday. But it was Thanksgiving, so it's also kind of tomorrow."

"Indy," I crooned, my hands going to cup her cheeks again.

"He was my twin, and I loved him"—she cut off on a sob—"so

much. We were nothing alike, but still inseparable until college. He was my best friend, and we loved to drive my mom crazy . . . probably just because she gave us such horrible names."

I smiled and brushed at a tear. "I love the name Indy."

Her watery gaze drifted over to me. "My brother's name was Ian. Indy and Ian . . . Indy-Ian. All our friends just called us Indian instead of trying to say our separate names." She laughed softly and shook her head. "He got a scholarship to play football in Texas. It was the first time we'd ever been away from each other, but I didn't get accepted there, and there was no way he wasn't going. It was like a dream for him. He'd always been so focused in school and football . . . my parents had always been proud of him."

Her eyes got a faraway look as heavy tears slipped down her cheeks.

"Our freshman year Ian said he couldn't come home for Thanksgiving, and our parents never really liked me, so I decided to stay here with Dean." She must have seen my skeptical expression, because she added, "Ian always had to tell my parents to back off because they were never happy with me or anything I did. My grades were never as good as his. My boyfriends never measured up to Ian's perfect girlfriends. My dad always said I dressed like a whore, but he congratulated Ian when he lost his virginity. It was always difficult with them. They practically paid me to move away from them."

"Are you serious?"

She choked out a depressed-sounding laugh, and even in the dark I could see her eyebrows rise in confirmation. "So apparently Ian just told my parents he couldn't come home because he wanted to come hang out with me here so we could have time without our parents fighting over how I wasn't making them proud the way Ian was. He called me the night before Thanksgiving to tell me he was boarding a plane with a friend who lived in the area, and would be catching a ride, and not to tell Mom and Dad. There was some crazy snowstorm, and he got stuck in Chicago."

The tears came harder, and for long minutes Indy didn't continue the story. After taking a few large breaths in and out, she looked up at me and gave me a depressed smile.

"I was woken up the next morning by a phone call around six. I was alone in my dorm room, my roommate had left for the break, and I remember it smelled like her perfume. I don't know why I remember that. It's just something that has always stood out, because I hated that fucking perfume, and it's all I could smell as I listened to my mom sobbing on the other end of the line. Ian and his friend had decided to try to drive since there were no flights, and it was only about four hours. We're from Chicago, so Ian called his friends all night until one of them agreed to come get them at the airport and drive them. They didn't make it forty-five minutes before they, and another car, hit a huge patch of black ice and spun out of control. They both went off the road and into a ditch. The driver was paralyzed from the waist down, Ian's friend broke his collarbone, and Ian's side of the car was pinned underneath the other car. They said he lived for about ten minutes after the crash. They didn't say the exact words, but it wasn't hard to figure out how much he'd been suffering for those ten minutes. And he'd been coming to see me."

"But, Indy . . . that doesn't make it your fault."

"I know that," she cried. "But I'm not sure my parents do."

"You don't—"

"My dad said, 'It should have been you' when I was finally able to make it home."

I flinched back. "What the fuck?" I breathed. "Indy, I—I don't. God, I'm so sorry about Ian. But your parents, they're wrong."

She nodded absentmindedly, her jaw shaking as she did. "Through everything, all I could think about was that Ian suffered. That he was in pain for those ten minutes, and I wasn't there for him when he'd been there for me my whole life. I—I just lost myself after that. I clung to my relationship with Dean because my parents hated me even more, but nothing took the pain away. Over and over I relived that phone call, the smell of that horrible perfume, and the fact that he suffered— and I started cutting."

My chest felt hollow and my stomach dropped. "Indy, no. . . ."

"Somehow it made sense to me. Like if I felt pain *for* him, I was taking away what he had gone through. I never did it to kill myself. It was always on my legs, and I knew where not to cut, but I couldn't stop. It became addictive. Every time I thought about him, I'd have to do it. Dean tried to get me to stop, and I tried—God, I tried so fucking hard, but I felt like I'd failed Ian," she cried. "I know none of this makes sense, but at the time it did. My parents never even found out—I was able to stop before sophomore year ended—but when I had to go home over summer . . . it was horrible. It was like even though they didn't *know*, they knew that I was refusing to cope, and they just got tired of having to deal with their disappointment. I found my bags on the driveway when I came home from the gym one morning, the locks to the house changed. So I came back to school early and found Dean and Vanessa having sex." She took a deep breath and I could tell she was trying to steady herself.

"I hadn't been there for Ian, I was never a good enough daughter for my parents, so much so that I can't go home anymore, and I found out my boyfriend—the only person who knew what was happening and was trying to help me through it—had wanted to dump me and hadn't done it yet because he was just afraid to upset me." I started to say something, but she cut me off. "*That* is why I'm trying to tell you it can't work. *That* is why I'm telling you you'll leave. Everyone does. And you think you want to save me, but it's not your job to save me, Kier. I need to save myself, and I'm trying. The drinking—it's bad, I know. But it's done. It has to be, just like I stopped cutting for Ian. I can't keep drinking to forget a guy who never cared about me. But while I'm trying to save me, you shouldn't have to get caught up in the mess that is my life. Do you understand now?" she asked, her voice breaking on the last word.

I thought for a minute before responding, and when I did, I took her face in my hands and pressed my forehead to hers. "I know what you're saying, but you're not scaring me away. I hurt for you, Indy. I hate what you've been through, and yes, I wish I could take it all away. But I know I can't do that, and I'm sorry. That will always be hard. You'll always miss him. Your parents—they can go to hell if they can't see how amazing you are. I still stand firm on my opinion of Dean, even more so now. But what you've been through? What you did to yourself? You're not scaring me, Indy. Everyone struggles with something. Everyone has different ways of dealing with the shit that happens in their life. Yours was destructive, yeah. But you? You realized that and stopped it and have been fighting it alone. Do I wish you hadn't ever done it? Of course. But do I admire you? Hell yeah. You're the strongest person I know for stopping."

"You're making it seem like I'm someone better than I am."

"No, I'm not. I told you," I whispered against her lips before placing a kiss there. "I see people, and I see you. Now I know what you've been hiding, and I still see the same girl I want to take care of and spend my time with. Nothing's changed over here. I'm just waiting to see if you're going to give me more reasons why you think I should run."

She huffed and rolled her eyes. "I've given you plenty."

"Well, not running."

"Kier . . ."

"Tell me something. Yesterday when I was here, you'd been crying, and you didn't want to see me. Did that have to do with me, or did that have to do with this week and Ian?"

Her eyes roamed my face in the shadows. "Ian. I was—I was struggling."

"Understandable." Placing a soft kiss on her throat, I moved away from her and spent a few minutes burying her under her blankets before grabbing the ones I'd been using and wrapping them around me. When I was done, I moved so I was lying next to her and she laughed at the amount of time it was taking me to do this. "Now that we're not going to freeze, why don't you tell me about Ian?"

Her smile fell. "What? What do you mean *about* him?"

"This is a hard time of year for you, and you were struggling alone yesterday. You told me tonight you didn't want to be alone, and you're not. So instead of struggling, why don't you tell me all the good things you remember about him?"

Her eyes shone in the dark as she stared at me in silence for what seemed like countless seconds before whispering, "Okay."

chapter five

Indy

Kier and I had spent the rest of the night doing just that. I'd told him stories about Ian as we lay bundled up in blankets, and eventually we fell asleep that way. The power kicked back on sometime early in the morning before we woke up, and at some point we'd shed our multiple blankets. We had woken up with two blankets covering us together and Kier's body curled around mine.

I hadn't woken up next to anyone since last school year with Dean, but even then it had never seemed as perfect as waking up with Kier. On the rare occasions Dean and I had spent the night with each other, it was always awkward, and when I woke I was uncomfortable—and that was if I'd been able to fall asleep at all. But my body seemed to fit perfectly against Kier's, his head resting just above my own, one of his legs fitted between mine, the arm he wasn't using as an additional pillow wrapped securely around my waist, his hand splayed across my upper stomach.

As I lay there enjoying my stolen moments with him, his pinky started lazily dragging back and forth against my stomach before he grumbled, "Power's back on?"

"Must be."

He made a tired sound in the back of his throat and rolled away from me. "Do you have anything planned today with your house-mates?"

I rubbed at my face and tried to hide how unhappy I felt about him moving away from me. "No, they've been gone working, so we haven't talked about doing anything."

"Do you want to spend the day with me?"

"Maybe," I said softly, my smile telling him my answer. "What'd you have in mind?"

His normally golden-brown eyes looked like they were shining from the light filtering in through the window as he studied me. A few moments later he said uncertainly, "A non-Thanksgiving day."

"Now that sounds perfect."

After I'd taken a shower and gotten dressed, I met him at the guys' house. He'd already started to cook breakfast for us. After a non-Thanksgiving meal, we spent the rest of the day talking, watching movies, and eating food that had absolutely nothing to do with the holiday. It was weird, and it was just as I'd thought it would be—perfect.

Yesterday he'd shown up not long after I came back from my run, and we bounced back and forth between the kitchen and living room as I read and worked on two papers I had due within the next couple of weeks, and he finished homework and studied for a test. He'd fallen back into his quiet self, and while I liked that he could spend an entire day with me just doing homework—not mauling me or even touching me, considering that he was always a couple of feet from me—as I tossed and turned last night, I couldn't stop thinking about it, and it started bugging me.

He'd even kept his distance on Thanksgiving—something I hadn't noticed until now because I'd been so busy feeling comfortable and safe in his presence. And when I thought back, I realized I couldn't remember him actually being close enough to touch me since we'd woken up in the pillow room.

Saturday morning I knocked loudly on the door to the boys' house until he answered, his face easily slipping into a smile when he saw me. He took a step back to let me in, shutting the door behind me.

"Good mo—" he began, but I cut him off by grabbing his hand and staring down at it. He watched me and asked, "Is my hand okay . . . ?"

"Why haven't you touched me since Thanksgiving morning?"

His laugh ended on a sigh. "Honestly? It makes it easier for me."

"Makes what easier?" I asked, looking up at him.

"Being near you."

My eyes widened at his blunt honesty and I bit down on the inside of my cheek, looking at where his fingers were playing with mine before glancing back up at his face. "You haven't kissed me since the night in the pillow room," I murmured.

"No, I haven't," he said simply, his golden eyes never leaving mine.

I didn't know what I'd been expecting—for him to grab me in his arms and kiss me right then, to try to make an excuse for not wanting to kiss me anymore, something . . . but I hadn't expected him to just agree. I blinked quickly and dropped my gaze and hands as I felt my cheeks burn. "O—um . . . okay."

He didn't say anything, and my embarrassment only seemed to build. I turned and started for his door, only stopping when his hands came down around the top of my arms, his chest pressed firmly against my back. "You came over to say those two things, and then leave?"

"Uh, yeah . . . pretty much."

His laugh was quiet and deep, the sound sending vibrations from his body to mine. "What did you want me to say?"

"Nothing, I didn't have any expectations."

"Liar."

I gritted my teeth and dropped my head to stare at the floor, and my eyes fluttered shut when the faintest touch of his nose trailing up the back of my neck had a shiver going through my body.

"You didn't ask why, so I didn't tell you why. But I could already see your mind working in ways that are dangerous for both of us, and I'm not gonna let you leave when you're thinking up some kind of bullshit that has you prepared for me to leave you."

"We're not dating—technically you can't leave me," I whispered, and he laughed against my skin.

"Now you're bringing technicalities and labels into this?" His hands moved down my arms to wrap around my waist, and he leaned in to speak in my ear. "And you and I both know people don't have to be together to leave each other. But us? No, we don't have a label. I don't need one, but if you do—we can talk about that on a day that isn't today. I'm your safe place, and when you're ready, you'll be mine. If you ask me, that means more than a bullshit label."

"Again with the 'when you're ready'?" I asked, and turned in his arms to look up at him.

Kier gently pushed me back until I was pressed against the door, and rested both his forearms against the wood, leaning in so our foreheads were resting against each other's. "It'll always come back to waiting for you to be ready, Indy. You weren't ready to tell me about Ian, or face what you were doing to forget Dean—because you weren't ready to get over him—so you weren't ready to know what I was doing for you. I kissed you, partly because I thought I would go insane if I didn't, but mostly because I needed you to be able to see what you were doing to me, to get a glimpse of what you've come to mean to me, and to see that no matter what you could possibly have told me, I wouldn't run."

I brought my hand up to his stomach and grabbed at his shirt, bringing his body closer to mine. "So why stop?"

"Because you told me everything. You laid yourself bare. You had to feel vulnerable after that, and I didn't want anything I did to feel like I was taking advantage of you. So now everything's out there, and now I'm waiting for you to be okay with that—to be okay with moving on from Dean and not keeping Ian a secret anymore. I won't push you to get there, and I won't kiss you until you are there. Not to speed things up, and not to make you think I don't want you, but only because I'm waiting for you to be ready. Once you're ready, I'm taking you and I'm not giving you back. You're going to be mine, Indy. I'll keep you safe from yourself. I'll be there for you when you struggle with urges and what happened to Ian . . . but there won't be anything between us. No Dean . . . no worries of me leaving you. Do you understand now?"

I swallowed past the tightness in my throat and nodded. My breathing was rough from having Kier this close to me, and hearing his words. That alone had me straining not to close the inches between our lips—but I knew what he was saying, and I knew I would wait.

No guy had ever talked to me the way Kier did, or said the kinds of things he said to me. No guy had ever been as considerate, and no guy had ever known me better than I'd known myself. And though I wasn't in love with Kier yet, I loved him for what he was doing for us.

"And after I've barely tasted you, it's hard not to. That's why I haven't been touching you. Not because I don't want to, but because being this close makes it harder to keep reminding myself why I can't have you yet."

He pushed away from me, that crooked smirk crossing his face as he stepped back farther into the house, his arms crossing over his lean, muscled chest. With a slight raise of his eyebrow, his golden eyes darted to the space next to him. "So, are you leaving or staying?"

I bit back a smile and took a step toward him before pausing. "I shouldn't stay."

His eyebrows pinched together, but he didn't say anything.

"Because right now I keep looking at your mouth, and I'm going to convince myself I'm ready if I don't get some space from you for a little while."

He automatically wet his lips before a challenging smile crossed his face, and my fingers twitched as my heart raced.

"Leaving! I'm leaving."

I turned and bolted from the house, his deep laugh following me as I ran down the porch and away from him.

• • •

Kier

School started up again two days later, and the rest of the semester began passing quickly with the winter break approaching. The classes were the same, the work still sucked, and for the most part I kept to myself. Except now Indy was filling my days and nights.

In the last week and a half, I'd spent more of my time with her than I had alone. It was the sweetest form of torture being near her and still never touching her, but it was worth it to see her opening up to me the way she had been. Even through classes, homework, and the stress of finals around the corner, she seemed to relax more in that time than I'd ever seen her in the last year and a half. Indy was a master at faking a smile—and she looked beautiful when she did. But, God, Indy just smiling was amazing.

And as the real smiles became more frequent, and fake smiles became only a memory, I just sat back and counted down the days until she would be mine. I knew she was ready; I was just waiting for her to know, too. Judging by the tension between us, and the fact that she no longer set foot in my room, it wouldn't be long.

Now as we walked across the campus toward my car, she wrapped her arm around mine and pressed her body close to my side. She slipped her hand into my jacket pocket to grip my hand, and her body shivered against the cold air. But even with that, she smiled up at the lightly falling snow.

Exhaling loudly, she sent her smile over to me. "Done. Finally!" she groaned. "Now all we have left is finals next week, and then nothing for almost three weeks."

"You know, most people don't get this excited until after finals are over."

She rolled her eyes and looked ahead. "Well, I'm not . . . most . . ." But she didn't finish, and her body stilled against mine.

I looked down to see her eyebrows pinched together, a curious expression on her face. As I followed her line of sight, my shoulders sagged and I swallowed roughly when I saw Dean standing not twenty feet away from us.

Maybe I was wrong about her being ready.

Her hand tightened against mine when he glanced over from the group of guys he was talking with, and his eyebrows rose when he saw us. And if it hadn't been for the fact that it would look bad for her if I were to do it, I would have let go of her right then and continued walking—letting her follow if she wanted to.

I didn't need to test her. I told her I'd wait until she was ready, and I would. But if she was still not over her old boyfriend, then I didn't want her using me as a crutch when she saw him. But I didn't let go of her as I started walking again, and she kept up without any hesitation.

"I haven't seen him in a month," she finally said when we got in my car.

I turned to face her before driving away, but she wasn't looking at me. "And?"

She blinked a few times, her face still in that curious expression she'd had looking at him. "It was weird."

Indy didn't offer anything else, and I didn't ask. I pulled out of the parking space and drove us back to our houses, neither of us saying anything the entire time. I didn't know if she could sense how frustrated I felt that after going so far forward, we seemed to be right back where we'd started, but she never said anything about it. She just stared out the windshield like she was trying to figure something out, and I tried to tell myself that I needed to calm down.

It wasn't working. My jaw felt like it was going to break by the time I pulled up in front of the houses, and my hands were gripping the steering wheel so tight that my knuckles were white.

When we got out, she made it halfway to her house before she realized I wasn't following her.

"Aren't you coming over?"

"Yeah, just let me go drop my stuff off. I'll be over in a minute."

Her brow furrowed, but she nodded as she backed up toward the girls' house, and I turned to go into ours. As soon as I was in my room,

I noticed I didn't have any "stuff," and I realized why Indy had looked so confused.

Raking my hands over my face, I fell back onto my bed and groaned. I didn't want to deal with this; I didn't want to deal with Dean. I wanted to be sure of where we were, like I had been ten minutes before we saw him. I wanted to ask her what she'd been thinking when she was staring at him. But I knew I couldn't ask her, I knew I had to wait for her to tell me—and it was killing me.

She was supposed to be mine, and I'd thought she finally was until I realized she still belonged to him.

When I'd calmed down, I got off my bed and walked over to the girls' house, letting myself in and up the stairs toward Indy's room. When I didn't find her in there, I didn't hesitate; I climbed the stairs to the attic and carefully walked across the death trap of a floor until I was next to her and wrapped another blanket around her as I sat.

She didn't look at me as I did, and she didn't say anything for long minutes as she stared at the snow falling outside the window. "You didn't have anything you needed to put down."

"I know."

Her eyes drifted away from the window and down to the pillows. Nodding a couple of times, she flickered her green eyes toward me for a second before saying, "I'd rather you not drag anything out for my benefit, Kier. If you're done, just say it. I appreciate honesty so much more."

"God, Indy, seriously?" I cupped her cheek and turned her head so she was looking at me. "You really thought that was what all that was about?"

She didn't respond, but her eyebrows shot up and she made a face, like what else should she have expected?

"I needed time to calm down. You just shut down the second you saw him, and I had to watch you staring at your old boyfriend who I want nothing more than to beat the shit out of. That was hard for me to watch, but I really can't expect anything else from you. You were with him for two years, and it's only been a few months since you guys broke up. I was afraid I'd say something, so before I could, I gave myself time to calm down."

"You think I still want him?" she asked, her voice cracking. "You think I'm still having a hard time dealing with what happened between Dean and me?"

I shrugged, and my fingers slipped from her cheek. "Yeah."

"Do you not see how much you've helped me—changed me—in the last couple weeks? In the last month? Even before I knew how I knew you, you were all I thought about and I wanted you. Not Dean. Yes, it was still hard then, but talking with you, finally getting everything out . . . well, it's not hard now. I told you when I saw him today that it was weird, and it was. Because for the first time it didn't hurt, it was almost like I was looking at a completely different person and it threw me off. Every time I've seen him or Vanessa, I've been close to panicking. Today, I wanted to laugh, but I think I was too shocked by the whole thing to do anything other than just think about the differences."

"Differences?"

Now Indy moved closer to me, her hands maneuvering out from her blankets for her fingers to wrap around the sides of my neck, her thumbs brushing my jaw. "In how you treat me, and how he treated me. In how you make me feel, how I thought I felt with him, and how I actually felt. And then it just hit me. Like, I was upset because of him? I'd gotten wasted weekend after weekend, had sex with nameless guys . . . because of *him*? And it just blew my mind."

For the first time since first buying Indy a loaf of garlic bread, I felt like shit for jumping to conclusions about her.

"He never saw me as anything more than an inconvenience. He told Vanessa that I was a mess, not that he was wrong about that then. To him I was useless, needy, and frustrating . . . and I know just by the way you look at me that I'm none of those things to you. From what you've said, I had plenty of Saturdays to frustrate you, but you never backed down, and you never stopped trying to take care of me. You've helped me in a way no one has since Ian died. You look at me and I know I've found exactly who I need. Who I want."

There was the slightest pressure on the back of my neck, and I didn't wait for anything else. That statement, that small pressure, was all I needed to know she was ready. I pulled her to me and captured her mouth with mine, and she met the kiss greedily. Her lips parted on a soft sigh, and I took the opportunity to deepen the kiss. Letting her hands fall from my neck, she fisted them in my jacket before she was pushing it off my shoulders and unzipping my hoodie. I only pulled away from her long enough to get them off my arms before she was grabbing the front of my shirt and tugging me back toward her as she lowered herself onto the pillows.

Moving the blankets away from her so I could press my body against hers, she hitched her knees up around my hips, and a groan formed deep in my chest when I involuntarily rolled my hips against hers. When her hands moved down my back, and her fingers played with the bottom of my shirt, I planted my palms on the pillows around us and lifted myself off her enough that she could slowly inch my shirt up my body and over my head. One arm at a time, I untangled myself from the shirt, and the tips of her fingers grazed the muscles low on my torso, causing them to tighten.

Indy smiled against my kiss, but when her fingers dropped lower, I knew I needed to stop this before it could go any further. I wanted her. I wanted her so fucking bad my head was spinning. But there was still so much between us that I couldn't do this to her—not yet.

Reaching down, I grabbed her hand and curled my fingers around hers as I moved her arm away. "We can't," I grumbled when I pulled back. I saw the heat and want in her green eyes and wanted to take that back. *Yes. Yes, we fucking can.*

"Why? You already know I'm not a virgin," she whispered, her cheeks filling with heat.

"I know."

Indy rolled her eyes and shot me a look. "Let me guess, are you going to follow this up with something along the lines of you think I'm not ready and you're going to wait until I am?"

I smirked and kissed her quickly, biting down on her bottom lip as

I pulled back again. "No, actually, I'm not." She raised an eyebrow but waited for me to continue. Only problem was it took me a solid minute to think of a good enough reason not to go back to where we'd just been. "I'm not having sex with you in this house when I just passed Misha coming in here. And I'm not having sex with you in my house, because I'm not letting any of those guys hear what you sound like when I make you come."

Her mouth opened with an audible huff, and her eyes widened. Her breathing deepened, and I dropped my head to kiss a line up her throat.

"So after finals next week, you're packing a bag and we're going someplace where it'll just be us. When we get there, I'm not letting you leave the bed for days." I listened to her breathing hitch before asking, "Now, are you okay with that?"

She swallowed and nodded, and I smiled against her soft skin before gently biting down on it. "Good."

chapter six

Indy

had never hated finals week as much as I hated this one. It never seemed to end, and it was only halfway done. It had been six days since the promise of what was to come. I'd finished my second day of finals, and I still had two days left. Well, technically one and then turning in a paper on Thursday morning, but Kier still had a final Thursday afternoon, and we weren't leaving for wherever he was taking me until after that.

Studying had been nearly impossible Wednesday and Thursday. No matter where we were, we ended up going to the pillow room, one of our rooms, or to his SUV to practically attack each other. After we realized that even being in public didn't change anything, we started staying away from each other. I saw him once in the morning, afternoon, and right before one of us went to sleep, but only for a couple of minutes each time. Anything more than that and studying went out the window all over again.

Not that I would have minded.

"I need to go," he whispered against my lips.

"Probably." I slid my hands inside his shirt, grazing the tips of my fingers over his muscled V in a way I was quickly learning drove him crazy.

Kier growled and backed me up against the wall of the entryway as he deepened the kiss. "Five more minutes."

"Thirty. Pillow room is free," I suggested, laughing when his golden eyes flashed open before narrowing.

"Indy," he said in warning.

Hooking two fingers inside his jeans, I pulled him closer and he put one of his hands against the wall to stop me.

Quick footsteps sounded on the stairs, and I frowned when Kier smirked. "Two more days, Indy." Cupping my cheek with his other hand, he leaned in for a slow kiss.

Chloe cleared her throat, her eyes wide when Kier and I pulled away from each other, and I was pretty sure I looked like a kid who got caught with her hand in a cookie jar—but then Kier's thumb brushed against my cheek and I kind of didn't care anymore.

"Time to go. See you tonight," he whispered. Kier nodded toward Chloe before giving me one more light kiss and walking out the door. I had a stupid, giddy smile on my face when I turned toward her again.

"When did that happen?" she asked, her face full of surprise as she pointed at the door.

I shrugged. "It's kind of been happening since the middle of November, but Thanksgiving break is when it all changed, I guess."

"Where have I been?"

I shot her a look. "Uh. Work?"

She glared at me for a few seconds before moving her hand so she was pointing in the direction of the guys' house. "Don't get me wrong, because he's—*damn*—but don't you find him . . . weird? He doesn't ever talk to anyone."

"He doesn't talk to anyone *else*," I said as I began walking toward the stairs, a sly grin now replacing the giddy smile. "*I* can't get that boy to shut up. Have fun at work!" I called over my shoulder as I ran up the steps.

• • •

After taking a hot shower and bundling back up in multiple layers of sweats and jackets, I hopped on my bed and tried to study. *Tried* being the keyword there. If it weren't for the fact that it was snowing outside, and our heater could only do so much with the drafts that came in through our house, I would have stripped back down and taken a cold shower because of the way my imagination was getting me so worked up.

I was lying back on my bed, books, study cards, and laptop forgotten as I thought about Kier's muscled body. I wished I'd gotten more time to run my hands over the planes of his chest and the lean muscles in his arms before he put his shirt back on last week. *Two days, Indy. Two. Days.*

"Hey."

I jolted at the sound of his deep voice, and looked over to find him in my doorway, a sad smirk playing on his lips.

"Looks like you're getting a lot of studying in."

Sitting upright, I glanced at everything scattered around my bed and tried to figure out an excuse before shrugging. "Yeah, not really. Are you okay? You can't already be going to sleep, and you left just a couple hours ago."

Kier shut the door behind him and walked over toward my bed, dragging the chair from my desk behind him and sitting down in it.

"I could've cleared off—"

"I need to talk to you."

My body stilled and I straightened my spine when I saw the haunted look in his eyes, and realized that he wasn't even sitting close enough to the bed for me to lean over and touch him. "Okay . . . ," I said warily, drawing out the word. "Should I—should I be worried?"

His eyes had fallen into his lap, but at my question, they snapped back up to me. Hunching over, he clasped his hands, letting them hang between his knees as he shrugged and slowly shook his head back and forth. "Honestly, Indy, I'm the one who's worried right now . . . because I don't know how you're going to react to this."

That didn't help relieve any type of worry at all. I scooted back so I was pressed against my wall, facing him, but didn't say anything else as I stared at him—waiting for him to begin whatever it was he needed to talk to me about.

"I haven't been fair to you, Indy. The last year and a half I couldn't help noticing you. You're beautiful, you have this smile that makes other people around you smile, and you always *seemed* happy. But even then I somehow knew it was an act, knew there was something you were trying to hide that was controlling your life. I wanted to save you even back then, but you were with Dean, and our paths just weren't meant to cross then. Then this school year began, and this whole semester all I wanted to do was take care of you, help you, save you . . . be with you. Even before you finally started noticing me during times where you weren't drunk, I was already falling for you so hard."

There was a "but" coming; I knew there was. Because none of this sounded like a bad thing yet, and all of it I already knew. And by the tone of his voice and the look in his eyes, this was about to be bad.

"And then I kept putting everything on you, letting you make the decisions, waiting until you were ready, because—well, like I've said, I knew there was something you were hiding behind and needed to get out before I'd push you into any form of a relationship with me. But the thing is . . ."

There was that "but," and now he wasn't talking, and I had this feeling creeping through my body like ice and fire were flooding my veins at the same time. Kier swallowed roughly and sighed before looking back up at me.

"The thing is, I've been kind of hiding behind my own shit. Keeping things from you, things that have made me into the guy you know, and into the guy who wanted nothing more than to save you. And I knew I had to tell you, but after you told me everything about your life—I felt like I couldn't. I was afraid if I did you wouldn't be able to see me the same way."

My eyebrows slammed down and my mouth popped open with a huff. "And you thought I didn't feel the same? You thought I wasn't terrified that you wouldn't be like, 'Yep, she's not worth it,' and just leave?"

His lips tilted up in the faintest of smiles, but he looked anything but happy. "No, I knew that was exactly how you felt. But I knew that nothing you could say would change my mind."

"And nothing you—"

"Indy"—he cut me off—"you can say that, but you've barely known my name for a month. I've been waiting for you for a year and a half, knowing that whole time that you were going to have something in your past. It's different. And as much as I want Thursday afternoon to be here, I've been dreading it," he groaned. "Because I knew I couldn't take you with you not knowing about me."

When he didn't continue for a while, I scoffed. "Well, what is it? Unless you somehow caused my brother's death, I can't imagine anything that would make me not want to be with you anymore. And seeing how they slid off the road, I'm positive you didn't."

"I didn't kill your brother, Indy."

"Then just tell me, Kier!"

"I killed someone else!" he shouted, and then grabbed at his hair, turning to look at the bedroom door before dropping his elbows to his knees—his hands still firmly gripping his thick black hair.

I was frozen. I couldn't move, couldn't breathe, couldn't blink. That—that couldn't be right. I must have misheard him. Because the Kier I'd come to know wasn't a—I couldn't even think it. Not because it was too terrifying a thought, but because it didn't fit what I knew of him at all.

"What?" I finally choked out. "You—no."

When Kier looked back up at me, his eyes were glassy and tortured. "*I* didn't pull the trigger, but I made him do it."

The fistlike vise that had been tightening on my chest slowly started letting up, and I blew out a deep breath. "What do you mean?"

"A guy from my school committed suicide because of me."

My heart sank. "Kier, no. No, I don't know what happened, but you can't think that—"

"Indy, it was in his note. I was the reason he did it. Cops questioned me, they showed me the note, his parents—fuck, his dad put me in the hospital when I walked out of the police station that day."

"But it was his decision—"

"Stop." He raked his hands down his face and leaned forward, only to sit back in the chair again. "You know how you always told me that I was quiet? That I don't talk?" When I nodded, he asked, "Did you think it was because I was shy, or . . ."

I shrugged. "No, you didn't seem shy, just like you didn't want to talk. Like what everyone was doing was bothering you in a way."

He huffed and shook his head. "I was popular in high school. I was the quarterback of our football team. I was dating the hottest girl in school. My parents gave me anything I wanted and were never home anyway—so my house was always the party house. I don't think anyone ever liked me. They liked what I was . . . if that makes sense. Rich, cocky, varsity QB . . . the whole bit. Everything back then was a label—it was dumb. But I was such a dick back then I wouldn't even have liked me."

I tried to see it, but I couldn't. Kier was handsome in a way you only ever saw on silver screens, but he was always in the background, never letting anyone get close to him . . . except for me. And the kind of guy who was quiet and in the background was the exact opposite of who he was explaining now.

"I made fun of anyone who wasn't 'us' basically, but there was this one kid, Alan Schwartz—God, I don't know why, but I just wanted to ruin his life. He never did anything, he stayed away from me, shit, he'd *run* when he saw me . . . but I just had it out for him for some reason. Picked on him about everything. His weight, his looks, and the way he dressed—and it was constant. Every day, every time I saw him. I think because my buddies wanted to seem cool around me, or something, they all started picking on him, too, and soon he had half the football team after him. We'd have our girls put tampons in his locker. We'd steal his clothes during P.E. and sometimes replace them with girls' clothes. And he wasn't gay; we were just doing anything to embarrass the shit out of him. He started missing school, and that's when I should have started realizing something was different about him. But I didn't notice anything; I just kicked up embarrassing him on the days he was in school.

"Spring came, he kept wearing long sleeves . . . and now that it's all over and I look back on that time, I remember how dead he looked. He didn't cry anymore when we embarrassed him, he didn't run away from me anymore, he just stared—like nothing mattered anymore. But when it was happening, I didn't notice. I noticed the long sleeves, though, and, of course, I made fun of him for wearing those, too, when it was hot outside. Every. Day. Never. Stopping. I was on my way to my junior prom when I got a call from my parents saying that the police were looking for me, and that they would meet me at the station. Funny that I thought they were joking when they said the police were looking for me, but as soon as they told me they would meet me somewhere, I knew they were serious. My parents were never anywhere for me. They only care about themselves; there was always some party or resort they had to go to with colleagues or friends.

"I took my girlfriend to the prom, told her I would be back soon, and left. Alan had been cutting his wrists for months apparently, and that night, he shot himself. There was a letter on his bed addressed to me. Asking what he ever did to me to make me hate him, to torture him, and to make him wish he'd never been born. He said he'd tried to ignore me, then hoped I would see what I was doing to him, and then finally gave up . . . saying he couldn't take it anymore. At the bottom, he wrote a line to his parents saying he loved them, and it wasn't their fault—they did everything they could. It just wasn't enough."

"Kier," I whispered, and had to swallow past the tightness in my throat. "I—I don't know what to say." The anguish in his voice as he retold the story couldn't be faked. He hated himself for what had happened with Alan.

"I couldn't even leave the room after that. I just lost it. Everything— everything I'd ever done came rushing back to me and I would have given anything to take it back. I wanted to die, I wanted it all to be a joke like they were just trying to give me a wake-up call for how I was ruining people's lives, I wanted to apologize to Alan . . . I wanted to redo the previous three years all over again. But it wasn't a joke," he mumbled, and worked his jaw for a couple of minutes. "My dad's attorney informed us that Alan's parents were going to take us to court for a civil suit—since there wasn't anything they could charge me with for picking on someone. My parents were still standing inside the building talking to their attorney when I walked outside. Alan's parents were there and his dad attacked me, and I didn't even try to stop him. I wanted to hurt, I wanted him to kill me, I wanted to take Alan's place. By the time he was pulled off me, I was unconscious. I ended up in the hospital for a week because of it, and I felt like it hadn't been anywhere near enough.

"But because of it, we never went to court because my parents could have actually pressed charges on him. While I was unconscious, they'd all agreed on no charges from either side . . . and my parents *paid* his parents off as way of an apology." Kier looked up at me, his golden eyes dulled. "You can't fucking pay someone for something like that. 'Sorry our kid forced yours to pull the trigger. Here's a hundred grand.' Who the fuck does that?"

"Did Alan's parents take it?"

"Yeah, and they started a foundation in Alan's name. After that, I dropped out of football, stopped hanging out with my so-called friends. It wasn't hard. Once I was off the team and stopped throwing parties, none of them talked to me again anyway. My girlfriend broke up with me because she said I was too different. No one even fucking cared about Alan. They were just pissed that they had to find a new place to get wasted every weekend. And that's when I just stopped talking to people." He shrugged and held my gaze.

"Because of Alan," I said.

"Because my words had ended someone's life. Because I was so self-absorbed that I couldn't see when he needed someone to be there for him, when he was getting too low and was crying out for someone to bring him back up. I should have seen, and I just pushed him more."

Kier dropped his head into his hands, and his shoulders shook as he cried silently. I stared at him for a few moments before finally crawling off the bed to stand in front of him. Lifting his head with my hands, I placed a soft kiss on his lips and dropped my forehead onto his.

"Don't say it wasn't my fault," he pled.

"I won't. I'm also not going to say it was your fault. It just . . . *was*," I breathed.

He shook his head. "How can you—"

"Because if it weren't for all that, you wouldn't have been looking, and you wouldn't have seen that you needed to save me."

Kier removed my hands but kept his eyes locked on mine. "Indy, you cut to escape the pain of your brother being taken from you. I *made* a guy cut and then take his own life. Your parents are horrible to you and kicked you out. My parents don't care about anyone except for themselves, and now I avoid them because as much as I hate myself for what happened, I hate them even more for not caring about him and trying to make it go away with their goddamn money. Things you struggle with, I've made happen. Why aren't you asking me to leave?"

"I just told you."

"No, Indy—"

"Because you aren't that guy anymore, Kier. You *were*. You *did* those things, and you're obviously still paying for them. You'll never forget Alan, and even though I can see you aren't there yet, I hope you forgive yourself one day. You have changed, and just like you say you can see me . . . I can see your heart. You're not at all like the guy you described to me. You're the quiet guy who saves me from myself, gives me bread, and locks my door so no one can get to me. You're the guy who won't let us go to any next step until you're sure I'm ready for it, even though you and I both know it's nothing I haven't done before."

His lips tilted up and one of his hands lifted to brush against my cheeks. "You don't see me very clearly."

I smiled sadly and twisted his own words back around on him. "I see you just fine."

chapter seven

Kier

Glancing over to where Indy was sleeping in the passenger seat, I let my eyes roam over her calm features, and a strange feeling unfurled in my chest. Something close to a mix of possession, admiration, and pride. She was mine. If you had told me a year ago she would be in my SUV with me, on the way back to my house for winter break, I wouldn't have believed you. She'd been untouchable then . . . she'd been untouchable for a long time. But she was here; even after finding out about my past, she was choosing to be with me.

I shook my head as I looked back at the road, and a smile curled at my lips. *Amazing.*

The smile fell quickly as I pulled off the freeway and began driving down the familiar streets of the city I'd grown up in. While it was familiar, none of it felt like home. It felt like a crushing reminder of the life I'd left behind. It felt cold—and it had absolutely nothing to do with the weather outside. But every winter and summer, I still came back. There was something I had to do.

Pulling into the parking lot, I unbuckled my seat belt and leaned over the center console to brush Indy's cheek. Her eyes blinked open, and she sank back into her sweatshirt as her forehead scrunched together.

"The bank?" she asked hoarsely.

"I just have to pull out some money. I'll only be a couple minutes, but I didn't want you to wake up and find me gone."

"Okay." She glanced at me and smiled. "Are we almost there after this?"

"Yeah, just about ten minutes away." I brushed my lips against hers before pulling back and stepping out of the vehicle.

Jogging up to the bank, I opened the doors and was immediately blasted by the heat as I stepped in. A banking officer smiled as she approached me.

"Welcome. What can I help you with today?"

I sent her a polite smile back. "I'm here to see Frank."

Her eyebrows shot up and her eyes took in my appearance for a second before her face slipped back into her polite smile. "Of course, let me see if he's available."

Less than a minute later they were walking out together, and Uncle Frank was putting his arm around my shoulders as he led me back to his office. "I've been wondering when you would get here. How've you been?"

"Good. Things are good."

He shot me a look. "Really? Finals go okay?"

"Yeah, they went pretty well. I left as soon as I finished my last one today."

Nodding as he shut the door behind us, he moved to go sit behind his desk. "That's good, then. But I haven't had you tell me things were good . . . ever."

I drummed my fingers on the arm of the chair I'd sat in, and sighed. "Yeah, well, things were hard for a long time, Uncle Frank, but they're getting better." When he just continued to look at me with a suspicious glare, I added, "There's a girl. She's waiting for me in the car."

"Really?" He smiled widely at me. "Do I get to meet her?"

"No, you don't. I don't want to scare her away just yet. Maybe at my summer visit, okay?"

He laughed and nodded as he began typing on his keyboard. "Okay." His fingers stopped abruptly and he leveled me with another look. "But you're treating her well."

I fought back a smile. "I am, don't worry. So, how much do I have left in the account after this semester?"

"Checking right now," he mumbled, his eyes already glued to the screen again.

My parents had had their own ideas for where they wanted me to go to school. Dad's master plan was for me to go to Dartmouth like he had done. He'd just figured football was a phase for me in high school and since he and the dean of admissions were close, I didn't have to apply. How convenient. By my junior year of high school, I was already being scouted for USC football and had wanted nothing more than to follow that one to the other side of the country.

Obviously that hadn't happened, and Dartmouth had never been in my sights, since all I'd wanted to do was play. When my life had changed so drastically, I applied to University of Michigan. It wasn't much more than three hours from Columbus, but no one I knew was going there, and it was another step in getting away from my original plans. My parents had thought I was joking even after I'd moved into the dorm my freshman year. Whether they didn't pay attention enough to care, or they were hoping I'd realize I was missing out on an opportunity in not going to Dartmouth, they continued to put the tuition for Dartmouth in my account every semester, along with "living money." And living money, for them, was fucking ridiculous and felt like another one of their bribes—which led to me visiting my uncle at the end of every semester.

"Looks like you still have over thirty thousand." Uncle Frank sent me a look. "How much do you want to keep for yourself? Two thousand like always?" I just nodded. "Okay, let me get everything ready for the transfer."

"Have you seen them lately?" I asked hesitantly, and he and I both knew I wasn't asking about my parents. He wasn't exactly a fan of them, either.

"A few times in the last couple months when they've come in to handle funds for the foundation," he responded without looking at me.

"How are they?"

Turning, he sat back in his seat and nodded. "They're doing great, Kier, I promise. The foundation has really taken off. Mrs. Schwartz goes around the country now speaking out against bullying and little punks like you."

My lips tilted up, and I laughed weakly. "That's good."

Uncle Frank smiled. "Yeah, they're both moving on as best they can, trying to turn what happened into the only positive they could find."

"Good." I sat back and looked away.

"Name?" Uncle Frank asked a couple of minutes later.

"Do they still see the donations?"

"Yes."

"Then anonymous," I breathed. "Always anonymous."

I looked up and stood when Uncle Frank blew out a heavy breath. "On behalf of the Alan Foundation, I thank you for your *anonymous* donation. I know the Schwartzes are thankful for it, too. And as your uncle, I love you, and your aunt and I are proud of who you're becoming."

I nodded and gave him a quick hug. "Merry Christmas, tell Aunt LeAnn I'll stop by sometime over break."

"Bring that girl with you!"

I huffed and winked as I backed up out of his office. "As long as you promise not to run her off."

Indy

pulled my legs up underneath me and leaned onto the center console as Kier played with my fingers. I was getting anxious to get wherever we were going, but we'd left the downtown buildings and we were now in a neighborhood with absurdly huge houses.

"Uh . . ." I started to ask again where he was taking me, but my jaw dropped when he pulled into a driveway, stopping in front of the gate to enter a code. "No. No, no. I, uh . . . Is this your house?"

"Parents' house."

"Right. Um, I'm not so sure I'm ready to meet . . . them. Yet." I felt like I was going to hyperventilate. After the horror of my parents, and hearing about his, I didn't really want to meet them. Our relationship was in a new phase; it definitely wasn't in the whole bringing-the-other-home-for-Christmas phase.

"Indy, relax," Kier crooned. "I told you, I avoid my parents. They won't be here this entire break. They have a place in Washington where they spend a good four months out of the year. My dad's business has a branch out there and in California, and they split the year between the three houses."

"So that trip over Thanksgiving . . ." I trailed off.

"No, they actually took a trip to Italy."

I sat back in the seat and looked at the house in front of us. Trips to Italy just weren't something I ever thought could be said in a way that seemed like it wasn't a big deal. But looking at this house, and knowing they had two others, I got it. To them it wasn't a big deal.

Kier's fingers curled under my chin, turning my head in his direction. "Don't judge me based on this, or them. All this"—he gestured toward the house—"used to mean something to me, but it doesn't anymore. I just stay here during the breaks."

Nodding, I leaned forward and captured his lips for a few seconds. "I know it doesn't."

"Come on, let's get in there. It's gonna be cold, but I'll turn the heat up and get a fire going."

As I followed him out of the car and up the walkway to the door, everything about the massive house faded from my mind as I remembered what our arrival here meant. We were finally away from the houses in Ann Arbor, we were alone, and good God, Kier couldn't open that door fast enough.

"Balls, it's cold!" I screeched when we stepped inside.

"It will be warm in no time. Give it maybe ten minutes. It'll be perfect. Come on, I'll show you where our room is."

Our room. *Our* room. Again everything slipped from my mind as heat rushed through my veins in anticipation.

Kier stopped twice on the way to change thermostats before we entered a room that was as big as three of mine back in the Ann Arbor house, and that wasn't including the bathroom attached to it.

Pressing a kiss to the side of my neck, he gripped at my hips before whispering in my ear, "Get settled in. I'm gonna go check everything and start a fire."

"'Kay," I said breathily, swaying a little when he moved away from me.

When he was gone, I looked around the room for a couple of minutes, but there wasn't much of Kier's childhood in there—and I figured that had more to do with him wanting to forget it than it did his parents not being a big part of his life. I walked into the bathroom, and my eyes widened when I saw the massive garden tub and shower, and I thought I'd died right then and gone to heaven.

Looking into the bedroom, I worried my bottom lip as I eyed the shower again. Not letting myself think on it any longer, I reached in and turned it on. With how cold it was in the house, a hot shower in *this* shower was too good to pass up—especially when we'd been in a car for close to four hours.

I waited until steam was billowing out above the glass before stepping out of my clothes and piling my long hair on top of my head. My body shook as I tested the temperature of the water with my fingers before stepping in, and the sting of the heat against my freezing skin burned for long moments until my body got used to it—and then I was in heaven. I hadn't even seen the closet and it didn't matter—this shower was all I needed to decide this was my favorite room. Ever.

The door to the shower opened, and I instinctively covered myself as I turned away from where Kier was standing. My eyes widened as my gaze trailed down his long, naked body. My breathing deepened when his golden eyes heated and he stepped inside the shower, shutting the glass door behind him. I swallowed roughly as he pressed himself behind me, and looked up just in time for him to drop his head and press his mouth firmly to mine.

A moan moved up my throat, getting lost in the kiss as his tongue teased mine in unhurried strokes. His hands moved around to the front of my body, sliding over where my arms were still covering myself—and at the reminder, I shakily moved them away, bringing my hands up to fist in his hair as he deepened the kiss.

One hand made a path down my stomach as the other moved up to my breasts, and I broke away from the kiss on a huff when his fingers spread me apart, stroking me and circling my clit just as slow as his tongue had been circling mine. I widened my stance, and my back arched off him when he pressed two fingers inside me.

"Kier," I breathed before his mouth captured mine again.

His arm was pressed against my wet breasts, trailing up my chest so his hand could lightly trace the front of my neck as he demanded more from the kiss, and I gave everything I had. My hips rocked against his hand and his thick erection pressed against my bottom as hot water pelted down on us. I felt like I was losing myself in Kier, and I loved it and the way it felt like he couldn't get enough of me.

For the first time in a long while, I was enough for someone . . . more than enough.

My head fell back against his shoulder as the knot in my belly grew, and the hand resting on my neck slowly trailed down toward my chest as he nibbled on the soft spot behind my ear.

"Come on, Indy. Let go for me."

His thumb pressed against my clit as his fingers moved harder, faster, and I fell apart with a cry as my body shattered. When I was limp in his arms, he reached in front of us to turn off the water before turning me around and wrapping his arms tight around me.

I looked up to see him smirking at me, his golden eyes bright as he stepped out of the shower with me still in his arms. Grabbing a towel, he dried us off through lingering kisses before dropping the towel on the floor and taking my hand in his, leading me back into the warmed-up bedroom.

He started to let go of me, his body moving in the direction of a set of dresser drawers, and I knew what he was doing. Not pushing me, but making sure I wanted this just as bad as he did. Holding tight to his hand, I pulled him back to the bed and pushed him down until he was sitting on it.

"Are you—"

"Yes," I said, cutting him off. "I want this. I want you."

Leaning forward, I teased his lips as I climbed onto the bed, placing a knee on either side of him. He smiled through the kiss and scooted back on the bed before lying down and bringing me closer to him. I took the tie out of my hair, letting it fall down around my shoulders and back as I curled my body over Kier's and positioned myself above him. He ran his hands through my hair, letting them trail down my waist to my hips, his fingers flexing against the skin when he got there, and then he guided me down on top of him.

Kier groaned as I took him inch by inch, and when I was fully seated on him, he kept me there—not moving—as his eyes held mine, his chest rising and falling heavily before he quickly sat up, crushing his mouth to mine.

A surprised gasp left me and turned into a laugh, and then a moan when he gripped my hips harder and moved me off him, only to push me right back down.

"Oh God," I whimpered against his lips as I took control and started moving on top of him.

Soon kissing became too difficult as we struggled to breathe, and I pressed my forehead to his seconds before Kier rolled us over. Dropping his head into the crook of my neck, he trailed his hand up my leg to curl around my knee, bringing it up around his hip as he moved inside me. His pace quickened and his grip on my body tightened before he stilled above me as he found his release.

As his body slowly relaxed, he placed a line of kisses across my collarbone and up my throat until he reached my lips, his body stilling when he saw the tears in my eyes. "Are you okay?"

I brushed my hands through his hair and smiled against his lips. "More than okay."

"Indy," he crooned, and cupped my cheeks. "Then why do you look like you're about to cry?"

My head shook back and forth as I tried to find the right words to say, and finally I just locked my eyes with his and whispered, "Thank you for saving me."

His body sagged in relief, and he kissed me soundly. "I'll always save you."

fouling out

Tiffany King

chapter one

Courtney

"What can I get you?"

"How about something hot and spicy like you?"

"Really? That's the best line you got?" I asked the guy who'd been hitting on me the last couple of nights. "I think I heard that one from a balding used car salesman back in high school when I waited tables at Denny's."

His friends, who'd been egging him on a few seconds ago, hooted with laughter. "Dude, I told you you'd be toast again," one of them said, clapping him on the back.

Mr. Flirt didn't seem to mind the razzing, shooting me a slow grin as he sat back in his seat. I bit back a snort. Guys were so typical. They gave you a little wink and a smile and somehow convinced themselves your panties would drop. I played the game, though, and gave him a coy smile in return. "Besides, you're not ready for this kind of heat. I'll bring you some volcano wings," I added, bumping his shoulder with my hip. Just the mere suggestion that he had any kind of chance lifted his spirits once again as everyone at the table high-fived like they had just scored some sort of victory. It was all part of the waitressing game. Tease them just enough that they keep coming back for more, all in the name of good tips. It really wasn't much of a hardship for me. I'd been waitressing since I was fifteen, so I was a pro at working the customer. Not that I didn't deserve the tips I earned. I worked my ass off, always had. Even back in high school, my manager at Denny's loved me because I never called in sick or missed a shift. At fifteen, I'd been more responsible than most of the employees he kept on staff.

Things were the same at Gruby's, the loudest and busiest sports pub around campus. I'd only been working here for a couple of months, but my manager, Chris, pretty much gave me any hours I wanted. With money always so tight, if I wasn't in class or sleeping, I tried to be here, squeezing in homework and studying during breaks. The holidays had basically wiped me out financially, so I'd been working non-stop since Christmas. For the past three weeks, the only time I'd seen my three roommates was to say a quick good-bye on my way out, or a tired good night when I got home. Lately, the house we all shared had become nothing more than a place for me to shower and then fall into bed.

I finished taking the guys' orders around several more innuendos before walking away. I could feel their eyes all over my ass without turning around to look.

"How's it going?" my best friend and fellow waitress, Amanda, asked, grabbing a bottle of ketchup from the servers' station.

"Typical. They're all God's gift to women with heaven in their pants."

"It's jock syndrome. Don't you just love basketball season? I swear this school acts like the sun rises and sets on their players' asses."

"It's all about the money, babe. The university isn't stupid." Not that I didn't agree with Amanda, one hundred percent.

"Preach it, sister."

Amanda was putting on a show for my benefit. I knew from experience that she was all about the basketball team. She was one of those hard-core supporters who painted her cheeks for every game and cheered as loud as anyone when the games were televised on the big screens scattered throughout the restaurant.

"Who are you trying to kid? We all know you love the players in more ways than one," I teased, wagging my eyebrows. I filled my drink order and placed the glasses on the round tray I was expertly balancing on my hip. "I bet you're already scouting for your next recruit."

She grinned. "Well, now that you mention it . . ." Her voice trailed off as she looked over her shoulder.

"Come on. Don't keep me in suspense."

"I'll fill you in later. I need to deliver this check to table six before they have a fit."

I shook my head, watching her walk away. Over the past year that we'd been friends, I'd watched her fall for at least half a dozen guys. She claimed dating someone taller than her was a must, which was why she always went for athletes, especially basketball players. I tried to put myself in her shoes, but I couldn't see anything bad about being a long-legged five-foot-nine goddess. At five foot nothing, I was shorter than pretty much every guy on campus. Mom called me pixie cute, which was a nice way of saying I was short.

After delivering drinks to the flirty table, I headed over to greet another group that had been seated in my section. Within twenty minutes, the restaurant was packed as the dinner rush began. Amanda and I didn't have another chance to talk other than to exchange notes on particularly difficult tables, especially those that felt the need to be touchy-feely. Ass grabbers were nothing new. Gruby's was located on the outskirts of campus, so it attracted a combination of college students and local residents. Mainly middle-aged men sporting beer guts and receding hairlines believing they still had enough game to close a piece of college ass. That is, if they ever had any game in the first place. They were usually the best tippers, but the problem was you had to put up with a lot more shit, including "accidental" ass grazes or boob brushes. They were all the same. Most didn't even try to hide their wedding rings. Of course, the waitstaff at Gruby's had our own way of keeping them in line, like spilling drinks in their laps, or a plate of food in the crotch if they'd taken too many liberties with their hands. Thankfully it didn't have to come to that very often. A little flirty banter was usually all it took to keep any guy in check, no matter how old he was.

Five hours into my shift and my feet were begging for a break. Today had been a long fourteen-hour marathon. An early cram session at the library had me out of the house earlier than normal, followed by art history class and then more studying before my final class of the day.

As the dinner crowd slowly trickled away, I stood out of view of the few remaining patrons and rolled my shoulders, trying to work out a kink in my neck. Feeling marginally better, I left the drink station to hand over the check to what would hopefully be my last customer of the night.

As luck would have it, Felicia, everyone's least favorite hostess, squashed that thought as she walked by. "Hey, Court. I just sat another group at table twelve in your zone." Like I needed her to tell me table twelve was in my zone. I had worked here long enough to know the layout of the dining area.

That was Felicia. She was a witch who had an annoying habit of telling everyone how to do their jobs. Worst of all was the way she would brag about how they used to do things at the last sports bar where she'd worked. After several not-so-subtle hints, Amanda had finally told her to go back to her last place if it was so fabulous because maybe she'd be happier there. Felicia missed the hint. She was on the verge of having her mouth taped closed, but thankfully we felt her days were numbered since she'd called in sick twice in two weeks. Chris had a low tolerance for employees who missed shifts. We were already planning the celebration party.

I straightened up and pasted a smile on my face to greet my new table.

"Welcome to Gruby's. I'm Courtney, and I'll be taking care of you tonight. Drafts are buy one, get one for another twenty minutes," I parroted, finally looking at the occupants as I pulled my notepad from the pocket of my half apron. My eyes widened and my mouth went dry when I took in the group sitting at the table. Actually it was because of one person in particular. I knew there was a chance this day would come. I was just hoping to be better prepared for it.

Dalton Thompson, my first best friend and onetime crush, sat in front of me, flashing his signature grin that I knew all too well. It had been years since that grin was aimed in my direction, but it was forever burned in my brain. Not that I could forget it, considering where I went to school. That same cheeky smile could be found on banners splashed all over campus, along with local TV news stations and even the national sports channels. Dalton was the face of the university's basketball team. After he'd won two state championships in high school, every big-time program in the country wanted Dalton, but he chose to stay home and play for Michigan. He was practically a legend to everyone in the local community, and one day in the not too distant future would be a top ten pick in the pros. To me, he was so much more. At least, he was at one time. When I decided to attend the same college as Dalton, I figured I was safe because the chances of us running into each other were pretty slim, and yet here we were.

chapter two

Dalton

"'ll take the Gruby's burger, medium, and an extra order of fries."
I handed over the menu to Courtney Leighton, recognizing her
right away even though I hadn't seen her in years. We were best
friends when we were kids. Then we drifted apart and it was like she
became a ghost. We stopped talking and even though we went to the
same schools, we never seemed to see each other.

Checking her out now in her short skirt and tight black T-shirt, I
was surprised at how much she had changed. She definitely wasn't the
tomboy I remembered who used to climb trees with me or trade
Pokémon cards. She was still short, but her body had developed and
filled out the package nicely. Who would ever have thought she'd grow
up to be such a knockout? As a matter of fact, the longer she stood in
front of me, the cuter she was getting. The height difference might be
weird. I bet if I stood up she'd barely reach my chest, which actually
could make for some interesting possibilities. She had a tiny waist with
a gorgeous ass that looked like it had been crafted for my big hands.
Not to mention she was completely stacked. I shifted in my seat since I

was suddenly more than a little turned on just looking at her. I needed to get a grip. This was Courtney. How weird would it be if we hooked up after all these years?

She took everyone else's orders but still hadn't looked at me. It was like she didn't recognize me. I remember being pretty bummed back in seventh grade when we started drifting apart, but at the time my dad was riding my ass hard, claiming my days of screwing off were over and that I had to get serious about my game. After that, he made sure I had no time for anything in my life except basketball.

"Anything else?" Courtney asked, finally looking at me like she was bored.

Her expression threw me off. Maybe she did recognize me and just didn't care or was too embarrassed to say anything. Even though this was a different situation, I'd had my fair share of awkward encounters with women. I always tried to be up front with any girl I met, but sometimes they wanted more than I could give them. Unfortunately basketball took up the majority of the free time I had after classes. That was why I'd never gotten serious with anyone. I never made false promises about where any relationship was going. Up to this point most ladies had been cool with that.

I decided to go for broke. "It's good to see you, Courtney."

"Hey, Dalton." She looked extremely uncomfortable. I guess that answered my question as to whether she remembered me.

"It's been a long time. Do you go to Michigan?" I was doing my best to break the ice, but she still wouldn't look me in the eye.

"Yeah, I do. I'll get your orders in." She hastily tucked the menus under her arm and flashed the others a smile before hurrying away. I got nothing.

"That was a little cold. Is she an ex or something?" Collin asked once she was out of earshot.

"Man, I wish I could have ordered a beer," Dave muttered.

"Nah, we knew each other way back in grade school," I answered. "And don't even think about it, Dave. You never know who's watching." Coach had laid down the law now that the season was heating up. No drinking and no staying up late chasing ass. Dave, who was hoping to get more court time, had taken those words to heart. He'd given up partying and even dumped Jessica, his girlfriend for the past six months. That was why we came to Gruby's tonight. We hadn't been here in a couple of months and figured good food and hot waitresses in skimpy uniforms would do him some good.

"That's cool. Talk about some small-world shit, though," Collin commented about Courtney. "I had to ask to make sure I wasn't about to eat a burger that had been dunked in toilet water or something, you know?"

"Damn, dude. Give me a little credit. I've never had a chick hate me that bad."

"My ass. You don't remember—damn, what was her name?" He paused, snapping his fingers. "We called her Black Widow."

I slapped the table, nearly falling backward out of my chair. "Oh, shit. You mean Aubrey. Okay, but she was crazy." Collin did have a point, though. Aubrey was cool at first, but after a while I had to cut it off because she got seriously possessive. She would pick fights with chicks that did nothing but look at me. After I told her we were done, she spray-painted the word *asshole* down the entire hallway of the dorm where I lived at the time.

"This fucking sucks," Dave whined, checking his phone for a text that obviously hadn't come in. He tossed the phone on the table like a total pussy.

"Dude, I don't think Coach meant you needed to break up with your lady. He just didn't want anyone hanging out at the bars all night trying to score," I pointed out as he picked up his phone on the off chance a message had come through in the two seconds it was out of his hand.

"Yeah, you look like a total pussy whip," Collin added, elbowing him.

"Fuck off, Collin," he said as Courtney approached the table carrying our drinks.

I flashed her a smile when our eyes met, but her glance slid right on by like she wasn't even aware I was there.

"Here you go." She smiled at Dave as she handed him his Coke. Collin got the same greeting, but when Courtney turned to me, her face was blank.

"Thanks," I said as she set my drink down. She nodded in response but turned back to Collin and Dave. "Your food should be up in a few minutes. If you need anything, ring the buzzer," she said to them, pointing at the buzzer attached to the wall. It was supposed to sound like the time-out buzzers at the arena, but it sounded more like some annoying horn you'd find in a smart car or something.

My eyes focused on Courtney's backside as she walked away. I'm not going to lie. I was completely puzzled by her attitude toward me. Collin was right. She was acting like someone I'd had a bad breakup from, not someone I had once been friends with. Sure, it was a long time ago. Hell, she was the first girl I'd ever kissed. Although calling it a kiss was a stretch. It was more like me awkwardly smashing my lips against hers without asking when we were ten years old. We were watching a movie at her house and I took a shot. Courtney retaliated by socking me in the arm. I never tried to kiss her again after that.

chapter three

Courtney

"Hey, Chuck, how much longer on my order?" I drummed my fingers on the serving counter, staring off into space in the crowded kitchen.

"Coming up."

I was so ready for the evening to be over, and past ready to get rid of Dalton. Having him grin at me and act like we were still friends was making me shaky and off-kilter. Obviously he didn't remember how he'd tossed me aside like I was no longer important. He moved on, leaving me behind without my best friend. More important, I was confused about the feelings I had started having for him. One moment I was daydreaming about us becoming boyfriend and girlfriend and then, poof, he was gone.

I had tried convincing myself I hated him for ditching me, but I couldn't do it. I had a crush. What could I say? Over the years I'd watched him from afar, but we never really ran in the same circles again. In eighth grade his talent on the court earned him a lot of attention, and in high school basketball had made him a legitimate star.

When I saw him in the hallways, he always seemed to have a new girl on his arm. I found my own circle of friends in high school, and eventually I realized I had romanticized our friendship into something it wasn't and I got over him.

Facing him now while he attempted to flirt with me like I was a typical girl he'd just met was seriously screwing with my head. I could see why girls were into him. It took all my concentration to ignore his come-hither looks and deep, sexy voice. How one person could be blessed with so many gifts was beyond me. Most men would trade their left nut for even a smidge of his talent on the basketball court, but combining that with rugged good looks and a voice that would make any girl's panties wet was just unfair.

Amanda interrupted my inner whine-fest, snagging a fry from one of the plates waiting to go out. "So, how's it going?"

I smacked her hand without hesitation, making the fry drop to the floor.

"Hey." She reached for another in spite of her complaint, but I slid the plate out of her reach.

"You know Chris will have your head if he sees you munching off the customers' plates." I didn't know why I had to remind her. She knew the rules as well as I did.

She pouted, folding her arms across her chest. "You're such a brownnoser."

"And you should know how gross that is. I'd hurl if I found out someone had their fingers in my food. You know Chuck would make you something if you asked."

"I don't want a whole dish of something. I'm on a diet, hence why I was only after one fry." She patted her model-thin waist for emphasis. I was tempted to throat-punch her. I wasn't fat. I just had more curves than I would have preferred. My waist was tiny, but my ass seemed determined to be seen. I was okay with my boobs being on the larger side, although at times I worried they were too large for my frame. Maybe I wouldn't mind my figure as much if I were taller. Being five foot nothing made my hourglass curves look like they had been smooshed in a compactor.

"Thanks, Chuck," I said, placing the last plate from my order on my tray.

He tipped his chef's hat in response. "Anytime, sweetheart."

"I saw that you lucked out with table twelve," Amanda said, opening a package of saltines since I had deflected her attempts at taking a fry.

I balanced the heavy tray on my palm before heading for the swinging door to the dining area. "Lucked out?" I asked incredulously before reminding myself that she knew nothing about my history with Dalton. In the year and a half that Amanda and I had been friends, I never once let on that I knew Dalton before he became the basketball savior of the university.

"Are you kidding? You're waiting on my own version of a dream team there." She shot a lustful look toward my zone.

Understanding dawned on me at seeing her hooded eyes. "Of course." Her next fascination was sitting at the table. For a horrible moment I wondered if it was Dalton. Not that it should matter. Dalton wasn't mine. He never had been.

I returned to their table with their food, resolved to make the best of the situation.

"So, how have you been?" Dalton asked as I dished out their plates. "It's been ages since we had a chance to talk."

"I guess some of us just got busy." My answer had a little more snap, despite my intent to play it cool.

He frowned, rubbing a hand over his head. It was a habit I remembered him doing when we were kids. It meant he was confused. "Yeah, I guess so."

I excused myself, telling them I would be back in a few minutes to refill their drinks.

Somehow I managed to keep it together for the rest of the service. I checked on them a few times and inquired about dessert, but I could barely suppress the pent-up breath I'd been holding when they paid their checks and headed out.

After Gruby's finally closed for the evening, I spent the last hour of my shift doing side work and cleaning the restaurant with Amanda and Chuck while Chris headed to the office to take care of whatever managers did. Chuck handled the kitchen and prepared a bucket of water for Amanda, who tried to bribe me into taking her turn at mopping. Throughout our closing duties, I finally learned that Amanda had set her sights on Collin. I didn't know anything about him other than having just served him, but Amanda was absolutely gaga.

Once the restaurant was prepped for the following day, we all headed out together. Amanda followed me to my car since I was her ride home. She was from sunny Phoenix and had chosen to leave her car with her parents while she attended school in Michigan. I'd become her unofficial chauffeur after we became friends. I didn't mind as long as she didn't complain about Lucy, my car. Lucy was old and had been labeled a piece of crap by Earl, the mechanic I'd been taking her to for years. "Don't call her that," I had to chastise him every time I took Lucy for an oil change. "You'll hurt her feelings. She may be older than all the other cars you work on, but she's the toughest," I'd point out, patting her rusty hood. I loved Lucy. I purchased her after I turned sixteen. I logged more hours at Denny's than I cared to think about and even fit in some babysitting jobs on the side, all so I could buy Lucy free and clear. She might not be as pretty as she once was, but she sure as hell was reliable. I'd kick anyone's ass that dared to argue.

"Gaaaaaaaaah, what is with the heat in this car?" Amanda wrapped a scarf around her neck and face until only her eyes and forehead were visible. I should have expected her to complain considering the frigid nighttime temperature.

I fiddled with the controls, hoping to coax a little more heat from the vents to pacify her. "You mean *Lucy*, and she doesn't want to spoil you." Lucy was a bit temperamental when it came to certain things, like heat and air-conditioning. Both wheezed from her vents like she was struggling to breathe. Earl claimed it was because she was going to drop dead at any moment. He'd been saying it for years, so I didn't put much stock in his words. Deep down I think he liked Lucy.

By the time I pulled up to Amanda's dorm building on the east end of campus, Lucy was slightly warmer than the current temperature outside, but Amanda's teeth were still chattering. "I'm buying a blanket to keep in here."

"It could be worse. You could be freezing your ass off waiting for the bus," I reminded her, smiling sweetly as she stuck out her tongue before slamming the door so it would close properly. Lucy was a bit temperamental about that, too.

Whipping a U-turn, I headed toward Hamilton Street, where I shared a house with my friends Indy, Misha, and Chloe. We'd been strangers when we all moved into the cute house, but we quickly found out how well we meshed.

All the lights except the living room appeared to be off at Hamilton House, which was the name we christened our abode with when we moved in. (I wasn't the only one who liked to name inanimate objects.) I pulled into the driveway, parking Lucy in my usual spot in front of the house, and got out to trudge through the foot of snow that had been too stubborn to melt since Mother Nature dumped it on us the previous week. I slid my key into the lock and stomped the snow from my boots before quietly pushing the door open. It was almost one a.m., which was the only downfall to working at Gruby's. Thankfully my earliest classes were at ten on Tuesdays and Thursdays. The other days I didn't have anything until noon, so I was able to get some sleep in.

Misha was on the couch reading a thick novel with her boyfriend's head in her lap as I quietly closed the front door behind me. "Hey," she greeted me softly after sticking a bookmark between the pages.

"Hey, what are you guys doing up so late? Don't you have class at like eight tomorrow morning?" Placing my gloves and hat in the pockets, I hung my heavy pea coat on the rack by the door, draping my scarf on the hook along with it. It was a routine Mom had trained me into years ago after I kept coming home with either my hat or one of my mittens missing. Raising a kid on a shoestring budget meant every cent counted, so lost mittens and hats were never a good thing. Mom had a good job that she loved at the Department of Children and Families, but the pay sucked. Still she had always managed to stretch the money so I never went without. Not that designer clothes or electronic gadgets ever showed up under our Christmas tree, but I never missed them. I admired Mom greatly for the work she did. Lots of kids were less fortunate than I was.

"The class was canceled, so I figured I'd catch up on a little reading. I've been dying to finish this new novel." She stroked a hand over Darryn's forehead, gently waking him.

"Lucky you. I wish one of my classes would get canceled. Professor Zeal is trying pretty damned hard to ruin early American history for me. He couldn't be any more boring if he decided to start showing bowling videos in class. His voice is the most monotone thing I've ever heard."

Misha chuckled as Darryn opened his eyes and grinned sleepily at me. "Consider it future practice for when you're poring over classic art or whatever other things you would do as a museum curator."

"But that won't be boring. That will be—" My words ended with a sigh. My lifelong dream of working in an art museum seemed distant at the moment. Getting through the required classes had become daunting. Who knew history professors would be so freaking boring?

"Don't worry. You got this. You ready for bed, babe?" she asked Darryn, rising from the couch and reaching down to help him up. He stretched and yawned before draping an arm across Misha's shoulders, pulling her close. "Are you heading to bed, too?"

"Yeah, after I wash the fried food stench off me." She clicked off the lamp in the living room as I walked away, waving.

The sounds of smooching filled the darkness almost immediately. They were a cute couple, and I loved Misha to death. I was happy for her. I switched on the hallway light so I wouldn't kill myself walking down the hall. "You guys have fun."

"Night, Court," they said in unison, which would have been nauseating coming from any other couple.

"Night, MD." I could hear more face sucking as I headed wearily toward the bathroom. Hence the nickname. They were always attached at the hip anyway. Admittedly I felt a tad envious even though I had no energy for a boyfriend. The only thing on my agenda was a shower and bed. Not that thoughts of Dalton hadn't crept into my head. I was sure tonight wouldn't be the last time I saw him. I would do my best to avoid him from now on, and we could continue on the separate paths our lives had taken.

Early American history the next morning proved to be as boring as always. Taking endless notes on my iPad while Professor Zeal droned on about the first transcontinental railroad would have been interesting if he could have injected any kind of enthusiasm into his voice.

My afternoon was spent in the campus library working on a paper I had due the following week. I got so wrapped up in research I nearly forgot to head to work. Luckily I managed to make it through the front doors of Gruby's at five o'clock on the nose, despite the snow flutters that had started midday.

"Wow, for a minute there I thought you were going to be late," Jill, one of the hostesses, greeted me as I walked in shaking a light layer of snow off my jacket.

I grinned, knowing I had probably ruined a bet for someone. "I'm never late," I said, draping my jacket over my arm and heading to the back room to stow my belongings.

"It could happen," Jill called after me before turning to greet three middle-aged men dressed in business suits.

Her words cracked me up. The staff had a standing bet on when and if I'd ever show up late. In all the years that I had been out in the workforce, I'd never been late. Only once when I was a teenager and working at Denny's had I ever called in, and that was because my mom was sick with pneumonia and refused to go see a doctor. I practically bullied her into going, and had to drive her there myself to be sure.

The kitchen was buzzing with activity as I walked through the swinging doors that separated the back from the dining area.

"Hey, girl, how they hanging?" Jimmy, one of the line cooks, called out.

"No flies on me," I responded with my normal answer. Jimmy roared with laughter like it was the first time he'd ever heard me say it. At seventy-six years old, he should be sitting on a porch, people-watching or tinkering with some old car, but instead he was working at Gruby's. He always said he wouldn't know what to do with himself if he sat at home all day. We were the lucky ones since he kept the kitchen lively and was a blast to have around. He had basically become an honorary grandpa to all the servers, allowing us to pour our college woes out to him. With more wisdom than all of us put together, he had an answer for every dilemma.

Any time the school's basketball game was on TV, it meant Gruby's would be packed, and tonight was no exception. Every TV in the restaurant was tuned to the same channel. You could barely hear yourself talk as loud, eager fans erupted in one fashion or another, depending on whether something good or something bad happened to the team.

I followed the game as best I could while I worked, managing to notice each time the announcer would mention number nineteen, which around here, unless you lived under a rock, you knew was Dalton. Judging by the constant mention of his name, it was obvious Dalton was having a great game. Rolling my eyes, I continued to take orders and hand out food. It seemed like there was no escaping Dalton Thompson as long as I was working at a sports bar. I guess I should have considered that when Amanda got me the job here. My old restaurant went belly-up right before the holidays. Nothing says merry Christmas like unemployment. Needless to say, I jumped at the chance to work at Gruby's. Although right now the job had lost some of its luster.

As my rotten luck would have it, the waitressing gods not only screwed me over, but also kicked me in the teeth that night. Three hours into my shift and an hour after the game ended, the restaurant erupted into loud cheers when a handful of the players walked through the front door, including Dalton, who was leading the show. He grinned at everyone chanting his name and waved like he was the Prince of England or something.

Biting back a groan, I headed to the kitchen to avoid the spectacle.

"What's going on out there? Did the president of the United States just walk in the door?" Jimmy asked, wiping his hands on the dish towel that was stuck in the waistband of his apron.

I snorted. "I'm not sure he would have gotten that kind of welcome. Some of the team just walked in. You know—the ones who feel they deserve to be worshipped."

"Sweetheart, you might as well accept that basketball is sacred around here and those that do it well will be worshipped as gods," Jimmy drawled, winking at me.

"You're as bad as everyone else. So they can get an orange ball through a hoop, who cares? Let's see them carry a tray with twelve drinks and two appetizers without dropping it and maybe then I'll worship them," I grumbled, grabbing table five's order before heading back out. I shook my head when I saw that the players now inhabited table seven in my section. Several curse words silently tumbled from my mouth as I spotted the back of Dalton's head. It was official. The waitressing gods hated me.

chapter four

Dalton

Adrenaline coursed through my veins as the guys and I pushed our way through the double doors of Gruby's. I owned that court tonight. I'd been in the fucking zone, and I was still completely pumped. At times like this I couldn't help feeling invincible, which was why I talked the guys into hitting Gruby's to celebrate. I'd been unable to get Courtney out of my mind all day. Knowing she was at work maybe watching each shot I nailed made me a beast on the court, getting me a triple double for my efforts.

This time when the hostess greeted us, I specifically requested Courtney's zone. The guys tried to give me shit when I made the request, but I didn't care. I was bound and determined to get her to acknowledge our past friendship.

She studied the seating chart before answering, "I hope you don't mind waiting a few minutes."

"Do what you have to do."

People I didn't know began coming over to shake our hands, congratulating us on the win tonight. It was a weird feeling at first, but after two years, I'd gotten used to it. Scanning the area, I smiled when I spotted Courtney on the other side of the restaurant. She was chatting with an older couple. Even with the distance separating us, I could tell her actions were animated and her eyes sparkled. She threw her head back, laughing at something the elderly gentleman said. Last night I'd thought she was pretty, but in a cute way. Seeing her so carefree, I realized she was downright beautiful. I didn't remember her being this attractive back in school. I found myself envious of the older man. I wanted to be the one to make her laugh like that. I'd never had any trouble getting a girl I was interested in, but right now the only person I wanted was acting like I didn't exist.

"Your table's ready, guys," the hostess said, approaching us.

"Bro, you were fucking insane tonight," Chad said after we sat down. "Don't get me wrong, you're always a badass on the court, but tonight it was like you were channeling Kobe Bryant or something. What was up with that?"

I shrugged modestly. "I don't know. I was in the zone, I guess."

"No shit," Collin agreed, looking up when Courtney approached our table. I flashed a smile, but she didn't even bother to look at me.

"What can I get you guys?"

My eyes followed her hand that pulled a pad from her slinky apron. Her waist was tiny. I bet I could have circled it with both my hands. I considered trying, but I wasn't overly convinced she wouldn't stab me with a steak knife. I brought my eyes back up slowly. I'm not going to lie. They might have lingered on her breasts for a moment before finding her face. I could tell my appraisal hadn't gone unnoticed. "What can I get you to drink?"

I shifted in my seat, tugging on my jeans that were becoming uncomfortable at the moment. Using my coat to cover the evidence, I willed my mind to think of anything that did not involve the luscious blonde in front of me. It took a second to make my body respond to the images of wrinkly old people in bathing suits. It was a trick I'd learned when I was fourteen and my parents took me to Daytona Beach. It was the only way I could keep from sporting a constant hard-on from all the chicks in bikinis walking around. Trust me, that is not something you want your mother to see.

"I'll take a Coke," Collin answered. He looked at me like I was nuts.

"Me, too," Chad piped in.

"Me three." I could have kicked my own ass. It sounded funny in my head, but I wished I could have taken it back the moment the words left my mouth.

"Got it. Do you guys know what you want to eat, or do you need a few minutes?"

"I know what I want," Chad said as he began to rattle off his order.

"I need a few minutes." I interrupted him before he could finish, picking up a menu that I probably could have recited with my eyes closed.

"Bro, are you kidding? Since when do you not know what you want?"

I kicked him hard in the shin under the table.

"What the fuck, dude?"

Courtney cut her eyes toward me, eyeing me suspiciously before shrugging. "Okay, then, I'll go get your drinks while you make up your mind," she said, pulling her eyes away.

"Why the hell did you kick me? You always get a burger," Chad demanded once she walked away, reaching a hand down to rub his shin where I'd kicked him.

"Sorry, man. I felt like something different." What was I going to do, admit it was all a lame ploy, an excuse to have her come back to our table? Maybe I could also hang a *bitch* sign around my neck for good measure. I didn't know why I cared so much. If I was just looking to get laid, I could get that by standing up and proclaiming that I was looking for company. This was something else. Maybe I was feeling nostalgic about a time when everything didn't revolve around basketball, and Dad wasn't constantly breathing down my neck. When Courtney and I had been friends, everything just seemed so much easier.

Chad looked at me skeptically but refrained from saying anything else.

"Hey, am I the only one who thought those guys were about ready to bawl when you drained four three-pointers in a row?" Collin crowed, changing the subject. That was Collin. He was the peacekeeper.

"Couldn't have done it unless you pulled down all those boards," I pointed out, sharing the glory of the game. "I actually felt bad for them once we went up twenty-five points."

"Not me. They can go back home and maybe take up knitting jock-straps or something," Collin added.

Chad and I laughed. Collin was ruthless on the court. It was what made him a great player. You had to be aggressive to make plays, and he could be a game changer when he wanted to.

We were still trading insults about the other school when Court-ney returned with our drinks. Our voices had gotten loud, and several tables around us had joined in on the roast. I was in the middle of laughing at an inappropriately mean comment about the only balls they should be dribbling when my eyes met Courtney's. Her animosity was hard to miss. It was clear she was pissed. Maybe she had turned into some religious nut that was easily offended by swearing and harm-less razzing.

The laughter dried up in my throat. I tried smiling to let her know we were kidding. She, of course, didn't return it. This chick was seri-ously hard-core immune to flirting. Her nickname should be the Brick Wall.

"Are you guys ready to order?" she asked impatiently, placing our cups on the table harder than necessary. Coke sloshed over, soaking the stack of napkins she had set down. "Oh, fuck me," she muttered, wiping up the mess before it covered the entire table.

"Is that an invitation?" I said the words without giving conscious thought to them. It was like an instinct.

"No, thanks. There's no telling what I would catch."

Chad hollered as the rest of the guys erupted into laughter. "Shit. That's harsh. You just got served, dude."

Courtney ignored his comment and stood disdainfully, waiting for us to place our orders. It was as if one of our moms were standing in front of us.

Chad, Dave, and Collin cleared their throats and put in their orders, leaving me for last.

"I'll take the half-court burger with extra cheese," I ordered without opening the menu.

"Fries or tots?"

Chad grinned widely but refrained from commenting when I kicked him under the table again. "Tots," I answered.

"Anything else?"

"How about your number?" I figured I might as well take the shot since she had already blasted me in front of everyone.

"Why?" For the first time, I had her undivided attention.

She didn't say no, which was a small victory. I savored it for a second before answering, "Normal reasons—talking, for example, and so I can ask you out sometime." I flashed my full-wattage smile, taking advantage of having her attention.

For a moment I thought I was making headway until she looked like she wanted to puke. Was the idea of dating me really that appalling?

"I don't date jockstrap wearers." She turned to leave before I lobbed back my response.

"Lucky for me, basketball players don't wear jockstraps."

She paused midstep but didn't turn back to look at me.

"Bro, I'm going to fuck you up if you kick me again," Chad threatened once she was out of earshot.

Collin snorted, clapping him on the back. "You wish. Dalton would wipe the floor with you. One time when we were all playing a game at the rec center, some dipshit thought he could keep pushing our man Dalton here. Dalton tolerated his shit for the first fifteen minutes or so, but then the dickhead knocked Dalton out of bounds with a cheap shot. My boy didn't even hesitate. He clocked him so hard he was out for the count. It was classic, baby. Dalton is the fucking man."

"What are you, his manager? Or maybe it's something else. I didn't know you swung from that tree. Do I need to leave you two alone?"

"Shit, I'd make you my bitch, fool. Believe that. Everyone wants a piece of the Collin Man," Collin bragged, making a show of kissing his own biceps.

"Right. You and Tater Tots here are both shooting zero-for-two at the moment. I don't need to kick Dalton's ass, 'cause Courtney is doing it for me."

"Fuck that," I piped in. "I'm just getting started, Smalls. Don't worry about me. I'll be closing that shit soon enough." It wasn't meant to sound cocky, just confident based on my experience with the ladies.

chapter five

Courtney

pushed through the swinging kitchen door and leaned against the wall, trying to clear my head. The dirty dishes slid off my tray, crashing to the floor. Mercifully they didn't break. Dalton Thompson had just asked for my number. He had to be screwing with me. He'd never looked in my direction the whole time we were at Grant High together and now suddenly he was interested. I felt like I was being *Punk'd*.

"Wow, my princess. You break-a my dishes, you break-a my heart. What has my little tigress so upset?" Jimmy asked, drying his hands on his apron and slinging a fatherly arm across my shoulders. "Whose ass do I need to kick?"

I bit back a shaky smile. "Just some jockstrap who thinks he's God's gift to women. He can't seem to take a hint."

"Someone harassing you?" Chuck asked as he joined us. Standing six foot three, Chuck was a beast. His frame was like a grizzly bear's, so when his chest puffed up, he was quite intimidating. I briefly entertained the idea of what Dalton would do if I sent Chuck out in my place. The thought definitely had its merits, and would give me some satisfaction.

At least it might dim his inviting smile, that hypnotic voice, and those warm eyes. That was the part of him I remembered the most. I'd always loved his eyes. There was something about seeing him in person again, and the sparkle in his eyes, that didn't project from any of the banners hanging around campus.

I patted Chuck's arm, smiling. "Easy, big fella. I'll handle him."

"Maybe I should go out there and emphasize that when a lady says *no*, she means *no*," he added, cracking his knuckles. "Tell me who needs a little reminder."

I laughed at the thought of Chuck confronting Dalton in my honor. That was all we needed, to start a brawl with the school's basketball savior. Chuck's sentiment was sweet but would be the end of Gruby's. "It's Dalton Thompson, but don't worry. I can handle him."

"*The* Dalton Thompson? All-American, conference champion, future lottery pick—that Dalton Thompson?"

"Seriously? You, too?" I snorted with disbelief. "Please tell me you're not riding the Dalton bandwagon like everyone else around here."

"Honey, I'd drive that bandwagon if they'd let me. Dalton is one of those once-in-a-generation types of players. He's got more talent in his pinkie than everyone else on the team combined. We were lucky he chose to come here to play ball. Trust me, that kid has a huge future."

"Oh Lord. So the guy is good at basketball. Why put him on such a pedestal?"

"Dalton isn't just a phenom on the court, he's a good guy. Believe me, with his talent he could be a prima donna, but he seems to have a good head on his shoulders. My nephew went to his basketball clinic last summer, and let me tell you, that guy has the patience of a saint. I love my nephew, but let's face it. Seven-year-olds can be little shits. Any guy that can tolerate a gym full of rug rats at one time is some kind of kid whisperer. Trust me. There's probably not many other players of his stature giving up their spare time to give free basketball clinics to kids."

I digested Chuck's words. Grudgingly I had to agree. It was a decent thing for Dalton to do.

"Do you really not like him?" Chuck inquired.

"I don't dislike him, per se. He's just not my favorite person. I'm not interested in becoming part of his entourage. And I definitely don't consider myself a basketball groupie."

Chuck laughed. "I can't deny he seems to do well at attracting the ladies, but from what I've seen here, he's respectful."

"Respectful, meaning he doesn't push them out of bed without saying good-bye first?" My snarkiness continued to amuse Chuck.

"Well, I can't speak accurately about Dalton Thompson's bedroom behavior. All I can offer is my opinion of what I know about the guy from observing him here. I'm just saying don't judge the guy before you really get to know him. Regardless, I think my offer to intervene was a little premature. You obviously have a handle on the situation." He winked at me, heading toward his office.

The problem was I did already know him. Taking the chicken's way out, I talked Amanda into trading tables with me. I could tell she was puzzled by my request, but she readily agreed. She was more than happy to have a chance to chat it up with Collin.

I dropped off the check at the table I'd taken over from Amanda. The guy handed over his credit card without even checking the bill. That was a surefire sign that a customer was ready to go. I cashed him out swiftly before heading to my table of tipsy sorority girls who were flagging me down for another round of drinks.

"Another refill, ladies?" I asked, grabbing the empty margarita pitcher.

"Woot, woot, heck yeah. Keep it flowing," one of the girls hollered, flashing a wide smile. At least they were happy drinkers.

"Coming right up." I left them to their not-so-private conversation about some guy who they heard had piercings in some interestingly inconspicuous places.

"Hey, Paul. Can I get another pitcher for table five?" I perched myself on one of the barstools to wait.

"Sure thing. Give me a few seconds." He filled two shot glasses for a couple of women dressed in business suits. The lanyards around their necks indicated they worked for the university in some capacity. They clinked glasses before sucking down the contents. One of them started coughing as the whiskey burned a path down her throat, making her friend laugh while she patted her on the back. "You'll get used to it," she chortled. "If we're going to play with the big boys, we need to be able to hang, or they'll crush us." She signaled Paul, who was putting the finishing touches on my margaritas.

"What's up with that?" I whispered.

"Battle of the sexes. From what I gather, the school treats the men a little better than the women."

"Shocking," I said sarcastically. The world treated men and women differently. Why should our university be any different? Especially when it came to athletics. You could be at the highest end of the spectrum in academics, but you were still a second-class citizen when compared to big-time sports programs. "I'm surprised the president of the university doesn't walk around with his lips stuck to the players' asses."

"Who says he doesn't? You have any idea how much money the sports programs generate for the school? As harsh as that sounds, the money allows for programs at the college that might be cut otherwise," he pointed out, sliding over to refill the ladies' shot glasses.

I knew what he said was true, but that didn't mean it didn't sometimes feel like they were rubbing our noses in it. Still, I guess twenty thousand people weren't filling an arena every few nights to see an art exhibit or a science experiment. I knew I was just being overly sensitive. Seeing Dalton two days in a row had me a little cranky.

Shaking my head, I grabbed the freshly mixed pitcher and headed back to my table of girls, who had begun chanting my name while I was gone.

"Here you go, ladies," I said, sliding the pitcher on the table.

"You're the best, Courtney-y-y. I seriously love you," Misty, one of the girls, drawled as she snagged my hand. She pulled me into the booth and slung her drunken arm across my shoulders. "Don't you guys just love Courtney? She's so cute and sweet." She planted a wet kiss on my cheek, making me blanch slightly, but I allowed it. I knew Misty from a few classes we had taken together. She was harmless. We had one of those kinds of friendships where we acted happy to see each other and always made promises to hang out, but neither of us ever took the extra step to do so.

"If I ever went gay, I'd totally want it to be with you," she continued.

"That's the sweetest thing I've heard all night, but you'd probably have a fight on your hands. I've been propositioned by my fair share of friends," I said, standing.

"Aw, I get it. You're a tease," one of Misty's friends declared.

"Oh, look, Cass is totally falling asleep," another of the girls said, elbowing Cass in the arm.

"I am not. I was resting my eyeballs for a moment. They were tired of looking at you." They all giggled when her friends pouted in response. "I'm kidding. I love you like a drunk loves to drink."

"Gee, thanks. Why can't you say something sweet like Misty said to Courtney?" She rolled her eyes and took another swig of the drink in her glass.

I laughed but left them to their drunken compliments.

Travis, one of the busers, snagged my attention as I walked by. "Hey, Courtney." He was busy clearing one of my previous tables.

"Hey, Trav. How's the band?" Travis belonged to a kick-ass band, but they would constantly fight and break up because of their tempers.

He sighed before providing the inevitable answer. "We're on a break again. I swear to God, I feel like I'm in some fucked-up relationship with a chick, as much as we fight."

I clucked my tongue sympathetically, running a rag across the surface of the table. "What is it this time?"

"Slick thinks we should all wear spandex to our shows. Ripped spandex to be exact."

"Um, eww."

He sighed again in defeat. "I know, right? Marcus told him he was high as a kite. Needless to say, the conversation didn't end well."

"I'm sorry, Travis. They'll work it out." I patted him on the back as he set off with the tub of dirty dishes in hand. I used my rag to clean off the bench seat, brushing any crumbs to the floor.

"Hey," Amanda said, sliding into the empty booth I had wiped down. I could tell she wanted something by the way she fiddled with the saltshaker. "So, you remember how grateful you were when I got you this job?"

"Yes," I answered apprehensively, sensing I wouldn't like where this was going.

"And how you claimed you would owe me big-time?"

"If I remember right, you said it was no big deal."

"True, but then you insisted. As a matter of fact, I distinctly remember you saying I saved your life."

I didn't say anything this time. Judging by the way she was laying it on thick, this was going to be a doozy.

"The way I figure it, saving someone's life is a pretty big deal. I'm guessing it would mean that person would do anything to repay the debt."

"You mean like chauffeur that person around every other day so she doesn't have to walk or wait for the bus in the frigid temperatures?"

She paused. Obviously she hadn't considered that before approaching me with whatever this big request was going to be. "No, it needs to be something bigger."

"Spit it out, then. What do you want?"

"Go on a double date with me."

"Are you asking me out?" I teased, placing my hands on my hips.

"You wish, sugar lips." She laughed and ducked her head when I swung the rag at her. "I want you to go with Collin's friend."

"Which friend?" I asked, already knowing the answer.

"Dalton! Can you believe that? He's totally into you. I know you have that crazy 'I don't date basketball players' thing, but this is Dalton Thompson. If I didn't like Collin, I'd be totally jealous."

I was already shaking my head before she could finish her statement. "Amanda, I can't."

"Why not?" She stood up from the booth, glaring at me with her hands on her hips.

"Because, Amanda. You just said it yourself. I don't date basketball players." In all honesty, I would have said yes if she had picked any other basketball player for me to go out with.

"Is this a short person thing?"

I swatted at her. "Don't be an ass."

"Well, unless it's something legitimate, you don't have a viable excuse. Don't make me play the 'you owe me' card. Just think. If you go, we'll be even."

I was still shaking my head, but her pitiful expression was crumbling my resolve.

"Please, Courtney. I'll be your BFF."

"You're already my BFF and we're not in grade school."

"Say you'll go," she pled. "Ple-e-ease."

I had to say yes. I'd be a complete bitch otherwise. I nodded as Amanda squealed, dragging me in for an excited hug as she jumped up and down. I was screwed.

chapter six

Dalton

t was a complete stroke of genius to crash Collin's date with Amanda. At first I'd been disappointed Courtney didn't come back to our table, until I realized Amanda was a friend of hers. I seized the opportunity to pump her for information. When Collin and Amanda started making plans to go out, I shamelessly jumped onboard, suggesting we should double-date. This time it was Collin's turn to kick me under the table, but I ignored him. He owed me.

The next night I swung by to pick up Collin on the way to get the girls at Amanda's dorm. "I still can't believe you latched on to my date. Why didn't you just ask this chick out yourself?"

I shrugged. "Desperate times call for desperate measures. Besides, I volunteered to drive, didn't I?"

"How the hell does that make up for cock-blocking me? What is it about this girl that's making you act like such a pussy?" He adjusted the vents in the car so the heat was directed at him.

"It's nothing. We were friends once and now she's acting a little weird. I figured this way she wouldn't be able to run off without talking to me."

"You obviously can't hear yourself. 'Oh, I hope she talks to me.'" He batted his eyes, making his best attempt to sound like a girl.

I couldn't help laughing even though he was making fun of me. That still didn't mean he didn't get sucker punched in the arm as we pulled into the parking lot of Amanda's dorm.

"Hey, dick. Just be a man and admit you want to tap that. Own it." He rubbed his arm, complaining.

"Don't worry about what I want," I warned as we trekked through the snow toward the building.

"Take a pill, Nancy. You should be kissing my ass anyway for letting you tag along."

I would have answered, but I spotted Courtney and Amanda walking toward us from the common area inside the building. Amanda flashed a brilliant smile at Collin. Courtney, on the other hand, glared at me. One way or another I planned on getting to the bottom of her animosity tonight. "Hey," I greeted her.

"Hey," she answered without looking up at me. I think the only reason she acknowledged me was because Amanda nudged her with her elbow. Things quickly became awkward as we stood facing each other with no one saying a word.

"So, everybody knows each other, right? Collin, Dalton—Amanda, Courtney," Amanda said, pointing back and forth. "This ought to be fun, don't you think?"

"You're crazy, girl." Collin laughed, throwing his arm around her shoulder. We fell into typical two-by-two double date formation with Courtney and me trailing behind as we all walked to the car. I had a ton of shit I wanted to say, but I felt tongue-tied. Collin was right. I was acting like a wuss. I never got tripped up around the ladies. Of course, I'd never had one treat me like such a dirtbag.

Amanda and Collin climbed into the backseat, leaving Courtney to ride shotgun. I could tell by her hesitation that she wasn't happy about the arrangement, but she never spoke up.

Amanda kept the car ride from becoming uncomfortable by maintaining a running commentary, mostly about basketball. I had to hand it to her. She knew her shit. Courtney didn't say much despite my efforts to coax her to open up. By the time I pulled into the parking lot of the bowling alley, I was about over it. It was cool seeing her after all these years, and even though I was curious about what her problem was, I wasn't going to put up with the attitude all night.

I waited until Collin and Amanda entered the bowling alley ahead of us before snagging Courtney's hand to pull her to a stop.

She jerked her hand free, looking like she could have taken a swing at me. "What the hell?"

"Shouldn't those be my words? What's your deal?" I shoved my hands into my pockets in frustration. "Are you completely forgetting that we were friends once?"

"Me? You're the one who forgot that." She turned toward the building until I reached out and snagged her hand again.

"What's that supposed to mean?"

"Are you really that dense? I didn't think basketball was a contact sport, but you must have taken some shots to the head."

"What are you talking about? I mean yeah, we stopped hanging out, but we were kids. I don't understand why we have to be enemies now."

"Yo, are you guys coming?" Collin yelled from the front door.

"In a minute, bro," I called back.

Courtney snorted with disbelief before shaking her head, muttering, "Stopped hanging out? Let me clue you in, sport-o. *We* didn't stop hanging out. *You* did. One minute we're friends and the next you're gone. All you cared about was basketball. I know that was important, but you just dropped me."

She stomped off toward the entrance and I let her go this time as I processed her words. Her reasoning felt crazy. We were just kids. What happened to our friendship had been mutual. Well, my dad had a lot to do with it, but she was forgetting all the times I tried reaching out to her. She was the one who acted like she had other shit going on that didn't concern me. She was the one who became distant. I hadn't thought about anything from back then for a long time, but it was all suddenly coming back to me now. My dad was all over my ass. Every day it was practice, practice, practice for hours. I remember needing someone to talk to, but the few times I tried with Courtney she pretty much dissed me. I always assumed us drifting apart was a mutual thing. It floored me that she felt I was responsible.

I jogged after her, shaking my head with disbelief. I caught up to her as she was trying to pay for her shoe rental.

"Hey, what are you doing?" I asked.

"Uh—getting my shoes. What do you mean?"

"Like it or not, this is a date. There's no way in hell I'm letting my girl pay."

"I'm not your girl," she said as the pimply-faced teenager behind the counter grinned at us, obviously enjoying the free show.

"Hey, aren't you Dalton Thompson?" he asked enthusiastically.

"Oh brother," Courtney said, snatching her shoes off the counter.

"Yeah, what's up? I need size fifteen and I'll cover both." I handed over a ten-dollar bill.

"You think I could get your autograph?" He held up a pen and notepad after placing my change and a pair of bowling shoes on the counter.

I signed the notepad and caught up with Courtney, who was seated at a table changing into her bowling shoes. "Look, Court," I said, falling back on the nickname I'd used when we were younger. "I didn't realize you thought I had ditched you. I mean, you remember how my dad was. I guess I always assumed the way basketball sort of took over my life that we both just got busy and stopped making time for each other."

"It's no big deal." The way she tightened up her laces made me think otherwise.

"It is a big deal. Look, I'm sorry if I was the asshole in this situation. I know the past is the past, but it doesn't mean we can't be friends now, right? Come on. Friends?" I asked, holding out my hand.

She studied my outstretched hand for a moment before reluctantly placing hers on top. "Fine, friends."

What I didn't admit was that I wanted to be more than friends. Everything about Courtney appealed to me. I wanted to discover everything I'd missed over the last eight years.

"Are we playing or what?"Amanda hollered from a nearby lane, interrupting our private chat.

Courtney at least loosened up after that and became marginally warmer as the evening progressed. She surprised me by being a kick-ass bowler and wickedly competitive, like me. I used it to my advantage by goading her into a wager.

"You're not going to welsh when I seal the deal on this last ball, are you?" I asked, waiting for my ball to return from my first attempt. I should have felt a little remorseful for hustling her phone number out of her, but she didn't have to take the bet.

"Just roll the ball." She sat with her arms folded across her chest, knowing she had been defeated. Amanda seemed to find my persistence hilarious while Collin eyed me like aliens had taken over my body. He'd never seen me go to this much trouble chasing a chick. I'd have to corner him before he ran his mouth off to all the guys.

I had to hand it to Courtney. She paid up fair and square. I felt the date had gone well, which only left one thing. I'd given a great deal of thought to the good-night kiss. I had a whole plan worked out, but Courtney dashed it before I had a chance to put it into effect. She practically leaped from my car as soon as we got back to Amanda's dorm. One minute she was next to me; the next she was gone, like the Flash. She must have tipped off her friend ahead of time, because Amanda didn't even comment. Collin looked back at me, grinning as he walked Amanda to her dorm. No doubt he'd get a kiss. I was tempted to leave his ass.

I told Collin before dropping him off he'd pay if he harassed me about Courtney in front of the guys, but truthfully I was kidding. I knew he wouldn't do that. When I got home I pulled out my phone and scrolled to Courtney's number. Hitting her up this soon would look desperate, and yet I couldn't put the phone down.

Hey, I texted, feeling like a fool.

Hey yourself. The reply was almost instantaneous, like she was holding her phone.

What R U doing?

Getting ready for bed. U?

And didn't that conjure wonderful images?

Vegging on my couch.

Fun. Did U need something?

Ouch. She didn't mess around. Nah, I just wanted to tell U
I had fun tonight. U jetted out so quick I didn't get a
chance to mention it. I'd like to see you again. Soon.

Oh, I had fun, too.

But??? I knew a brush-off when I saw one.

No but. I'm just really busy and don't have
much time for the whole dating thing.

I studied her message for a minute before replying. I'd been expecting this. Even though we had made progress tonight, I could tell
she had been holding back. I'm not asking you to marry me.
We can keep it casual.

Her return text was slow to come in. I groaned when it did. I had
walked right into that one. I'm sure casual is the only word
you know. No, thanks.

Come on, I didn't mean it like that. When did
you become so elusive?

By elusive you mean why don't I fall over on
my back with my legs spread?

Ouch. Harsh, babe. I wouldn't let U fall.

Nice try.

You're tough. What does a guy have to do to
get a break?

Maybe not hit on every girl he meets.

Who says I do that?

Please. I've seen you in action.

The truth comes out, you've been stalking me.

U wish. You've been a player since high
school.

High school? Give me some credit. I'm more ma-
ture now. Scout's honor.

Ha, you were never a Boy Scout.

Doesn't mean I'm not a good guy.

So you say.

R U always so distrustful?

Only with basketball players that try to play
games off the court, too.

I'm not that guy.

Right, and I'm not rolling my eyes.

I'm going to prove I'm different.

I don't see how.

I hope you like surprises, because I believe
in go big or go home.

We shall see. Lots of guys overestimate their
appeal.

I'm **wounded.** My thumbs flew across the screen. Despite her
harsh judgment, I was enjoying myself immensely. She was quick wit-
ted and funny in a sarcastic way.

I'm sure. I better go. I have stuff I need to
catch up on in the morning.

Okay, I'll text you tomorrow.

Don't you have a game or something?

I do but there will be some downtime.

I'll probably be busy all day.

That's fine. U can text when U have time.
Night, Court.

She didn't respond again, but I didn't let it affect me. Chasing
Courtney had become more fun than anything I'd done in a while. It
was like playing in a big game. I enjoyed the challenge. I thrived on it.
I was sure the guys on the team wouldn't understand, but I didn't care.
Let them chase their own chicks their own way.

chapter seven

Courtney

The chime of an incoming text message woke me. Reaching over to my nightstand, I fumbled around for my cell phone with my eyes still closed. My hand closed around the phone, and I tried to pry my heavy eyelids open to peer at the screen, but they refused to cooperate.

I let my arm fall to the mattress, still clutching my phone in my hand. I needed to get up. There were a million errands to fit in before my shift at Gruby's tonight. Of course, needing to get up and wanting to get up were two different things. Ignoring the voice of responsibility in my head, I burrowed deeper into my blanket. It was freaking freezing outside, and my bed felt too good. The sound of my phone chiming again made my eyelids spring open. Who could possibly be texting me so early?

Peering at the screen, I saw another text from Dalton. I couldn't believe how persistent he was. It was hard to let go of all the hurt I'd allowed to fester into anger over the years, but he'd made a good point during our date last night. When Dalton had gotten too busy for me, I

could have put up a fight. Instead I wallowed in self-pity. The few times
he tried to call I'd always acted like I was too busy. After listening to
his side of the story, I probably owed him the same apology he'd given
me. That being said, clearing the air the way we had didn't make it any
easier to start dating him.

Morning, Sunshine. I snorted reading the message as a sensation of warmth filled my stomach.

Who is this?

U wound me.

I bet.

Seriously. Your words are like a knife to my
tender heart.

Oh Lord. It's getting deep in here. Where R U?

At the airport.

Fun.

Honestly, traveling is the worst part of the
season.

You mean you don't have fans everywhere you go?

Sure, sometimes. It's still not like being
home. Plus some of the guys are more responsible than others.

What about U?

I listen to Coach. Whatever he says goes.

What about when it comes to girls? How would your coach feel if he knew you were texting me, trying to get in my pants?

Hey! Whoa! Who said I was trying to get in your pants?

Do I have idiot stamped on my forehead?

Not sure. I'm not there.

Let's assume I don't. We both know what's going on here. My words were blunt, but that was my intention.

We do?

Dalton, don't be coy. It doesn't suit you.

Fine. I like you, Court, and I want to go out with you even though you're just trying to get in my pants. A startled laugh left me after reading his text. He was seriously incorrigible.

You're a mess.

By mess you mean adorable, right?

Were you dropped on your head a lot as a baby?

Go out with me again. He switched gears, no longer dancing around what he wanted.

That would be a little hard since you're out
of town.

I mean when I get back.

That probably isn't a good idea.

Why not?

Because I'll spend the whole time trying to get
in your pants. I could feel the corners of my mouth lifting, knowing
he had just read my text.

That's a risk I'm willing to take. Is that a
yes?

The smile left my face as I studied his words. I felt like I was
standing on the edge of a cliff. If I took the plunge, there was a
chance it would leave my heart bleeding and broken on the rocks
below. The kicker to the situation was that I did want to go out with
him. His attention over the past week was a heady experience. More
than half the female population on campus would gladly switch
places with me. Maybe if I kept the date fun and casual without allowing my heart to become involved like before, I would be more
comfortable saying yes.

Court???? R U still there?

Yep.

Will U?

How do I know you're not toying with me? I hated

that I felt the need to ask the question. It made me sound like some
insecure little girl.

> You're going to have to trust me. I'm not go-
> ing to hurt you again. I promise.

> What are you willing to do?

> U mean like to prove myself?

> Yep.

> Sounds like you already have something in
> mind.

> Maybe.

> Let me guess, you want me to tie myself to a
> flagpole and declare my love for you in front
> of everyone?

Sounds like you're the one who had something in
mind, I teased. It's a good idea, but I had something
else in mind. I couldn't help giggling as I filled him in on what I
expected him to do. If he actually went through with it, there would be
no way I could say no to a date with him. I wasn't even sure I would do
what I asked if I were in his shoes. Regardless of the fun I was having,
I reluctantly told him I needed to get going.

Our text conversation played through my head the rest of the day
as I tried to cram a week's worth of errands into a few hours. Saturdays
were always my catch-up day since work, classes, and homework consumed my time during the week. Sunday was completely devoted to
Mom. We'd made a pact years ago that we would always make Sundays
our day to get together. We weren't religious or anything. Mom just

strongly felt Sunday should be a family day. It didn't matter that it was just the two of us. It was because of her that I never missed not having a dad. Mom played both parental roles and she did it flawlessly. We had a special relationship.

Not surprisingly, Gruby's was packed to the gills. Tonight's game was nationally televised, which drew a lot of attention. There wasn't a single empty seat in the place, meaning a great night of tips for me.

The game hadn't started yet, but the pregame show was blaring from every TV. I was busy handling numerous tables but managed to catch snippets of the announcing crew discussing the team's chances of being a number-one seed in the upcoming March tournament. My ears especially perked up when I heard them mention Dalton's name. I stopped for a moment to watch the clips from the previous game showing Dalton shooting one three-pointer after another. The crowd in the restaurant cheered loudly with each swish through the net like it was happening live.

It felt strange to watch everyone react so strongly to everything he did. Like they were all worshipping Saint Dalton. I wondered what it must feel like knowing the hopes and dreams of an entire university rested in your hands. I felt the stirrings of doubt as I began to second-guess my decision to give him a chance. How could someone like him be interested in me? Of course, that was if he actually went through with his end of the bargain. If not, I'd have my out. The chances of him backing out had to be high. My request was admittedly ridiculous. Surely he'd come to his senses and move on to the next girl.

The sound of the announcers laughing on the TV grabbed my attention once again. "What does Dalton Thompson have painted on his face?" I pivoted around, groaning when I saw the glaring evidence of my dare on the giant six-foot screen. "Is that a heart?" one of the announcers asked incredulously.

Everyone in Gruby's stared at the TV screens, trying to make sense of what they were seeing. I couldn't believe he went through with it. A laugh bubbled up in my throat. He had risked making himself a bit of a spectacle to his teammates, coaches, and even the media to go out on one date with me. There was no way I could back out now.

Amanda squealed, sliding up next to me. "Holy shit. Why does Dalton have a heart stenciled on his cheek?"

I tried to look innocent, but the goofy grin on my face gave me away.

"Slap my ass and call me a tramp. You're responsible for this?"

I clamped a hand across her mouth. "Shush, you don't have to announce it to the whole restaurant."

"Why is he wearing a heart?" she mumbled through my fingers.

"I sorta told him I'd go out with him again if he painted a bright red heart on his cheek for the game." I admitted it but felt more than a little embarrassed about my request.

"OMG, that is fucking hilarious."

I grinned at her. The announcers were still speculating about the heart. One commented maybe it had something to do with Valentine's Day, even though that was a few weeks prior. The other suggested maybe it was for his mother. Regardless, the fact that Dalton Thompson did it made it news.

Amanda gushed now that my hand wasn't wrapped around her mouth. "Holy crap. You're going out with Dalton again?"

"And that's the reaction I was worried about. One can't simply go out with Dalton without everyone speculating. Can you imagine the shit he's going to get?"

"What are you talking about? Any guy would be lucky to date you."

I snorted. "Right, because I'm so knockout gorgeous."

"Shut up. You have to know you're a bombshell. Sure, maybe travel-sized, but beautiful nonetheless. You're proportioned just right. Trust me. Girls are jealous of your knockers and ass."

I laughed at her choice of words even though I was sure she was blowing sunshine up my ass. Long-legged twigs were what guys were looking for, in my opinion. I wasn't sure what Dalton's deal was with me. Maybe he had a list and he had reached short and curvy.

"How else do you figure you got a recognized player to paint his face for a nationally televised game? I couldn't even get my douche-canoe ex to stick around."

"Well, he was an ass. It seemed like you and Collin hit it off last night, though."

"We did. We're supposed to go out again when he gets back, but . . ."

"Oh no. What's wrong with him?" I knew that tone in her voice. "You didn't even give him a chance," I said, thinking about poor Collin. Amanda's dating track record was less than stellar.

"I don't know. He seems a little too good to be true. I'm waiting for the second date to see if his true colors come out."

"Oh my. God forbid he's a good guy."

"Ha. You're a fine one to speak. You've got the team's all-star jumping through hoops and you're all like, 'I'm too ugly.' Seriously?"

"Don't be a jerk." I chuckled, swiping at her. "I bet Collin would do the same for you."

She smirked. "I'm not so sure of that. Dalton is pursuing you like you're holding the golden ticket to Wonka's Factory. He wants your candy."

"Shut it." I frowned at her with butterflies dancing lightly in my stomach.

The heart on Dalton's face was a popular topic the rest of the evening. Especially since Dalton played great, as usual. As the last few minutes of the game ticked away, the announcers declared the heart a lucky charm and speculated whether Dalton would repeat it for every game. I could have spoken up and at least set everyone at Gruby's straight, but I kept my lips tightly closed.

chapter eight

Dalton

Did you see? I texted Sunday morning.

    See what? The reply came back almost immediately, making me smile. I liked that Courtney responded so quickly. She must be at least a little interested in me.

    Very funny. I have proof in case you missed it.

    Okay, I might have seen it but I'm not sure the size justifies a date.

    Nice try. I'll pick you up at three tomorrow afternoon. I'd already prepared myself in case she tried to back out. There would be no chance of that.

    What if I have to work?

U don't. U told me yesterday U were off.

Aren't you going to be tired from your trip? Her
last-ditch attempt was cute, but I wasn't budging.

Nope, I'll be all rested up.

R U always such an eager beaver when U go out
with someone?

Normally I don't have to work so hard.

Great, so I'm like some conquest for sporty-
boy who normally gets everything he wants just
by smiling?

Well, my smile is pretty amazing.

Oh Lord. I think I'm coming down with a stomach bug.

Look, you're not a conquest.

Then what am I?

A refreshing change.

I may have just sprained my eyes from rolling
them.

You're still going. I'll be there by three.

Don't you want my address?

I chuckled, earning a grin from Collin, who was sprawled across the seats next to me in the airport. `I have my ways. Hamilton Street, right?`

`Really? How?`

`Can't reveal my sources.`

`Typical.`

We were getting ready to board our plane, so I had to say good-bye, which was probably a good thing. The way my luck had started with Courtney, I'd say something she would take out of context and I'd be in the doghouse again.

"Bro, you got it bad," Collin observed.

He didn't know the half of it. He'd really think I was a pussy if he saw all the messages we'd exchanged.

"You're just jealous."

"You wish. I got my own thing working."

"We'll see. Amanda is known for chewing guys up and spitting them out."

"That's because she's never rode the Collin train," he said, cracking a smile.

"Wow, you should tell her that. I bet she'd tear her clothes off."

"Do I look stupid?"

"Well, now that you asked . . ."

He chucked his empty water bottle at me, which I slapped away easily.

Collin was cool, but I had my own girl issue to worry about. For whatever reason, tomorrow felt like the most important date I'd ever gone on. I didn't want to screw it up. Over the past two days, my initial relationship with Courtney had changed from pursuit to genuine interest. Through the course of our text-messaging, I'd gotten a small glimpse into the person behind the force field she seemed to have up when she was around me. I was definitely intrigued. Tomorrow I would get to see even more.

The drive from my apartment to Courtney's house on Hamilton Street took less than ten minutes Monday afternoon. I felt something in my stomach that I could only have guessed was nerves. It was a feeling I wasn't used to. Even before big games, one of my strengths was that I stayed as cool as the other side of the pillow. The roads were icy from another cold front that had moved in overnight. Winter in Michigan translated to freeze-your-balls-off cold. I blasted the heat, coaxing it to warm up the car to a suitable temperature before I pulled up to Courtney's house.

There were several cars in the driveway. I parked behind a car that looked like it was being held together by chewing gum and maybe some spit. The thing was so rusted out it looked like it belonged in a garbage heap. It had a college parking sticker in the window, so it must have worked.

I made my way up to the front door and stomped my feet on the welcome mat as I rang the doorbell. The sound of voices hummed through the door just before it was thrown open. Courtney hopped on one foot, working to zip her boot that stopped just below her knee. "You're early."

"Nope. It's one minute past three, to be exact," I said, trying to act cool over the sight of Courtney dressed in tight jeans. The denim hugged all her assets, highlighting them in a way that should have been illegal. The tight pink sweater that strained across her large full breasts was almost my undoing. A clear mental picture of what lay underneath filled my head and was enough to make my mouth go dry. I took the opportunity while her head was down to shift my boys while I still had some control. All I could think was that it was a good thing my coat ran past my waist.

"Indy, I'm leaving. Do you want me to lock the front door?" Courtney called down the hall.

"No, Kier is on his way over."

"Okay, see you later." Courtney closed the door, shrugging into a short jacket that stopped at her waist just above her amazing ass. Tonight was going to be like a medieval torture exercise on my body.

"So, that was one of my roommates," Courtney commented as I took her elbow to guide her down the icy sidewalk. It was a move Mom had instilled in me when I was ten. Always open the door for a lady, and let her go first. I was unprepared for how I felt touching her. There were at least two layers of clothing separating skin-on-skin contact, but I could still sense the warmth of her arm.

Courtney looked down at my hand. "Are you afraid I don't know how to walk?" she asked, although she didn't pull away.

"My mom always taught me it was polite to escort a lady over treacherous terrain."

"And you think this is treacherous terrain?" She patted the rust bucket of a car when we passed it.

"Sure. It's icy and the sidewalk slants slightly. Besides, it gives me a chance to hold on to you so you can't bolt," I stated, opening the car door for her. "So, is that your car?" I asked skeptically, climbing behind the wheel of my car.

"Yeah, that's Lucy." She turned to glare at me, clearly challenging me to say something derogatory.

"Lucy?" I asked playfully, sidestepping the fact that it was a complete piece of junk.

"Yeah, Lucy. Are guys the only ones allowed to name their vehicles?"

"Well, no. It's just, *Lucy* doesn't quite seem appropriate for that car."

"Maybe not to you. There's nothing wrong with Lucy. Sure, she's not as pretty or fancy as some cars, but she's reliable, and I don't have to worry about any dings or scratches."

"Damn, extract the claws from my ass. I wasn't criticizing."

"Right. Everyone picks on poor Lucy. So, where are you taking me?"

"Twelve Acres Vineyards."

"Nice. That's not too far away."

"Have you been? Wait—do you even like wine? I guess that information would have been vital for me to check on before I made our reservation."

She started laughing at my question.

I couldn't help smiling with her. She had a great laugh. "What's so funny?"

"You asking me if I like wine. My roommates would bust a gut. They call me a wine snob since that's usually the only alcoholic beverage I drink. Well, besides an occasional shot."

"Really? What about beer?"

"Yuck, I hate beer. The taste and smell make me want to gag."

"I hate to break it to you, but you know you work in a sports bar, right? Beer is kind of a staple item at a place like Gruby's."

"I've learned to block it out. It's not like I'm sticking my nose in everyone's glasses."

I chuckled at her explanation. It was sound reasoning.

"What about you? You don't exactly look like a sommelier."

"Ah, that's where you're wrong. I am quite gifted at wine tasting and pairing." I grinned when she looked surprised. *Sommelier* wasn't a word that was thrown around much on a college campus. "You're surprised I know what a sommelier is?" I teased, resting my hand on hers. I expected her to pull away, but she shocked me by turning her hand over and lacing her fingers through mine. It was just holding hands, but it was a step in the right direction.

"Okay, I'll admit I'm a little surprised. Even I hadn't ever heard of pairing when it comes to wine. So, where did you get your knowledge?"

"My parents took me on a tour of wine country in California when I was fourteen. It was supposed to coincide with an important basketball camp, but I broke my hand and couldn't go. I remember my dad was pissed because most of the best players my age were going to be there. He wanted to cancel, but the trip was already booked, so they dragged me along while I pouted the entire time. I complained bitterly, wondering why we couldn't go to a theme park instead since we were going to be in California. After a few days, I discovered wine country wasn't all that bad."

"What was her name?" Courtney asked.

"Excuse me?"

"What was the girl's name who still makes you grin like a goof? No boy would have fond memories of wine country over theme parks if a girl wasn't involved. Spill it."

"Touché. Her name was Honey."

Courtney snorted loudly. "Sorry, did you say *Honey*? Why am I not surprised?"

"You like busting my balls, don't you?"

She smirked. "You're an easy target. I'm sorry for interrupting. Please tell me about Honey."

"Anyway, I met Honey at a bed-and-breakfast we were staying at for a couple days. Her parents owned it. You'll love this part. She lived up to her name. Her skin was the color of honey, and she wasn't afraid to flaunt it. Being a young lad of fourteen, I definitely appreciated the short shorts she traipsed around the vineyard wearing. They left little to the imagination and within hours of meeting her, I came up with any excuse I could to trail around after her.

"She was sixteen, and I guess you could say way more experienced than any other girls I knew. Because I was tall for my age, she assumed I was older. Being the bright boy I was, I didn't bother to correct her. On our second day at her parents' vineyard, Honey pulled me into one of the dim barns, away from prying eyes. We were just about to round second base when my dad busted us.

"He had no qualms about throwing me under the humiliation bus by totally blurting out my age, and that I was way too young to be fooling around in some barn. Honey was horrified that she almost got felt up by a fourteen-year-old, and stalked off after informing me I was nothing but a boy. Dad thought the situation was funnier than I did. I remember wishing a pile of wine barrels would fall on me and put me out of my misery."

Courtney had started laughing halfway through my story, and was now wiping tears of laughter from her eyes. "Oh my God, that's hilarious. The great Dalton Thompson strikes out thanks to his daddy. Now, tell me. What is your idea of second base?"

"You don't know what second base is?" I shook my head in mock disbelief.

"I know what I think second base is. I want to hear what your idea is."

"Second base is tongue action and northern touches."

"Northern touches?"

"Yeah, you know, copping a boob feel." I felt my cheeks flushing slightly. Who would ever have thought I'd be embarrassed over talking about feeling a girl up? In my defense, it wasn't normally a subject that came up with girls.

"You poor thing. So Daddy busted you before you could actually cup anything?" She smirked, obviously finding humor at my expense.

"The sad thing is I was right on the verge. The tips of my fingers had just grazed the lace of her bra when he walked in. It's not funny," I added as she started laughing again. "Okay, now it's your turn to tell me something embarrassing that happened to you."

"I was perfect and escaped any embarrassing moments unscathed."

I could tell she was full of it by the way her mouth twitched. "I don't believe you. Spill it. I told you mine. Now you tell me yours. Sharing is caring."

"Oh boy. It's getting deep in here. Did you just say *sharing is caring*?"

"I did. I can own it. Now stop stalling."

chapter nine

Courtney

Dalton found my embarrassing tale of how I'd once flashed a life-guard at a water park one summer very amusing. At least my story killed the rest of the time it took to get to our destination. I recounted how, unbeknownst to me, my chest had been on display for the world to see. I'd just gone down one of those twisty water slides when I splashed hard into the pool of water at the end. Standing at the bottom of the slide, I'd been too busy trying to get the water out of my face while making sure my hair wasn't a total wreck to worry about the cool breeze on my chest.

It was only when my friend shrieked my name that I discovered the horrifying truth. The lifeguard was standing not two feet away from me. His eyes were locked on my chest, which was insanely large for my petite fifteen-year-old body. I hit the deck like a sniper had taken me out. Ducking beneath one foot of water, I tried to stuff my goods back into my skimpy top that had seemed so perfect when I picked it out at the mall.

"So, you're telling me you didn't realize both of your . . ." He paused, searching for the politically correct term. "They were hanging completely out?" he asked, pointing to my breasts.

"Boobs. And no. Not until my friend called my name. I'm not kidding when I tell you at least an entire minute passed while Lifeguard Boy got quite the eyeful."

"Lucky guy. I bet you made his whole summer." Dalton's eyes drifted to my chest before returning back to the road.

"It was single-handedly the most mortifying moment of my life." I couldn't help joining in his laughter as he pulled into the parking lot of 12 Acres Vineyards. "I never went back, by the way."

"Trust me when I say you were probably a pool legend after that. I bet he told every guy he knew. I wish I was there."

"You were too busy being a basketball star by then. Hanging out with me was no longer cool." The words left my mouth before I could stop them and I felt like a total bitch. It didn't help to keep dragging up our past. He'd already apologized. I needed to let it go. I opened my car door, welcoming the cold blast of frigid air that smacked me in the face, swearing under my breath when I stepped out.

Dalton rounded the car and placed an arm across my shoulders, tucking me against his side. "I really am sorry." He pulled me closer as we stood in the parking lot.

I tilted my face up to look at him. "You don't have to keep apologizing. I'm a jerk for bringing it up again. We were twelve. I'm embarrassed I allowed it to color my opinion of you for so long." I ducked my head back down when a new blast of cold air hit me in the face.

Dalton covered my face with his arm, leading me toward the building, away from the wind. The size difference between us was somewhat awkward for a moment, but somehow we made it work. Surprisingly we fit like two pieces of a puzzle. I burrowed closer against him as we walked, enjoying the closeness. The smell of his cologne and the soap he used encircled my senses.

Somewhere along the way, without realizing it, I'd stopped fighting my attraction to him. It would probably be a mistake. Unintentionally or not, the chances that we would last long term were probably slim. He was destined for stardom, going places outside my comprehension. I would remain here, trying to scrape by until I could finish school and get a job that would support Mom and I.

Understanding our different destinies didn't make me pull away, though. Maybe it was the familiarity of being childhood friends or the way we both opened up during the car ride today, but being with him felt comfortable—natural. Whatever the reason, I'd decided he was worth the risk. The fact that I was physically attracted to him was icing on the cake. It was a small reminder of the feelings that had just begun to spring up when we were twelve. Of course, the attraction now was a far cry from the preteen attraction I had felt for him then. My desires now were very much in the adult capacity.

The warmth inside the building was soothing after walking from the car outside. I felt mildly disappointed when Dalton dropped his arm from my shoulders, until he reached for my hand. As we strolled along, I became hyperaware of how something as innocent as hand-holding could become somewhat erotic while sipping wine together. Dalton slid his thumb across the top of my hand in slow methodical strokes before gently caressing my pulse point. The hairs on the back of my neck felt as if they were standing on end. Each sweep of his thumb was a sensual dance with my sensitive skin, making it tingle.

It was becoming apparent to me that it might have been a bad call on my part to skip lunch. Between the scent of Dalton's cologne and the alcohol I was consuming, I was already feeling slightly intoxicated. I nibbled on a few cubes of cheese to attempt to alleviate the buzzing in my head. Dalton's breath teased my neck, making me shiver in a good way. I should have put some distance between us so I could regain my bearings, but instead I snuggled closer to him, wishing we were somewhere else with a lot fewer people around.

All the air escaped my lungs as Dalton slowly captured a bead of wine from my bottom lip with his finger. I watched with bated breath as he moved the finger to his own mouth, sucking the drop of wine. It was all I could do not to moan as my insides turned to putty.

"You need to stop looking at me like that," Dalton murmured in my ear.

"Like what?" I licked the rest of the wine off my lip with the tip of my tongue.

This time it was Dalton who groaned softly. Placing his hands on my hips, he slowly backed me into a dim corner, away from prying eyes. "Like you're thinking how great it would feel if I hoisted you up on that wine barrel table over there with your legs wrapped around my waist."

"Are you sure that's not you thinking that?" My hips responded almost instinctively as he pulled me snugly against his body. I could feel him, rock hard, pressed to my stomach. The wanting desire I had been keeping at bay from the moment he showed up at my house looking practically delectable with low-riding jeans and a black V-neck sweater that accentuated his well-toned chest was threatening to explode.

"Bet your ass it's what I'm thinking." His hands cupped my butt, pulling me close, just as his lips crushed down on mine.

I wasn't entirely sure what came over me after that. I would like to blame the wine and Dalton's tormenting caresses. One moment my feet were planted on the floor, and the next I was scaling his body like some damned horny monkey climbing a tree. Maybe it was his soft lips, or his large hands that were more than willing to get me where I wanted to be.

There was nothing tentative about our first kiss. It was hot and consuming like a forest fire. His tongue took control of my mouth like he owned it. My own tongue responded boldly as the heady taste of the wine he'd consumed teased my taste buds. Dalton's hands held me in place as I moved against him. I was close to the point of no return when the sound of a clearing throat behind us finally broke through my wine-induced sexual intoxication. Heat crept up my neck as Dalton slowly lowered me back to the floor and turned toward the manager, who looked less than pleased.

I had tunnel vision as the manager escorted us on a walk of shame out the front door. The cold air sobered me up quickly. Neither Dalton nor I said anything as we walked to his car, but I was quite sure my face was as red as a tomato. Dalton was still a gentleman, holding the car door open and then closing it once I was seated. I looked out the window so I wouldn't have to see his face as he climbed in and adjusted his seat belt. My actions were completely mortifying. To say I had behaved like a dog in heat would have been putting it mildly. Sex-starved prisoner would have been more accurate. I had totally made Dalton my prison bitch.

An unexpected bubble of laughter rose up my throat even though I was still embarrassed. I tried to clamp it down, but it escaped nevertheless. Dalton joined me in laughing. At least we could both appreciate the humor of the situation. It took several minutes to get it out of our systems. Tears streaked down my cheeks, and my stomach ached from laughing so hard.

"So, I guess we can never go back there," I finally choked out.

"I would think not, but hey, they got a good show."

"You're not embarrassed or mortified like I am?"

"Embarrassed? Are you kidding? Erotic—yes. Mortifying—no."

His words heated me from the inside out. *Erotic.* The word was heavy with meaning. "Come on. You weren't even the slightest bit embarrassed when the manager escorted us out?"

"Hell to the no. I just wish we would have been in a less conspicuous place, because I'm interested in how far it would have gone if we hadn't been interrupted." He winked at me, making me blush again. There it was, hanging out there like a golden carrot. Did he know how close I had been to the big O? Only the fact that he had called the experience erotic saved him from getting a sock in the arm.

"Yeah, well, I don't normally act like that on a first date."

"Technically this is our second date. I was expecting to get to second base tonight."

"Oh Lord. I'd say we came pretty damned close in there."

"A few seconds more and it would have been a home run," he teased. Little did he know how close to the truth his words were.

"Didn't you say your mom taught you to be a gentleman? A gentleman doesn't kiss and tell."

"That was a whole lot more than kissing, sweet stuff," he murmured, resting his hand on mine. "If it helps, I was just as into it as you."

"That does help a little."

"Are you hungry?" he asked.

"Definitely. Maybe if I'd eaten before I drank a gallon of wine, I wouldn't have tried to devour you."

"So you're telling me if I want to round more bases I shouldn't feed you?" he teased, merging into the far right lane toward the highway exit. No more than a couple miles up the road, he pulled into the parking lot of a popular Italian restaurant.

"Are you allowed to talk about baseball so much when you're a basketball player?"

"Good question. I can count on you to keep my secret, right?" He closed his door and walked around the front of the car to hold my door open. I had to admit, I was already getting used to that routine. He pulled me up from the seat so I was facing him with his long arms bracketing me on either side.

"Hmm, I don't know. That's an awfully big secret to keep. What do I get?" My eyes moved to his lips. Here we were in yet another public place and all I could think about was jumping on him again. He must have had the same thoughts since he lowered his mouth to mine. This time the kiss was probably what our first attempt should have been. It was tender and sweet and slow. So slow I thought I would melt into a puddle at his feet.

After a moment, he pulled away. "Are you sure you're hungry?"

"Yes. No." My words were a jumbled mess. "Wait, doesn't food fuel the brain? I think I might need that. I'm still feeling a little bit tipsy from the wine."

"Are you sure it's the wine you're feeling?"

"Nope. Not at all," I answered as he put his arm around me and led me toward the restaurant.

The innuendos and sexual tension that still radiated between us made dinner a very pleasant experience. Our conversation flowed easily as we exchanged first date bios. We caught up on things we had missed out on while we weren't friends. A lot of what he said I already knew since I had basically watched him from afar over the years. I almost regretted admitting that juicy tidbit considering how thrilled he looked.

Eventually the conversation moved to our classes. We each had professors who were particularly difficult.

I was happy to hear that Dalton didn't have classes like Intro to Basket Weaving. I'd heard that the school went easy on student athletes where academics were concerned. But Dalton definitely took his classes seriously and was smart. He was majoring in business, because he thought it would help him later in life after basketball ended or if, God forbid, it didn't work out for him. He was definitely realistic about the future. Not that it dimmed his aspirations.

I was no different except for our goals. He had NBA dreams, while I wanted to secure a position in a museum where I could pore over art all day. One of Dalton's admirable qualities was that he wasn't afraid of hard work, especially if it got him to where he wanted to be.

Our conversation turned playful when we started talking about animals. We both preferred dogs to cats. I confessed that my feelings weren't based on actual experience, since I'd never owned my own pet. Dalton had a tough time wrapping his brain around that one.

"So you never got a pet? Not even a gerbil or a goldfish?"

"Nope. Not even a stray cat. You remember the apartment complex Mom and I lived in. They always had a 'no pets' policy."

"That's right. I do remember that. That sucks. My parents gave me Riley for Christmas the year I turned fifteen. It was instant love. Right after our dog, Gretchen, died. Do you remember her?"

I nodded. I did remember Gretchen. She was the closest I ever came to having a pet of my own.

"She was a great dog, but Riley's special."

"Like runs-into-the-walls-and-tries-to-eat-his-own-tail special?" I teased.

"He has been known to chase his own tail, but that doesn't mean he's not wicked smart. Take his fixation with my mom's shoes and no one else's for example. We all feel he blames her for sending me away to college." He pulled his phone out to show me a picture of a beautiful golden retriever gnawing on a woman's pump.

"Maybe he just likes the taste of the leather of her shoes better. You're going to have to give me more than that."

He tapped his chin for a moment, thinking. "Got it. Riley can play basketball."

"Hmm, resorting to fibbing now?" I asked after he paid the check and helped me into my jacket.

"No, seriously. He's a good shot."

We left the warmth of the restaurant behind, moving quickly to his car.

I shook my head, climbing into the vehicle. "You're such a goof-ball."

"I'll have to prove it to you one of these days."

He smiled as he closed his door and started the car. The quiet intimate atmosphere was a bit awkward at first after the restaurant. I couldn't help thinking about our kiss at the winery. A new wave of heat washed over me as the mental picture filled my head.

By the time we pulled into my driveway and were standing outside my front door, I was torn over whether to invite him in or not. I wanted to spend more time with him, but I knew I should kiss him and send him on his way. I wasn't the type who gave it up that quickly. If I had sex with him tonight, chances were he would move on to his next conquest, and I would feel like a total tramp.

He pulled me close for a good-night kiss. His lips were warm and soft as they settled on mine. I couldn't help moaning slightly as his tongue swept into my mouth. A cold blast of wind blew against us, but I barely noticed, not wanting the kiss to end.

Dalton took matters into his own hands and pulled away. "You better get inside before you catch pneumonia. Can I see you tomorrow?"

"I work until nine."

"That's okay. We can grab a late dinner," he said as another gust of wind whipped against us.

"Okay," I answered through chattering teeth as he leaned in to give me one last kiss. This time he pushed me against the door so his body was blocking the wind. The cold became an afterthought as I felt every hard inch of him pushed against me. I struggled against my shaky resolve not to ask him in.

He pulled away. "Go inside. I'll pick you up at Gruby's tomorrow night."

My hand shook as I fumbled to get my key into the lock. He placed his hand on mine, steadying it as the key slid effortlessly into the lock.

"What do you know? It slid right in," he whispered into my ear. My knees nearly collapsed out from under me. He turned the doorknob and propelled me inside. I leaned against the door once I closed it, trying to catch my breath.

"Holy hell, that was hot."

chapter ten

Dalton

Courtney was waiting for me when I pulled up in front of Gruby's the next night. She opened the door of the restaurant and hurried to my car since the weather still sucked.

"Hey," I said, placing a long, lingering, heated kiss on her lips. It had been less than twenty-four hours since we were together, but she was all I could think about. The text messages we exchanged throughout the day didn't help matters. Now that we'd gotten past our initial hiccup, our texting had taken on a sizzling quality. I had quite the vivid imagination and Courtney had it working overtime.

Unfortunately my lack of concentration had carried over into basketball practice, earning me a chewing-out from Coach. That combined with a call from Dad had taken most of the wind from my sails. Having Court in my arms now made it all worth it. The feeling was foreign to me. I couldn't remember the last time I'd looked forward to any part of my day that didn't involve basketball.

"Hey yourself," she greeted me, breathing in a rush when I finally pulled back.

"I was thinking we could eat at this new steak restaurant I discovered a couple weeks ago."

"That sounds good. I'm starving."

"You don't munch on food at work?"

"Sometimes, but usually I don't have time. How was your day?"

"Okay," I lied. I couldn't muster up enough enthusiasm to sound convincing.

"Why does your 'okay' sound anything but okay?"

I smiled ruefully at her insightfulness but didn't answer. Lacing my fingers through hers, I changed the subject by asking about her day. I could tell she knew what I was doing but went along with it anyway. I would deal with my problems later.

Courtney seemed quite taken by the dim lighting and intimate feel of the restaurant. My hand found the small of her back as the waitress led us to a table in a secluded corner, adding to the ambience.

We sat across from each other while the hostess placed menus in front of us. Reaching under the table to adjust my jeans, I found Courtney's knee, making her gasp when I gave it a squeeze.

"Uh, enjoy," the hostess remarked, giving Courtney a sideways glance before walking away.

"Nice, creep," Courtney choked out as my hand slowly moved up past her knee.

"Very nice," I said. She reached under the table, squeezing my hand in a death grip.

"Be good," she murmured. "You don't have to move it all the way off," she added when I pulled my hand away. Courtney was cool as a cucumber, looking up to smile at the approaching waitress.

The tone of her voice indicated she had enjoyed my hand on her leg as much as I did. Maybe she wanted to continue what we had started at the winery the day before. My body responded immediately, urging me to move closer if not for the damned table. When I decided I wanted more than a friendship with her, I had no idea it would be me struggling to keep a clear head.

The entire meal felt like one long foreplay session. Courtney allowed my hand to remain on her thigh while she tortured me with the look in her eyes. Without saying a word she had me more turned on than I'd ever been in my life.

"Is everything okay?" the waitress asked, bringing Courtney another Diet Coke.

"What's that?" I asked. Her question caught me off guard. For a second, it seemed like she had read my mind.

"Is the steak cooked correctly?" She pointed to my plate. I hadn't even noticed that I had barely touched my food.

"Oh no. I mean, it's fine. I just wasn't as hungry as I thought. Can we get the check, though?"

Courtney laughed at my expense, watching the waitress, who looked at us like we were drunk.

Neither of us spoke as I drove away from the restaurant, but there was a clear sense of anticipation in the air.

I didn't help matters during the drive back to her house. My hand never stopped touching her. It seemed to have a mind of its own as my fingers stroked up and down her thigh. I had to bite back a groan when she instinctively parted her legs, giving me better access to her inner thigh. I almost ran off the road. By the time I pulled into her driveway behind Lucy, I was so turned on I was almost in pain.

Courtney must have felt the same since we both practically jumped from the car at the same time. The porch light loomed in front of us.

"You want to come in?" she asked with her hand on the door like she already knew the answer.

"You sure?" It pained me to do so, but I gave her an out.

She nodded with a finger to her lips. Taking her lead, I followed her to her bedroom, softly closing her door behind me. Her room was dark except for the moonlight streaming through the partially open curtains. It took my eyes a moment to adjust before I spotted Courtney standing next to her bed. She looked self-conscious, making me feel a little like an ass. I knew what a leap of faith it was for her to invite me in. Because of our past, she still seemed to be holding on to the notion that the two of us together would be a bad idea.

She didn't know how wrong she was about me, but I was on a mission to show her.

Originally I'd planned to play it cool and take things slow, but I had never expected what happened at the vineyard, or to be standing here now for that matter. Every signal she was sending me said that she wanted this to happen.

She stood nervously wrapping a lock of hair around her finger, waiting for me to make the first move. I closed the short distance between us without taking my eyes from hers. Without saying a word, I cupped her face and tilted it up toward me, moving slowly to ease her fears. Her lips parted with anticipation as I brought my mouth inches away from hers. She whimpered slightly. I smiled with satisfaction when she stood on her toes to close the distance between us. The moment my mouth met hers she knotted her hands in my hair. Her intent was clear. She wanted this as bad as me. Moving my hands to her waist, I lifted her off the floor as she wrapped her legs around me. I became instantly hard, rubbing against her thighs. She moaned as my hands found her ass once again before I lowered her back to the floor.

Without breaking eye contact, I reached for the hem of her sweater, lifting slowly as she raised her arms. The sweater slid effortlessly over her head and dropped to the floor. She reached forward and I watched as she seductively unclasped my jeans and then invited me to return the favor. Grasping her jeans and barely there panties together, I shimmied them down her hips until they rested at her feet. She kicked them off while she lifted my shirt as far as she could reach, and then planted a string of kisses along my abdomen, causing me to moan as I yanked the shirt over my head.

Reaching a hand behind her back, she unclasped her bra, exposing her full spectacular breasts. I honestly didn't remember taking my pants off after that, but somehow they ended up in a pile on the floor. A smile rose from her lips like she knew what I was thinking. Grabbing my hand, she guided me to her bed. That was the last time she led that night.

The moment we hit the mattress, I took control, exploring every inch of her body with my hands and mouth, smiling with satisfaction when she arched her back after I tugged hard on her nipple with my mouth. My free hand moved between her thighs, where she was wet and ready. Her knees fell apart as my finger stroked her light hair before slipping inside the dampness. Her moan smothered into my shoulder as my tongue continued to swirl around her nipple, moving at the same pace as my finger buried deep inside her. Her hips moved against my hand. I knew I had her on the verge of climax, so I gently tugged on her nipple with my mouth to help her get there. She responded by moving her hips faster and burying her hands in my hair, pulling me tightly against her breast. Before she could finish, I left her tantalizing nipple and moved to her mouth. My tongue found hers and she whimpered with need before shuddering in my arms.

She was still shaking when I rolled on a condom before entering her in one swift movement. I slid in easily, rocking against her as she worked to remain quiet so her roommates wouldn't hear us. I wanted badly to prolong the moment, but all the foreplay wouldn't allow me to stretch it out. I was ready to explode. After a few thrusts against her, I finished harder than I ever had. I collapsed, taking care not to crush her.

Her eyes slid closed as she collected her breath. "Well, that was something."

"You can say that again," I panted, resting my forehead against hers. "I feel like I just ran an hour of stair drills."

"I'll take another something, please." Her words made me laugh and did interesting things to our bodies that were still locked together.

woke up early the next morning since I had practice. The way Courtney looked wrapped in the sheets, I was tempted to skip it and give us both a pleasant morning instead. Reluctantly I forced myself to leave. If I missed a practice, shit would really hit the fan.

The last thing I needed was to give Dad another reason to ream my ass. I was still feeling the sting from being chewed out over the heart on my face.

"This is your year, Dalton. Everything we worked for is within our grasp. No NBA team is going to take you seriously if you don't stop dicking around."

"Don't you mean everything I worked for?" I rarely spoke up when Dad was giving me shit, but after ten years of hearing it, I was pissed off.

"You don't think everything I've done for you has been work? All the practices, A.A.U. tournaments, staying on top of the coaches, making sure the recruiters knew about you. You think you'd be where you are if it wasn't for me? I'll be damned if you're going to waste the talent we spent all these years building."

This was the extent of our conversations anymore. He was the reason Courtney and I had stopped being friends when we were twelve. He'd called me a fairy boy, because my best friend was a girl. He pulled me away from her and made sure all my spare time was spent on basketball. I thought once I got into Michigan he'd get off my ass once and for all. I should have known better. Now it was all about the NBA.

That was still my dream regardless of Dad's bullshit, but at times I hated it all. I could walk away, but what would that solve? That was why I enjoyed the junior summer clinics I had taught for the past few years. It drove him absolutely nuts that I would "waste my time," as he would say, but it was how I stayed connected with what I truly enjoyed about playing basketball. For the kids I coached, it was still a game. Not the business it had become for me.

With one last longing look at Courtney, who had fallen back to sleep, I crept from the house. The only thing keeping me going was that I'd be seeing her again later that night.

As luck would have it, I didn't get to see her again that night or the rest of the week. Our crazy schedules made meeting up damned near impossible. Between classes, her job, and basketball practice, I was becoming increasingly annoyed. I was tempted to duck out of practice, but Coach would send out a search party and then have my head. Especially since we had the conference tournament ahead of us. My concentration was a mess. All I wanted to do was be with Courtney. Instead I was at practice going through endless drills I could do in my sleep, and yet I also felt like I was letting the team down. They expected my leadership, and my focus was elsewhere.

Courtney didn't complain about our lack of time together nearly as much as I did. She reassured me that once the season ended, we'd have plenty of time to connect. In the meantime, we made do with endless text messages. I planned on hanging out at Gruby's on Thursday night while she worked, but with more practices and team meetings, I just couldn't find the time.

Friday, I was on a charter bus for the two-hour drive to Indianapolis for the conference tournament. The only solace I found was in Courtney's text messages.

You've only been gone for an hour and I miss you already.

Not half as much as I miss you.

I wouldn't bet on it.

How was work?

Slow tip day.

That sucks.

That's all right. We'll be busy for your game.

U work too hard.

Such is the life of a poor college student.

If I was already playing in the NBA, U wouldn't have to work another day. The text was intended as a joke, but as soon as I hit SEND, I regretted it. We'd only been together for a week.

Knowing how skittish Courtney was, I figured a text like that could send her running for cover. I was in the process of typing that I was joking when she sent a reply.

> I'm sure you'll have a whole harem of women to take care of by then. I better not quit my day job.

Obviously she was kidding, but with all the pressure I'd been feeling, it annoyed me. For whatever reason, she still doubted that I could be exclusive. Our relationship was still new, but I wondered how long I would have to work to earn her trust. To make her realize that what I felt for her was special. Somehow I would have to show her. Mom always said actions spoke a thousand words or some bullshit like that. That definitely applied to me and Courtney. I changed the topic and we continued to text for another half hour until it was time for her to get ready for work.

I didn't get a chance to text her the next day since practice bled into some media obligations and then pregame preparations. The team hit the court and as I made my way through warm-up drills, I wondered if Courtney would be watching the game at Gruby's.

"Dalton," a loud voice boomed behind me. I turned to see Dad standing near the bench. He clapped his hands, urging me to focus.

"Come on, Dalton, this is your night," Coach Riley yelled from under the basket.

"I'm cool, Coach." I launched toward the rim, spinning into a reverse dunk for good measure, which elicited a few cheers from the crowd.

Maybe it was fate, or then again, it could have just been me dragging ass, but the first quarter of the game wasn't my best effort. The second quarter wasn't much better. I was laying up enough bricks to build a house. At halftime, I got my ass handed to me by Coach, who reminded me I wasn't an NBA star yet and I'd better get to work. Collin shot me a knowing look but kept his mouth shut.

The second half went much better as I stepped up my game. That was why I was so successful. I refused to lose. The team jumped on my shoulders as I drained four buckets in a row, pushing us past the opposing team we'd been trailing the entire night.

In the end, the game came down to my final shot. For an instant, I was afraid it wouldn't fall. The ball circled the outer edge of the rim, teasing me and the onlooking fans who waited on the edges of their seats. With one final rotation, the ball rolled inward through the net. The rest of the team erupted off the bench as the cheerleaders jumped up and down in celebration.

The players clapped me on the back, waving towels in the air. Looking up in the stands, I could see Dad's frown from where I stood.

chapter eleven

Courtney

My stomach was in my throat the entire time I watched the game. Dalton was having an off night. My chest pinched uncomfortably each time he missed a shot. Watching the game surrounded by groaning fans made the experience even harder. I knew how important basketball was to Dalton and I found myself silently cheering him on. The second half of the game he seemed to come alive and they were able to pull ahead of the other team. The noise level in Gruby's went up to a whole new level as the restaurant erupted with cheers with each basket. In the end, the last shot was up to Dalton. We all waited with bated breath as the ball slowly circled the rim before sliding through the net. Everyone in the restaurant roared with approval.

Amanda gave me a crushing hug as she jumped up and down with excitement. My own happiness waned when I saw the dejected look on Dalton's face on the big screen. He was being interviewed on the crowded court by the sideline reporter, but he didn't look as happy as you would think he'd be. His shoulders slumped and his face was completely defeated as the camera showed him jogging off toward the locker room. It was obvious something was wrong.

I had to fight the urge to grab my phone from my pocket. Even if I called to check on him, he probably wouldn't answer anyway. His phone would likely be turned off. Besides, I wasn't sure he would want to hear from me. Maybe our relationship hadn't reached that point. Things were moving fast for us, but we'd only had three dates and one night of unforgettable sex. Technically we'd only been together a few weeks. I figured I'd just call him later after my shift was over.

The rest of my shift felt like I was walking underwater as the night dragged. The clock seemed to taunt me with each hour passing in slow motion. My nerves were stretched to the limit as the look on Dalton's face kept flashing in my head. It was killing me not knowing what was wrong. I was sure it was just game stuff, but they'd still won. My hand closed around my cell phone for about the hundredth time since the game ended, but I forced myself to drop it back in my pocket. I would wait.

Closing duties were like an exercise in hell. I couldn't seem to do anything right. Like spilling water all over the entryway carpet when the wheel on the mop bucket got stuck, or dumping an entire tray of premade burgers on the floor as I was trying to slide them into the industrial-sized refrigerator. By the time Amanda and I left, I was in a foul mood and anxious to drop her off so I could finally call Dalton.

I was dialing his number before Amanda had even closed the car door. I bit back a groan of dismay when it went straight to voice mail. "Shit," I muttered to my empty car.

I stepped on the gas a little too hard, spinning out as I pulled away from Amanda's dorm. I called Dalton again once I got home. It went right to voice mail. Fifteen minutes later, voice mail again. I lay on my bed and typed a frustrated text message, telling him to call me when he got a chance.

The next morning, I woke to find my message hadn't been returned. No missed calls or voice mails, either. More than a little disappointed, I tossed my phone aside and climbed from bed. A burst of energy had me stripping my bed before heading to the laundry room with an armful of linens. Once the sheets were in the wash, I headed back to my room and gave it a whirlwind cleaning. I needed something to keep my mind occupied.

After changing out of my pajamas, I tried to call Dalton again with the same result as the night before. I sent him another text message before leaving my clean room behind. The nagging thoughts creeping into my head were beginning to frustrate me. I did my best to ignore them, heading to the kitchen to grab some breakfast before going over to Mom's for the day. Honestly it probably wasn't fair to think Dalton could be giving me the brush-off once again. I was freaking out over one night of unanswered calls and text messages. There had to be a reasonable explanation.

The kitchen was noisy and crowded when I entered, tempting me to hit a drive-through instead. It was great that Indy and Misha were both in love, but seeing them wrapped around their guys first thing in the morning after the sleepless night I'd had wasn't all that appealing. Kier gave me a nod, looking uncomfortable amidst the chaos. In the small amount of time I'd spent with him, I had discovered he was quiet and not overly comfortable in loud settings. I smiled at him sympathetically before grabbing a package of Pop-Tarts and heading back to my room.

"Hey, where are you going?" Misha called after me. "Darryn decided to cook us all breakfast. Isn't he a sweetie?" she asked, patting Darryn's butt.

I snorted at her term of endearment. Darryn was known for being a badass and had even been thrown out of his last place for fighting, but he was downright docile in Misha's hands. At the moment, it was just too mushy for my stomach to handle.

"Wait, I thought I was just making breakfast for you," he joked, pulling Misha in close.

Chloe and I exchanged looks. They had it bad.

"Shoot. I'd like to stay, but my mom is expecting me." It wasn't a complete lie. Mom was expecting me, just not this early. Edging out of the kitchen, I made my escape, breathing a sigh of relief as I closed the front door behind me. I really was happy for my roommates, but at the moment I had too much drama going on in my head.

Mom was still in her pj's reading the paper when I arrived at her apartment forty minutes later. She was the only person I knew who still had the Sunday paper delivered to her house. I found her sitting on her living room couch with her legs folded up under her while she sipped her coffee.

"Hey, you're early," she said as I bent down to give her a hug.

"Things were a little crowded at Hamilton House this morning." I pulled off my jacket and tossed it on the recliner. Mom raised her eyebrows. I knew what that meant. Sighing, I picked up the jacket and walked to the closet to hang it up. Even now that I was an adult, one of Mom's looks still got me to jump into action.

Once my coat was stowed away to her satisfaction, I joined Mom on the couch and grabbed the sales ads. Not that I was a big shopper, but I liked to skim through each one. One of these days I wouldn't be a poor college student anymore, and hopefully would have the money to actually buy something frivolous. That was if I could find work after graduation. I had this terrible fear that I would finish school only to discover there were no jobs available. I was forever second-guessing my major. Art history was a narrow field, to say the least.

Mom left me to my reading for a few minutes before playing the mom card. "So, who do I need to hurt?" She set her empty coffee mug on the table.

"What?" I asked, feigning innocence. I buried my face in the newspaper. Mom always had the uncanny knack of being able to read me. She said I was like an open book and she could see my every feeling as if they were words on a page.

I sat stoically silent, willing myself to remain strong. As long as

I used the paper as a shield, she wouldn't be able to see my face. The silence stretched on, and finally I couldn't resist peeking over the newspaper to see if she'd given up. It was a classic mistake that had bitten me in the butt numerous times growing up. I should have known. Mom never gave up. Lowering the paper, I found her eyes on mine.

I made a production of dramatically sighing and folding the paper before answering. "It's no big deal."

"If it wasn't a big deal, you wouldn't be keeping it from me." That was her mom wisdom in action. There was no arguing with her reasoning.

"I'm a little confused," I finally muttered, getting up to grab a Coke from the refrigerator.

She waited until I returned with my soda before asking. "About what?"

Her question was simple enough, but it opened the floodgates. Before I knew it, I was pouring out every detail to her: Dalton's sudden interest, the text messages, the heart on his cheek that had earned him a date in the first place, and finally the look on his face after last night's game and how he wasn't returning my calls or messages. I didn't mention that I had slept with him, and luckily she didn't ask. I expected her typical parental advice about how we all learn from our mistakes, but she surprised me.

"There may be a simple explanation for what's going on. I would wait until he calls before making any snap decisions."

I looked at her incredulously. It wasn't like she was a man-hater, but she'd always kept the guys she dated at arm's length.

"What if he doesn't call?" I asked, voicing my worst fear. "He did it before."

"Oh, sweetie, he was just a boy back then. If I can bestow any of my wisdom onto you, I would encourage you to be patient. There might be things going on with him that you don't know about. After your father, I always assumed every man would hurt me like he had. When any relationship after that would encounter a bump, I would walk away without a backward glance. I thought it was the only way to protect myself from getting hurt again. The older I get, the more I see the mistakes I've made. Not only did I push away a few promising relationships, but I also passed my distrust of men onto you. You're young, and yet I already see you acting under the same assumptions I did."

I couldn't believe the words pouring out of her mouth. All my life I thought she was so strong the way she would see through the men who tried to hurt her. To hear her take responsibility felt wrong. She was just trying to protect her heart. How could she blame herself for that?

"You were always so strong."

"Honey, I wasn't strong. I was scared. Too terrified to give my heart to anyone after your father broke it. Now I'm a lonely old woman who wonders what I could have had if only I'd allowed myself to trust someone. I'm happy enough, but I feel like I missed the boat. You understand what I mean?"

"You're not old," I argued, moving to the couch to hold her hand.

"I feel old. But sometimes I'm just downright lonely."

My heart ached at her words. "I'm sorry, Mom. I didn't realize you were lonely. I can come over more often. We'll do more stuff," I said as her eyes filled with tears.

"Sweetie, you've always been so good to me. I treasure every moment we spend together, but I know you're busy with school and work. Besides, this kind of loneliness is different. I ache for companionship."

I silently gnawed on her words. In a million years, I never would have expected to hear that kind of admission from her. I'd always admired Mom for her strong sense of independence. I wanted to be like her. Now I found myself reeling, not knowing what to believe.

She changed the subject, and for the rest of the afternoon we continued to chat like we did every Sunday, but we stayed away from the sticky subject of relationships. Only when I was pulling on my jacket to leave did she tell me to take her words to heart.

The next day Dalton still hadn't called or texted. My doubts increased. Despite Mom's big revelation, I was starting to think my instincts were right. Dalton had got what he wanted from me and he had moved on. I ended up skipping classes that morning and moping around the house.

I was debating watching a *House Hunters* marathon or taking a nap when my phone finally chimed. I nearly dropped it in my haste to answer when I saw Dalton's name on the caller ID.

"Hello," I answered. My voice was harsher than I intended.

"Courtney?"

"I see you found your phone again." The sarcastic reply tumbled from my mouth before I could even think of retracting it.

I heard him sigh over the phone before he answered, "I'm sorry about that, Court. I know in light of our history that didn't come off well."

His voice sounded defeated and my sudden flare of anger completely dissipated. "What's going on, Dalton?"

He hesitated, exhaling deeply before answering, "Just a bunch of crap."

"With the team?" I sat on the edge of the couch on pins and needles waiting for him to get to the point.

"Nah, I wish. This is the same shit I've been dealing with for years. I guess you could say it finally came to a head."

"Is it anything I can help with?" My heart was starting to ache from the pain I could hear in his voice.

"You're doing it, babe. Just talking to you makes me feel so much better."

"I wish I was there," I said wistfully.

"Nah, you don't. There's nothing good about the place my mind is at right now. I would drag you down."

"Dalton, can you tell me what's wrong? Maybe talking about it will make it more manageable."

He sighed again. "It's just the same old family drama, trying to live up to the expectations of my asshole father."

"You're kidding, right? Your dad's a sports guy. Aren't you like a sports dad's wet dream? Excuse me for putting it that way, but how the hell could you not be living up to his expectations?"

He chuckled wryly. "Shit, now I do wish you were here. I like hearing you all fired up. I bet you look seriously adorable right now, all ferocious." He sounded marginally happier. "My father's just always demanded the best from me. Sometimes I think he wants my basketball career more than I do. Every once in a while I get sick of hearing his shit. That's basically what happened this weekend, but times ten." His voice trailed off.

"What happened?" I was sure I sounded pushy, coaxing him along, but I wanted him to continue opening up to me.

"I pretty much told him to fuck off."

"Wow."

"I couldn't stop myself. I've got enough going on in my head with the tournament without him coming to my room to tell me I'm fucking up by obsessing over some girl who means nothing. I lost it. I swear I wanted to rip his head off. Collin talked me down, but in the end I told him I was done with his abuse, that I was done with basketball. Coach Riley showed up. It turned into a whole thing."

"No," I gasped. I couldn't believe things could escalate to that point. To think Dalton would be willing to walk away from basketball.

"I meant it. I'll finish out the season, but I'm done trying to carry his dreams. It's stopped being fun."

"It could still be fun, Dalton," I said. "If your dad would take your not so subtle hint and back off, maybe you could start to enjoy the game again. And I'll be there, cheering you along."

"You will? I was worried you wouldn't forgive me for not calling. I just couldn't until I got my shit together. My head has been seriously messed up the last few days. I'm sorry for doing that to you, babe."

"Dalton, I understand. You don't have to apologize. Want to know the truth? I had my doubts, but that's my lame-ass insecurities."

"Damn, I got to go. Coach is calling me."

"Go. Call me when you get a chance. And, Dalton?"

"Yes?"

"I'll be watching you tonight. I expect to see you enjoying the moment. And kicking some ass."

He laughed. "You know it, babe." He went silent, making me think he'd hung up already.

"Courtney?"

"Yes?"

"Thank you."

"Hey, girl. Why aren't you answering your messages?" Amanda demanded to know when she showed up for her shift.

"Did you text me?" I pulled my phone from my apron pocket. "Crap, it's dead. I forgot to charge it after I talked to Dalton earlier. What did you need?" I asked as I plugged the phone in behind the bar. I definitely needed a charged phone.

"All I know is Collin told me you have to watch *SportsCenter* tonight."

"What time?"

She pulled her phone from her apron to check the time. "Oh hell, like now," she said, grabbing one of the remotes to change the channel on the TV that was closest to us.

"Hey," a middle-aged guy nursing his third beer tried to gripe, but he was in over his head at the moment.

"Shush," Amanda said, glaring at him.

Any other time, I would have chastised her for being rude to a customer, but my eyes were glued to the TV, where the announcer had just said Dalton's name. I wasn't sure what I had been expecting, but it definitely wasn't this. Dalton was once again sporting a painted face, but this time it was nothing but the letter *C* on his cheek.

A giggle bubbled up through me. I was certain that *C* was for me. Dalton had found a way to make sure I was there. Beer Belly Dude muttered under his breath that Dalton was turning into a pansy, which earned him another glare from Amanda.

We turned up the volume so we could hear the interview.

"Dalton, I have to ask. What does the *C* stand for?"

"All I can tell you is that it's meant for someone very special to me." With his answer, Dalton looked directly into the camera and held up his hand in the shape of the letter *C*.

The interview was short. Less than sixty seconds, but it was all I needed. With tears in my eyes, I grabbed my phone, which luckily by now was partially recharged, and sent him a message even though I knew with the game starting he wouldn't get it for a while. I just hoped he used a password for his phone, because the message was definitely for his eyes only, making it pretty clear what my plans were for him when he returned.

Three days later, the team returned home conference champions, just like Dalton promised. There was a buzz throughout Gruby's since everyone knew the team would be showing up tonight to celebrate. I bounced around the restaurant, feeling carefree and light as a feather. Dalton and I had talked a lot over the last few days and had grown even closer. He and his dad were still on the outs, but I could tell Dalton felt better after finally confronting him. He still had the big national championship tournament coming up and the team had earned a number-one seed, so expectations were at an all-time high. Somehow I knew Dalton could handle it. It was who he was. With or without the pressure from his father, Dalton was a leader. Only he knew what direction he was going to take with basketball, but he vowed it would be fun again.

I was busy dropping an order ticket off in the kitchen when I heard the whole restaurant explode into cheers. Hurrying out through the swinging door, anxious to see him, I didn't see the obstacle in front of me until it nearly knocked me on my ass. A large warm pair of hands gripped my shoulders, steadying me on my feet. Lifting my eyes, I found Dalton peering down at me, making my heart race.

"Dalton," I breathed, trying to give the appearance that I was perfectly calm. "How's it going?" I knew the question sounded stupid the moment I'd asked it.

"Uh, good."

Of course it was good. I thumped myself on the head before Dalton grabbed my hands. "Sorry. That was a dumb question. Congratulations. I'm so proud of you." My words were heartfelt. I wanted him to know that his dad might be a douche, but there were some of us who truly appreciated what he did.

"Thanks, babe." He reached down to stroke my cheek. "What time do you get off?"

"Why?" I teased him playfully, but seeing him for the first time in several days, I was thinking the same thing.

"Because the only person I want to celebrate with is right here. And the kind of celebrating I have in mind is best done without an audience."

"Let them look." I threw my arms around him as he lifted me up and planted a deep kiss on my lips. Loud cheers and catcalls erupted through the sports bar. We would never learn. "We seem to have a thing for making out in very public places," I whispered, blushing as the staff whooped with delight.

He pulled back slightly. "They're just jealous. Hey, did you catch my interview?"

"What are you talking about?"

He looked momentarily confused until I winked at him. "Always busting my balls." He chuckled. "So, I'm thinking a statement like that surely earned me some serious brownie points."

"Oh, you think so, huh? It really wasn't all that big. I mean, you're the one who said, 'Go big or go home.'" I planted a small kiss on his chin even though we were still being watched.

"Damn. You like making me earn it. Okay, you know I don't back down. I'll have to think of something else. You never did say, though. When does your shift end?"

"A few hours."

"Hell with that. I'm ready to cash in now." He lifted me into the air again. I couldn't help squealing with delight.

"You're the best girlfriend a guy could ask for," Dalton murmured before kissing me again.

My heart beat a happy dance. Dalton might be the star basketball player, but as far as I was concerned, I was the one who had gotten a slam dunk.

beneath your layers

Christina Lee

chapter one

Chloe

flipped the sign on the door to CLOSED and breathed a sigh of relief.

A bunch of college freshman had just stormed in last minute, trying on everything in creation, and then walked right out having purchased nothing. And now I was left to clean up their mess. I began by straightening the rows of cotton shirts on the front table and then I'd head back to tackle the dressing rooms.

A tap on the glass door startled me. I turned to see Blake-freaking-Davis standing outside, and my shoulders immediately stiffened. Perfectly square jaw, flawless body, and gorgeous caramel eyes. I dipped my head, focusing my attention on the shirt I was folding so he wouldn't catch my exaggerated eye roll.

He usually walked around with a cocky grin and no-cares-in-the-world attitude—except when he was sharing the same air space as me. Tonight his teeth were clenched and he appeared to be biting the inside of his cheek to keep his pained expression neutral.

The feeling is mutual, baby.

I grabbed the keys off the counter and sized up his flannel shirt, frayed cutoffs, and black work boots as I swung open the door. He must've just gotten off his shift.

"Jaclyn's not here," I said briskly. Jaclyn was Blake's aunt and the owner of the shop.

"I figured," he said, twirling his keys in his hand. "I'm a few minutes early."

"Early for what?" I bit out. "It's closing time."

"She asked me to meet her here about some project." Blake did odd jobs for Jaclyn from time to time, so that information didn't surprise me. But usually it was on the weekend when he was free from his construction job.

"Oh . . ." I stepped back to allow him entrance. "You can wait for her."

"No, you know what?" he said, edging away from the door. "Since I have extra time I'll swing by Common Grounds to grab a coffee. Be right back."

I knew Common Grounds well, since I made it my daily mission to consume as much of their iced hazelnut coffee as possible.

I was just about to push the door shut when he twisted back to look at me. "Do you, uh . . . want something?"

My jaw dropped open. First, because this was the most he'd spoken to me in like ever. Usually we just ignored each other. And second, because he was actually being considerate. "No, I'm good."

Once he was gone, I worked faster on the vintage tees table so that I could leave more quickly. The less time I had to spend with Blake, the better.

Smoothing out a Beatles T-shirt, I folded back both sleeves before creasing the sides in the exact way my grandmother had taught me years ago. I was raised in her home after my mother had become pregnant with me and left her fashion career behind.

I'd practically memorized all of my mother's portfolios, and the looks she'd created for the models in those shoots had been timeless. When the craze was low-riding pants, she'd put them in men's high-waist trousers—and pulled it off. I planned on following in her footsteps. It was what was expected of me.

Luckily we shared the same passion for style. If we didn't, I'd feel way more pressure from her than I already did to pick up where she'd left off.

I loved working at Threads and was thrilled that my professor approved it as internship credit. I needed the cash; plus it helped me keep my finger on the pulse of the industry. And Threads offered a little of everything I loved—new styles mixed with trends that stood the test of time.

Those freshmen who'd blown through here earlier didn't appreciate vintage for what it was—they thought it was just a fad. But sporting a sixties Chanel skirt and handbag was like creating fresh art in my book. Thankfully my mother and I wore the same size. She had retained her closet full of originals from back in her heyday as a wardrobe stylist in New York.

I'd never met my father, but given the hushed conversations over the past several years between the strong and independent women in my life, I thought that he was a deadbeat. My mother didn't feel men were a necessity, and I couldn't agree more. They were fun to make out with and hook up with. Come to think of it, I hadn't even experienced that hookup part in more than a year, but I could live with that. I was way too busy anyway.

Plus my mother would've gotten on my case about having a boyfriend before I finished my degree. She liked to stick her nose in every facet of my life in order to keep me on the right path. Which was sometimes *her* path. But I only had to suffer through it for another year of school before I moved to New York City to stretch my own wings.

I couldn't stand to leave the front tables disheveled. So I finished that task before I sorted through cash register receipts one last time. Soon I'd be walking back to the campus housing I shared with my three roommates to study for a merchandising test. One of the girls would have a boyfriend over—they usually did—even though the same time last year, we all had been unattached. Now I was like the third wheel, depending on who was home. But I was cool with that. Between classes and work I didn't have time for extracurricular activities.

I heard a key turn in the lock and Jaclyn breezed through the door. "Hi, hon. Did Blake show up yet?"

"He's around the corner getting coffee," I said, heading toward the fitting room. "I didn't realize you were coming back tonight."

"Last-minute idea," she said.

I began picking up discarded pieces of clothing off the floor and placing them on hangers.

"Chloe, I e-mailed Professor Jenkins with an idea for your final project today," Jaclyn said, handing me the last two hangers off the rack. "She was completely on board."

"What is it?" I gulped.

Jaclyn was the coolest boss, but she was also very demanding.

I hung the dresses on a nearby display and then we both headed toward the counter.

From beneath the register, I pulled out the fresh pack of Post-its with a stilettos watermark that I'd just purchased, so I could be ready for her. I was a meticulous list maker; it was the only way I knew how to keep organized.

"You know how we have that Made in the Arbor street sale coming up next month?" she said.

The event happened every spring and drew in huge crowds not only from this part of town but also from the surrounding counties. I rummaged around for my new packet of red ballpoint pens. I could tell this was going to be important.

"Of course. I just printed off more fliers." Which reminded me. I pulled out another list and crossed off *print fliers* with a black Sharpie. So satisfying.

"I have an idea I've been considering for a long time," Jaclyn said, tapping her finger to her chin. "I own a space around the corner on Liberty Street."

"You do?"

She nodded. "I haven't done anything with it yet and I've decided this event is the perfect opportunity."

Pen poised on my new sticky pad, I said, "I'm listening."

"I want to create a pop-up shop."

My lips parted and my heart rate accelerated. Music to my anal-retentive ears.

Before I could form coherent words, Jaclyn continued. "I want you to build the set for the sale and open the shop as if it were your own that day."

I felt a cross between excitement and utter fear of failure. "Seriously?"

"Yes, seriously," she said, looking me in the eye. "I trust you, Chloe. You're independent, hardworking, and in a short year you'll be knee deep in your own career somewhere. I have complete faith in you."

"I appreciate that." My head felt all spinny from the compliments. My mother would love hearing about this bit of news as well. Maybe it'd keep her lip zipped for a while. She was constantly asking if I'd gotten in touch with her old contacts from the business.

"So . . . what did you mean by building the set?" I asked Jaclyn. "Like go buy shelves and set them up?"

"Not exactly," she said, looking over the receipts I'd bundled together. "That's why I invited Blake here."

My stomach clenched. It was so infuriating that I could never think straight whenever I heard that name. I tried not to sound too panicked. "Because . . . Blake . . . ?"

"Opening a new space costs money and I'm still deciding if Liberty Street would be a good location for a store. So I've asked Blake to help you out." She paused to look at me. I kept my expression neutral. "He used to be a theater and design major here at the university. Now he works construction during the day. He'll be able to get wood at cost from the lumberyard and then he'll consult with you on how to build it. Sound reasonable to you?"

"Yes," I said, swallowing back my disdain. "Of course."

I didn't mention that I'd heard the rumors about Blake—that he couldn't hack his classes, so he dropped out of college. The girls in the Art and Design Building had certainly talked about it enough, with the way they had been constantly drooling over him when he was around.

After Blake fell off the radar, a part of me wanted to ask Jaclyn what had happened to him, why he quit school, but I knew it wasn't my place. She'd be hard-pressed to tell me anything about her nephew, I was sure.

"I expect you to be very involved in the building side of the project, as well as the design. You're very creative and I know the space will look amazing," she said, and then her eyes scaled down to my black pumps. "But you'll probably also have to stain and sand wood."

"Got it." I followed her gaze as she took in my outfit. I had on my favorite pair of Manolos that I scored for a sweet price off eBay.

"Do you own a pair of sneakers, Miss Fashionista?" Jaclyn appreciated my fashion sense and wore some expensive pieces of her own.

I shook my head as she reached behind the counter and pulled out a box. "Size eight, right?"

She opened the carton that contained a brand-new pair of pink Converse Chucks, like the ones we had arranged in our front window display. Pink was definitely my favorite color, but I still wasn't keen on the idea of wearing them—they *were* sneakers after all, and I didn't do sneakers.

She handed the box over. "These are on me. You'll need them."

I fingered the laces, suddenly feeling out of character. "Thanks."

Working in close quarters with somebody who irritated the hell out of me *and* wearing casual clothes? Brilliant.

"You'll be graded on creativity, organization, and overall visual presentation."

I nodded, jotting those points down. I wondered just how in the heck I was going to pull this off with someone like Blake, who didn't seem to put much stake in a career or grades. He had the potential to ruin this project for me.

"You two will probably work well together," Jaclyn said, obviously never noticing how much we tried ignoring one another. "Maybe even become friends. He could probably use one right about now."

My eyebrows shot up and when I looked at her she was lost in deep thought.

"What do you mean?"

"Oh, nothing, honey," she said, sighing. "I shouldn't have said that." She walked toward the back room, leaving me reeling.

"And don't worry, I'll speak to your mother about all of this, too." Jaclyn and my mother had attended the university together, though I wouldn't call them friends. "Since she's on the Chamber of Commerce Committee."

chapter two

Blake

rolled my neck side to side, waiting for my turn in line at Common Grounds. My muscles were definitely feeling it today from pounding nails into a frame. Physically, construction was one of the hardest jobs I'd ever had and probably one of the most underappreciated. Hell, we were building people's homes. Their foundations. Their dreams.

Aunt Jaclyn asked me to give her a hand at the store every now and then and I always did, mostly because of Mom. Aunt Jaclyn knew I needed the money and that I'd never take a handout from her or anyone else. I'd taken the year off school so I could work, to help with the mounting rehab bills. And I'd do it again in a heartbeat in order to keep Mom sober.

Besides, Aunt Jaclyn had always been good to me, and this project seemed pretty important to her. I'd have to fit time in after work in the evenings, but that didn't bother me—it would give me something else to focus on.

I stepped up to the counter. "Iced hazelnut, please."

The barista was someone I'd hooked up with briefly last year and she smiled coyly at me now.

"How's it going?" she asked.

"Good, thanks."

I hadn't gotten laid in a few weeks, but honestly, I had more important things on my mind. When I reached for my coffee, her fingers slipped over mine and her eyes told me she'd be up for more of the same if I were willing. But I pulled away before giving her the wrong impression. Caring for my mom was enough female interaction for right now.

I walked back to my aunt's shop, hoping her pretentious employee, Chloe Brighton, had already left for the night. She was cute with that wavy blond hair—a little on the short side for me—and her huge blue eyes. But she didn't dress like a regular chick her age, in jeans and T-shirts. She was always in a skirt or a dress with stilettos, like she should have been born in a different era or something. The heels always made her shapely legs stand out and that was hot, I'd give her that. But her attitude still ruined it for me.

The only time I'd seen Chloe look totally relaxed and comfortable in her own skin was this one day a few months back when she walked past the construction site of the new housing complex on First Street. Her cheeks were rosy and her mouth was lifted in a half grin—as if there was something happy she'd been thinking about just then. I'd never even seen her expression that peaceful and open, even at the design building at the university.

She had on this tight straight skirt that went to her knees and I could see the outline of her perfectly round ass. Her blouse was fitted and the buttons at the top undone enough that I could just make out the outline of her tits. Hot damn. She looked like some 1940s pinup model.

But the guys quickly got out of hand with their shouts and whistles. She glowered at them and when they began yelling shit about being uptight and needing a good fuck, I came to her defense. Instead of seeming grateful, she glared at me like I was some kind of trailer trash.

Screw her, man.

Since then I'd done a good job of ignoring her anytime she was at my aunt's shop. Not that it'd been difficult—she'd gone on snubbing me as well.

I spotted Chloe through the front window and groaned. She still hadn't left for the evening.

As I pulled open the door, Chloe regarded me like I was the nasty dirt beneath her fingernails. She looked at my drink and then her eyes darted to a similar empty cup and straw on the counter. "Is that . . . an iced hazelnut?"

"Yeah," I mumbled.

"That's exactly what I order. I take it with cream and sugar."

"Same," I said. We stared at each other like two creatures from different planets who'd found middle ground. As minimal as it was.

"Blake, honey," Aunt Jaclyn said, emerging from the back room. "Thanks so much for helping out on this project."

"Not a problem." I wondered why Chloe continued standing there. Didn't she have somewhere else to be? Like maybe out with her snooty fashion friends?

"So, we have the street sale coming up and Chloe needs a final project for her internship," she said. My head snapped up to gape at Chloe. She was biting her lip, looking all panicky. *No way.* "I figured you guys could team up. You'd be helping both of us out."

Neither of us spoke as we each tried looking elsewhere. Me—at the wall; her at those damned sticky pads she was always carrying around.

"Let's walk down and check out the space," Aunt Jaclyn said, grabbing her keys from the counter. "Then I'll leave you two alone to discuss your plan of action."

My shoulders slumped as I followed Aunt Jaclyn to the door. Then I reluctantly turned to hold it open for Chloe. Eyes cast down, her shoulder brushed against my chest as she passed by and I could smell her strawberry shampoo or lip gloss or something.

On the first step of the stoop, her heel caught on a nail and she stumbled. Before she went sailing, my instincts kicked in, and I hooked my arm around her waist to keep her standing. As soon as our eyes met, she bristled against me. I should have just let her fall on her damned face.

"I . . . um," she said. God, this chick did not know how to show gratitude. This was the second time I'd helped her and she couldn't even say thank you.

My biceps was right below her ample chest and I let go of her like she'd been on fire. "Maybe you should wear more practical shoes."

She rolled her eyes. "Whatever. You wouldn't know fashion if it smacked you over the head."

I shrugged. "At least I can keep myself upright."

She kept going as her cheeks tinged pink. I'd shut her up. *Good.*

She turned suddenly and headed back toward the door. Over her shoulder she said, "Wait, Jaclyn, I forgot my notepad."

My aunt stopped one storefront down to wait for us and I smirked as I held the door open for Chloe again. Her and those ridiculous sticky pads. You'd have to be blind to miss the lists she always left everywhere around the store.

She glared at me. "What?"

"Nothing." Her cheeks darkened further and I had to admit that I liked pushing her buttons.

"You making fun of me?" Her eyes narrowed. "At least I know how to *take* notes."

Ouch, what a bitch.

"I don't need notes," I spat out. "I can remember everything in my head."

She strode over the threshold into the store. "That explains a lot."

We walked the rest of the way in silence. Aunt Jaclyn opened the new space and we stepped inside. It was a bit of a mess with boxes, old fixtures, and paint swatches strewn about. We'd need to clear it out before we could build or decorate much of anything.

"All yours." Aunt Jaclyn dangled the keys in front of Chloe. "I'm heading out. You're welcome to any props I have in the back room of either shop."

After she left, the room grew so quiet you could hear the voices coming from the deli next door. We stood speechless side by side, staring at the clutter in front of us.

"So, what are your ideas?" I said, trying to move us along so I didn't have to spend one more minute with a person I didn't care for.

"Considering I just got the info five minutes before you walked back through the door," she said, opening her notes to a fresh page, "I'm still formulating it in my head."

"You want my two cents?" I asked, shoving my hands into the back pockets of my jeans.

"No," she said too quickly. And then she turned to me, grinding her teeth. "I mean, sure."

"Obviously we need to clear this mess first. I can bring a workhorse, tools, a circular saw, and the lumber," I said, moving through the space around a couple of boxes. "You just need to tell me what your vision is so I can get to work."

"Makes sense, I suppose," she said, clutching that pad of paper like it was her lifeline. Probably was, seeing how uptight she was.

"So, what does your schedule look like the next few days?" I asked.

"*Classes,*" she said, her fingers already sketching something on the page. "And homework. *Obviously.*"

Another dig. I'd choose the higher road and ignore that little comment. "So, when's the next time you can meet?"

"Tomorrow night, same time?" she asked as she shifted her eyes grudgingly toward mine. And then bit down on that damned lip.

"I can't tomorrow. I have . . . a thing." No fucking way was I going to share that I had a family session with my mom. "The night after next works for me."

She gave a swift nod and said, "See you then."

I turned on my heel and strode out the door.

chapter three

Chloe

My six-inch Manolos clacked all the way down the cobblestone street to the new space. For a couple of hours last night, I had sketched and planned the shop in my notebook. I was tense about showing Blake my idea because even though he frustrated the hell out of me, he also made my stomach do this weird flippy nervous thing. He was easy to dislike from a distance, but up close I felt vulnerable and probably acted like a silly little girl.

And I was so not going for it. He had the potential to ruin my grade on this assignment and I didn't know who the hell he thought he was.

I brought the pink Chuck Taylors in my bag and planned to put them on as soon as I stepped inside. They clashed horribly with my outfit today. I supposed I could have worn something else, but I looked darn good in this Prada skirt and blouse that I had gotten on sale at Nordi's. Maybe there'd been some small part of me that wanted to look my best for Blake as well. Maybe I wanted him to see me as a capable and confident woman.

When I rounded the corner, I saw Blake leaning against his truck. He must have gone home to change after work, because tonight he wore dark-wash jeans and a light blue T-shirt. His hair looked slightly damp, like maybe he'd just showered, and his fingers gripped two cups of iced coffees from Common Grounds.

As I approached, his eyes skimmed down my body and landed on my heels. His jaw ticked in irritation, but I didn't plan on allowing him to intimidate me.

When I reached him he met my gaze, straightened himself from the car bumper and thrust a container at me. "I got you a hazelnut coffee."

I looked down at my cup and saw he had added cream and maybe some sugar. He'd remembered how I took it. "Cool," I said, trying to shake away the effect the sentiment had on me.

He stared hard at me, as if willing me to say something else, before finally nodding and heading toward the door. What the hell had that been about? I dug out the key to let us inside.

Silently I opened my sack, slipped off my heels, and then laced up the sneakers. When I looked up, he was watching me with a damned twitch at the corner of his lip.

"Shut it," I said, and then yanked my notepad out of my bag.

"At least you decided to be sensible," he said as I got to my feet. Sensible. There was no use for that word in the world of fashion.

My eyebrow shot up. "I've never heard a guy complain about a woman wearing heels."

His gaze slowly slid up my legs. Great, I'd just given him a reason to check me out.

My heart beat erratically upon his inspection.

"True," he said, finally meeting my eyes. "They do make women's legs look amazing. But they also look like they might hurt."

"The things you do for fashion," I mumbled, and then jerked open my notebook, hoping to change the topic.

"I've been working on my idea the last couple of nights."

I turned to the page where I'd made all of my notes. I scanned down the list to remind myself what I'd written because suddenly my throat had gone dry. "I was thinking of an Old Hollywood theme."

He nodded and looked around the space as if picturing it. "Okay."

"I want to use old film reels and hang them in a few different spots. I figured I could pull out the yards of tape from each spool and string them all around the space. From those pipes, for instance," I said, motioning to the exposed brick wall and the industrial ducts hanging low. "Then I'll pin some things for sale on the strands, like our vintage jewelry."

His fingers rubbed along his jaw and I found myself holding my breath waiting for a response. Any response. He'd been a theater major after all, so he knew about staging. Or maybe he sucked at it or hated it. Maybe that'd been the reason why he dropped out.

"Are you a fan of old movies?" he asked.

"Well, duh," I said, trying to level my voice so I didn't sound like an excited child. "*Casablanca, Sabrina, Roman Holiday.* I want the effect to be like an old black-and-white film and the props will reflect that."

"Sounds all right, I guess . . . pretty cool idea, not that I've ever seen those classic movies," he said, and I pumped out a breath. Well, that wasn't a breaking news story. "But I've definitely been a part of stage productions that had sets from different eras."

I turned the notebook sideways to my sketch of the space. "This is what I was thinking as far as shelving goes."

He moved behind me to glance over my shoulder and I could smell his clean soap scent and a hint of cologne or aftershave. He leaned forward and I felt his breath on my neck. It'd been some time since I'd even allowed a guy to get this close. Especially a completely frustrating, albeit good-looking one. "That's a pretty good sketch."

"I *am* in the School of Design."

"Believe me, I didn't forget," he huffed. "You seem to remind me every chance you get."

I gasped and looked up at him, only to see annoyance reflected in his eyes. "I do not."

"Okay, you don't." He tugged the notebook from my fingers and I wanted to grab it back and tell him to go screw himself, but I kept myself in check.

What in the hell had he meant by that comment anyway?

He motioned with his hand. "So you're thinking an A-frame shelving unit against this wall here and then a circular display in the center?"

I nodded and twisted a lock of hair in my fingers.

"Sounds fine," he said. "There's only one thing wrong with your logistics."

"What's that?"

"It would be impossible for the kind of unit you designed to hold any kind of weight." He pointed to my drawing. "It would implode once you placed anything heavier on it—even a stack of clothes."

"I guess that's where you come in," I said, throwing up my hands. "You're supposed to help steer me in the right direction."

"You mean you trust my judgment?" He narrowed his eyes at me. "I'm not just some deadbeat that pounds nails into wood?"

My pulse picked up. "I never said that."

"You didn't have to," he scoffed. "I can see it in your expression."

I clenched my fists. "No, you can't!"

"Just drop it," he said, handing back my notes.

"No, I don't want to drop it. Tell me what in the hell you mean."

He glared at me for a long, painstaking moment before finally speaking again. "Do you remember that day a couple months ago when you walked by the construction site where I was working?" I nodded. "The guys were getting rowdy. That's what they do—they work hard all day and blow off steam by acting stupid."

I folded my arms, unsure of where he was going with this. "Nice way to make excuses for them."

"That's not what I'm trying to do. Just telling it like it is," he said, gritting his teeth. Obviously I frustrated him the same way he frustrated me.

"I could tell what you were thinking by the damned look on your face," he said, pacing around the space.

"They were being pigs," I said, trying to defend myself. No way was I in the wrong. "When guys act like that, they don't deserve my respect."

"Point taken," he said. It looked like he was going to say something else, but then he restrained himself.

"Whatever. Let's just get moving and clean this space up," he said in a clipped voice.

It sounded like he wanted to get a million miles away from me, and I still didn't understand what I'd done wrong.

I remembered that day he'd just brought up vividly. I'd been walking home from Happy Hour at Gruby's, where my roommate Courtney worked. I hadn't been out in a long time. Fact is, I rarely went out. But my other roommates, Indy and Misha, convinced me to meet them there and I had a really good time. When their boyfriends showed up, I took off to walk home, feeling pretty lighthearted.

When I turned the corner and passed this construction site, I began hearing catcalls. I scowled and ignored those hard-hatted idiots until they began shouting stuff that really struck home. Things that reminded me of rumors my only boyfriend in high school spread about me—after he took my virginity and dumped me.

"She's got a stick up that fine ass."

"Bet she's never been laid properly."

"I could show her a thing or two."

And then a voice rang out. "Guys, knock it off."

I turned toward the sound. It was Blake Davis and I was stunned into silence. He was sporting stubble, dirty fingernails, and clunky work boots. He looked so different from his casual clean T-shirt and jeans attire from his days at the university.

"Don't pretend you wouldn't do that girl in five seconds flat," the guy sitting next to him had blurted out.

Blake's gaze met mine, his eyes hard and unyielding. "Never in a million years. Not my type."

My breath had caught. His words made me feel lower than the mud on his shoe. I forced my chin up high and continued walking home. My hands shook the entire way.

Since then, I'd always wondered why his words had affected me so much.

Add that to his confrontation tonight, and I wasn't sure we'd ever be able to come to enough of a mutual understanding to work together on this project.

We spent the next hour in silence as we moved boxes to the back room. Well, technically, I slid them toward the back and he lifted and carried them. He was surprisingly strong, and as he raised each box, I couldn't help appreciating his taut and muscular forearms. Working construction obviously had its benefits.

I decided we needed a bucket and supplies to give the place a thorough scrub-down. I wrote down a list of items and headed out the door to the small market down the street that stayed open past nine. Blake followed, mumbling about getting some bottles of water.

As Blake and I moved through the aisle that displayed detergents, he pointed to the floor cleaner in my hand that had a bright pink label and said, "Did you plan to match your cleaner to your outfit?"

I gaped at the pink Converse sneakers I'd completely forgotten I was wearing. With a skirt. Like some used-up fashionista on someone's worst-dressed list.

"Stop thinking so hard," he mumbled close to my ear. "I was only joking. Lighten up."

I spun on him. "Pretty sure you could use some lightening up of your own."

Just then I heard someone call my name. I looked up and saw my mother's committee friend heading down the aisle toward me. Her heels were high, her lips bright red, and her outfit immaculately put together. I glanced at Blake as my skin broke out in a panicked sweat. Sure enough, she'd tell my mother she'd seen me out late with some guy, looking disheveled, and then I'd be subjected to the Spanish Inquisition.

Blake seemed to pick up on my rising alarm and in a huff he said, "Don't worry, princess, you can pretend not to know me and I'll do the same. Meet you at the cash register."

Before I could even react, he was gone, and my mother's friend was in my face asking me questions. I could barely concentrate because I'd been too busy thinking about Blake's words. Was I really that uptight? Why did I care so much about how I looked or what people thought about me? At what point had my life become so orchestrated?

As soon as my mother's friend was gone, I snatched a different floor cleaner from the shelf and met Blake at the front of the store, where he stood with a bucket and mop. I placed the sponges and soap on the counter and turned to look at him.

He stepped in front of me, before I could say anything else. "I've got it. You can hand my receipt in to Jaclyn so I can expense it."

I opened my mouth to protest, but his eyes tore into mine and I clamped my lips shut. "Don't even say it, princess. I make way more money than you do. Unless you're living off your daddy's trust fund or something."

I drew my hands into fists as he greeted the cashier. I stood behind him, breathing heavily and staring at the back of his head. His hair was perfectly wavy and for the first time I noticed a piercing on the top of his ear. It was a silver hoop and I had the urge to yank on it and tell him he was wrong. So very wrong about me.

We walked back in silence, me fuming beside him and refusing eye contact. As soon as I stepped back into the shop, I got busy cleaning the floors. An hour later we were both on our hands and knees scrubbing the baseboards and I was silently cursing the fact that I was getting my Prada outfit dirty. I probably did look like a princess, constantly rolling up and adjusting my skirt. It was my own dang fault for refusing to change into different clothes.

Out of the corner of my eye, I could see Blake scowling. All at once his arms shot to the back of his neck, and he began tugging his shirt over his head. His flat and tight stomach was on full display before the second shirt that was hidden beneath fell back over his abs.

I pretended not to look too long and instead took a deep breath, focusing on my task. Suddenly that same shirt was in front of my face. "Here, put it under your knees."

"What? No, I don't need—"

"Yeah, you do," he said. "I can tell you really care about your clothes. They probably cost a lot more than my damned T-shirt."

Was this his way of apologizing or making fun of me?

"It doesn't matter," I whispered.

He thrust it closer to me. "Please, take it."

I stared at his shirt a few moments more before grasping it, smoothing it out on the floor, and then placing my knees on top of it.

"It's my mistake for not bringing a change of clothes," I mumbled.

He turned away and continued working on the far wall in silence.

I wanted to redeem myself, or at least say something to break the ice. I looked back at him. "I noticed your piercing . . . um, earlier. I like it."

I held back a cringe. I was usually more of a fan of clean-cut guys.

He barked out a bitter laugh. "Really?"

"Where, um . . ." I struggled to come up with a question to keep the conversation going. "When did you have it done?"

He heaved a deep sigh. "A couple years ago . . . on a dare."

My eyebrows shot up. "A dare?"

"Yes, a dare. Bet you've never even done anything on a dare, princess," he muttered. "Bet it's too spontaneous for you."

"What the hell, Blake? Of course I have," I spat out. Now I was seething.

He squinted at me. "Yeah?"

I shrugged and met his eyes in a challenge. "And stop calling me princess."

"Fair enough." Then a devious glint registered in his eyes. "So . . . truth or dare?"

chapter four

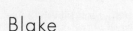

Blake

didn't know why I was being so obnoxious to Chloe; she just seemed to bring it out of me. I knew I had her now, though. No way would she play this game with me. She was too damned uptight.

"What?" she sputtered. "Here . . . now?"

"Yes, now." I laughed. She was slightly endearing when she was so flustered—when she let her prim and proper mask slip. "You've got somewhere else to be?"

"I . . . barely even know you."

I could see her pulse pounding at her neck. She was getting even more nervous. Was it because she was trapped here with someone like me or because I was calling her out of her comfort zone? I let the minutes tick. We were about to find out.

"Fine." She took a fortifying breath and then said, "Truth."

I turned away, trying to hide the pulse in my jaw. I *knew* it. She'd chosen the safer response.

"Here's hoping for honesty," I said, meeting her eyes.

She nodded and twirled a lock of her hair, looking unsure of herself again.

Something about her made me want to dig deep, to find out what she was really made of. There had to be a different person—a decent, compassionate person—under all of that restraint. I'd already seen glimpses of her. But maybe I was only headed for disappointment. "Since you didn't think I made a fair assessment earlier, tell me what you were *really* thinking the day you walked past the construction site."

Her eyebrows rose to her hairline. "Like I said, I . . . I was pissed and disgusted. When you came to my defense out of nowhere, it stumped me."

She thought she was done, but I planned on getting more out of her if I could. I just had this natural curiosity, despite being completely frustrated by her. Because when she was caught off guard—like she'd just been by my question—she became more *real* and I wanted more of that.

"And?"

"A . . . and . . . well, first, I wondered what you were doing there."

I looked down, avoiding her gaze. No way could I talk about dropping out with this girl. Unless she gave me more—showed me more.

"And second, what you said about me—the 'not in a million years, not my type' part . . . well, it . . . it *sucked* to hear you say that."

I met her eyes while her chest heaved. I had affected her back then? Because truth be told, I was completely captivated by her vulnerability right now.

"Okay," I said softly. I needed to make sure that I played this situation carefully, because I didn't want to scare her away. I cleared my throat. "I get it. Makes sense."

I got busy on the other wall, effectively dropping the subject, and letting her off the hook. Letting us both off the hook. For now.

We were silent for a few more minutes before I heard her tentative voice. "Your turn. Truth or dare?"

She probably expected me to say dare because she figured we were so different. I studied her eyes and then moved down to her lips. They were red and shiny like her tongue had just skimmed across them. She was a pretty girl. And right now, all soft and uncertain, she was even more gorgeous.

I shook that foreign thought from my head. "Truth."

Chloe's lips parted and she stared at me for a long moment until she finally recovered. I immediately regretted my decision. Especially if she was going to ask me why I dropped out of school. If she did, I probably wouldn't answer.

"Why did you . . . say that about me . . . that day?"

She looked past me to the wall, wringing her hands. It made me want to soothe her, put my fingers over hers to still them. Never in a hundred years would I have guessed that my reaction that day would still be bothering her, months later.

"I hear catcalls all day long. So when it happened again, I looked up to see who their next target was."

"Target," she said, scrunching her face into a grimace.

"And then I saw you. And I got it—you're a great-looking girl, Chloe. Plus that outfit you had on that day really . . ." I needed to stop talking before I dug myself a grave. She'd probably think I was having dirty thoughts about her. And I wasn't. At least not more than a couple of times.

"What?" Her face was relaxed and open like she truly wanted—or maybe needed—to know what I thought of her. For reasons I might never begin to understand.

"It just . . . it showed off your curves, okay? The guys were going nuts. Like big fucking apes or something." I laughed and shook my head thinking about what a bunch of dumb-asses they could be. And most of them were older than me. "Even still, they were being idiots, and girls shouldn't have to put up with shit, which is why I came to your defense."

She stared at her sneakers, a rose hue stretching across her neck and up to her ears. Then she reached out her hand and patted mine, just once. "Well . . . I guess I owe you a thanks for that."

Something in my chest gave way, like a release of my pent-up frustration over this girl.

"And . . . I wasn't really being honest when I said that about you . . . ," I said. "I was just pissed at the way you responded, like you had lumped all of us together."

She nodded and our gazes clashed for one long moment. Like we'd finally found some authentic middle ground, other than sharing similar taste in coffee. "Truce?"

She shot out her hand and I took it in my own without hesitation. Her fingers were warm and delicate, a contradiction to the impenetrable shell she'd presented this entire time. I figured this was our way of starting over and I was cool with that.

Tonight I stood in line at the Common Grounds and was about to order two iced hazelnut coffees when Chloe walked through the door in her work attire and spotted me. Her cheeks glowed pink like she'd had the same idea about getting us drinks for our night ahead.

We had worked on the space three more times these past two weeks. She progressively became more relaxed, allowing her dry sense of humor to shine—and even swapped out her outfits, so I didn't have to give any more of my T-shirts to the cause.

She'd change into jeans—designer, of course—with those pink Converse sneakers as soon as she got to the space, using the small bathroom in the back. It was hard not to notice her perfectly round ass in that tight denim, and I looked every chance I could get. I *was* a guy, after all, and I knew how to appreciate a woman's body.

But no way did I want her to know that I thought she was hot. Not that it mattered anyway. We were way too different and she wasn't the kind of girl that would be down for a casual hookup. She was very driven and expected a lot of herself, and maybe her mother did as well, given the phone calls she was constantly fielding from her.

When Chloe heard her name ring out from a table near the coffee shop door, her eyes darted around nervously and then back toward me, as if she'd wished she hadn't spotted me in the first place. A couple of impeccably dressed ladies sat drinking cappuccinos and as she trudged over to them, her head bent as if in frustration.

As I placed our drink order, I noticed how she gave one of the women a quick kiss on the cheek. She had Chloe's same coloring and eyes, so I could only assume it was her mother. Given their hushed conversations by phone, I gathered her mother liked to hear the details of her daily life. I might kill for that kind of attention.

I looked down at my dingy cutoffs and heat prickled my neck, as my instincts told me that Chloe wouldn't be comfortable with me stopping by her table. I hadn't had time to change out of my construction boots today, but at least I'd brought a fresh T-shirt to pull over my head as soon as I got into my truck. So I walked past Chloe and out the door without another glance in her direction.

When I returned to the space, I left Chloe's coffee on a large box near the shelf she had stained dark brown, and then got busy sawing more wood on the other side of the room.

Chloe and her mother seemed very close and I tried to imagine what that kind of intense attention would feel like from my own mother. Especially since I was more like the expectant parent in my family, always reminding Mom of her AA meetings and therapy sessions, checking hiding spots in the cupboards and smelling her breath for any hint of alcohol.

I gave Chloe the silent treatment when she walked through the entrance, but couldn't help noticing how quickly she clicked the lock in place and drew the shade down even farther.

"Avoiding someone?" I asked through clenched teeth.

Her back against the door, she shut her eyes momentarily as if getting her thoughts in order.

"I . . . lied to my mom," she said, glancing over her shoulder, as if she was being followed. "Told her I was going home to study instead of coming here so she didn't ask to tag along and see the space."

I made harsh markings with my pencil as I measured another piece of plywood. "Why?"

She shook her head, melancholy lacing her eyes. "I . . . just want this to be my project for now. I'll surprise her with it when we finish."

I didn't understand this girl at all. I was still seething from how unwelcome I felt in the coffee shop and I wanted to find out right this instant what her deal had been.

I stood up, releasing the measuring tape from my fingers, and stalked toward her. "Truth or dare?"

I had figured we were getting somewhere these past few days. I was beginning to enjoy working alongside her on this project. I thought we were forming a friendship, and instead she'd left me confused all over again.

The question was, why did I care so much?

As I drew nearer, her breath hitched. I stared her down as the puzzled look on her face changed to worry. She bit her lip, aware that I was annoyed about something.

"Truth," she whispered, and then blew out a shaky breath. Not having changed from her designer work clothes yet, she'd left her top three buttons open, exposing her silky skin. I could see the outline of her lacy white bra through the sheer material.

Some part of my brain went haywire and I imagined her panting against that door while I reached out to unclasp those buttons with my grimy fingers. I'd get that shiny white material all filthy and then I'd rip it down the center, exposing her to me.

Damn, where had that thought come from? It was like my anger toward her had became murky and twisted and had developed into a complete turn-on. It spurred me to step even closer to her. Like I had something I needed to prove. Except I didn't exactly know what.

"What was the shit you just pulled in the coffee shop?" I said. "Afraid to be seen with someone like me?"

"It's not that." Her shoulders sagged. "It's . . . look, maybe you haven't noticed, but my life is already scripted. My mom made huge sacrifices for me and she reminds me nearly every day. She wants me to finish what she started—making a name in the industry—and the plan doesn't include any boys."

"Christ, it's not like we're dating or anything," I said, ruffling my fingers through my hair. "We're working together on a project."

"It doesn't matter. She's in my business on a daily basis. It wasn't always like this, not until I was deciding on colleges, and lately it's been worse than ever. . . ."

It was true that it sounded that way when I'd overheard their conversations. Her mother seemed to expect a play-by-play. Still it was a stark contrast to the mess I had going on in my own family, so it was hard for me to wrap my head around.

"Jesus fuck, you're an adult, Chloe," I said. "You don't even live at home, which is more than I can say, and you have your own life on campus."

"Do you know how much ass-kissing I had to do for her to allow me to live off campus and not commute from home?" She met my gaze and her eyes blazed with resentment. "I work to help pay for my books and rent, but she and my grandmother pay the bulk of my tuition. We get a discount because she's on the board of the design school, and yeah, she throws that in my face as well."

She pushed off the door and brushed past me. "I just have one more year to be the good little daughter and then I'm leaving, moving to New York City, and I'll be far away from her."

But even she looked uncertain about her own statement. Like she was trying to be tougher and more confident than she really was. Something settled in the center of my chest. Something that felt like empathy, but I pushed it way down.

"I understand wanting to get away and live your own life, believe me," I mumbled.

She rounded on me. "Yeah? So what the heck is *your* story?"

"I'm not sure I want to tell someone like you, someone who walks around like she's got a stick up her ass. I mean, I get that you have mommy issues, but believe me, princess, it's light-years away from what I'm going through," I practically growled.

As she stood there, her eyes glassy and hurt, I had the desire to pull her against me and show her exactly how worked up she was making me.

I rubbed my fingers over my eyes. "I'm pretty sure I don't need your judgment on top of everyone else's."

She slowly shook her head in defeat, her lips seemingly unable to form any words.

I walked toward the stacked wood. "Why the hell do you care anyway?"

"Believe it or not, I'd like to get to know you," she said so quietly I almost didn't hear her. "I don't . . . I haven't . . . been around a guy in a while and you kind of . . . unnerve me."

I looked back at her and gulped down my surprise. "How?"

"I can't really explain it. It's just ever since . . . you know." She wrung her hands again like she was wound so darn tight. And the look in her eyes—like a wounded animal. My chest tightened in response.

What I wouldn't give right now to have a do-over of that one day she was referring to now. And this time, our eyes would meet and we'd find acceptance and understanding in each other's gaze, instead of so much damned misinterpretation.

chapter five

Chloe

took a brave step forward. Blake lifted his gaze to mine and I got lost in his soft caramel eyes—the same eyes I'd gotten used to seeing over these past few days and, if I admitted it, looked forward to seeing as well. "Let me start again. Truth or dare?"

Earlier he'd had this momentary look of vulnerability in his eyes—like I'd hurt his feelings in the coffee shop—and I'd never seen that from him before. I'd only ever been on the receiving end of sarcasm and frustration and brief glimpses of gentleness these last couple of weeks together.

"Truth," he mumbled, and looked down at the specs he'd drawn on the wood. Lately he only ever said *truth*, possibly because my dares had been pretty lame. By now, he'd probably grasped how courageous I really was, which was not a whole lot. My dare last week for him was to sing the tune he'd been humming out loud. He'd only rolled his eyes before belting it out.

I hesitated, looking at him a long minute before asking my question. "Why *did* you . . . leave school?"

He got this resigned look in his eyes like he knew it had been coming. I prayed he didn't think I'd overstepped bounds. Because what he
thought was beginning to matter even more to me.

"I had to drop out . . ." He heaved a long sigh. As if he'd finally
decided to let it all hang loose. "And move back home to take care of
some . . . responsibilities."

That hadn't been the answer I was expecting.

"I know a little about responsibilities," I said, keeping my voice
smooth and low. "What kind?"

He lined up the wood under the saw, ignoring my question. I
waited him out. When he simply drew the safety goggles over his eyes
and began cutting, I decided to try a different approach.

As soon as he placed the piece of wood to the side and gathered
another in his fingers, I said, "Do you . . . have any brothers or sisters?"

His hand paused on top of the lumber in order to look at me. "One
brother who's in high school."

"Does it have to do with him?" I asked, tentatively. "Do your mom
and dad need some kind of help?"

"I only have a mom, and yes, she needed help," he said, looking
back down at his task.

"I only have a mom, too," I muttered. "Never met my father."

"Well, I guess we have something else in common." He got this
faraway look in his eyes before the corners crinkled in irritation. "I've
only met my dad once. He's a musician and travels all the time. I used
to have a pipe dream that I'd join his show after graduation—as a
roadie—but screw that. Besides, I need to stay close to my family."

"Wow. I often wonder who my father is," I said, thinking about
how closemouthed my mother had been about him. I'd always fantasized that he was some famous celebrity she'd dressed for a shoot one
day. More than likely, he was some photographer or model she'd
worked with regularly.

Sadness and surprise filtered through his eyes. "You don't know?
Gosh, that would be tough to live with."

I nodded. "I haven't pressed her about it in a while. But hearing you talk about it makes me think that I should try again."

"I think you have that right, Chloe," he said. "To know where you came from. *And* to decide whether to be your own person."

"Yeah." I fingered the edge of my shirt. "The truth is, sometimes I don't even know how to act when I *am* able to step from beneath my mother's shadow."

I had no idea where that revelation had just come from. He tilted his head to the side while his gaze softened and I suddenly wanted to take the focus away from me.

"That's incredibly cool that you're helping your family," I said lamely.

He looked into my eyes as if searching for something—maybe pity—but I showed him none. All I felt at this point was admiration. Had I taken the time to get to know him earlier, I would've realized that he was kind of special.

"*My* truth is that I had to drop my classes to help with my mom's mounting medical bills. Insurance only paid for thirty days of rehab and she needed to continue outpatient treatment."

He paused and I tried to keep my lips in a neat straight line. He didn't need me reacting to his news right now. He needed support and I would try to offer it.

"I would have finished my theater degree this year, but now it's delayed." He shrugged. "I moved back home to make sure my brother was keeping up his high school grades while Mom secured an AA sponsor and attended daily meetings."

"Gosh, Blake, I'm sorry that I . . . that you . . ."

He held up his hand, effectively cutting me off. "No, it's okay. You don't need to say anything."

He trudged to the back room without uttering another word. I wasn't sure if it was in an effort to get away from me or to discontinue the conversation. I couldn't help feeling bummed that he had gone through that with his family. How brave he had been to take all of that on.

When he reemerged with a broom and dustpan to clean the saw-dust off the floor, he didn't look my way again.

He flipped to a station on his iPod, and the low sound of classic rock filled up the space. I headed in back to change into my casual clothes and then got busy staining wood.

After another thirty minutes of working in silence, his voice star-tled me. "What do you think?"

He'd already put together one of the A-frame shelves and it was leaning against the far wall.

I walked over to it and slid my fingers along one of the lower shelves. "It looks great."

"Cool," he said. "Then I'll start working on the middle piece until your stain dries."

When I looked back a few minutes later, Blake was sitting on the same box that'd been supporting his lumber, trying to fit angled pieces together. My hands were stained and messy and I bent down to change brushes, in order to garner a smoother finish.

"Truth or dare?" His voice rang out above the din of "Back in Black" by AC/DC.

I lowered my hands so I could catch a better glimpse of his eyes. He looked calm and perfectly relaxed, a contrast to an hour before.

"Truth," I said rather easily now. He knew it would be my answer anyway. But one day soon I planned to surprise him. When I got up enough nerve.

"Do you ever go up to the Cedar Mountain Theater to see those old movies that you're so fond of?" he asked in a soft voice.

I was surprised that he even knew of the place. Not many of my friends were familiar with it. The theater was tucked away in an old corner of the town. It'd been there for years and had somehow sur-vived, even though it only showcased the classics. Every now and again, it featured art deco films and probably drew a larger crowd.

"I used to go all the time," I said. "By myself, of course. Not many people I know like those movies."

He hummed a little of the tune piping through his device. "What do you like about them?"

No one had ever asked me that question. But I knew my answer straightaway. "I like how they're set up. The lighting, the mood, the music. It's all staged perfectly."

I took a step toward him without even realizing it. "Plus there's just something about those old-time romances. The special looks, the anticipation of a simple touch. I think it's way more of a turn-on than the sex scenes in modern films."

He quirked a seductive eyebrow at me like it was a question or a proposition—or just that he was being adorably playful—and I liked that side of him. I felt a rash of heat break out over my cheeks and neck.

I cleared my throat. "Your construction buddies could learn a thing or two from those movies."

His laughter echoed around the space—pure and open and real. And I loved hearing the sound of it. It made me want to summon that noise from him as often as possible. Especially in light of his somber news.

"Do you like musicals or plays?" he asked, curbing his entertainment.

"Not really a fan of live theater." I shrugged. "I like my stuff *staged*, remember?"

"There's plenty staged in live theater. Obviously," he said, motioning with his hands and reminding me in his own away that he used to build sets.

"Sure, but I don't know," I said, standing back and trying to decide if the lumber I was working on needed an additional coat of stain. "Live theater kind of makes me nervous."

"How?" His eyebrows scrunched together as he reached for the hammer and nails.

"Too many things can go wrong," I said, my voice suddenly dry. Somebody shut me up before I gave away just how unbelievably anal-retentive I truly was. Too late. "The actors can forget their lines. The backdrop can . . . fall apart."

I even sounded neurotic to my own ears.

He grinned knowingly. As if he had me figured out. And I probably already told him too much. From this point on, I'd just have to have faith that he wouldn't make fun of me.

But he had told me some personal things as well. So maybe it was about mutual trust.

After he hammered a nail into the wood, he said, "But theater is where all the magic happens."

I replaced the lid on the can of stain and reached for a rag to wipe my hands. "What kind of magic?"

"When things are spontaneous—that sensation of something happening that's so unexpected you feel it dead center in your chest—your heart is pumping hard, your stomach starts buzzing."

He made it sound so enticing. Still I wasn't buying it. But the way his lips moved over the words gave me this warm and strange twinge in my chest. He looked so alive and animated. I almost wanted to experience that, too. *Almost.*

"Sounds dreadful," I said, and he laughed hard in that unreserved way that made me feel light-headed.

"You should try it sometime," he said, reining in his amusement. "Being spontaneous, that is."

"Maybe," I said, circling the wood to catch the light for flaws.

He stared hard at me, finger brushing his chin, puzzling away at something. "Wouldn't you consider your outfits spur-of-the-moment?"

"No way," I said. "I plan what I'm going to wear the night before."

"Of course you do," he said with a twitch to his lip.

God, how pathetic was I? So basically I'd just made myself sound like some tragic spinster girl who sat at home watching old movies and deciding with great effort what clothing to lay out for myself for the next day.

I was about to tell him I was done for the night so I could go home and lick my wounds.

But then he got this solemn look in his eyes. "You're kind of like a canvas that needs to be studied." In order to prove this point, his eyes scaled painstakingly slowly from the top of my head all the way down to my toes, catching every last nerve ending on fire.

"Your lips and eyes and how you style your hair—even down to those sexy heels you wear."

My lips trembled as he stepped closer.

"You're like a work of art."

Normally I'd think he was making fun of me, but his gaze seared straight through me as he moved nearer still. I could feel my breaths flying out in fluttery whispers and I tried to tamp them down.

His fingers reached for a stray piece of hair that had come loose from my vintage barrette and he gently moved it behind my ear. Then he leaned forward and whispered, "Truth or dare?"

And I didn't know what it had been—my mood, our closeness, how we seemed to bridge the gap between us by sharing personal information, or the beginnings of my undeniable attraction to him—but I stared him dead in the eye and said, "Dare."

He looked momentarily dumfounded before relief washed over him, relaxing his features. As if I'd said the one thing he'd been dying to hear.

And then as though maybe I would change my mind, he gripped my arms and said, "I dare you to go see a theater performance with me."

"Um . . . sure," I said, relieved it was something that needed to be planned, tickets to be purchased. My head was not screwed on straight in that moment. "When?"

"Right now."

chapter six

Chloe

t'd been a long time since I let a guy lead me anywhere. But there we stood in front of a tiny lopsided playhouse that looked like it might collapse in a heap at any moment.

"I think you'll love it," Blake said, clutching my elbow and steering me to the ticket window.

I looked around the dreary and deserted streets and wondered just who in their right minds would want to come to this theater. "What is this place?"

"It's a different kind of live theater," he said almost in awe. "It's amazing. You'll see."

He led me through doorway into a very dark room, and next thing I knew, I was being jostled by this crowd of people milling around and looking toward the ceiling. No seats to be had, it was standing room only, and I felt very out of my element. Nervous about what I was about to experience. "Can't you at least give me a heads-up?"

"There's no way to describe it." His eyes were glowing with excitement. "You just have to experience it."

But as soon as the first trapeze artist came floating down from the ceiling quoting Shakespeare, I was utterly mesmerized. For the next hour these thespians-artists continued to impress me with their capabilities of swinging, tumbling, and hanging upside down all while reciting their lines. My heartbeat was erratic, my cheeks were flushed. It *was* like nothing I'd ever experienced before, and truth be told, I loved every minute of it.

Blake moved us into the far corner against a wall. He stood behind me, as if in protective mode. I felt safe with him, but also completely turned on. I could feel the heat of his body and I welcomed every nudge or bump—whether by accident or on purpose, I didn't know.

Regardless, I wanted more of it. As he explained what was happening above us, his hot breath fanned against my neck and then in my ear, and I longed for his lips to drift across my skin.

It'd been ages since I'd had this kind of feeling about a boy. Every time his fingertips came in contact with my body, my skin broke out in a fresh trail of goose bumps.

At the end of the performance, he gave me a heads-up that the artists were about to spray water into the audience and then his hands formed a shield to protect my head. But in a daring move that came from some other girl trapped inside me, I slipped from beneath his shelter. Not because I wanted to get away from him, but because I had this undeniable urge to be free, bold, alive.

I held out my arms and turned my face to the ceiling as water splashed down upon me. It was shocking and liberating and it helped douse the flame burning me alive from the inside. When I looked over my shoulder, Blake was grinning, his eyes wide with astonishment.

We spilled out of the theater in a sea of people, laughing and joking and wet. Well, at least I was wet. Blake only had a few beads of water in his hair. For the first time in forever, I realized I hadn't even looked over my shoulder to see if I recognized anybody from campus or from my mother's circle of connections. Regardless, nobody I hung out with would go to such a place off the beaten path.

"Wasn't so bad, was it?" Blake asked, almost tentatively.

I grinned. "It was pretty great."

Suddenly I wanted to know more about him. Much more. "Do you miss it?"

His steps faltered. "What?"

"The stage," I said, feeling bold again. "I could see it in your eyes—the way they lit up."

"I do miss it, but I don't stress about it," he said in a low voice. "Because I know I'll be back . . . someday."

I liked his optimism. He didn't hang on too tightly to one emotion or idea, it seemed. Given his family situation, he probably needed to be ready for the unexpected. I could use a similar lesson. My life felt too scripted—too suffocating—and though there had been a time that I'd reveled in that security, lately I felt too molded in place. Too pinned to plans. Too damned much under my mother's thumb.

The only thing I could look forward to was breaking away next year. Even the idea of that scared the hell out of me. Would I really go through with it?

Maybe next year, there would be room for a boy like Blake, when I'd be venturing out on my own in a new city and trying to make a life for myself. I had Blake to thank for showing me what I might have to look forward to—but I knew I needed to wait until the time was right. Because now? The time didn't seem right, for either of us.

A kind of melancholy set up camp, heavy in my chest, but I ignored it.

"Is set design the kind of career you've always seen for yourself?" I asked.

"I think so," he said, turning the corner to where his car was parked. "Maybe on a Broadway set or in a smaller production around here."

I couldn't imagine Blake leaving his family to seek out Broadway any time soon. Maybe we'd keep in touch after our project was over with. I'd like that.

We lapsed into a comfortable silence, each lost in our own head. I looked at my phone and saw two missed calls from my mother and was transported back to reality too soon.

"Thanks for a great night," I said after he drove me to my car, which was still parked in front of Threads. "Next time it's my choice— you get to come see a classic movie with me."

Heat crawled up my neck. I couldn't believe I'd voiced that hope out loud. Without practicing how it would sound first.

"Deal," he said without any hesitation.

And a couple of nights later that was exactly what we did. We saw the ten o'clock show at the Cedar Mountain Theater and ate buttery popcorn while I explained how much I loved all the vintage clothing in those productions. He didn't even raise an eyebrow at me.

Every time his thigh brushed against mine, I felt the urge to turn and practice one of those old-fashioned kisses that I was so fond of in these movies.

In fact, during the kissing scene, I held my breath as my imagination took over. In my side view I noticed how Blake's gazed skimmed over my face and then landed on our hands, which were so close together I could feel the electricity between our skin.

But it was so ridiculous to have those fantasies when our lives were so different—so scripted by our families, in completely different ways.

I'd even seen one of my mother's society ladies near the concession stand before the movie. I immediately pulled out the notebook I carried everywhere, just in case, and fabricated the idea of a class project. I told her the assignment involved the study of costumes and that we were meeting more of our classmates near the entrance, the exact place where Blake had set up residence.

He pretended to study the door in order to spot our friends arriving and didn't even question me about it afterward. It was as if we'd come to an understanding that our time together wasn't real; it was just the tucked-away moments we shared while working on this project and there was no use wasting time discussing it any further.

chapter seven

Blake

By the following week our space already looked fairly put together. All of the lumber had been stained and the shelving units created. The only two tasks that remained were the staging and decorating. I'd finished building days ago and I didn't *need* to help with anything else, but all I wanted to do was steal more moments with Chloe in the pop-up shop.

Even though our time together had an expiration date, this project felt as much mine as hers and I wanted to see it through. Plus it kept my mind off what was bothering me at home.

My mother was beginning to act strange—like she was hiding stuff from me. I'd been through this too many times to count and knew all the signs of someone heading down that dark road again. All I could do was make sure my brother's life wasn't disrupted. Thankfully he had a full schedule of school and sports activities to keep him busy. But he wasn't stupid—he knew the score as well as I did.

I was pretty sure Chloe figured out that I didn't need to hang around anymore, either, but she never said a word. Every day that I showed up, she looked grateful. And happy to see me. And that kept me coming.

"Can you hoist the tape over the top of this pipe? I can't reach," Chloe said.

"Bet you're missing those heels," I said, grabbing the roll of filament from her grasp.

"Bet you are, too," she countered, arching a playful eyebrow.

We'd been doing this a lot more lately—flirting with each other. It made me nearly desperate for the opportunity to touch her.

What that meant exactly, I wasn't sure. We were great in our confined space together. I was fairly certain that she didn't let anyone else know what we were up to, besides my aunt Jaclyn—and especially not her overbearing mother. Nor that we had hung out a couple of times. That bothered me at first—really bothered me. But now I got it. She had been kept on a short leash and pretty sheltered.

After hanging a few of the silver movie reels on opposite walls, I said, "Truth or dare?"

She seemed so at ease tonight, it actually surprised me when she said, "Truth."

Darn. I had hoped I could convince her to go somewhere with me on a *dare*. I'd have to try a different approach.

"Hmm . . . if I asked you to come see my friend's live band at Club Utopia . . . would you say yes?"

She immediately began twirling her hair around her fingers and I almost regretted trying to persuade her into going out with me at all.

It felt like an entire minute had passed by before she finally agreed. "Yes."

I appreciated that she was remaining open to ideas and I really liked seeing that fire in her eyes—that small flicker that was awakened when she took a chance and tried something that was outside her comfort zone.

As we made our way to the door, she swept her hands down her clothes as if to smooth them out and said, "Is this okay—what I'm wearing?"

She had on a vintage Coca-Cola T-shirt from my aunt's shop, tight jeans, and her pink Converse sneakers. I reined in my dirty thoughts about how amazing her breasts looked beneath that thin cotton material and how the denim stretched over her womanly hips.

"Actually it's perfect for where we're going."

I could practically hear her gulp and that made me grin.

When we got inside the club, she nervously looked around the lively joint. The opening band was hard rock, the speakers were blaring, and the floor was packed with fans trying to get as close to the stage as possible.

"Can I . . . get you something to drink?" I said, against her hair. She shivered, as if I'd surprised her by being so near.

She placed her mouth next to my ear and I nearly crawled out of my skin. Her lips were warm and as she spoke they buzzed against my flesh. "I don't really drink. I don't like—"

"Feeling out of control?" I said, finishing her sentence.

She nodded, biting her lip, as if I'd think she was a freak of nature, when in actuality I admired that type of self-discipline. How could I not? "No biggie. At *all*."

I'd actually been nervous about becoming an alcoholic myself, but after reading all the literature and going through this with Mom too many times to count, I knew that I could stop after one or two beers. That was the difference. Now I just needed to keep a close eye on my brother.

"Can I just take a couple of sips of whatever you're having?"

"Sure." We moved over to the bar, where I ordered my beer. She took two grateful swallows for some form of liquid courage and handed it back. She seemed to have no problem placing her lips where mine had just been, but I couldn't stop thinking about her mouth—especially her full bottom lip—as I sipped from the bottle after her.

My friend Nick, the drummer for the headline band, sought me out in the back of the bar and clapped me on the back. "Thanks for coming, man."

When I introduced Chloe, she politely said hello, but I got the impression that she wanted to disappear from his scrutiny.

After he left to begin his set, I said, "You feel out of your element here, don't you?"

She nodded. "Kinda. Sorry."

Before I could respond, the music started and the place erupted over the first song. People began yelling and swaying and Chloe looked around in awe. I stood behind her against the back wall, and just like at the live theater production, I felt this insane need to protect her, to create our own little personal zone.

But by the third song, she seemed to get into the music and was swaying back and forth as they covered a popular tune. She mouthed a few of the words, which was so damned sexy. My arm kept brushing hers as I took sips of my beer, and I felt almost desperate to tangle our fingers together.

What would she think if I did? She was such a "play by the rules" kind of girl that I was pretty sure she might freak. Still our time together was coming to an end and I felt the burgeoning desire to get closer to her, to see what this chemistry was all about. You could probably walk on the tightrope of tension between us.

After I finished my first beer, I felt a little bolder. I wasn't feeling a buzz quite yet, but my confidence and yearning to test our attraction hit its peak.

When I carefully placed my fingers on her shoulders, I studied her reaction. Her body seemed to tremble beneath my touch, and that only egged me on.

"Truth or dare?" I asked, and her eyes met mine, holding the connection strong as cement.

A rash of color sprinkled across her cheeks and she looked so damned irresistible. A momentary guise of uncertainty crossed her features before she took a deep breath. "Dare."

My lips sought her ear before she could change her mind. "Your pick. Do something spontaneous."

Her gaze swept around the bar unsteadily before something seemed to click and settle in her eyes. I could see her ticking through the idea in her brain. She nodded and then stepped forward out of my grasp.

She made her way to the middle of the writhing bodies, closer to the stage. Her back was to me and I noticed the tightly coiled tension in her shoulders. She stood there for several long minutes, watching the band and the people around her. Then to my utter astonishment, she lifted her arms in the air and began swinging her hips in time to the music.

Her ass looked sweet and if I had been standing directly behind her like I'd been moments before, I wouldn't have been able to keep my fingers from sliding around her waist and moving in close. So damned close. The front of my jeans tightened in response.

Some dude with long hair dancing next to her turned in her direction to check her out. His eyes slid from her breasts down to her crotch and I balled my fists in response. Damn, was I really feeling jealous over this girl? The same girl who had driven me up a fucking wall for so many weeks?

Now the guy stepped in front of her, shifted his hand to her hip, and matched her efforts. She bristled in response, and just as I was about to head over and push him the hell away, she brought her hand to his shoulder. In her profile, I saw her nod and grin.

After a minute more, she turned away from him and searched for my eyes across the room. She held my gaze steadily as she swayed her hips seductively in my direction.

Hell, this girl was hot. Especially when she was letting go and owning her sexuality.

She danced the entire song with this guy close behind her—a little too close—but her eyes remained glued to mine. I couldn't look away even if I tried. When the number was over and she began moving toward me, I felt something spring loose in my chest. The kind of feeling I hadn't had for a girl in months. Maybe years.

I wanted her. But I wasn't sure if she wanted me in the same way. Not outside of our time together on this project. And I needed to be okay with that.

She giggled and threw herself into my arms, pulling me in for a tight hug. "That was fun."

"Yeah?" I said against her neck. Fuck, she smelled good—like strawberry shampoo. "You looked like you were having fun. I'm surprised that dude didn't ask for your number."

She pulled back to look at me. "Why would he?"

"Because you're hot, Chloe." I drew her closer to whisper in her ear, "You might not even realize how damned hot you are. Especially when you're not thinking too hard—when you're lost in the moment."

Her lips parted and her eyes met mine. She seemed at a loss for words, so I decided to change the subject. I wanted to give her an out. Maybe I'd said too much.

I motioned for the bar. "Want me to get you a soda or a water?"

She stared at me for another long moment before she said, "No, thanks."

We listened to the next song quietly standing beside each other, lost in our own thoughts. Until she turned to me and said, "Truth or dare?"

"Dare," I said, almost breathless. Given her mood, maybe she'd give me something good this time.

"Your turn," she said. "Do something spontaneous."

My fingers trembled from wanting to touch her so badly and all I could think about was doing just that.

"You sure that's what you want?" I said, turning and backing her against the wall.

"Yes," she breathed out.

"Something spontaneous or something I've been thinking about doing for days?" I said, my lips coming closer to hers. "Maybe weeks?"

Her breath caught. "It . . . it's your call."

My head swung forward, our foreheads practically touching.

Fluttery breaths were escaping her lips. I place my arms on either side of her head and she bit down on her lip. My heart thrashed in my chest and all I could think about was how desperate I was to kiss her, and how nervous I was to blow this opportunity.

So I attempted to read her signals and they were definitely mixed. Her eyes flitted between panic and lust.

When I pinned my hip against hers, I could've sworn I heard a low moan in the back of her throat.

"Please," she rasped out. "Please . . . don't . . . Blake."

My stomach was in my throat. Fuck, either I'd scared her or I'd been reading her wrong. I leaned back to give her space, but her fingers suddenly skimmed across my waist, clenching my shirt and drawing me nearer.

"Don't what?" I asked in confusion. She was *so* fucking messing with my head.

"Don't . . ." She was panting now. "Don't *stop*."

The air rushed from my lungs and I flattened my body against hers.

Gathering her face in my fingers, I brushed my lips hesitantly across hers. "You sure?"

"Yes," she said, shutting her eyes. "Please."

Her voice was so sexy, so pleading, it was all I could do not to lift her in my arms and take her to some quiet back room. Or out to my truck. Somewhere I could have her all to myself.

I pressed my lips firmer against hers, more insistent.

When she opened her mouth and flicked the tip of her tongue out to meet mine, I couldn't help groaning. Her lips were like velvet and I grasped her neck securely, my thumbs skimming across her throat as I dipped my tongue fully inside her mouth. Her fingers moved up and wound tightly in my hair as her tongue lapped insatiably against mine.

"Fuck, Chloe." My hips ground against hers—once, twice. "See what you do to me?" I was certain she could feel my arousal now.

Our tongues were tangling in a frantic pace and she was moaning into my mouth.

"God, Blake." She opened her eyes in a panic and a lust-induced haze. "What are we doing?"

She asked this as she continued kissing me, teasing my bottom lip with her tongue. She was so contradictory. Always thinking, even while in a state of passion. Probably making lists in her head. Maybe already trying to redefine the rules.

"Close your eyes and stop thinking, goddamn it," I said in a gruff voice. "Just *feel*. Don't worry about later or tomorrow. This is me and you. Just here and now."

She responded by grinding into me. Holy hell.

My hand slid up to cup her breast, my thumb slipping across her nipple, while I nibbled on her lips—until I remembered where we were.

I drew away and looked around the bar. Though we were tucked away in a corner against the back wall, it wasn't like we were invisible. And sooner or later, Chloe would realize that as well and more than likely feel mortified.

I leaned back in and kissed her lips tenderly, combing my fingers through her hair.

"That was some dare," she mumbled.

I knew this was temporary. Only for this moment. Still I wanted to make sure she knew how amazing she was. "You are so fucking gorgeous. And sexy as hell. Don't ever forget that."

I kissed her deeply, one final time, wishing it could last all night.

chapter eight

Chloe

For the next two days I kept touching my lips repeatedly, remembering what it'd been like kissing Blake against that wall in the club. Hot damn. Had I ever been kissed that way before? Like he'd wanted to consume me? Classic movie kisses be damned!

"What's the deal?" my roommate Courtney asked, pouring herself a big old glass of vino. Courtney loved her wine. She looked at the clock above my head, probably wondering why her boyfriend, Dalton, was running late.

My other two roommates, Misha and Indy, were getting ready to go out for the night—Misha to some new Italian restaurant with Darryn, and Indy next door to her boyfriend Kier's place, where they cocooned themselves in a lot. Kier was quiet but perfect for Indy. So maybe opposites really do attract.

"What do you mean?" I asked, not meeting their eyes.

"You're walking around all dreamy," Indy said, laughing. "Must be a boy. At least I hope it's finally a boy."

I tried to deny it, but then I broke down and told them. About

Blake and the kiss. "But it was just a dare. It's not like we'd ever date for real or anything."

Misha raised an eyebrow. "Why not?"

"Because we have different . . . plans for our lives." Plus he'd made it clear that his family was a huge responsibility and that he'd taken time off from classes to focus on them. Hadn't he? My emotions and thoughts were so jumbled up at the moment.

"And he can't figure into your plans?" Courtney said, just as there was a knock at the door. She moved toward the front entrance to let Dalton inside. "He won't make it onto one of your sticky notes?"

I laughed because damn, Courtney was so right. I went upstairs to change into my jeans and a T-shirt. I was meeting Blake at the space tonight and I had a plan—one that was out of my comfort zone—and I never would have thought of it had it not been for Blake and his invitations to see live shows. I just hoped he'd agree with it and not see it as some last-ditch effort to keep him around an extra couple of days.

Even though it actually might've been.

After I arrived, I glanced around the space and was thrilled with how well it had all come together. It looked magical, really—with the Old Hollywood posters we'd hung, along with the film reels and fedora hats in different locations.

I pasted the note I'd scribbled for Blake near the doorknob before heading across the street to buy us our iced hazelnuts.

Be right back—getting our coffees. I have an idea! See you in a few minutes.

When I returned, he was standing against the far wall, one ankle crossed over the other, looking amused. And jeez, how much hotter could he get, wearing a tight pair of dark jeans with that fitted red T-shirt? He looked fresh out of the shower, which meant he'd have the clean soap scent that I couldn't seem to get enough of.

Not only that, but I was having extreme difficulty tearing my eyes away from his lips. I needed to cut that crap out and act like the other night was just what it had been—something fun and daring.

"What's so funny?" I asked, trying to rein in my smutty thoughts.

"The fact that I was finally subjected to one of your sticky notes."

"You should feel special." I winked.

I thought it was going to be more awkward between us after what had happened at the club. Instead it felt natural, outside of the electricity buzzing in the air between us. The same current that vaulted me toward him.

"So, what's up?" he asked as I handed him his coffee.

"I had a last-minute idea," I said, and then nibbled on the inside of my lip, already doubting myself.

"Do you need to consult your notes?" he asked with a glint in his eye.

"Ha, very funny." I actually had considered grabbing for my notebook on the box across the room.

"What is it?" When he straightened to step closer to me, I held my breath.

Hands shoved in his pockets, he was close enough to kiss. I forced that thought from my mind. "What do you think of the idea of building a short runway?"

His forehead furrowed. "For real?"

"Let me show you my sketch," I said, heading across the space. He followed on my heels.

I lifted the notebook and flipped to the right page. He was standing directly behind me and I could smell his fresh laundry scent. I tamped down the urge to turn and kiss him senseless. I wondered if he was having the same trouble, because he made some kind of noise in the back of his throat before covering it up with a cough.

"We can build it in the back and then move it outside during the sale," I said, spinning to look at him.

"As long as you're okay with a very basic design, shouldn't take more than a couple of nights."

His gaze darted between my lips and my eyes as a warming sensation slid from the center of my chest to the depths of my stomach.

"Yes," I said, sounding too breathy. "That'll work."

He kept his eyes fixed on my face, his expression cloaked.

"I figured we could model the clothes," I continued with some effort, trying to pull away from his heavy gaze. "Maybe it would lead to more sales."

He straightened himself, rubbing his fingers along the stubble on his chin, as if thinking it through. "You have access to models?"

"Sure, from the design college. They use models all the time and most of them are students," I said. "A few of them might jump at the chance for this opportunity."

His eyes lit up in approval. "Good thinking."

"I bet you'd do well on the runway, too." From what I'd felt the other night, he was rock solid and smooth. I tried not to allow my eyes to rove too much over his body. "Your height, your stature."

"Keep dreaming," he said, shaking his head. "Though I *have* modeled before. It's decent money."

"No way," I said, nudging his shoulder. "You are full of surprises."

"See what happens when you take the time to get to know someone?" His gaze lingered on mine, amusement dancing in his eyes.

My cheeks burned at the allegation. "Touché."

He grinned. "Your idea actually surprises the hell out of me."

I took a quick sip of my coffee. "Why?"

"You've been part of runway shows before, right?" he asked. "The mad chaos that takes place behind the scenes, trying to get the models into the next set of clothes and back in front of the audience?"

My palms felt clammy as I remembered the two shows I'd been a part of in the School of Design. I was a dresser, which meant I stood by my model's assigned rack and waited to help her between changes. I was extremely organized and had laid out my model's next outfit at just the exact time so she could slip right in. But he was right—it was sheer pandemonium back there, people yelling out sizes and number order and rushing the models to get their butts back in line.

I didn't know how my mother had done it on a regular basis. It was the one part of the business I was sure I'd absolutely avoid. While my mother had been extremely driven, I was extremely methodical.

I was cool with shopping and pulling clothes for regular shoots or shows, but throwing together this kind of production, where thinking on the fly and timing were everything, was something that made my heart jackhammer too wildly in my chest.

But if I quieted down and listened—and admitted some things to myself—I would find my own truth. That beneath all of that panicky anticipation, it absolutely *did* feel magical, to embrace the unexpected.

Just like Blake had described theater. Just like he'd shown me by taking me to a couple of performances. Sure, one was a rock-and-roll gig, but it was still live—and completely exhilarating.

And deep down, I wanted to experience that again—that unpredictable, unbridled sensation—all on my own.

"This show would definitely be run on a much smaller scale," I said. "Only one outfit change."

"Ah," he said, looking at me appraisingly. "Still, I'm proud of you for even attempting to take it on."

I could feel the color rising in my cheeks. "Thanks."

He cleared his throat. "Let me see if I can round up some stray pieces of lumber." He walked away, leaving me to catch my breath.

When he reemerged, he said, "I don't have enough here to make do. I can come back tomorrow night after a trip to the lumberyard. Sound reasonable?"

"Absolutely. And thank you," I said. His eyes seem to light up when I showed gratitude, which made me feel even more terrible about the kind of person he thought I'd been before.

"Although . . ." I bowed my head, suddenly unsure of myself and this ridiculous new idea. I didn't want to look him in the eye. "You've probably got other responsibilities you need to finally get back to. Like with your family."

"Not exactly," he said hesitantly. "Besides, it's been nice . . . keeping my mind occupied. I like being here."

I looked up and met his gaze and saw desire blazing in his indigo eyes. And it had been placed there by me, which was so hot. If I only had that one thing to take away at the end of this experience—that I'd turned this amazingly sexy guy on—that would be cool by me.

"Tonight I can help hang those curtains in the front windows, if you want."

"That would be great." I smoothed out the silky material that I'd just begun pressing. Thankfully Jaclyn had an extra steam machine in the back. It saved us time and a trip to the other store. "If you can start screwing in the brackets, I can hand you these when you're ready."

He carried a stepladder to the front of the store, where all of the windows were covered with thick butcher paper, and got to work. After drilling holes in the wall, and screwing in the brackets, I passed him the rods that were draped with freshly hung curtains.

Now all that was left was fixing them to my liking.

Stepping down the ladder, he said, "I'll trade places with you."

He held the ladder steady for me while I climbed halfway up the rungs. I gathered the material in my hands, trying to tie the one end while he watched from below.

"Shoot, this side is stuck," I said, trying to jiggle it loose from the strut.

"Here, let me help." He took a couple of steps up the ladder and placed his arms on either side of me to help pull the curtain off the nail. His chest was right up against my back, his lips near my ear, and I couldn't help it; I let out a throaty sigh.

"Chloe," he said in a rough voice.

I lowered my head in defeat and I could feel his jagged breaths against my hairline.

"I know the other night was . . . fun," he said. "But getting you out of my head during the day hasn't been so easy."

My skin pebbled from his revelation.

"Truth is—you turn me on so much. It's hard not to think about . . . touching you again. For whatever that's worth."

"Blake." His lips skimmed across my neckline and I shivered from the contact. "I've . . . never been kissed like that before. For whatever *that's* worth."

"Ah hell." His voice was thick and husky, as if he were struggling with his last measure of control. The area between my legs prickled like it had short-circuited. "Chloe, what are we—"

His sentence was effectively cut off by his phone ringing. He stepped down the ladder in a jerky motion. "It's my brother. I need to take this."

After he answered, he listened attentively and then said through clenched teeth, "What about Mom picking you up?"

He listened some more. "Don't worry, I'm on my way. Tell your coach I'll be there in ten minutes."

We made eye contact, his eyes dark and stormy, before he turned and sprinted out the door. I just nodded; there was no need for further explanation. I knew he had other pressing responsibilities, no matter how much he tried ignoring them when he was here with me.

My heart ached for what he was going through. But my body continued responding to what he'd admitted to me on the ladder.

It took the next hour for my skin to stop prickling. And even longer for me to fall asleep that night.

chapter nine

Chloe

"Truth or dare?" Blake asked casually as he sawed wood for the new runway structure. As if the response to that one question hadn't already placed us in compromising positions.

I took what had become the easier route tonight. "Truth."

Besides, it looked like there was something he had been working through in his mind. Maybe we finally needed to talk this crazy attraction thing through.

"What you said last night, about never being kissed like that before . . . what did you mean?" he asked. "When was . . . the last time you had a boyfriend?"

"In high school. He raked my name through the mud right after he wore me down to have sex with him." I sighed. "I was a virgin and we did everything else for months. And then when I finally gave in, he dumped me and spread a bunch of rumors about me being an uptight prude."

"Damn," he said. "What a bastard."

And then his eyes widened as realization seemed to sink in about what he'd said to me weeks earlier about having a stick up my ass. "Oh man, Chloe."

"It's okay. Because it's mostly been true," I said, admitting to my own faults.

"No. I'm sorry I had the wrong impression," he said. "And I'm glad we got to know each other and became . . . friends."

"Me, too," I said, relief spreading through my chest.

"I know after our time here is done . . . we won't see very much of each other." He paused and swallowed. My heart strained painfully. I was desperate to ask him why not, but then I remembered my rule about focusing on college and my career. I was the one who pretended not to be associated with him whenever I saw the women from my mother's circle, after all.

Besides, if he affected my brain this much only from a kiss, what kind of mess would I be if we tried dating? Not that he was saying he wanted to.

"But if you ever need anything . . . ," he said, his voice trailing off. "I mean, the way you transformed this space is amazing and I know you have a great career ahead of you."

"Well, you certainly helped," I said. "I couldn't have done it without you. But . . . thank you."

We were silent for a bit and then I said, "Your turn. Truth or dare?"

His cheeks lifted into a small smile. "Truth."

"Girlfriends?" I asked.

"Not really. My first love from high school pretty much stomped on my heart, and since then, I've just been dating here and there," he said. "But I also have a lot of responsibility on me right now. So I guess I don't really have the time or energy to dedicate to it."

And there it was. He had his reasons laid out as well. "Well, I definitely understand that."

"Have you dated anyone . . . since . . . ?" He stared into my eyes. "I mean, when was the last time you . . . you know, a guy made you feel good?"

"Um . . . not sure." My breaths sputtered out. "I've been with a few guys. But it's . . . been a while."

"Fuck." He squeezed his eyes closed as if painfully trying to restrain himself.

"What . . . what about you?" I asked, almost afraid of the answer. But also to keep him talking, because I was about to become a puddle on the floor from watching him alone. "When's the last time a girl . . ."

His gaze blazed into mine and then he took a step closer—so close he could've reached out and pulled me into his arms, if he'd wanted.

"Made me feel good?" he muttered. "The other night . . . with you."

"God, Blake . . ." My head rolled back and my breath became fluttery. "What are you saying? We didn't do anything besides kiss."

"But I went home knowing how your skin and your lips felt against mine and that . . . almost satisfied my fantasies for the night."

A whimper burst from my lips. "You're not the only one."

His eyes widened and he moved even nearer.

His fingers slipped up my arms, making the hairs stand on end. "Truth or dare, Chloe?"

As we stared each other down, I couldn't have answered any other way even if I tried.

"Dare," I whispered. My heart was pounding against my rib cage.

"I . . . dare . . . you . . . to close your eyes." He paused and waited for me to slide them shut. Then I felt his warm air against my lips. "And just *feel*."

I gasped and my lids fluttered open.

"Keep them shut." His voice was like a command and I responded by slamming my eyes closed.

My body began trembling. I was craving him—craving his touch. My heart was in my throat as I waited to see—to feel—what he was about to do.

Also because it was very difficult for me to give up this amount of control.

"You're so pretty," he said as his hands wrapped around the back of my neck and his lips grazed my throat. "Let me make you feel good."

It was a foreign feeling to have my eyes closed to the surrounding world and just experience someone's touch. His lips closed around my ear and I felt emboldened and alive, much like that night at the club. As his fingers slinked down my arms to my waist, I pressed my chest against his. My nipples were erect and my breasts felt dense and full.

As if he'd taken the hint, his thumbs brushed across my buds and I sighed in relief.

His fingers traveled beneath my shirt to my bare skin. "Do you like when I touch you here?"

"Yes," I said. "Please."

He groaned, and just as his hands fully cupped my breasts, his mouth captured mine in a bruising kiss. His tongue slashed past my lips as his finger moved across my back to unhook my bra.

"So sexy." In one swift motion he lifted off my shirt and then tugged off my bra. I stood before him naked from the waist up. "God, Chloe . . . you look amazing."

I kept my eyes clenched tight. It was easier that way. If I opened them, I might've chickened out.

His mouth kissed and licked down my throat to my collarbone. "Can I keep touching you?"

I nodded and then suddenly had a moment of unnerving uncertainty. The last measure of my control crumbling. "Can anybody see us?"

"The windows are covered, remember?" His mouth swiftly moved down and captured one of my nipples—maybe in order to keep my mind off the previous subject. "You're safe with me."

My knees nearly buckled from the sensation of his hot mouth on my skin. When he moved to the other side, I moaned and grasped at his hair. I didn't remember ever being this turned on in my entire life. I ground my hips against him, needing to get closer.

"Ah hell," he blurted out, and then slowly backed me against the wall. The brick felt cool against my fiery skin. All I could hear was the distant sound of the traffic buzzing by on the street and his heavy breaths at my neck. I felt secluded, protected, and unbelievably stimulated.

As his hand hovered on the button of my jeans, his lips found my ear. "Can I touch you everywhere?"

I was momentarily petrified, my knees quivering, but that gave way to my blazing arousal. All I could do was nod—my body was so bombarded by sensation.

I whimpered as he unzipped my jeans and then his hand slipped down the front of my underwear. I was so completely wet and nearly mortified that he'd soon discover that.

"Oh damn," he grunted out in a tortured voice. "You're so turned on, aren't you?"

"Completely," I said, letting go of any shame.

He pushed my jeans to my knees and then his fingers nudged inside the edges of my underwear. "Did I do this to you?"

I was shuddering and panting. "Yes."

He swore as his fingers found my center and the sensation was like being suspended off the edge of a cliff. My heart was thrashing and my pelvis was pulsing and all I wanted was to take that leap of faith. With him.

A low growl emitted from his throat and the sound was so visceral I almost let go right then and there. Almost. But still I hovered over the precipice of my own orgasm, nearly embarrassed by how long it had been and how easily I was giving up control from the simple brush of Blake's fingers.

"Have you been thinking about me in bed at night—like I've been thinking of you?"

I quavered as his fingers continued brushing over my nub and then slipped firmly inside me. "Every . . . single . . . night."

He groaned and sucked expertly on my nipples. "This moment, right here with you, is my fantasy come true."

"Oh God . . . Blake." There was an upsurge deep in my belly, like sparks sending a heated footpath up and down my legs and then biting at my center.

All it took was another swipe of his thumb for me to fully and completely detonate. He grasped on to my waist as I shook and mumbled and kept my eyelids firmly shut.

Blake kissed my neck and ear and lips as I became more fully aware of myself and my surroundings. With my lids still closed, mortification began to bear down. I was basically naked, up against a wall with Blake—in my employer's place of business.

"Open your eyes," Blake whispered against my lips.

I did so, reluctantly. I found him staring at me in wonder, his eyes bright and clear.

His thumb traced against my throat. "You're beautiful."

chapter ten

Blake

I t'd been a miserable day. That morning, I'd found my mother passed out on the couch, an empty bottle of wine hidden in the wastebasket. When I began rummaging around, I also found vodka hidden in the back of the cupboard above the stove.

I stood over the sink dumping the contents of the bottle as a storm of emotions swirled inside me: shock, anger, and defeat.

After I drove my brother to school, I nudged my mom awake. "Have you started drinking again?"

"Don't you dare accuse me of anything," she snapped.

But then I held up two empty bottles of vodka and immediately saw a flash of mortification in her eyes, before her face fell into her hands. As the realization sank in that she'd been caught and had most certainly fallen off the wagon, she began blubbering and mumbling incoherently.

We'd been here before. Several times. But the sting of it was no less wounding. Though I was beginning to become numb to this feeling of loss I'd experienced practically my entire life, this time was particularly painful, because we had come so far and I had given up so much to get here.

It was always so difficult to hear my mother's gut-wrenching sobs.

I handed over her cell phone and encouraged her to call her sponsor and attend an AA meeting today. "The counselor said this could happen, Mom. It'll be okay. You just have to do the work to get to a good place again."

"I will," she said, not meeting my eye. "I promise."

was so distracted at the construction site that I cut my finger with a putty knife. Thankfully it was Friday and I was supposed to meet Chloe tonight to put the final touches on the runway.

That girl had somehow gotten under my skin. I couldn't get her out of my fucking head. The noises she made when my fingers were inside her. I could get used to that sound every night. Damn, I was already beginning to miss her, knowing that this might be one of our last nights together.

I went home to shower and change after work and made sure my brother had gotten to his buddy's house for the night. There'd been a note from my mother that she was out with her sponsor and would be attending her second meeting of the day. Still I wondered why she hadn't answered her phone or responded to my text, so I drove past her favorite watering hole on the way to meet Chloe.

When I didn't find her car parked anywhere nearby, I blew out a breath of relief even though something still felt off. Dread had settled dead center in my chest, and my fingers trembled on the steering wheel as I imagined what I might find when I got home later that night.

The moment I stepped into the store, Chloe took one look at me and her jaw went slack. She could sense something was wrong, which didn't surprise me—anxiety was pressing in on me from all sides. We had been in this confined space together for weeks and had come to know each other's moods. Why I thought I could gloss over my feelings tonight was beyond me.

"Blake." She'd begun staining the runway black, but now she set her brush down and approached me cautiously. She wore hip-hugging skinny jeans with a vintage ABBA T-shirt. Her blond hair was loose from her usual dainty clip, the curls framing her face, and damn, she looked sexy. "Talk to me."

I momentarily shut my eyes and shook my head. For a second I was afraid she'd think it was something she'd done, but I was pretty certain she realized it had to do with something else. "No. I'm okay. Everything's okay."

"Please," she said, stepping closer. "I want to help."

"You can't help. Nobody can," I said, feeling a flash of frustration. "It's just . . . things are a mess again."

"Your mom?" Her voice was low and careful.

I scrubbed my fingers over my face. "Yeah."

She moved behind me, her fingers reaching for my shoulders. "You're so tense."

Then her hands began working some kind of magic by deftly massaging my neck and my shoulders. My arms braced the wall in front of me and I let out a moan.

"Feel good?" she said.

"Yeah." I rolled my neck back against her fingers. "Thank you."

"What else can I do?" she asked cautiously.

"I . . . I don't know." My eyes practically spun in the back of my head from her hands moving over my skin. "What you're doing is . . . *amazing.*"

Her fingers slipped beneath my T-shirt as they began kneading the muscles between my shoulder blades. "You want to tell me about it?"

"N . . . No." My voice stuttered as her hands journeyed down my spine to my waist.

"Take this off," she said in a soft and tentative voice. After I pulled my shirt over my head, she smoothed her warm fingers over my flesh, as if savoring it.

Her hands traveled to my stomach and it quivered from her touch.

I immediately felt hot and solid for her despite all the chaos going on in my life.

"Blake," she whispered. Her fingers skimmed up and down my chest and her nails lightly scratched my abdomen.

My hard-on fought against the material of my jeans. "Damn, that feels incredible."

I just wanted to get lost in this girl.

Her lips found my ear and I shivered from their closeness. "I only want to make you feel good," she said as her teeth grazed my neck and then trailed down to my shoulder. I pumped out a heavy breath. She turned me on so damned much.

When I felt her breasts flatten against my back and her hand brush over my erection, my arms flexed against the wall. I didn't even try stopping her. Because hell, I wanted her to touch me.

She unbuttoned and unzipped my jeans, and without hesitation slid her delicate fingers inside. When her small but sure hand gripped me firmly, I groaned loudly.

"Chloe. God," I strained out. "I've imagined you doing this on so many nights."

Her hot lips began sucking on the back of my neck as her fingers worked me in the front.

After so many days of pent-up sexual frustration from just being around her—smelling her, tasting her skin and lips—I was already close.

I probably should have twisted to look at her, to kiss her sweet mouth. We weren't even making eye contact, but somehow this felt so damned intimate. To have someone to lean on when everything in my life was going to shit.

Besides, I knew her pretty well by now. Had I turned to face her, she might have balked. More than likely, not seeing my eyes, my expression, made her feel brave—and I didn't want to ruin this. I needed her fingers on my skin, wanted it so damned badly.

"Christ, I love feeling your hands on me." My words spurred her on as she gripped tighter and stroked faster.

"Let go," Chloe mumbled, kissing between my shoulder blades. "Just let it all out."

And that was exactly what I did. I unleashed all of my frustration and sorrow. And I allowed my uninhibited passion for this girl to sweep me away into a mind-numbing orgasm.

chapter eleven

Blake

When I came through the door carrying two coffees the following night, Chloe was lighting the last of dozens of tea lights she had spread across the room.

It gave the space this magical, almost ethereal glow. She'd also laid down a plaid blanket and wicker basket in the center.

"Wow, what's all this?"

"I thought we'd have a picnic tonight," she said, biting her lip and looking incredibly sexy. "After we finish painting. It'll be our reward."

"Sounds great." Her actions were exceptionally sweet and considerate and I just wanted to pull her against me and kiss the hell out of her.

There would be time for that later, but first we needed to finish applying the second coat to the runway. The street sale was at the end of this week.

"How are things . . . at home?" she asked, her voice tentative.

"Um, I . . ." I shook my head. I didn't want my mood to permeate the night the way it did last time, but I guess I couldn't help it—I was currently living under a dark cloud.

"Please, Blake," she said, her gaze searing into mine. "Talk to me."

Being with Chloe the previous night had somehow helped. Like I had someone to lean on and get lost with. Maybe it was okay to allow her to be my anchor. Just for right now.

"Not much better," I said truthfully. "Mom's sponsor spent the day with her and got the treatment center involved. We have a family session in the morning to discuss the next steps to her sobriety."

"I'm sorry." Sadness filtered through her eyes. "How's your brother?"

"After his game tonight, he begged me to stay over at his friend Matt's house again," I said, thinking about how I sat there, seething in those stands, because my mother wasn't able to attend his game with me. She hadn't been to a game all week. "I was about to say no, but his parents had walked over and told me it would be fine by them."

"You're a great big brother."

"Thanks," I said. "What's new with you?"

"You mean besides the fact that my mom got on my case about not attending an art and design fund-raiser last night?"

My jaw went slack. She had been with me. Essentially taking care of me. "You ditched out on that last night?"

"I did," she said with a strong voice. "And it felt darn good."

Her grin was wide and open and I couldn't help smiling right along with her. She was fighting her own kind of battle and I wanted to be a support for her as well.

We left the second coat of paint to dry on the runway and then sat down on the blanket. She opened the basket near her knees and said, "I thought maybe we needed something strong tonight."

My eyebrows shot up as she pulled out a bottle of Baileys.

"I thought you didn't drink."

She shrugged. "I said I usually don't. But this kinda tastes like chocolate and goes great with coffee."

"Where'd you get it from?"

"My roommate Indy let me swipe it from her."

I grinned and opened our coffee lids while she changed the station on her iPod. A slow and soulful Adele song came on, and to my utter amazement, Chloe reached for my hands. "Let's dance."

We did a toast with our Baileys-laced coffees and then I pulled her into my arms as we swayed to the moody song.

Her skin was soft, she smelled like strawberries, and I felt all the tension unraveling in my chest at having her nearer. I wasn't sure how I was going to walk away from her after this week, and maybe I didn't have to.

Maybe if I got things squared away with my mom again, I could ask her out on a real date.

But for now, I just wanted to be next to her. In this moment.

I looked into the dark blue depths of her eyes. "Thank you," I said.

"For what?"

"For . . . being here for me, the last couple of nights."

"No problem. I . . . look forward to being here . . . with you."

I leaned forward and pressed my lips to hers in a heated kiss, showing her just how much I liked it, too. Within a couple of minutes our kisses became more insistent, our tongues tangling frantically as our bodies overheated.

Next our shirts came off and our bodies were molded together, chest to stomach to hips, and I was beyond turned on. I wanted to strip off the rest of our clothes so that I could feel all of her smooth skin next to mine.

"Blake," she whispered. "It's been a long time, but I want . . . I need . . ."

My stomach tightened in anticipation. "What?"

"I want to be with you . . . *tonight.*"

My breath caught in the back of my throat because I wanted nothing more in that moment than to be with her, connect with her, in that way.

I cupped her face and then deepened the kiss, my body flattening against hers more urgently. I kneeled down on the blanket and tugged her with me.

I nibbled her ear and then along her neck, making my way to her breasts. She arched up against me as I pulled one of her nipples into my mouth and then gave the other side the same attention.

"Please," she urged, grasping me through the front of my jeans.

"Oh God, Chloe," I rasped out. "Are you sure?"

"Yes, I'm sure." My mouth captured hers in a bruising kiss and we continued grinding up against each other. In another minute, both of our jeans were off and I could barely catch my breath. She was so gorgeous—kneeling there completely naked, her skin soft and glistening in the dim light.

Our hands were roaming everywhere—in hair, over chests and backsides, between legs, working each other into a panting and reckless frenzy.

She was so wet and I was so damned ready my hard-on was straining against her stomach. It'd been so long since I felt so connected to someone that I was desperate to be inside her. But I needed her to be sure.

"*Now*, Blake, please," she mumbled, while kissing my neck and gripping me in her fingers.

I reached for my wallet and pulled out the condom I'd always kept there, just in case.

I slid it over my very hard erection and then nudged her back on the blanket. I took my time kissing her soft lips, all the while looking deeply into her eyes. "You're so damned pretty, Chloe."

I positioned my head at her entrance and she shivered from the contact. I entered her partway and then paused, hissing through my teeth. She was so tight and wet and warm.

It felt incredible being inside her, so I wanted to take my sweet time.

I noticed her trembling lips and her flushed cheeks. "Are you okay?"

"Yes," she strangled out. "I'm perfect. This is perfect. Please, I want you."

I slid in farther, inch by inch, and she cried out as I filled her completely.

As soon as she became adjusted to the feel of me inside her, I began moving in and out at a solid pace, keeping eye contact with her. Everything in this moment felt so right, so amazingly fucking flawless. I didn't want it to end.

I could feel her climax building slowly—her skin pulsing, her warm center squeezing more tightly—as I reached my thumb down to roll over her swollen nub.

She yelled out my name, trembling and grasping at my hair, and I stilled myself to watch her get her release, before pumping into her more firmly to chase my own.

We stayed wrapped in the blanket for a long time afterward, just gazing into each other's eyes—talking, laughing, and stealing kisses. It was one of the most unforgettable nights of my life.

chapter twelve

Chloe

Today was the day of the Made in the Arbor street fair and I had gotten an early start to prep for the long hours. I hadn't seen Blake in a few days and was basically going out of my mind.

We'd never exchanged phone numbers, just always shown up at the space to work together. I figured his disappearing act had something to do with his mom, because of what he'd shared that last night we were together.

I squashed down the notion that he didn't return because of me—that I'd given him what he'd wanted and he was done. Or maybe it didn't live up to the fantasy he'd said he had of me. I wasn't very skilled in that department, but he certainly made me feel like I'd been.

No matter how busy I made myself, I couldn't get him out of my head—how his skin smelled like fresh linen or the way his lips fit so perfectly against mine.

Jaclyn seemed more than impressed with what we had accomplished at her other store. She said that it would be a shame to take it down and that she knew the sale would be a hit. She began officially calling the new space Fibers, which matched nicely with Threads.

I couldn't help telling Jaclyn that I was concerned about Blake and that I hoped he was okay. I was sure she could see my feelings for him in my eyes, in the emotions I was trying desperately to rein in. It must have been obvious how close we'd grown over these past few weeks.

That was probably the reason why, despite her extreme privacy, she had given me a hint that his family was indeed in full-on crisis mode again. I stopped short of asking for his number—I figured when he was ready he might reach out to me. Every time the bell above the shop door jingled open, I prayed he'd step through it, but it never happened.

I was lost working at Fibers without him. There hadn't been much left to do except attend to last-minute touches to prep for opening day, but in each corner I looked, he was there. From the filament strands wound around the pipes, the curtains that hung in the windows, to the shelves and the runway he'd built by hand, his presence was everywhere. I was lonely for him as I'd never been for any other guy.

Mom would've had a field day with that one. As it was, she'd been frustrated with me for being distant these past few weeks. I told her I was busy with the project and classes and felt bummed that I couldn't confide in her about Blake—so I had my roommates to thank for trying to lift my spirits these past few days.

My mother had arrived to the sale early and was mingling with the other shop owners and Chamber of Commerce Committee members outside. She was poised and perfect and I'd always admired her natural charisma when it came to interacting with others. I usually had to work harder at it.

I'd admit it had felt good to see her utter astonishment about what I'd created, when she first stepped inside the store. And when she told me it looked incredible, my chest ballooned with pride.

She seemed hesitant around me today, though, as if we were navigating new territory together. One that didn't include her knowing or commandeering every single facet of my life.

The fashion show was taking place at noon, when the street would be the most crowded from lunchtime traffic. Jaclyn was thrilled with my runway idea and I was able to secure some models from the School of Design. Jaclyn had called in all of her seasonal part-time help to work the sale, so there were more than enough hands to assist both inside and outside the shop.

Before I knew it, the morning had flown by and the models were showing up and heading to the back room to get instructions from the other classmates I'd roped into helping out with the show.

I'd been busy securing the edges of the runway with netting, but then I moved behind the desk to grab my notebook, which contained a running list of the day's activities. I reached for my thin Sharpie to cross off the tasks I'd accomplished, and I noticed it lying uncapped on the counter.

I mentally scolded the person who had been so careless until I saw a yellow sticky note—fresh from my pack—sitting atop my pad. Words were scrawled across in red marker, and when I read them my chest constricted, my breaths faltering.

I've missed you.

I gazed toward the sidewalk, looking for the one person I'd hoped had written that note. But the street was only riddled with customers picking through the sales racks.

I lifted the notebook and paged through my event notes with shaky fingers. As I flipped the sheet over, I found another sticky note.

I'm sorry I've been gone. Things have been a mess at home. But I thought of you every minute of every day.

My bottom lip trembled in relief. I nearly burst into tears at his revelation.

But where in the hell was he now?

I felt something bulky on the next page and found yet another note.

I keep hoping you miss me just as much and that somehow—despite your very detailed life plans—we can make this work. Please say YES.

I closed my eyes as my chest practically burst open with emotion.

I wanted so badly to make it work, and I'd only realized it at just that very moment. That what I'd been feeling so desperately these past few days was the yearning to be with him.

All the time.

Maybe Blake was outside waiting for the show to begin. I needed to find him immediately afterward. I hugged the notebook to my chest and heard Jaclyn's voice ring out.

"Are we on schedule?" she said from the rear of the store. "The models and dressers need more direction back here."

"Yes, of course," I said, swallowing thickly. "It's almost showtime."

When I passed by her, I could've sworn I saw a glint in her eye.

The back room was bordering on chaos and I seized one moment to take a fortifying breath before stepping into the middle of the floor.

Despite my initial panic, I was feeling calmer in the center of this storm—thanks in part to Blake, for opening my eyes and daring me to see what was hidden inside myself.

"There you are," Julie, one of my volunteer assistants, said. "I just wanted to double-check the order with you. Seems there's been another change." A model had bailed on us yesterday, but I was able to delete his number from the lineup.

"What kind of change?" The model in front of me was struggling with her shoe, so I bent down to help her adjust the strap. "I didn't approve of anything."

That was when I heard his voice. Low and throaty and raw. "Chloe."

My head snapped up painfully as my heart battered in my chest.

Blake was as gorgeous as ever in his relaxed jeans with freshly washed hair.

His blue eyes bored into mine. "Can you tell me what I'll be wearing?"

I straightened on shaky knees and brushed off my skirt. "What do you mean?"

"Aunt Jaclyn called," he said. "She said you were down a male model and could use some help today."

I scanned through the crowd in the back of the room and found

Jaclyn, gathering some prize baskets for the sale. When her eyes met mine, she winked.

My gaze darted to the number ten rack that we had pushed to the side last night. The clothing I had pulled to dress that model still hung there and I pumped out a breath. I could definitely make this work.

As soon as the initial shock of seeing Blake wore off, I went into action mode. "Fit him in at the end of the lineup," I threw over my shoulder to Julie. "Amanda can dress number three, but I'm dressing number ten."

I led Blake to the tenth rack and pulled it from against the back wall.

"I was going to skip this number, but since you're here . . . ," I said, grinning like an idiot now. "What are you waiting for? Strip."

He didn't even bat an eyelash as he tugged his shirt over his head and then pushed his pants down so that he now faced me in his gray boxer briefs. Yep, he'd certainly done this modeling thing before. *Hot damn.*

I caught my breath as he slid on the pair of designer jeans I held out for him, which, of course, fit like a glove.

When he had them zipped up, I finally looked him in the eye, but I couldn't help gaping at his lean chest and stomach.

His gaze stayed fixed on mine as he pulled on the tailored shirt and fastened all but the top three remaining buttons.

"Chloe." He stepped into my personal space and I tried to act professional, but I struggled to manage any bit of self-control.

My fingers were trembling; that was how badly I wanted to touch him. "I . . . I've missed you, too."

His thumb brushed over my cheek and I closed my eyes to revel in the feel of his skin coming in contact with mine. "So, does that mean *yes?*"

Now both hands held my face as he forced me to look at him. "Because not talking to you or seeing you really sucked," he said. "And I wasn't exactly sure where we stood . . . after all this was said and done."

I swallowed roughly. "Is everything okay at home?"

A flash of pain registered in his eyes. "It's getting there. Mom's back in treatment. I'll explain more later, because I just want to make today about Fibers and you."

"I'm sorry."

Oblivious to the swirl and chaos around us, we were trapped in our own little bubble. My fingers skimmed around his waist, and his fingers tunneled through my hair. "So, what do you say? Can we try to make this work?"

"Yes," I breathed out.

"Ah hell." His lips stretched across the space between us to press against mine. "I've been miserable without you."

He kissed me again, this time more firmly. His fingers grasped the back of my hair securely as if he was unwilling to let me go.

"God, Blake," I mumbled, nibbling at his bottom lip. "I've been miserable, too."

He groaned, deepening the kiss, his tongue licking over my lips and then dipping fully into my mouth. Everything happening around us faded into the background as my fingers fisted the back of his shirt and tugged him nearer.

For the first time in *ever*, I didn't care what anybody else thought. The only thing that mattered was that Blake was here and he wanted to be with me as badly as I wanted to be with him.

I tore my lips away from his, realizing just how unproductive I'd been in the last several minutes. Especially before a huge event. It was so unlike me.

I needed to call out the model order. I had a grade to earn and people were counting on me. My stomach tensed, taut with familiar panic, as I attempted to break his hold and smooth down his designer shirt. But Blake tugged me back against him for a final tender kiss.

Just then I heard a whoop from the middle of the room, and when I looked up, my three roommates, Courtney, Misha, and Indy, were standing there grinning at our display. I walked toward them and they pulled me into a group hug, congratulating me on the store and giggling about Blake. They backed away, saying they'd wait outside to see the show.

Taking a deep breath, I turned and called the lineup. This was the easy part. The timing and the dress changes were the chaotic parts. But I felt good, like I had this in the bag. I walked up and down the row to be sure clothes were straight and hair was in place on each model.

When I got to number ten, Blake grinned and laced his fingers through mine, pulling me in for a brief and chaste kiss. "Good luck. You're going to rock this."

The show went off without a hitch and I was on a high—feeling so alive and confident in my own skin as I took a bow at the end of the set to roaring applause.

As the models filtered off the stage and headed to the back room to change, I was surrounded by my roommates and other design students, who had wanted to congratulate me on a job well done.

The storefront was empty when I walked back inside, but I could still hear the buzz of the crowd from the street and customers combing through the racks that had been brought outside.

"The show was a hit. Fantastic job," Jaclyn said, rounding the corner from the dressing area, and my cheeks lifted with the swell of pride. "And what you've done to this space is simply amazing."

"Thank you," I said, heading toward her. I heard the door swing open and chatter from customers behind me, but I was riveted by the serious look in Jaclyn's eyes. There was something else she wanted to say.

"I know your plan is to move to New York City after you graduate, Chloe. But I want you to know that you have another option, too," she said, fixing a rack of dresses near the back wall. "I'm willing to offer you the job of managing this store. It belongs to you anyway and I'd like to see if this location takes off."

Hearing her offer unleashed a swirling kaleidoscope of emotions inside me. It'd been the first time I'd ever allowed the possibility of having this job as a career inhabit my brain. I really enjoyed the merchandising aspect of running a storefront, but I never saw it as an option for me—and neither did my mother.

"That's an incredible compliment," my mother's voice rang out from across the room, and my shoulders immediately hunched up. It was the tight, professional sound I'd come to recognize all too well, when she was holding herself back from being something other than polite. "I agree what she did was amazing."

She took a deep breath and I knew what was coming next. "But Chloe has classes and schoolwork and will eventually have résumés to fill out with my contacts in New York. I wouldn't want her to get bogged down with the idea of having to manage an entire store when that's not what she's been working toward."

"Chloe is excellent on the business side of things," Jaclyn said, essentially shutting my mother down. Watching two strong women going toe-to-toe was like waiting for the outcome of a tense tennis match. But I was beginning to feel like a child standing there in silence, and I needed to get my mouth unstuck. "I'm her boss and I'd like to give her this opportunity. She can make up her own mind and I'll respect whatever she decides. And I hope you will, too."

For a brief moment I was too dumbfounded to move. But I quickly got my wits about me, because I couldn't allow Jaclyn to fight my battles for me. If Blake could face the crisis in his family head-on, it was time for me to do the same.

"Mom, we need to talk," I said, effectively ending their conversation. I had to face up to my own truths, and now was the perfect opportunity to do it.

I spun to confront my own mother. The woman who made me my heart tremble and soar at the same time. I always had so much respect for her, but lately she'd become too overbearing. She needed to hear how I felt about how she'd been treating me. I had allowed it to continue for far too long. That blame was all mine.

Jaclyn simply squeezed my shoulder as she passed, her face set in quiet admiration.

I inched toward the front of the shop, my feet nearly pasted to the floor. My mother stood perfectly still, her eyebrows creased together in indignation. "How dare she think that I don't—"

"She's right, you know." My heart was hammering in my chest.

She stared at me as her face traveled through a series of emotions, from shock to sadness, and finally landing on something that resembled regret.

"The reason this is the first time you're seeing the store," I said, feeling like a traitor to my own mother, "is that I wanted to finally have something of my own."

Her shoulders drooped as her head fell forward. I didn't want to hurt her, but I needed her to know exactly how I'd been feeling.

"Please understand, Mom," I said, my voice quavering. "I know you only wanted what was best. I'm so thankful for everything you've done for me. But lately . . . you've been so insistent . . . pushy . . . and I . . . I should have spoken up sooner."

"Oh, honey." She stepped forward suddenly and pulled me into a hug. "I'm sorry. What have I done? I must have really gone overboard if you didn't even want to share what you'd been working on with me. We used to tell each other everything."

"I *did* want to share it," I said, tears burning the back of my throat. "Just not until after it was completed. I wanted you . . . to be proud of me. Proud of what I'd accomplished on my own."

"I *am* proud of you. Very proud," she said, squeezing tighter. "It's just . . . I felt you pulling away from me. And I guess I tried holding on tighter. It's like I blinked and you became this responsible young adult. I . . . I was afraid you wouldn't need me anymore."

"I'll always need you, Mom," I whispered. "Always. But you need to give me the space to make my own decisions . . . and mistakes."

"I'm beginning to understand that," she said, her voice clogged with emotion. "I . . . I'll support whatever you choose to do with your life, Chloe."

"You don't know how relieved I am to hear you say that." When I opened my eyes, I saw Blake headed from the back room with a handful of models, looking unsure of whether he should even approach.

"Blake!" I called over to him.

My mother released her hold to look behind her. "Is that him?"

"What . . . What do you mean?"

"The boy you've been spending all of your time with?" she said with a half smile. "I wasn't born yesterday, you know."

"Mom, this is Blake," I said as I motioned for him to join us. "He's worked just as hard on this space as I did. For weeks, he helped me bring it all together. All of the shelves were built by hand."

"Very impressive," my mother said.

"It's your daughter who's impressive." Blake smiled at me and then shot out his hand. "Nice to meet you. I've heard a lot about you."

"Have you?" Surprise filtered through my mother's eyes, quickly followed by relief—maybe that I didn't totally disregard her, after all.

"It's a pleasure, Blake," she said. Then she turned to me. "I'd better head back out there to the other committee members. How about dinner on Sunday? Maybe Blake can join us."

Even though I knew she probably just wanted to find out more about him, I was secretly thrilled at her offer.

"Thank you," Blake said. "I'd like that."

As my mother left the shop, Blake moved behind me and slid his arms around my waist. "Are you okay?" He pulled me firmly against him.

I smiled. "I'm actually pretty darn good."

As a group of customers entered the store, Blake spun me around and gave me a heated kiss that was too short for my liking.

"When can I get you alone?" he whispered against my lips, and my skin prickled with longing.

"Let's meet back here later tonight," I said, and his eyes ignited with desire. "I think we have a runway to christen."

....

Samantha

My phone rang with the special chime, the one reserved just for him. I rummaged around for it in my purse, which was tucked in the basket at the front of the cart as I was browsing through the aisles of Target. The grin taking over my entire face was completely uncontrollable. I just couldn't help it. Talking with him—seeing him—was always the highlight of my day.

Running my thumb across the plate, I clicked the icon where his message waited. I'd never even heard of the app until he'd convinced me I *had* to get it, teasing me I was living in the Stone Ages, which to him I was pretty sure would date all the way back to 2011. I couldn't begin to keep up with all the tech stuff he loved.

I held my finger down on the new, unread Snapchat message from *gamelover745.*

An image popped up on the screen, his face all contorted in the goofiest expression, pencils hanging from both his nostrils as he bared his teeth. I choked over a little laugh. The joy I felt every time I saw his face was almost overwhelming as it merged with the twinge of sorrow that tugged at my chest.

Quickly, I shoved the feeling off. He told me he couldn't stand for me to look at him or think of him with pity. I had to respect that. He was so much braver than me, because seeing him this way made me feel so weak.

I forced myself not to fixate on his bald head and pale skin, and instead focused on the antics of this playful boy. The little timer ran down, alerting me I only had five more seconds of the picture, so I quickly read the messy words he scrawled across the picture.

I'm sexy and I know it.

On a muted giggle, I shook my head, and I didn't hesitate for a second to lift my phone above my head to snap my own picture. Going for my silliest expression, I crossed my eyes and stuck my tongue out to the side.

So maybe the people milling around me in the middle of the busy store thought I was crazy, or some kind of delusional narcissist, but there was no place inside of me that cared. I'd do anything to see him smile.

I tapped the button so I could write on the picture.

Love you, goofball.

I pushed SEND.

Seconds later, my phone chimed again. I pressed down the plate to receive his message. This time he was just smiling that unending smile, sitting cross-legged in the middle of his bed, radiating all his beauty and positivity, and that sorrow hit me again, only this time harder.

Love you back.

Letting the timer wind down, I clutched my phone as I cherished his message for the full ten seconds, before our snap expired. The screen went blank. I bit at the inside of my lip, blinking back tears.

Don't, I warned myself, knowing how quickly I could spiral into depression, into a worry I couldn't control, one that would taint the precious time I had with him.

Sucking in a cleansing breath, I tossed my phone back into my purse and wandered over to the cosmetics section, taking my time, browsing through all the shades and colors of lip gloss. I tossed a shimmery clear one into my cart, then strolled into the shampoo aisle.

Apparently I was in no hurry to get home. It was sad and pathetic, yet here I was, twenty-three years old and passing away my Friday night at a Target.

Ben had texted me earlier saying he was going out to grab a beer with the guys and not to wait up for him. All kinds of warning bells had gone off in my head when I realized him leaving me alone for the night only filled me with an overwhelming relief. And that realization hurt my heart, because he'd always been good to me, there for me when I was broken and needed someone to pick up the pieces, patching me up and making me smile when I thought I never would again.

But with Ben? There had always been something missing. Something significant.

That flame.

The kind that lights you up inside when *the one* walks into the room. You know the one, the one you can't get off your mind, whether you've known him your entire life or he just barreled into it.

Was it wrong I craved one?

Maybe I'd be content if I'd never felt it before. If I'd never known what it was like to need and desire.

But I had. It'd been the kind of fire that had raged and consumed, burning through me until there was nothing left but ashes. I'd thought that love had ruined me, until Ben came in and swept me into his willing arms.

He'd taken care of me, a fact I didn't take lightly. I honored and respected the way Ben honored and respected me.

So maybe I never looked the same or felt the same after *he'd* destroyed something inside of me. But I'd survived and forced myself to find satisfaction with that, willed it to make me stronger instead of feeble and frail.

I tossed a bottle of shampoo I really didn't need into my cart, but it smelled all kinds of good, like coconut and the sweetest flower, and today I didn't feel like questioning my motives. In fact, I tossed in some body wash for good measure. I rarely treated myself, and I figured today I deserved it. The last four years had been spent working my ass off, striving toward my elementary-education degree at Arizona State University, and I'd finally landed my first real job a month ago.

Pride shimmered around my consciousness. Not the arrogant kind. I was just . . . happy. Happy for what I'd achieved.

I bit at the inside of my lip, doing my best to contain the ridiculous grin I felt pulling at my mouth.

Ben was always the one who took care of me. But he also took all the credit. Like my life would be miserable without him in it.

Finally . . . *finally* . . . I'd attained something that was all on me.

Slowly, I wound my way up toward the registers. I needed to get out of here before I drained what little I had in my checking account with all my *celebrating*.

I rolled my eyes at myself and squashed the mocking laughter that rolled up my throat.

Yep, livin' large and partying hard.

My life was about as exciting as Friday night bingo at the retirement home down the street.

But hey, at least my hair would smell good and my lips would taste even better.

Scanning the registers, I hunted for the shortest line, when my eyes locked on a face that was familiar but just out of reach of my recognition. Curiosity captured all of my heed, and I found I couldn't look away.

She was standing at the front of her cart, her attention cast behind her, searching. Obviously, searching for someone.

I stared, unabashed, craning my head to the side as I tried to place the striking green eyes and long black hair. She was gorgeous, enough to make any supermodel feel self-conscious, but she was wearing the kind of smile that spoke a thousand welcomes.

Two feet in front of her, I came to a standstill, which only caused her warm smile to spread when her gaze landed on me.

My attention flitted to the empty infant car seat latched onto the basket before it darted back to her face.

My stomach twisted into the tightest knot as recognition slammed me first somewhere in my subconscious, my throat growing dry when her name formed in my head before it swelled on my tongue.

"Aly Moore?" I managed, everything about the question timid and unsure. Well, I wasn't unsure it was she.

There was no question, no doubt.

What I wasn't so sure about was if I should actually stop to talk to her. My heart was already beating a million miles a minute, like a stampeding warning crashing through my body, screaming at my limbs to go and go now.

Still, I couldn't move.

Short gusts of sorrow were a feeling I was well-accustomed to, dealing with Stewart and all the sadness his illness brought into my life.

But this?

Pain constricted my chest, pressing and pulsing in, and I struggled to find my absent breath.

God, she looked just like *him*. I always did my best to keep him from my thoughts, all the memories of him buried deep, deep enough to pretend they'd forever been forgotten, when in reality everything I'd ever shared with him had been the most vivid of my life.

Seeing her brought them all flooding back.

His face.

His touch.

I squeezed my eyes, trying to block them out, but they only flashed brighter.

God.

"Samantha Schwartz." My name tumbled from her mouth as if it came with some kind of relief. She stretched out her hand, grasping mine. "Oh my gosh, I can't believe it's you. How are you?"

I hadn't seen her in years. Seven, to be exact. She was only two years younger than me, always sweet. Sweet *and* smart. Different in a good way, quiet and shy and bold at the same time. I'd always liked her, and some foolish part of me had believed she'd always be a part of my life. I guess I'd taken that for granted, too.

But that's what happens when you're young and naive and believe in promises that turn out only to be given in vain.

I swallowed over the lump in my throat and forced myself to speak. "I've been good. It's so great to see you." It was all a lie wrapped up in the worst kind of truth.

I dropped my gaze, my eyes landing on the diamonds that glinted from her ring finger where she grasped my hand, and I caught just a peek of the intricate tattoo woven below it, like she'd etched a promise of forever into her skin.

A war of emotions spun trough me, and I wanted to fire off a million questions, the most blatant of them jerking my attention between the empty infant carrier and her ring. My mind tumbled through a roller coaster of memories as it did its best to catch up on the years that had passed.

"Oh my God . . . you are married? And you're a mom," I drew out as I finally added up the obvious, and a strange sense of satisfaction at seeing her grown-up this way fell over me. It seemed almost silly, thinking of her that way, considering she was only two years younger than me. Now the years separating our ages didn't seem so distant. Not the way they had then, when I'd thought of her as just a little girl, a hundred years and a million miles behind me. It seemed now she'd just flown right past me.

With my assertion, everything about her glowed. She held up her hand to inspect the ring I'd just been admiring, her voice soft with a reverent awe. "Can you believe it?" She laughed quietly. "Some days I can't believe it myself."

The joy surrounding her was so clear, and I chewed at my bottom lip, both welcoming the happiness I felt for her and fighting the jealousy that slipped just under the surface of my skin. Never would I wish any sorrow on her, or desire to steal it away because I didn't have it myself. I wasn't viscious or cruel. But seeing her this way was just a stark reminder of what I was missing.

Happiness.

I bit back the bitterness, searched inside myself for an excuse to get away, because I was finished feeling sorry for myself, when Aly's face transformed into the most radiant smile, her attention locked somewhere behind me. There was nothing I could do but follow her gaze. I looked over my shoulder.

All the surprise at finding Aly Moore here shifted and amplified, spinning my head with shock when I found whom she was staring at. My knees went weak.

Jared Holt strode toward us.

The grown man was completely covered in tattoos, every edge of him hard and rough. None of the surprise I felt was attributed to the way he looked, because I'd been there to watch his downward spiral. Part of me was just surprised to see he was still alive.

But I recognized it the second I saw him. Joy. The way a soft smile pulled at his mouth and the warmth that flared in his eyes when they landed on Aly. He held an adorable, tiny baby girl protectively against his chest, the child facing out as they approached. She kicked her little legs when she caught sight of her mom.

My heart did crazy, erratic things, and the small sound that worked up my throat was tortured.

Someone was trying to pull a sick joke on me, dangling all the bits of my past right in front of my face.

It just had to be Jared.

No, he hadn't been responsible for any of the choices Christopher or I had made. Still, he'd been at the center of it. The catalyst that had driven the confusion.

The overwhelming feeling rushing me was altogether cruel and welcomed at the same time, because God, how many times had I lain awake at night, unable to sleep because I was thinking of Christopher Moore, wondering where he was and who he'd become?

Those questions always left me feeling sad and hollow, because I'd witnessed pieces of that man, the one who emerged after I was gone. Or maybe the one who'd been there all along—I'd just been too blind to see him for who he really was.

Aly must have sensed my panic. Again she reached out to squeeze my hand. "You remember Jared Holt, don't you?" She obviously knew I did. There was no missing the look that passed between the two of them, a secret conversation transpiring in just a glance.

"Of course," I whispered hoarsely.

"Samantha," Jared said as a statement. He handed Aly the little tube of diaper-rash ointment he must have gone in search of while she waited at the front of the store. He turned his attention right back to me. "God . . . it's been years. How are you?"

"Good," I forced out, wondering where in the hell that word had even come from because right then, I was definitely not feeling *good.* I was feeling . . . I blinked and swallowed. I couldn't begin to put my finger on it except to say it was disturbed, as if the axis balancing my safe little world had been altered.

"How are you?" The concern that involuntarily laced my tone was probably not needed, because he smiled at Aly as he situated his daughter a little higher up on his chest and kissed her on the top of her head.

"I'm perfect," he said through a rumbled chuckle.

Aly took a step forward and lightly tickled the tiny girl's foot.

The little black-haired, blue-eyed baby kicked more, the mouth that twisted up at just one side so obviously just learning how to control her smile as she rolled her head back in delight. She suddenly cooed, and her eyes went wide and she jerked as if she'd startled herself with the sound that escaped her.

Aly's voice turned sweet, the kind a mother reserved only for her child. "And this is our Ella . . . Ella Rose."

Ella Rose.

They'd even named their daughter after Jared's mother.

Affection pulsed heavily through my veins as I looked on the three of them, so happy to see their joy. As strong as that emotion was, it wasn't enough to keep my own sadness at bay, and my mind reeled with the questions I wanted to ask about Christopher.

But those questions were dangerous. It wasn't that I didn't want to know. I couldn't know.

Instead, I reached out to let their baby girl grip my finger. I shook it a little, and that sweet smile took over her face again, this time directed at me as she tried to shove my finger in her mouth.

I just about melted. I was pretty sure this little girl had the power to single-handedly jump-start my biological clock. "Well, hello there, Ella Rose. Aren't you the sweetest thing?" I glanced up at Aly. "How old is she?"

"She just turned two months yesterday," she answered. "It feels like she's growing so fast, but I can't remember what it was like not to have her as a part of our lives. It's such a strange feeling."

My head shook with stunned disbelief. "All of this is just crazy." I eyed them playfully as some of the shock wore away, as if being in their space was completely natural. "The two of you ending up together."

Aly blushed, and Jared watched her as if she was the anchor that kept him tied to this world. Then he slanted his own mischievous grin my way. "Don't be too surprised, Sam. This girl was always meant for me."

Turn the page for a sneak peek at the first book
in Molly McAdams's new Thatch series,

LETTING GO

Available wherever print and e-books are sold.

....

prologue

Grey

May 10, 2012

"Then over there is where the girls and I will be waiting before the ceremony starts," I said, pointing to the all-seasons tent just off to the side. "I think the coordinator said she'd get us in there when the photographer is taking pictures of Ben and the boys on the other side house, so he won't see me."

I glanced to my mom and my soon-to-be mother-in-law talking about the gazebo behind me, and what it would look like with the greenery and flowers, and I smiled to myself. They'd been going back and forth on whether we should keep the gazebo as it was or decorate it ever since Ben and I had decided on the Lake House as our wedding and reception site. And from the few words I was hearing now, they were still undecided. I honestly didn't care how it was decorated. I wanted to be married to Ben, and in three days, I would be.

"Grey, this place is freaking *gorgeous*. I can't believe you were able to get it on such short notice," my maid of honor and best friend, Janie, said in awe.

"I know, but it's perfect, right?"

"Absolutely perfect."

I grabbed her hand and rested my head on her shoulder as I stared at the part of the property where the reception would be. Ben and I had promised our families that we wouldn't get married until we'd graduated from college, but that had been a much harder promise to keep than we'd thought it would be. School had let out for summer a few days ago, and we wanted to move off campus for our junior year . . . together. That hadn't exactly gone over well with my parents. They didn't want us living together until we were married. I think in my dad's mind it helped him continue to believe I was his innocent little girl.

I'd been dating Ben since I was thirteen years old; the innocent part had flown out the window over three years ago. Not that my father needed to know that. After a long talk with all our parents, they'd agreed to let us get married now instead of two years from now.

That was seven weeks ago. Even though Ben had asked me to marry him last Christmas, we'd officially gotten engaged once we'd received the okay from our parents and started planning our wedding immediately. Seven weeks of being engaged. Seven years of being together. And in three days I would finally be Mrs. Benjamin Craft.

With how the last few weeks had dragged by, it felt like our day would never get here.

My phone rang and I pulled it out of my pocket. My lips tilted up when I saw Jagger's name and face on the screen, but I ignored the call. Putting my phone back in my pocket, I kept my other hand firmly wrapped around Janie's and walked over to where the rest of the bridesmaids were. My aunts and grandma had gathered around the gazebo-debating duo and were helping them with the pros and cons.

"So what are we going to do tonight?" I asked, hoping to get some kind of information about the bachelorette party.

"Nice try." Janie snorted. She started saying something else, but my phone rang again.

Glancing down and seeing Jagger's name again, I thought about answering my phone for a few seconds before huffing out a soft laugh and ignoring the call a second time. I knew why he was calling. He was bored out of his mind and wanted me to save him from the golf day Ben and all the guys were having before the bachelor party. Normally I would have saved him from the torture of golfing, but today was about Ben. If he wanted to go golfing with all his guys, then Jagger just had to suck it up for his best friend.

Almost immediately after ignoring the call, I got a text from him.

Jagger: Answer the goddamn phone, Grey!

My head jerked back when the phone in my hand began ringing just as soon as I'd read the message, and all I could do was stare at it for a few seconds. A feeling of dread and unease formed in my chest, quickly unfurling and spreading through my arms and stomach.

Some part of my mind registered two other ringtones, but I couldn't focus on them or make myself look away from Jagger's lop-sided smile on my screen. With a shaky finger, I pressed on the green button and brought the phone up to my ear.

Before I could say anything, his panicked voice filled the phone. "Grey? Grey! Are you there? Fuck, Grey, say something so I know you're there!"

There were a siren and yelling in the background, and the feeling that had spread through my body now felt like it was choking me. I didn't know what was happening, but somehow . . . somehow I knew my entire world was about to change. My legs started shaking and my breaths came out in hard rushes.

"I— What's happ—" I cut off quickly and turned to look at my mom and Ben's. Both had phones to their ears. Ben's mom was screaming with tears falling down her cheeks; my mom looked like the ground had just been ripped out from underneath her.

Jagger was talking. I knew his voice was loud and frantic, but I was having trouble focusing on the words. It sounded like he was yelling at me from miles away.

"What?" I whispered.

Everyone around me was freaking out, trying to figure out what was going on. One of my friends was asking whom I was talking to, but I couldn't even turn to look at her or be sure who it was that had asked. I couldn't take my eyes off the only other women currently talking on a phone.

"Grey! Tell me where you are. I'm coming to get you!"

I blinked a few times and looked down at my lap. I was sitting on the ground. When had I sat down?

Janie squatted in front of me and grabbed my shoulders to shake me before grabbing my cheeks so I would look at her instead of where my mom and Ben's were clinging to each other.

"What?" I repeated, my voice barely audible.

Just before Janie took the phone from me, I heard a noise that sounded weighted and pained. A choking sound I'd never heard from Jagger in the eleven years we'd been friends. The grief in it was enough to force a sharp cry from my own chest, and I didn't even struggle against Janie when she took the phone from me.

I didn't understand anything that was happening around me, but somehow I knew everything. A part of me had heard Jagger's words. A part of me understood what the horrified cries that quickly spread throughout every one of my friends meant. My family. Ben's family. A part of me acknowledged the sense of loss that had added to the dread, unease, and grief—and knew why it was there.

A part of me knew the wedding I'd just been envisioning would never happen.

chapter one

Grey

Two years later . . .
May 10, 2014

dressed in a fog and sat down on the side of my bed when I was done. Grabbing the hard top of the graduation cap, I looked down at it in my hands until the tears filling my eyes made it impossible to see anything other than blurred shapes. I knew I had to leave, but at that moment I didn't care.

I didn't care that I'd done my makeup for the first time in two years and I was ruining it. I didn't care that I was graduating from college. I didn't care that I had already been running twenty minutes late before I'd sat down.

I just didn't care.

Falling to my side, I grabbed the necklace that hadn't left my neck once in the last couple years and pulled it out from under my shirt until I was gripping the wedding band I'd bought for Ben. The one he should be wearing, but I hadn't been able to part with—almost like I'd needed to keep some part of him with me.

The last year had been easier to get through than the one before it. I hadn't needed my friends constantly trying to get me to do my schoolwork. I hadn't needed Janie pulling me out of bed every morning, forcing me to shower and dress for the day. I'd even taken off my engagement ring and put it away a few months ago. But exactly two years ago today, I'd been showing off the place where I was going to marry Ben. Completely oblivious to anything bad in the world. And Ben had died.

At twenty years old, his heart had failed, and he'd died before he'd even dropped to the ground on the golf course. He'd always seemed so active and healthy; no one had ever picked up on the rare heart condition that had taken him too early. Doctors said it wasn't something they could test for. I didn't believe them then, and even though I'd read news articles of similar deaths in young people, I wasn't sure if I did now. All I knew was that he was gone.

Heavy footsteps echoed through the hall of my apartment seconds before Jagger was standing in the doorway of my bedroom, a somber look on his face.

"How did I know you wouldn't have made it out of here?" One corner of his mouth twitched up before falling again.

"I can't do it," I choked out, and tightened my hold on the ring. "How am I supposed to celebrate anything on a day that brought so much pain?"

Jagger took in a deep breath through his nose before releasing it and pushing away from the doorframe. Taking the few steps over to the bed, he sat down by my feet and stared straight ahead as silence filled the room.

"I honestly don't know, Grey," he finally said with a small shrug. "The only way I made it to my car and your apartment was because I knew Ben wanted this, and would still want it for us."

"He was supposed to be here," I mumbled.

"I know."

"Our two-year anniversary would have been in a few days."

There was a long pause before Jagger breathed, "I know."

. . . .

"Where's Chuck?" Cameo asked, handing me a beer she had snagged from the coolers that lined the floors in the kitchen of the frat house we were hanging out in. The house was Gamma Phi—something or other. Honestly, I couldn't remember, and I didn't care. They were all the same to me anyway.

"Who knows? Playing darts with the guys, I think," I said. Hopefully, they were using his head as the dartboard.

"You two make up?" she asked, raising her eyebrows.

"I think you misunderstood me, sweets. When I said, 'Who knows?,' I meant, who cares? I hope someone throws a dart that sticks right in his egotistical ass," I corrected her, not feeling very appreciative of the guy who was supposed to be my current boyfriend. Of course, after only two dates, it didn't seem right to fall into that trap, as far as I was concerned.

She laughed, taking a long drink from her beer before answering, "Another one bites the dust." She held up her beer to toast.

"Cheers," I answered, shrugging, feeling no further comment was necessary. I twisted the cap off my beer as I surveyed the rowdy crowd around us. The decibel level at frat parties was always nothing less than near deafening. Not that I was complaining. I was in my element. The louder it got, the better. This was the kind of scene I hadn't seen when I still lived at home and went to community college near Woodfalls. Going to an actual university was like stepping into another world. A world that I took to immediately. I was loud and raucous. So what?

Cameo and I left the kitchen and headed outside to the patio, which gave us a front-row seat to all the action. The guys were entertaining the crowd by trying to one-up one another with one crazy stunt after the next. We'd already seen some idiot jump from the porch on the second floor, hugging a mattress. Cheers erupted on the front lawn as people hooted and hollered, yelling scores for his landing. He stood up with his arms raised in victory before bowing at the waist and tossing his cookies splendidly on two unsuspecting girls who stood off to the side. Both girls shrieked with disgust, which only invited more cheers from the onlookers.

Not to be outdone, a group of girls decided to get in on the action when the guys initiated a girl-on-girl mud-wrestling tournament. Within minutes of being soaked by hoses spilling water at full blast, the front lawn of the fraternity house was a sopping mess. Judging by the steady line of participants that had quickly formed, the nominated contestants seemed to be too drunk to care about being subjected to male gawking or the fact that it was too cold to be rolling around like pigs in shit.

"You going?" Cameo asked.

"Hell no," I answered, choosing to keep my seat on the sidelines.

I'd been there, done that and I didn't relish taking an elbow in the nose or having a handful of my hair pulled out to entertain drunken college guys. Chuck, who had finally appeared from wherever he'd been hiding, couldn't seem to get it through his thick head that I didn't want to participate. It took me stomping on his foot and threatening to twist his junk into a knot before he finally stopped trying to pull me into the fray.

"Aw, you mean you don't want to give your boyfriend a show and roll around and get all wet with another girl?" Cameo teased, breaking into my thoughts. She looked halfway past tipsy as she smiled at me.

We had been at the party for an hour and were nursing our third beer each. I could hold my liquor better than Cameo, who was a bit of a lightweight. Chances were I'd be dragging her ass home later since she'd barely be able to walk. She and I had made a pact when we'd first become roommates that we would never leave the other behind, unless of course a hot guy was involved. Little did I realize when I made the pact that it would be me shouldering most of the load.

Honestly, I didn't mind. I loved Cameo to death. I had completely lucked out when I found her as a roommate after being accepted into Maine State College's business program. I'd gotten in by the skin of my teeth since I wasn't exactly what you would call an "academic all-star." I had taken a full year off after high school because I didn't know what I wanted to do with my life. Finally, my mom talked me into at least trying community college, and somehow, I managed to drill into my hard-ass head that if I wanted to transfer to a state university, I would have to work hard. Not that I wasn't still having fun at the same time. I wasn't dead after all. My acceptance letter came at the perfect time. My best friend, Brittni, had moved to Seattle, and I was feeling lost without her. She was the voice of reason I didn't have that kept me in line for the most part, but without her, my antics in Woodfalls had hit an epic scale. After some of the shit I'd pulled over the years, I think the entire town let out a collective sigh of relief when I moved away for school. Even if MSC was only sixty miles away from Woodfalls, at least I was out of their hair. Now, in the almost two years that I'd been on campus, I'd managed to bring my reputation as a bit of a hell-raiser with me.

I pulled my thoughts back to Cameo, who was still waiting for my answer. "Please, you know I'd have no problem throwin' down in there. It's just too damn cold to roll around in the mud," I said confidently. "Besides, Chuck's been working to get in my pants. Little does he know, the Vagmart store is closed to his ass."

"Ha, your vag-store," Cameo snorted, setting her beer on an end table that was already overflowing with bottles. "Guys are so predictable. They think all chicks wanna get naked with each other and have pillow fights."

"Well, I know that's all I think about," I said, wagging my eyebrows at her suggestively.

"Gross. You perv," she said, slapping my arm.

"Oh, come on. You know you want this," I teased, running my hands down my curvy figure. I had to sidestep a couple who were too busy sucking each other's faces as they walked to watch where they were going. "Hey, get a room," I called after them as they stumbled into the wall.

"Where the hell do you think we're going?" the guy asked, dislodging his lips long enough to answer.

"Sorry. Shit, carry on then," I said, grinning at Cameo.

"See, that's why we will never have a party at our apartment," she stated.

"What, you don't want an orgy to break out on your bed?"

"Don't even finish wherever your perverted mind was headed with that," she advised, holding up her hand like a crossing guard.

I laughed loudly. Cameo was the perfect roommate in most aspects, but she did have a bit of an obsessive-compulsive personality, much to my amusement. Not that I didn't agree with her. I didn't want drunken college peeps using my bed to get nasty in either.

"Could it be you're just bummed that your bed hasn't seen any action in how many days now?" I teased, wincing as I watched two girls in the mud pit go for each other's hair. Why did girls always do that? Why couldn't we fight like men? With fists and punching instead of hair pulling and scratching. I'd much rather take a punch to the gut than have a handful of my hair pulled out.

"Whatever, you whore. It's been four days," she answered, watching the fight with interest.

"Whoa, takes one to know one," I laughed.

"Bite me, bitch. I just like guys."

"And sex," I added.

"Yes. So what, Mother Teresa?" She grinned, throwing out her beloved nickname for me.

It wasn't like I didn't enjoy sex. She knew that. Lately, I was just more selective about whom I fell into bed with. Take Jock-Strap Chuck, for example. A few months ago, I might have caved and given it up to him. But I'm getting sick of the games and acting like someone I'm not to keep a guy. I used to be a total boyfriend pleaser, especially back in high school, when I dated the same creep off and on for almost four years. I finally called it quits once and for all about a year ago. The relationship was toxic to say the least. Years of scathing comments about how I looked or what I did, and then he would push to have sex, only to lay a major guilt trip on me when he felt remorse after we did it. Jackson suffered from a serious case of being a momma's boy. We'd no sooner do the dirty deed than he would whimper about premarital sex and how disappointed his mother would be. Even after years of putting up with his shit, actually committing to break up with Jackson was difficult. He had been my first serious boyfriend. The one I had given my virginity to, or my V-card, as I liked to call it. That was a big deal to me, despite my wild-child persona and the way people perceived me on the outside. It's not like you can ever get that back, even when the guy turns out to be a douche. Jackson definitely became that and more, telling me when we broke up that I was worthless and that no other guy would ever want me. His words had cut me deeply and made me feel like I was lacking. His mom actually threw a party when we were officially over.

After leaving the Jackson mess behind me, I eventually found the confidence to try my luck with guys again, but after a sting of disastrous first dates, I began to believe that maybe Jackson had been right. He was as good as I deserved. If not that, then maybe the dating gods were punishing me for all my past sins. Like the time in seventh grade, when I talked Braxton Fischer into switching the video we were supposed to watch in Mr. Morton's science class with a porno he had found hidden in his dad's nightstand table. Mr. Morton made the mistake of leaving the room for almost ten minutes before he came back to see two topless, big-breasted girls washing cars on the TV.

"What the hell?" a shocked Mr. Morton yelled as he turned several different shades of red. The class erupted with laughter, and although none of my classmates ratted me out, Mr. Morton knew better and immediately sent me to the office. I could have argued. He had no proof it had been me, but my reputation had already been established.

The principal, Mrs. Jameson, called my dad to pick me up, which I thought was odd, considering she knew my mom. I finally understood when he showed up and she handed over the video to my dad with a scornful look on her face, like she was repulsed to even be that close to something so unholy. She thought the video was his, but my dad didn't skip a beat. He didn't flush with embarrassment or stammer at being reprimanded. Instead, he thanked her and told her he was wondering where he had left it, leaving Mrs. Jameson looking utterly scandalized.

The only lecture I had gotten on the way home was a reminder that some parents may not want their children to see movies about those kinds of car washes. That was the best thing about Dad. He always understood the person I was, never judging or scolding me. He would simply give reminders and pointers of what a better course of action might have been. I loved both my parents fiercely for their gentle restraint.

I wish I could tell you that had been the last prank I ever pulled, but my reign of stunts continued into high school. I would pick a victim and execute my prank with the precision of a surgeon. Dad always said if I would learn to harness that power toward school, I would be a straight-A student. That would have been tragic and a complete waste of fun, in my opinion.

Eventually, I mellowed when I was dating Jackson. He reminded me countless times that his mom would never approve of me if I was always causing trouble. Little did he know, I didn't want nor need his creepy mom's love.

For that reason more than any other, breaking up with Jackson had been necessary. Our relationship had been like a runaway train headed for a brick wall. Unfortunately, none of my relationships after that had turned out any better. My friends Brittni and Ashton said I had an uncanny gift of gravitating toward the only jerk in the crowd. I always shrugged off their comments. I dated guys who suited me, which usually meant they were as loud and wild as I was.

"Wow, did she seriously just push that girl's face into her boobs?" Cameo asked, pulling me back to the present. She stepped closer to get a better look at the two mud-covered girls, who had grabbed the attention of most of the male population at the party. As the crowd cheered the girls along, I noticed everyone watching had their cell phones out to record the wrestling match, so I pulled out mine too.

"You're not going to post that, are you?" Cameo asked as I moved in closer.

"Why the hell not? This is epic on a whole new level," I answered as one of the girls shoved the other to the ground and straddled her.

"Damn, that's hot," a warm male voice said behind me.

I grinned as I turned around, recognizing the voice of my friend Derek. "Really? I can score their numbers for you if you'd like," I joked.

"Honey, I'm talking about Tall, Dark and Shirtless over there," he answered, pointing to a well-toned guy who had removed his shirt so it wouldn't get splattered with mud.

"Right, here I thought you had suddenly decided to bat for the other team," Cameo teased Derek, looping her arm through his.

"Sweetheart, you could only wish," he said, dropping a kiss on her forehead.

"Damn straight," she giggled. "No pun intended," she added before frowning up at him. "Why do all the good ones turn out to be gay?"

"So we can have marvelous friends like you two without the mess of a romantic relationship. Just think, if I was straight, we wouldn't be friends."

"That's because we'd be lovers," I cooed, snuggling up to his free arm.

"I love you, Tressa baby, but you'd scare me in bed," Derek said, wrapping his arm around my waist.

"Oh, come on, I'd go easy on you," I answered, grinding my hips against his leg.

"Don't believe her. I swear the wall looked like it was going to collapse the last time she had a guy over," Cameo teased, sticking out her tongue at me as I swiped at her with my free hand.

"Whatever, Wonder Woman," I said, reminding her of the last guy she'd slept with, who'd had a fondness for comic books. He showed up at our apartment one night with a costume from the Halloween store. Usually, I didn't mind sticking around when Cameo had a guy over, but I had to leave for that one. The truth was, it had been months since I'd even considered being with a guy.

"Hey, what about the dude with the camera? I'm surprised you didn't take him up on it," she returned, talking about the last guy who had almost made it into my bed until he'd wanted to record us. He had to go outside to collect his camera and clothes from the yard after I threw his belongings out the window and kicked his ass out.

"Unlike you, I only do high-class porn," I threw back.

"As stimulating as this conversation is, I'd rather be dancing," Derek said, indicating the open door of the frat house, inside which the music had been turned up.

Cameo and I agreed, following Derek toward the music that we could feel pumping through our chests. Joining a crowd that seemed to be flowing as one, we let loose and lost ourselves in the music. Dancing came naturally to our trio, and it was something we enjoyed doing together. As in, just the three of us. Being in a large crowd, we would occasionally have to put up with some drunken dude trying to grind against Cameo or me, but Derek was good at stepping in. At six foot five, he was an imposing figure who could maneuver his body wherever he wanted to shelter us from unwanted advances.

After an hour, we were dripping with sweat, despite the nip in the nighttime air, which circulated through the open windows and doors. Pulling my damp hair off the back of my neck, I indicated with a nod of my head to Derek and Cameo that it was time for a break. It felt like we needed a shoehorn to squeeze through the jumbled bodies, but eventually we made it out of the room.

"Holy shit, talk about a cardio workout. I should be a twig after all that," I complained, snagging another drink. "I should effing hate you," I said, glaring at Cameo, who was practically a waif standing next to me.

"Don't be an ass. I'd take your boobs any day over these," she retaliated, cupping her smallish breasts in her hands. "At least you've got curves. I'm like a stick."

"Look, ladies, you can both be jealous of my perfect body," Derek interrupted, making a point of tossing his imaginary long hair. "Some of us got it, and some of us don't." Cameo and I laughed. Derek was a bit of a showboat, which made him perfect for our group. "I'm going to get a drink," he added, following behind Cameo, who was already headed in that direction.

I stayed behind, content with another beer I had pulled from a nearby cooler. It was nice to take a breather and observe the crowd a little. I became preoccupied watching a group playing a distorted version of spin the bottle when a pair of arms reached around my stomach, pulling me roughly against a hard chest.

"Are you ready to kiss and make up?" Chuck growled in my ear. He smelled like a distillery.

"Not really," I answered, stepping out of his grasp.

"Come on, girl. You're gonna let a little fight ruin this?" he said, sounding plastered.

I wanted to laugh, but that would probably have only egged him on further. I also wasn't in the mood for a messy scene tonight, so I went with a softer approach and a little more tact than he probably deserved.

As I spun around to face him, I couldn't for the life of me remember why I had gone out with him in the first place. He was a partier like I was and had seemed cool when I met him at Club Zero a couple weeks ago, but he was a meathead. I pretty much realized on our first date that we probably weren't going to make it. Mostly because he was a perpetual nut scratcher. I don't mean he would do the occasional subtle shift that some guys do with their junk. If that was all he did, I could have lived with it. He was an all-out ball scratcher and didn't seem to care who saw him do it. It could be the waitress who looked disgusted as she handed over our pizza, or Cameo or basically anyone who was having a conversation with him. If you stood next to Chuck, you would at some point see him scratch his balls.

"Chuck, it's not you—it's me," I said, cringing at the cliché I had chosen. How did you tell someone you would rather gouge out your eyes than see him play with his junk again?

"What the fuck? Who uses a bullshit line like that?" he declared, grabbing my arm so I couldn't move. I looked down at his hand, which was wrapped around my wrist. Seriously? Why did it always come down to this? Did I have the words *please manhandle me* tattooed on my forehead?

I saw Derek approaching from the corner of my eye. He wasn't hard to miss because of his size, and judging by the look on his face, Chuck wanted no part of what was coming. I held out my free hand to stop Derek before he could get involved. I might have an uncanny knack for dating assholes, but I also knew how to take care of myself when I needed to. I stepped on Chuck's shoe and slowly rolled my weight so my platform heels sank down on the softness of his toes. "In case you're too stupid to notice, we're done." He grunted in pain, making me smile. Sometimes it paid not to be a lightweight.

"Get off me, you bitz," he slurred. He wobbled so badly, I could have pushed him over.

"Why don't you go sleep it off?" Derek insisted, as he stepped in and pulled me protectively against him. This was why Derek was the best kind of friend. He wasn't a fan of violence, but you would never know it when it came to Cameo and me. Back home, I had always been the protector when it came to my friends. It was kind of nice to have a knight in shining armor. Not necessary but still sweet. I found it endearing that even though Derek had known me for only a year, he acted like we were lifelong friends. Derek was a perk that came with Cameo picking me to be her roommate last year. When I had transferred to Maine State, I knew I didn't want to do the whole dorm thing. Living at home my first two years of college had made me yearn for more independence. I wanted to let loose without so many restrictions. Living in an apartment with Cameo had provided the freedom I was looking for, and sharing her best friend, Derek, sweetened the deal.

Chuck looked like he wanted to retaliate, but in the state he was in, he was in no shape to attempt anything more. With a shake of his head and a look of bewilderment in my direction, he staggered off, scratching his junk the entire time.

"Honey, you sure can pick 'em," Derek said, shaking his head with amazement before turning away from the train wreck.

"You're a fine one to talk," I pointed out, punching him in his biceps. If it seemed like I was being picky at the moment when it came to guys, Derek was even worse. He claimed he didn't feel like wasting time on meaningless relationships. I think he'd missed the memo on what college dating was supposed to be.

"I'm searching for someone who understands me," he said dramatically, making us laugh. "Speaking of which, hello, Clark Kent," he added, looking toward the front door. "He looks like he could understand everything I have to offer."

Cameo and I pivoted around to see who had managed to snag Derek's attention. He could be a bit of a snob when it came to man candy. Anyone who caught his eye had to be something worth seeing.

"Oh, hell no," I muttered under my breath. He was the last person I had expected to see at a party like this.

Read on for a teaser from
Christina Lee's first New Adult novel,

ALL OF YOU

Available everywhere books and e-books are sold.

....

ove was like a loaded gun. You slid your bullet inside the cold metal chamber as a safeguard for the inevitable day that everything went to shit. At the first sign of trouble, you blew your opponent to pieces, long before their finger found the trigger. At least that's what my mother's string of failed relationships taught me.

I downed the warm beer and scanned the frat party from my armchair perch. The low moans drifting from the next couch over awakened a longing inside me. My best friend, Ella, and her boyfriend were going at it again. Our other friend, Rachel, an even bigger player than me, was in the far corner making out with another university jock. And I wasn't about to be the only one leaving empty-handed tonight.

Guys were easy to figure out—at least in the hormonal sense. You needed only to appear helpless or horny, and their pants instantly dropped to their ankles. Except none of the guys here tonight appealed to me. Maybe I'd text Rob for a booty call on my way home. He was always good for one, unless he'd already hooked up with someone else.

My gaze landed on the guy entering the back door through the kitchen. A red baseball cap was slung low on his head and inky black curls escaped beneath it. His arms were muscular, and his charcoal T-shirt hugged his lean chest. He was Grade-A Prime Meat and probably knew exactly how to put those full lips to good use.

I watched as he high-fived one of the guys and then propped his forearm against the counter. His smile was magnetic, and I pictured him using it on me in another five minutes, when he sweet-talked me. I stood up and straightened my shirt so that it revealed more of my cleavage—the little I had—and strode toward the keg with my plastic cup.

As I drew nearer, I saw how alarmingly gorgeous this guy really was. The one hand fisted in his pocket tugged at his jeans, revealing a small sliver of a taut stomach. The trail of baby-fine hairs leading downward made heat pool low in my stomach.

I tried catching his eye, but he wasn't going for it.

His friend was a different story, though. He practically growled in my direction.

The friend was cute, too, but paled in comparison to Hot Boy. But maybe his friend was my ticket in. Too bad I wasn't the type to take on both of them—that might be entertaining.

Bile scorched the back of my throat. *Hell, no.* Two meant more testosterone, less power. No telling what might happen, even if I *thought* I was in control. There was a reason I only did one willing guy at a time.

When I stopped at the keg, I overheard Hot Boy telling a friend that he was moving in the morning. Hopefully not out of state. No matter; I only needed him for tonight. His voice was low and gruff, sending a ripple of satisfaction through me.

Hot Boy's friend reached over and grabbed hold of my cup. "Let me help you with that."

Hot Boy looked up and our gazes meshed for the first time. Warm chocolate eyes pinned me to my spot. They raked over me once before flitting away, sending my stomach into a free fall.

He pushed aside the messy bangs hanging in his eyes and resumed his conversation.

I wanted to run my fingers through those unruly curls at the nape of his neck. I made a mental note to do that later, when he was lying on top of me.

His friend handed my cup back, filled to the brim. Hot Boy didn't look my way again.

"Thanks." I clenched my teeth and worked to keep my lips in a neat, straight line.

"So, what's your name?" he asked as he stepped closer. His breath was sour with beer and cigarettes and I knew I could've taken him oh so easily. As simple as the arch of my eyebrow.

But I didn't want him. I wanted Hot Boy. Just for one night.

"My name's Avery," I said, loud enough for Hot Boy to hear.

Hot Boy only paused at the sound of my voice without looking my way. *Damn.* Maybe he had a girlfriend, or maybe he was gay. The pretty boys always were.

"Nice to meet you, Avery. I'm Nate." His friend slid his hand to my hip, and I considered giving up the hunt and taking him upstairs. But for some reason, I just wasn't feeling it.

"I'll be right back." I left him swaying unsteadily on his feet.

I headed back to Ella and Joel, who were still hot and heavy on the couch.

"I'm going to head home," I said, close to her ear.

Ella came up for air. "No prospects tonight?"

"One." I glanced over my shoulder to the kitchen. Hot Boy's friend was still waiting for me. "But I'm not really into it."

"Bitch, you're always into it." Her lips curved into a devilish grin. "Gonna hook up with Rob tonight instead?"

"Maybe." I didn't want to disappoint her. I was ready for a good time most weekends. And, even though she didn't really approve, she was ready for all the gritty details the next day. Ella hadn't gotten me to change my ways in high school, and she wouldn't now. But if I wasn't in the mood, I didn't feel like explaining it to her.

I looked around for Rachel to say good-bye, but she was already somewhere private with jock boy. Ella went back to ramming her tongue into Joel's mouth.

She'd probably felt stranded by Rachel and me too many times to count, so seeing her with Joel actually thawed a corner of my frozen heart. A real live boyfriend was what Ella had always wanted. Someone who *got* her, she'd said. Whatever the hell that meant.

Hopefully Joel would keep treating her right, or he'd have to answer to me. I wasn't opposed to grabbing hold and yanking those balls down hard. My self-defense classes had taught me well.

I decided to give Hot Boy one last shot as I passed by him on my way out the door, luring him with my sexiest voice. Unfortunately that meant passing his friend, too.

"Excuse me." My mouth was close to Hot Boy's ear, my chest brushing past his arm. He smelled like coconut shampoo. Like warm sand, hot sun, and sex. I wanted to wrap myself inside of his arms, but I kept on moving.

"No problem," he said without even a glance.

Damn. Rejected again. That made me want him twice as much.

Just as my foot crossed onto the landing, I felt a warm hand reach around my waist. I almost fist-pumped the air. *Got him.*

I turned to greet Hot Boy, my breaths already fluttery. But the smile slid from my lips and slumped to the floor when I realized it was his friend who'd grabbed me instead.

"Hey, baby, where you going?"

"I'm leaving." I twisted away, hoping to break his embrace.

But he kept in step with me. "How about you hang with me awhile longer?"

"Maybe another time."

His hands frisked around to my stomach, and normally I'd accept that kind of action—initiate it, even—but for some reason I couldn't shake Hot Boy's rejection.

I was more of an emotional train wreck than even *I'd* realized. Despite Ella reminding me almost every fucking day.

And just as I was chastising myself and changing my mind about hooking up with his friend, I heard Hot Boy's low rumble of a voice. "Give it a rest, Nate. She said she was leaving, and I'm pretty sure that means without *you.*"

I blinked in shock. Maybe he'd noticed me after all.

His friend backed away with his hands raised. And then turned to the keg.

Hot Boy gave me a once-over. "You good?"

"Yeah, thanks."

Wait a minute. This was backward. I was thanking Hot Boy for being all chivalrous. And the boys I hooked up with were *so not chivalrous.*

Hot Boy nodded before turning on his heels and heading out of the room, leaving my ego collapsing on the cold, hard tile.

Chivalrous Hot Boy was so not into me.

I walked the two blocks back to my apartment alone.

I tossed and turned, imagining Hot Boy's lips on mine, a fire blazing across my skin.

My cell phone buzzed from the nightstand.

Rob: You in the mood?

Me: Not tonight.

Photo by Ali Megan Photography

A. L. Jackson is the *New York Times* bestselling author of *Take This Regret* and *Lost to You*, as well as other contemporary romance titles, including *Pulled* and *When We Collide*.

She first found a love for writing during her days as a young mother and college student. She filled the journals she carried with short stories and poems used as an emotional outlet for the difficulties and joys she found in day-to-day life.

Years later, she shared a short story she'd been working on with her two closest friends, and with their encouragement, this story became her first full-length novel. A.L. now spends her days writing in southern Arizona, where she lives with her husband and three children. Her favorite pastime is spending time with the ones she loves.

CONNECT ONLINE
aljacksonbooks.blogspot.com
facebook.com/aljacksonauthor

Molly McAdams grew up in California but now lives in the oh so amazing state of Texas with her husband and furry four-legged daughters. When she's not diving into the world of her characters, some of her hobbies include hiking, snowboarding, traveling, and long walks on the beach . . . which roughly translates to being a homebody with her hubby and dishing out movie quotes. She has a weakness for crude-humored movies and fried pickles, and loves curling up in a fluffy comforter during a thunderstorm . . . or under one in a bathtub if there are tornadoes. That way she can pretend they aren't really happening.

USA Today bestselling author **Tiffany King** has written a number of young adult titles: The Saving Angels series, *Wishing for Someday Soon, Forever Changed, Unlikely Allies, Miss Me Not,* and *Jordyn: A Daemon Hunter Novel.* She is also the author of the New Adult series the Woodfalls Girls, including *No Attachments, Misunderstandings,* and *Contradictions.* Writer by day and book fanatic the rest of the time, she is now pursuing her lifelong dream of weaving tales for others to enjoy. She has a loving husband and two wonderful kids. (Five, if you count her three spoiled cats.)

Christina Lee lives in the Midwest with her husband and son—her two favorite guys. She's addicted to lip gloss and salted caramel everything. She believes in true love and kissing, so writing romance has become a dream job. She also owns her own jewelry business, where she hand-stamps meaningful words or letters onto silver for her customers.

CONNECT ONLINE
christinalee.net